Were Wolves
THE MIX TAPE
A Tale of Urban Horror

Were Wolves
The Mix Tape
A Tale of Urban Horror

by

A.J. Harper

© copyright 2010 by A.J. Harper

This book is a work of fiction. Characters, addresses and events are the product of my imagination. Any resemblance to real people, organization, institutions or incidents is entirely coincidental. While the novel is set in Oakland some of the area's features have been altered for the purpose of telling this story.

www.urbanhorror.com

Dedications

To
LaRhonda Harper
Your life was a blessing, your memory a treasure...
You are loved beyond words and missed beyond measure

Acknowledgements

To the people who stood by me during a real tough time.
Ellen, Jaunita, Willie, Chief, Paul, Babe, Danny,
Rondi, Keven, Tanya,
Marcus, Patrice, Kyle, Katrina, Charmane, Macha,
Erika & Erik. Anita, Colleen, the Wilsons, Fred, Todd & Roz

Thanx

Part 1

Urban Hounds

"He who wants to eat with the wolves has to howl along with them."
German Proverb

1

March 27th, 1:03 a.m., Skyline Blvd, Oakland CA. Full Moon

"Do you think one day we will look back on this and laugh?" Lexus McDonald the exhausted, rust colored African American standing at 5 feet, 8 inches tall with a short, bleach blonde hair worn in a rounded bob whispered nervously to her friend, Maria Juaez with painful breaths.

"Nope, but I hope so." The equally winded Latina answered through teeth that chattered from fear rather than the chill of the night. The teens stood motionless, surrounded by two Doberman pinschers and an enormous gray wolf that appeared from nowhere. The sound of human screams seconds earlier only heightened their fears.

"Damn!" Maria the petite 5 foot 6 inch tall Latina evaluated their seemingly hopeless situation. "I never thought things would go down like this. I just knew things would only get better," she whispered feeling her long, dark brown feathered hair clinging to her face and neck from sweat. Her cream colored skin flushed red. Maria recalled the job notice she found posted on a *Craigslist* post that read

$$$$$$$$$$$$$ EARN BIG $$$$$$$$$$$$$$$
As a video dancer
You may have what it takes to start a career as a background dancer
in your favorite stars video

The two sixteen year olds replied to the posting from the Hannah's Home for Girls in Tulsa, Oklahoma. Lexus had spent the last eight years of her life in and out of foster homes while her mother continued her downward spiral with methamphetamine use, losing her home, teeth and finally custody of her daughter. Maria mother was murdered by a jealous lover and had spent the past four years at the group home, when the courts determined that her grandmother was too sickly from cancer to provide for her any longer. They received a response of interest regarding their Myspace photographs and You tube video of the two performing "Put a Ring on It" from Pepper the agencies talent scout, inviting them to participate immediately in one of the agency's casting calls. When the teens informed Pepper that they were living in a group home in and had no way to get to Oakland, Pepper replied that the company would pay for their transportation and housing and give them a living expense until they actually started working.

With prepaid Greyhound tickets in hand, the duo quietly packed their favorite items and slipped out of the 18-girl group home. When they arrived in Oakland, they were greeted by Pepper Brown. Despite her vibrant, red hair and large diamond stud in her nose, the petite Korean was professionally dressed, and well spoken. Everything about her appeared legitimate. Pepper gave the teens $100.00 in cash, manicures, pedicures, clothes and make up while hyping up the recording industry, informing the excited teens that Jennifer Lopez and even MC Sepulcher, who currently was ruling the charts, got their start as back up dancers.

After a whirlwind day the two were taken to the Jack London Motel where they were allowed to rest before their midnight video audition. When they arrived at the Oakland Hills home of a recording executive, the place was different from what they had expected.

Although there was a several rappers present, it was obvious to Lexus and Maria that Pepper had taken them to a party and not an audition for a rap video. The smell of marijuana and alcohol permeated throughout the house. Rappers and giggling females in revealing outfits snorted lines of cocaine on any flat surface available, others videotaped the lurid happenings. After several hours of shrugging off drugs, alcohol and request for sex, the two slipped out a side door of the house that sat atop the Oakland hills into the heavily wooded area. The teens painfully realized their happy dream of foster kids turned famous dancers had turned into a nightmare. The pair spent the following twenty minutes in tight fitting, lycra dresses and uncomfortable shoes wandering aimlessly down a dark, unpaved brush covered road, hoping to cross a major street that would allow them access to a bus that could take them downtown and back to their room at the Jack London Motel. When the pair finally made it to the road, they could see the headlights of an oncoming vehicle descending in their direction. Not knowing what to do, the teens remained frozen like deer, their eyes transfixed on the growing orbs of light. A silver *Mercedes C320* driven by an angry, cream-colored male, his hair styled in *Finger Waves* parked the car aside them. From the way he held the steering wheel as he stared menacingly at the girls, it was apparent he had long limbs and a short fuse. Pepper sat in the passenger side wearing a grim expression. Two heavily made up females, one white the other African American, neither much older than Lexus and Maria occupied the back. Another scowling cream-colored male, only with a bald pate parked a black Mercedes sedan behind the silver Mercedes. Sitting aside him was another African American female, her electric blue wig doing little to cover that she was under the influence of drugs or alcohol sat in the passenger seat. Three anxious Pit bulls occupied the backseat.

The teens remained silent as Pepper stepped out of the car, observing her every move. "Listen guys," the Korean explained, the diamond stud in her nose glistening from the headlights. "There's been a misunderstanding, get in the car and let's head back with no hard feelings. Okay?"

Realizing the gravity of their predicament, Lexus, in an effort to set things straight said to the occupants of the Mercedes, "We're sorry for the trouble we caused."

"Good, get in the car, we'll talk about this after we all have gotten some sleep," Pepper agreed.

"We cool, thanks anyway." Maria intervened, her arm blocking Lexus in mid motion.

"What are you talking about?" Pepper spoke in a more assertive tone. "You are in the middle of nowhere. Stop being silly, and get in the car."

"You didn't want dancers, all you wanted was some ho's," Maria fired back, "and we ain't ho's, so if you don't want to get to steppin, then we will!"

The large driver stepped out of the silver Mercedes, adjusting his hair with a violent gesture before moving toward the teens. "I'm sick of this!" he sneered, exposing his glistening silver-plated 45 Caliber automatic stuck in the front of his pants. Get in the car, 'fo I pop a cap in yo ass's right out here in these hills!"

The two froze at the sight of the pistol allowing the male to grab Lexus and attempt to force her into the car.

The other females got out of the car to grab Maria. "Bitch, get in the car" the black girl demanded.

"Maria, run!" Lexus screamed, as she struggled with the larger male, but instead of fleeing, Maria slipped off her stiletto high heel and used it to rake the face of the black girl that came near her. "I ain't nobody's bitch!" the Latina screamed.

The scared female dropped to the cold ground, screaming in agony while covering her blood covered face. Then filled with rage in heart and a stiletto in her hand, Maria charged at Pepper who retreated screaming with the other white girl behind the Mercedes to avoid the furious teen.

The henchman struggling to place Lexus in the back of his car turned his attention to Pepper and received a savage blow to the Adam's apple from Lexus. The large male went down gashing his waved head open on the side of the car door and was instantly unconscious by the time he hit the dew, covered ground.

Maria and Lexus quickly regrouped and scurried down the hill illuminated by the car lights toward a clearing. The frantic pair maneuvered down the hill, the sharp pebbles, mushrooms and twigs bruising and cutting into their bare feet. They could hear the frantic voices above saying they had to take Sweet and Sandra to the hospital right away." Seconds later the ebony blanket of night once again covered the hill and the teens could hear the barking of dogs. The second driver had released his Pit bulls on them. With piercing screams, Lexus and Maria ran even harder before tripping and tumbling down into the dark open field. The sound of the dogs was closer; the teens knew if they didn't get up and run the viscous canines would show them no mercy. The two aching teens stood to run, but instead the dirt, covered pair froze in stunned silence. In front of them they witnessed six glowing yellow orbs. Although they were aware of the menace behind them, the two watched in awe as the small globes that hovered three to four feet from the ground approached them until the teens could see that the glowing spheres were the eyes of a humongous wolf and two Doberman pinschers. Maria and Lexus remained motionless, frozen by fear. The canines stared at the teens before observing the Pit bulls that entered into the clearing, and like Maria and Lexus the three attack dogs stopped dead in their tracks at the site of the other canines with luminous eyes.

"This has nothing to do with you mindless domestics," the large gray wolf spoke to the Pit bulls in English with a deep and commanding voice, astounding Maria and Lexus. "Go back to your humans masters and live another day."

The Pit bulls, snarled at the massive wolf, approaching the teens, slowly but defiantly.

Maria and Lexus anxiously observed the muscular dogs, now aware that the pits and other canines were not of the same pack.

"Such useless loyalty" the wolf sighed. Turning to the Doberman pinschers, he instructed, "Leave no remains, including the occupants in the Mercedes."

Lexus remembered flipping her hair from her face and the Pit bulls were gone. Seconds later there were brief screams from atop the hill that sent her heartbeat off the Richter scale.

The teens did not know why they had been spared so far and remained motionless.

"I am Sandia," The enormous gray wolf spoke as he approached the teens, his deep voice reflecting intelligence and authority. "You have been selected to be part of the Union. Do you accept this invitation?" Not knowing what else to say, the teens nodded their head in agreement.

"Excellent," the wolf responded. "You have made a wise choice. When you awaken, you will choose your spiritual form, and you will be part of a pack that dates before human time."

Maria looked at the beast as if this surreal experience was a nightmare, when she watched Lexus pressed to the ground by a Doberman pinscher, seconds late she felt herself slammed to the ground. The last thing Maria remembered was the Gray wolf standing over her before going for her throat.

2

March 28th, 10:29 a.m., Unknown

Lexus woke with a start both her hands were around her neck ready to fight off the attacking hounds, but to her relief, there were no dogs or wolves in sight. "It was all a dream," she sighed. Then she realized that she was not in the small bedroom she shared with Maria at the group home, nor was she in the motel room where they settled in. In fact, she was in was a king-size bed, in a king sized room. "Where am I and where is Maria?"

Slipping out of the bed, Lexus recognized the dress given to her by Pepper lying across the arm of a worn, rust colored leather chair. That's when Lexus noticed the red, flannel Victoria's Secret pajamas she was wearing. I'm keeping these, the blonde, chocolate girl mused, admiring the fit and feel of the colorful ensemble in the full-length mirror that stood in the corner, wishing she had her cell phone in order to take a photo to later upload to her Myspace page. The teen again wondered, what happened to me? Sliding across the polished hard wood of floor of the rustic bedroom that looked similar to the rooms featured on HGTV. Lexus peered out the window and the view of the mountains and trees quickly informed her she was no longer in the city. In the driveway below was an expensive looking black, sports car parked in the driveway. With finding Maria at the forefront of her mind the sixteen-year old gently opened the redwood door as not to make a sound and noticed across the mid-sized hallway an ornate wooden door similar to hers. Tiptoeing across the Navajo runner, Lexus quietly opened the door; and as she had hoped, found Maria in the bed sleep, her dress also lying across a distressed leather chair.

"Maria?" Lexus whispered loudly to her sleeping buddy and immediately realized Maria was pretending to be sleep. She sat up and then slipped out of the bed. "Didn't we get attacked by dogs?" Lexus asked puzzled, noticing that her roommate was wearing canary yellow, flannel Victoria Secret pajamas, but preferred her own.

"See all the blood on my dress over there," Maria answered, pointing to her silver dress covered in blood stains. "I don't know what happened, but my knees and feet are no longer sore."

Lexus discovered that the same was true for her arches. "Where are we?" she whispered.

"I don't know," Maria answered, "but I'm sure it's time for us to leave".

"Check the closet to see if they have a jacket or something," Lexus spoke realizing that their dresses were tattered, and their shoes were never designed for walking.

"Good looking out" Maria replied opening the closet "Whoa!" she cried with surprised "There's hella stuff in here." Lexus peered into the closet and shared Maria's astonishment. The closet was lined with various tops, jeans, shorts and jackets. At the foot were sneakers, boots and slip-on's.

"They all seem to be in your size," Lexus added looking at the tops and jeans. What's in my closet? Lexus wondered, walking across the hall and finding that her closet mirrored Maria's. Changing quickly, the two crept down the stairs and stopped when they spotted a lone black woman sitting on green printed couch in a Santa Fe styled living room. The two began to quietly retreat up the stairs when they heard the seated woman sigh, then with a French accent say, "Enough already, I know you are there, come down, so we can get on with this."

The two looked at each other then cautiously descended the stairwell.

"Sit," she instructed the teens who bumped into one another as they headed for the couch across from the stunning, dark skinned black woman, although she was sitting, it was obvious that the statuesque, woman stood over six feet tall. She had a small pug nose and large full lips, a short Afro with a starburst of white in the center.

She had exotic eyes that immediately informed you that she was a no nonsense woman. She wore tight black slacks, and a loose fitting creamy white, chiffon blouse that forced attention to her ample cleavage and a tight fitting black leather vest. Her legs were crossed revealing black high-heeled alligator boots that added three more inches to her height. The woman sat on the couch as if she was posing for a high fashion shoot. "If you would allow me," the woman spoke gesturing her graceful left hand revealing diamonds on each of her long, polished, fingers, "I will answer your questions before they are asked."

"Where are we? And what do you want from us?" Lexus blurted.

The woman sighed, "If you allow me to speak, then I can answer your questions before I am deluged with an avalanche of pointless inquiries."

"Let her talk," Maria added.

"Okay," Lexus agreed.

"I am Josephine Morreaux. I am here to inform you that you have been honored to part of the Union, a group whose history dates back to nearly the earliest years of civilization."

"You guys are Jehovah Witnesses?" Maria asked forgetting that she was not to interrupt.

"No, we are not Jehovah Witnesses," Josephine replied with calm restraint. "If you would allow me to continue, The Union is an elite group of Le Loup-Garou, or how you say werewolves," Josephine smiled.

"Did you say join some werewolves?" Maria scoffed, "Lady you crazy. C'mon Lexus" she added standing from the couch, "We gone."

"That may be," Josephine replied, offering no resistance to their exit, "but I did not say you were asked to join. I said you were selected."

"That don't mean nothing to us," Maria jabbed, insistent that she have the last word before slamming the door.

"It will, when you asked yourself, how were you able to be attacked by a pack of werewolves and lived to tell about it without a scratch?" Maria heard Josephine's state before the door slammed, seconds later the door reopened, and the two walked back into the house and again sat in the couch opposite Josephine.

"How did you do that?" Lexus asked.

"As I was saying," their host continued, "You were selected by the Union."

"But why?" Lexus asked with frustration, her mind going back to the frightening experience.

"That question will be answered by Sandia one of the leaders at a later date; though personally, I would have never selected you as I cannot see your worth."

"Too bad it wasn't you," Maria chimed.

"Indeed," Josephine nodded in agreement.

"What do you mean by that?" Maria replied realizing she had just been dismissed.

"Look at you," Josephine smirked, as she waved her jewelry covered hand to outline the teens, "I suppose there is the promise of potential, and it is obvious that you two are attractive. Yet, you represent nothing, and you bring nothing to the table. Why I am here even entertaining you, is a mystery as much to me as it is to you."

"Ya mean, ya mama don't represent nothing, bitch!" Maria fired back.

"You know what?" Lexus fired back, "this could all be bullshit, we probably caught whiff of some powder and dreamed up that we got attacked."

"And she's just lying," Maria agreed.

Josephine broke into a loud laughter. "You flatter yourselves. Lying requires creativity and a concern for the person they would seek to deceive. Who are you that I would exercise my considerable creative wilds? No, my young friends what I say is as true as I knew that your pale taste in clothes would only be improved by the fundamental wardrobe I provided."

"I don't like em, and won't wear em" Maria replied.

"Now, who is using their creativity to impress?" Josephine asked with self-satisfaction before tossing each a colorful, Dooney Burke Wristlet purse. "You will find inside, five hundred dollars and the keys to this cabin." She spoke as the two opened the purses to inspect the contents. "If you choose to stay you will find that all the amenities that you could possibly desire are to be found here, a fully stocked refrigerator, big screen television with cable, laptops, hot tub, etcetera."

"What about a phone?" Lexus asked suspiciously.

"But of course, you each have your own Blackberry located in your nightstand."

"And just what are we supposed to do for you?" Lexus asked.

"Do for me?" Josephine replied with a chuckle. "No, my small loquacious one you couldn't possibly do anything for me for one, I will not be here."

"You don't live here?" Maria asked.

"This is one of seventy five homes that I own. It is for your exclusive use. Treat it with care as you go through your transformation. I will be at my Montmarte flat in Paris. Sherman, my property manager will come by once a month to see if you have need of anything, and my number is available if you should if you must communicate with me."

"Transformation? Lexus spoke alarmed, "you're really serious about this."

"Your wee brain is starting to grasp the complexities of your new found reality, this is good, but as I said, you both possess the potential for promise," she smiled at the teen's discomfort.

"You talk a lot of shit lady," Maria grumbled under her breath, growing tired of Josephine airs.

"Excellent, you are starting to feel the fire of the Le Loup-Garou fueling you with passion non?" Josephine smiled at Maria's comment. "Leaving you to question, could I best this woman who talks so much shit? I would advise you to try," she challenged. "But you will not, as the smell of your fear is nauseating, non, you would not do well against the leader of the Wolfen."

"The Wolfen?" Lexus asked seeing the opportunity to change the momentum of the moment.

"Yes, right on cue," Josephine turned to Lexus anticipating her interruption. "The practical one, you two will serve each other well. The Wolfen is a critical component of the Union that will also be explained in time." She looked at the two. "The transformation will take place regardless to where you are. It is your choice to stay or go. It will happen slowly with you first choosing your spirit form and shape then you will acquire powers that will be unimaginable. I must take my leave." Josephine stood towering over the teens as she headed towards the door.

"Wait a minute," Maria followed Josephine outside, with Lexus close behind "where are we? And how are we supposed to get around?"

"You will soon become accustomed to the outside, and you will find getting around an issue that requires little or no thought, but it is skill that must be put into practice. The chocolate Amazonian spoke sitting inside the black, Maserati Spyder parked outside. "Once that has happened you will need to go back into the city of Oakland for two purposes she spoke reaching inside the glove compartment and handing Lexus a piece of cloth, "This belongs to Joseph Madayag, the last member selected to join the Union, you will find him and set up a meeting with Sandia."

"How are we supposed to find him with this?" Lexus replied with incredulity.

"We don't know anything or anybody in Oakland," Maria added.

"It will come to you," Josephine assured her, revving the elegant vehicle.

"And what's the other thing we're supposed to do in Oakland?" Lexus asked.

"Let just say Le Loup-Garou never forgets an enemy, "Josephine shouted as she drove off in a cloud of dust.

3

Friday, April 2nd 1:03 a.m., Unknown

Not knowing what to do and having no place else to go, the teens skeptically remained at the cabin. After nearly a week of free access to the phone, frig, and internet, the duo became less edgy and began to enjoy their new home.

"Are you ready to head back to Tulsa?" Maria asked Lexus, as they channel surfed on the sixty-inch plasma, television, enjoying the lifestyle they imagined their trip to California would bring.

"I think I could get used to this," Lexus replied, blowing her golden bobbed hair from her face "and I'm certainly going to try." She smiled, tossing Maria the universal remote as she lifted her phone to text a friend. "Do you think Josephine and her stuff about the Union is on the up, and up, or is she just crazy?" Lexus asked while texting a friend in Tulsa.

"I don't know," Maria replied, catching the remote, "but if it allows me to live like this, I'll join," she laughed. She flipped to Animal Planet. A special on dogs from A to Z was in progress.

"Leave it on that channel!" shouted the program catching her attention. "Let's pick out the type of dogs we should get."

"Cool," Maria responded, but I already know what I would get. It would be a Samoyed, their white and fluffy, like teddy bears."

"I would have to get me a Pit bull" Lexus added. They continued to watch the show oblivious to the decisions they had made.

4

May 24th, Crest View. Oakland, CA

"This is Lisa Chow reporting from the Oakland hills at the scene of a grizzly and puzzling case. The remains of two mauled bodies have been identified as convicted pimp, Jerome Green better known as "Sweet Green" and his accomplice Lisa Kan better known as "Pepper. They are the third Oakland hills killing in the last two months. Kerry Benson known as "Teknique" of the rap group, Tax Kollektors, skeletal remains were found this time last month. With me, is Oakland police sergeant Norbert Bright who can hopefully shed some additional light on these horrific incidents." The camera pans out and standing next to the reporter was Sergeant Bright. "So what information do you have on these attacks? And I understand that Green and Kan had a history with the police."

"Both Sweet and Pepper have priors for pandering and pimping. Their modus operandi was soliciting girls online for their prostitution ring, under the guise of video auditions. They would arrange to get poor girls from out of town by paying their way and providing them with housing. The girls are then addicted to drugs and stay because of drug dependency. A witness whose name is being withheld because of their age, informed us that after being with them for several days and insisting on going home that Sweet held her while Pepper begin to hit her. Then from nowhere an enormous Pit bull and Samoyed crashed through the front door and drugged, the screaming, Sweet and Pepper out of the house and into the night."

The witness called the police, and when we arrived, we found the bodies of the two victims in the backyard. Their heads and necks had been eaten clear to the skull while their bodies were still intact."

"Is this normal behavior for wild dogs?" the reporter asked somewhat queasy.

"Do you believe they have a master that is putting them up to this?"

"This is not normal behavior for dogs and although they saved the life of an individual from two unsavory individuals, our experts say this is strange behavior for even the most rabid dog."

"Both incidents happened on a full moon, could this be the work of a serial killer or a full moon crazy with some extremely mean dogs?" The reporter asked.

"We have no concrete evidence to suggest anything at this time, However we are cautioning the public about being out on the next full moon night and to report any suspicious individuals or animals to the police."

The camera panned back to the attractive reporter. "This is Lisa Chow reporting live from Oakland."

Part 2

Dogs & Dawgs

Hate!!!
It's everywhere
Both near and there
So far away
What's worse it's here
It's got something 2 say
4 those who want 2 hear
Hate!!!!
Don't push it like weight
You want buff, just break
No love, just ache
Don't believe
Just wait!!!
Hate!!!
It's everywhere
Both near and there
So far away
What's worse it's here
Be aware don't fear
Remember the words of the seer
Hate!!!!!!

1

July 9th, 1:40 p.m., Los Amore Vineyard, Napa Valley, CA

"So you're like a vampire hunter or something?" Jennifer, Vietnamese teen questioned Dr. Flora Rodriguez.

"She's not a vampire hunter, dummy," Jamilah corrected her best friend, adjusting the gray and black striped Badtz Maru beanie worn atop her long, dark, curly hair. "She's a psychiatrist."

"Alright," Jennifer continued. Acknowledging her mocha colored peer's comments. "How many crazy vampires have you seen?"

After an hour on the road, another twenty minutes cruising past countless vineyards Diana Anderson, the mother of Tioni Anderson drove Omari and Jamilah Jackson, Jennifer Twan, and Joseph Babay Jr., (aka) Dragonbrush up a narrow road that led to a three-story, vanilla white, Spanish styled stucco house, surrounded by a vine covered, wall. Inside Diana introduced the teens to Dr. Flora Rodriguez, a tanned, forty-ish Latina, with a soft voice and easy going manner. Flora Stood at 5 feet and 10 inches tall, wearing an oversized, white, button up-blouse with the sleeves rolled up faded, blue jeans and bare feet. Throughout her long, black hair worn in a loose bun were generous streaks of gray. Flora led the curious teens to a spacious patio overlooking her orange grove, filled with shade trees, plush, patio furniture and soft Spanish guitar music softly streaming from the outside speakers. She invited the teens to enjoy the sumptuous, Mexican feast she had prepared for them while she caught up with her old friend Diana. When Flora returned, she found the group relaxing in the chairs gorged from the food and engaged them in lazy conversation.

"I'm not allowed to discuss my clients to others," Flora answered the question of the attractive, 16 year old Vietnamese whose long, ebony braid draped the top of her Chuck-E-Cheese uniform. "But, I can discuss you all. I understand that several weeks you were exposed to vampires. Jennifer you were transformed into one but cured, the Montgomery Ward building was destroyed and I understand members of both the Cobalt and Crimson gangs are missing. Pastor Charles Anderson and Sergeant Norbert Bright of the Oakland police department did well by bringing you all to me because incidents of this magnitude simply do not disappear from our lives on their own. As much as we would like to believe that we can make traumatic situations go away by ignoring them, the truth is, unless we work to rid our lives of their negative effects, they will continue to hinder our personal progress." With a cheery smile the doctor said, "That's it. I would like to see you all in a couple of weeks, take as much food as you want. I can't eat it all."

"That's it!" Jamilah blurted. "We came all the way out here to eat and leave? This whole thing was stupid." The mocha, colored sixteen year-old vented, looking at the others to see if they felt the same.

"Eating and leaving is cool with me." Dragonbrush added, reaching for another handful of tortilla chips from the table. The fourteen year-old Filipino was more concerned about his up coming court appearance than he was with remaining in Napa Valley a minute longer than necessary.

"What's the matter?" Tioni asked, the sun glistening off the fourteen year-olds, gray eyes and braces.

"We're not doing anything," Jamilah continued, "If you're going to a Dr., it should be for something."

"Give us an example of what a doctor should do?" Flora asked fascinated by the striking teen's observations.

"My stomach hurts allot," Jamilah explained, "not my head, and coming here is not going to fix that, so being here is a waste of time if you ask me."

"When you went to the doctor what did they say was wrong with you?" Flora continued questioning.

"Nothing," Jamilah answered.

"I would hazard to guess that your ailment was stress induced more than anything else," The doctor observed, "I have to ask, how many cups of coffee do you drink a morning?"

"I don't drink coffee, thank you very much" Jamilah corrected her.

"Then what is your morning drink?" Flora pressed.

"I drink Mochas or Starbuck's Frappachino's," Jamilah causally responded, it hadn't click that her favorite drinks were caffeine based.

"How many?"

"Two in the morning and sometimes two at night," she answered to the shock of her friends and brother

"Why do you think you too good to eat breakfast?" Flora asked before Jamilah completed her last word.

"I don't think I'm too good to eat breakfast," Jamilah replied with a curled lip. "I just eat breakfast at lunchtime."

"I bet you eat candy in the morning," the doctor challenged.

"So, everybody in this room eats candy for breakfast," Jamilah replied, outing the group.

"Who's this guy that you can't get off your mind morning noon and night?" Flora pressed. "How did you know I think about my daddy all the time?" Jamilah asked with widened eyes.

"Girlfriend must be psychic," Tioni interjected.

"So, Tioni, Jennifer," the doctor said breaking her concentration from Jamilah, "on a scale of one to ten how loud would you say Jamilah grinds her teeth when she's sleep?"

"Stop!" Jennifer shouted amazed. "You are reading my friend like she's was a kindergarten book!"

"But you didn't answer the question," Flora replied her attention completely on the lithe Asian. Tioni looked at Jennifer ignoring Jamilah, then turned to the doctor and said, "About an eight."

Jamilah placed her hand over her mouth amazed; she wondered why some mornings she would wake with her jaw hurting. "At least I don't talk in my sleep." She fired back, "you know what Tioni and Jennifer say in their sleep?" Jennifer be calling O-"

"This is not about them." Flora interrupted, before Jamilah could complete her statement. "This is about you. This is about helping, not embarrassing you." Flora looked at the red faced Jennifer then turned her attention back to the group. "As you can see, this room it's relatively large, but look at all of you all. You're sitting together in the center of the room inches away from each other, looking at Jennifer, Tioni and Jamilah "And you three are leaning over each other," she walked toward the door." You all trust each other more than you know, and that's a good thing. I'll be right back," she said walking out the room, with the crew splitting up and sitting at different locations in the room further away from each other.

"Don't be telling my business," Jennifer said throwing a balled up Kleenex from the table at Jamilah

"So, you guys were telling mine," Jamilah responded throwing it at Jennifer.

"No, she was telling your business." Tioni answered throwing it back at Jennifer.

Flora walked back into the room with a smile on her face, "I knew it." She chuckled, looking at the scattered five. She carried in her hands a box of tea and a bottle of Pepto-Bismol. She walked over to Jamilah and dropped the items in her lap. "This is what you should be taking," She said walking back to her hammock only to find Omari swinging in it.

"How did you know so much about her?" Dragonbrush asked, wondering could the doctor divine his personal issues.

"Believe it or not, Jamilah's maladies are not new," The doctor answered, deciding not to tell the comfortable looking Omari to get up. "In fact, they are quite common in teenagers. Most of you eat too many sweets in the morning, and not a proper breakfast." She continued while sitting in a large purple, velour beanbag with a smaller black, velour bag as a footrest. "But since Jamilah is so concerned about her father, and it's normally some person or parent, that racks our mind," she clarified to the nodding heads of the others, "placing large dosages of caffeine on an already stressed out stomach is where a lot of the pain is coming from. Chamomile or non-caffeine tea is better."

"Are you saying I can't drink my frappuccino's?" Jamilah asked.

"Just not on an empty stomach, that will reduce your pain, and you will have to learn to relax. Grinding your teeth at night is a sign that there is a lot on your mind," she looked around at the others. "And yes, Jamilah, you are right. The rest in this room are probably grinding their teeth talking and walking in their sleep. But, I'm sticking to my original promise," the doctor reiterated.

"When we next meet, I want each of you to tell me something that gets on your nerves."

"Next time?" Omari jumped in, his rust colored dreadlocks bouncing as he stood up. "Does that mean we are finished?" Seconds later he was walking toward the exit with Dragonbrush a close second.

2

3:44 p.m., Los Amore Vineyard

"That was short," Diana asked Flora impressed at how quickly the session had gone as they walked toward Diana's Escalade where the teens waited.

"My objective was to get the group to begin operating as a single unit. In order for that to happen," the psychiatrist explained, "they must first feel that this is a safe and comfortable environment. Fortunately, this group is already comfortable with one another."

"So you wanted to get everyone on the same page?" Diana asked giving her longtime friend a hug before getting behind the wheel of her vehicle. "Did it work?"

"You'll know if I succeeded in few seconds," Flora stated as Diana drove off.

"How was the session?" the pastors wife asked the group as they headed toward the orange groves.

"That was a complete waste of time," Tioni expressed, the others agreeing loudly.

She did it, Diana sighed, she got them all on the same page.

3

10:049 a.m., Lake Shore Avenue. Oakland, CA

It wasn't even noon, and Omari's day was already in the toilet.

Dragonbrush was so bummed out about his court appearance at 9:00 a.m. that Omari suggested they see a movie after. That was before Jamilah received a call from her mother in Seattle asking if it would be okay if in a couple of months, Mercedes the daughter of her boyfriend Jamal Brown (whom Jamilah hated) could share her room, once she was discharged from rehab. What followed was a screaming match of cosmic proportions.

With the assistance of his Aunt Ayanna and Uncle Uhuru, Omari was able to convince Jamilah to join him at the movies and to leave early in order to have breakfast. Afterwards, they could peruse the shops on Lake Shore before meeting Dragonbrush at the Rockridge BART station. Jamilah reluctantly agreed. Omari hoped his sister's mind would be so preoccupied with shopping that she would put her family issues on the back burner. Omari was right. When the two passed a clothing boutique that captured Jamilah's eye, she echoed those fatal words, "I'm only going to stick my head in here for a minute." One store became three. Happy for his sister, but not the least bit interested in shopping with her, Omari waited patiently outside where he could do more than just stand among a myriad of ladies, things looking stupid. The freckled face teen peered through the latest boutique's large, decorative storefront window and could see his older sister sorting through a sales rack of jeans, her lean, five feet and eight inch frame holding several pair of black jeans that seemed to melt into the black, skorts and black, long sleeve BeBe top she was wearing. Her long dark brown, curly tresses gracefully draping her back as she grabbed another pair of black jeans off the sales rack before heading into the dressing room. Turning his attention to the passing cars,

Omari heard the comments.

"Mommy, look! He must have chickenpox!"

The fourteen year old knew the comment was directed at him as Omari's bronze, red, dreadlocks and freckles that danced on his cream-colored face caused double takes and sometime out and out stares. Omari ignored it for the most part, but there were times when he wished his interracial features were not so distinctive. Omari's attention followed the squeaky, high-pitched voice, to a small, coffee colored girl about four years of age with two large Afro puff's pointing at him. Holding her hand was her mother, and behind them at the car was the older sister he assumed who was about his age.

"Those are freckles, not chicken pox," the little girls, mom corrected the youngster with a loud whisper, while smiling at Omari. The three made their way toward the store, obviously to stick their head in for only a minute Omari surmised.

"But Mommy, they're ugly." The girl continued, as her professionally dressed mother hurried her younger daughter past Omari and inside the store before the youngster could make anymore embarrassing comments.

I wonder if this be one of those days? Omari thought, stepping away from the entrance.

"Mom, I forgot something." The oldest daughter whose copper, colored complexion mirrored that of her mother and younger sister spoke before jogging back to their silver, Mercedes CL500 parked at the meter. Omari watched as the attractive teen's long ebony, flat-ironed tresses tangled with her large, gold hoop earrings, used her mother's car remote to open their elegant car. As she rummaged in the front seat of the car, Omari admired her round butt and long, shiny legs. She wore white, Banana Republic shorts and a tight, gray, DKNY sleeveless hoodie. Not wanting to be caught gawking, Omari turned his attention back toward the traffic. The attractive teen, trotted past Omari into the store. Not wanting to make eye contact, Omari turned his attention to the pavement when he heard her call, "Hey!"

Omari turned around and the girl tossed him a balled piece of paper. He caught it with both hands and heard the girl whisper as she walked further into the store "Your freckles and locks are so hot, call me." Omari could hear her giggling as she joined her mother who was sorting through a rack of blouses and her sharp tongued, younger sister. Omari opened the balled paper, and it read

"Are your kisses as hot as your freckles and hair? Call me and let me know? Makemba 112-2309."

Omari felt himself, blushing. He thought about what he was wearing, his sagging bluish gray, Ecko jeans, crisp, oversized white Oaklandish t-shirt, yellow and white, Air Jordan 1 Retro's, and wondered was his attire adequate. Removing his gray cap the teen gently shook his head allowing his dreads to fling, freely across his face. Then peering through the store front window Omari could see an impressed Makemba carefully giving him a smile before catching the attention of her mother who escorted the stunning teen and her younger sister to the opposite end of the boutique and out of view. Omari walked away from the store's window placing the balled paper into his pocket, then took another glance inside the storefront window. His attention was diverted by the powerful hum of a car engine. Turning to his left, he could see a deep green, vintage 1993 Corvette ZR-1, complete an illegal u-turn on Lake Shore Avenue then pulled in front of the teen.

"So you're dealing in front of woman's clothing stores now?" A familiar voice shouted from behind the dark tinted, driver side window, that was lowered, just enough to let the blaring music inside escape. As the passenger side window lowered Omari could see sitting past an unfamiliar bald, African American male occupying the passenger's seat, Justin Greenwald, better known as DJ Jedi, grinning from ear to ear. Justin was the son of a software developer and city councilman A lean, always polished, nineteen year old blonde, blue eyed, pretty boy, Justin's charms and million dollar smiled usually got him what he wanted.

"Man, how many cars do you have?" Omari asked, impressed by the Corvette.

"Just two. This one belongs to the old man," Justin bragged. "Omari, this is my partner Edwin, he's been hanging out in Miami for the last several months, but the call of the Town was too strong for him to ignore, so he's back."

"What's up man?" Omari greeted, walking to the passenger side of the Corvette then shaking the hand of the maple colored black male with a glistening baldhead, muscular build and a model's smile. Dark Ray Ban Aviator glasses covered his eyes. "You're still picking me up this evening?"

"Around 9:00 p.m." Justin responded. "You have time to ride with us to the music store?"

"Naw, I'm waiting for Jamilah, and then we have somewhere we have to be," Omari answered dryly. He knew that Justin didn't like Jamilah, and he didn't like Dragon either. Omari wondered if he liked any of his friends."

"Then do you have time to run and get a sandwich?" Justin pressed.

"I'm cool, I'll see you tonight." Omari answered waiving off even the slightest possibility that he would leave his sister.

"Not a prob, don't forget we have some music to drop off before the show." Justin responded turning his music back to its original, blaring state then continuing down Lake Shore.

Omari met Justin at the hip-hop themed burger joint, Old Skool Café. Omari and Dragonbrush were at the café turntables that were for public use discussing how scratch architect *Grand Master Flash's* DJ-ing style influenced so many of today's DJ's, when Justin, who was the café's guest DJ approached Omari, inviting him and Dragonbrush to see the Café's professional booth. Omari never seeing the inside of the professional booth agreed. Dragonbrush followed, but Dalton the café's security guard, told him, "Only one guest in the booth at a time." Justin told Omari that he had spied some of his turntable techniques and believed he had what it took to be serious DJ, and if Omari was willing to put in the grunt work, Justin would assist him in developing his skills. Seeing it as a cool way to make some extra money, Omari agreed. Justin had yet to win any major DJ competitions or even a record deal, but his DJing theatrics and growing popularity had made him an underground superstar. He could walk into any Rave or local party and get in on just face value. As far as Omari could tell, Justin was the epitome of successful DJ. He had it all, fame, fortune and the perks that fortune provided, like the latest, electronic equipment, an apartment overlooking Lake Merritt, the latest designer clothes, a red, 1966 Ford Mustang and a gray, Land Rover Defender for heavy gigs and a high demand for his mix-tapes which Omari spent most of his time delivering. Omari was learning a lot from his association with Justin, from how to operate the state of the art mixing board and sound systems. "It doesn't matter what equipment you use as it is along as it's by Pioneer or Stanton," to small details like in the heat of mixing, long sleeves have a tendency of touching the vinyl. Running with Justin was cool until it came to Dragonbrush. Justin said he only needed one helper and that Dragonbrush would be in the way. This was unfortunate because with Omari's late schedule and Dragonbrush's early morning paper route, the two spent very little time together. Omari wished Dragonbrush could work with him because as cool as he was, there was something suspicious about Justin that Omari couldn't put his finger on. Omari pulled out the small, crumpled piece of paper from his jacket and then gazed into the window. Makemba was walking into the dressing room holding a bundle of clothes. Omari prayed that Jamilah would leave the store before Makemba saw the two of them together, so he wouldn't have to explain that Jamilah was his sister or have to listen to his older sibling's criticism. Then his thoughts went to Jennifer. He didn't know why. They had gone out to the movies and to eat, but he didn't think of her in a girlfriend way, or at least he didn't think so. They never said anything about it. He placed his hand over the pocket that held the number and decided he would give her a call. Jamilah exited the store holding a shopping bag and a large grin.

"Can I ask a favor?" the gorgeous force of nature pleaded sympathetically.

"There's one more store I want to stick my head in for only a minute, maybe two." Omari looked at his sister and it was clear that she was having fun and not worried about their parents. How could he say no?

4

11:04 a.m., Lake Merritt BART Station

Dragonbrush was impressed by his free hand drawing of super heroine, *Darna*.

He couldn't wait to show off his cool poses once he met up with Omari and Jamilah at the Rockridge station. The young Filipino began penciling the Pinay version of Wonder Woman in his sketchbook he referred to as his "bible" while sitting in court. Dragonbrush completed outlining the pencils with a fine tipped sharpie in the Bart station while waiting for the train. Moving his shoulder length hair styled with Gatsby Hair Wax from his eye, the fourteen year old stood, and stretched his 5 foot, 5 inch, olive, brown frame. Dragonbrush possessed an artist's spirit, and was never truly happy unless he was creating, primarily on public walls. Looking down at his attire of paint splattered camouflage cargo pants, large black t-shirt that read *"Artist, Make Lousy Wage Slave,"* and hand painted Jordan', the words of Omari's Aunt Ayanna, came back him. "Don't you think your clothes are too passive aggressive?" He agreed to keep his shirt covered by wearing his gray, 594 hoodie.

Dragonbrush also remembered Omari telling him that if ever pissed him off, he would tell his aunt that 594 stood for penal code Section 594-625c 594. The code states every person who maliciously defaces damages or destroys property with graffiti or other inscribed material is in violation of the law. In retrospect, the hoodie was a bad idea also, and the judged called Dragonbrush on it.

Several months ago Dragonbrush and his friend, Yes, were apprehended while tagging a freeway underpass. When the officers spotted the tag "Dragonbrush," they instantly associated it with the same tag in countless other areas, and arrested them. The offense resulted in him standing before one of the hardest Judges in the county, Judge John Yamiguchi. Judge Yamiguchi could sentence 50 youth to juvenile hall or camp before lunch, then sentence another 50 by the end of the day and could be seen leaving the courthouse as if he didn't have a care in the world. Originally, Dragonbrush was scheduled to appear before Judge Patrick Rickman, whom Dragonbrush heard was lenient judge, but at the last minute he was reassigned to Yamiguchi's court. The harsh judge released Dragonbrush to his parents, but told Dragonbrush that, "he would be keeping an eye on him."

The Dublin/Pleasanton bound train arrived, blowing papers and dust through the station and blowing the teens, waxed hair, as he touched his hair, to see if any hair was out of place. Dragonbrush reflected on how much he hated the Judge. For one thing, he was forced to use his real name Joseph Madayag Jr. rather than his preferred street name, Dragonbrush. He also believed the judge hated Filipinos. While others got a simple slap on the wrist and let go, for doing the same crime (Yes was told to "leave his court and never return"). The Judge told Dragonbrush he would have to "pay for his crime." Dragonbrush knew that the judge would have given him some serious juvie time had it not been for Sergeant Norbert Bright acting on his behalf. Bright suggested to the judge that Dragonbrush and Yes use their time and talent for community service, by painting a mural at the Malcolm X Youth Center. This would allow the two to use their artistic skills in a positive way. The judge agreed under the conditions that Dragonbrush would appear before him monthly, so he could personally review his progress. At that time, he would also hear of any further incidents or complaints of tagging, or as he called it "vandalism." The judge also ordered that Dragonbrush parent's pay $2,500 for damages their son had cause, this resulted in Dragonbrush being kicked, out his house to live in the tool shed in the backyard and later from the house completely. For the past several weeks, Dragonbrush had been living with Omari, his sister and uncle and aunt. Last night was Dragonbrush's first night back at his parents.

Today was Dragonbrush and family's monthly check in at the Alameda County Court House Juvenile Division. It was then that Judge Yamiguchi explained that there was an accounting error and that instead of $2,500 the Madayags actually owed $13,000 in restitution fines.

When Dragonbrush's dad, Joseph Madayag, Sr. heard that, Dragonbrush thought his dad would choke him just like Homer did Bart Simpson whenever he was mad at him. When the senior Madayag argued that his son had "acted without his consent," the judge responded, "As his father, he was forced to pay the restitution regardless of whether his son did it "against his will or not".

Instead of reacting, Joseph remained calm and left the courthouse instead of getting dropped off by his furious father, Dragonbrush thought it wiser, that he catch BART to meet Omari and Jamilah and allow his parents to cool off."

Dragonbrush sat back on the bench in frustration. The additional fine couldn't have come at a worse time, it had been three months since his dad had been laid off from the bakery a position he had held for twenty years before getting a lesser paying position at Safeway and Dragonbrush's brother Lewis was in college depending on them for income, and his mom had just announced that she was pregnant.

Dragonbrush had recently got part of a paper route delivering the San Francisco Chronicle, which paid him $250 a month of which $200 went toward the payment of the restitution thiswould allow him to pay off the $2,500 in a year, but $13,000? He would be paying off that the rest of his life.

Loud laughter and obscenity laced words filled the station; Dragonbrush turned and could see they were originating from four males on the descending escalator. He recognized the four Cobalt gang members, Glock, Slimstyle, Coffy and Shady and felt a shiver run down his spine. Glock, a muscular, golden, brown African American, with dark brown hair cut in a Fro-hawk, a goatee, and bloodshot eyes that had given up on the value of his or anyone else's life years ago. Violence and intimidation were the tools the nineteen year old used to negotiate, and he saw no need to add anything else to his repertoire. A lieutenant in the notorious bay area Cobalt gang Glock one of the few people on earth that truly terrified Dragonbrush. The fourteen year old Pinoy had heard that Glock had recently been paroled from the San Quentin Sate Prison for assault with the intent to kill; for pushing a woman in front of an oncoming car on a dare. Dragonbrush's plans were to avoid him at all cost. Glock was wicked, his buddy Slimstyle was twisted. Slimstyle enjoyed watching Joe Pesci in the movie Good Fella's because his character was violent and unpredictable, which was how Slimstyle envisioned himself. Shady and Coffy were equally nice. Apparently one of them had a court date or had to check in with their parole officer. Glock and his posse were 4 good reasons to build more jails Dragonbrush thought, observing that by sitting at the far end of the station. He was in open view with nothing to hide behind. Forgetting the effort he placed into styling his hair, the Filipino pulled his hoodie over and his head and placed his sketchbook under his jacket hoping they would continue, in the opposite direction, allowing him the opportunity to catch whatever train, in whichever direction.

Dragonbrush was five years old when he first met the Glock. He remembered his older brother Lewis taking him to Saeed's corner market for sodas. Dragonbrush remembered Glock and Slimstyle approaching them from across an empty street, Slimstyle pushing his thirteen year-old brother to ground, and Glock grabbing Dragonbrush, placing a pistol to his head. Slimstyle handed Lewis a butcher's knife and told him that unless he took that knife into Saeed's store and robbed him, they would blow his little brother away. To prove their seriousness, Dragonbrush could recall Glock telling Lewis that there were two bullets in the chamber and he didn't know where before pulling the trigger to the gun at his temple and hearing the gun click. Dragonbrush remembered the terrified expression on his brother's face before he ran into the store and robbed Saeed's wife who was alone at the cash register before Glock could pull the trigger again.

Dragonbrush felt a chill as he reflected on the incident. He didn't realize how close to death he was until he got older, but the experience still gave him nightmares. A couple of hours later, Officer Norbert Bright the local beat cop found out what had happened from Saeed, after talking to he and brother, Glock and Slimstyle went back to juvenile hall on a probation violation without revealing that Dragonbrush and his brother snitched. Bright returned the money, his father never found out and they never went to Saeeds for anything after that. Fortunately, Glock and Slimstyle spent more time locked up than they did walking the street, but when he was free. Glock was the second most horrific thing that had ever happened to Dragonbrush.

The thugs sauntered causally from the escalator taking pride in their menacing appearance as the other wary commuters stood their distance. They migrated toward the opposite end of the platform where Dragonbrush hoped they would continue until he could sneak toward the up escalator and out of the station. Then, as if he knew Dragonbrush was on the platform, Glock turned around and met Dragonbrush's horror, with a wide grin. The young tagger had been made. Feeling butterflies rise in his stomach as the four approached, calling his name in laughter. Dragonbrush first thought was to run through the train tunnel to escape, but another fear gripped him, preventing him from running into the dark abyss.

The four surrounded the nervous Filipino, Glock leaned over Dragonbrush, opened his leather jacket, revealing a crisp fitted wife beater and the black handles of two 9mm Glock's placed in his white boxers and sagging blue jeans. Glaring from side to side, Dragonbrush could see that the others also had guns and remained motionless.

"I know what you are thinking," Glock grinned, "I won't shoot you in the station," he placed his hand in the small of his back and pulled out a hunting knife and placed the tip of the four inch blade between Dragonbrush's eyes. The teen froze as he could see his own frightened eyes in the shiny blade "If you try anything, this will cut your tongue out before you even scream." Glock used his knife to flip Dragonbrush's hood from his head then placing his face into Dragonbrush's asked, his "ya heard?"

Dragonbrush nodded in compliance, the smell of strong, alcohol, violating his senses.

"Good," the bully asserted. "We need you to make a few drop off's for us."

"I can't," Dragonbrush responded sheepishly, looking down to avoid eye contact with Glock giving his tormentor the opportunity to grab a fistful of Dragonbrush's coiffed hair, forcing him from the bench to his knees. "See fella's, this is how you treat your freak." Glock said mockingly, his grip so tight that Dragonbrush could only grimace in pain as tears formed in his eyes.

"I said," Glock spoke with anger at hearing the "no" word. "I need you to make a few drops for us, ya heard?"

"I can't, I'll get in trouble" Dragonbrush stood by his story, enduring the agony. "Slimstyle!" Dragonbrush heard Glock assert before he felt a savage kick to his stomach. His hardcover, sketch book absorbing most of the blow, but when his body collapsed, the teen cried in pain as he felt the roots of his hair pulled from his scalp the shocked teen looked at the passengers watching the entire incident at other end of the BART station and wondered, *Why are they just looking and not helping? Could they also be enjoying my humiliation?*

Dragonbrush's inner voice told him, they're really going to kill you. Do what you have to do to live. "Okay I'll go," Dragonbrush agreed weakly, noticing the destination sign flashing for a Fremont bound train. The almond toned teen knew that during the morning commute each train would have at least one police officer aboard that would help him. He resolved to wait until the last moment before the doors closed and make a dash for it

"So are we bringing him with us?" Slimstyle a cruel, eighteen year old transplant from Flint, Michigan with pimply chocolate skin and locks worn in two pigtails asked, wondering did they really want to deal with a commotion that Dragonbrush could cause while riding the 8-car train, arousing the curiosity of the passengers inside the train.

"Hell yeah, will let him take all the risk" Glock replied, placing his new, unlaced Nikes on Dragonbrush's thigh. "You don't mind do you?" he taunted, while looking defiantly at the occupants on board the train including the train operator as the train doors opened. Panic hit Dragonbrush like a bucket of cold water, instead of waiting for the last minute he rolled from underneath Glock's foot tripping him. The rest fell to the floor as they tried to catch their toppling friend. Dragonbrush bolted for the train and had taken several steps when his sketch book fell between his legs, tripping him to the ground. He quickly recovered grabbing his book, but the four were again standing over him Glock kneeled down beside Dragonbrush and again gripped a handful of hair.

"Next time," Glock sneered before releasing the teen to crumpled back to the shiny floor. Dragonbrush closed his eyes and braced himself for whatever punishment would follow, but after a few seconds he noticed that nothing had happened. He looked up, and could see that the four had boarded the train and were pointing in his direction letting him know that they would see him again.

What happened? Dragonbrush asked himself, wondering why the gang bangers would leave him. Turning to the opposite end of the station, he could see two officers walking in his direction. "Thank God," he sighed, as he set back on the bench. He looked at the now moving train and could see Glock and his menacing peers laughing at him.

Dragonbrush's heart jumped again as he recognized the black and white officers walking casually toward him as the officers he, and his friends Omari and Yes had a run in with weeks earlier. Dragonbrush hoped they had forgotten because, he was too hurt, nauseas and angry to run.

"I don't believe it," the wiry, walnut colored officer said with a scowl. "I know the person in need of assistance, can't be the same kid that flipped us the bird the other night?"

They remembered, Dragonbrush groaned. "I'm sorry about that, but those guys attacked me." He said, clearly shaken.

"Yeah, and I'm sure you started it," the taller and heavier white officer added. "I know your kind, little smart-mouths, an ass kicking is all you understand." He reached and touched Dragonbrush tangled hair "You got goop in your hair like a woman, you don't even respect the fact that you are a male. You had it coming." He looked at his partner. "I'm not even calling this in, this guy disgusts me."

"They had guns and a knife" Dragonbrush spoke trying to hold himself together.

"Yeah. of all the people at this station that they could have robbed, they chose you?" The black officer asked, unconvinced of Dragonbrush's sincerity. "Here's what I think. You saw those guys, said something stupid to them, and they beat the hell out of you. If they had guns and a knife and didn't use them on you, then be glad."

"I tell you what," the white officer added looking down at the shaken youth, "You go see a barber and cut that birds nest of yours to a reasonable length then we will see what we can do," he said with a laugh that was joined by his partner. Dragonbrush looked up, the Richmond train had arrived, and passengers were boarding and exiting. He rushed toward it and slid between the doors just before they closed. He looked at the still laughing officers and gave them the finger. The wounded teen lumbered to the back of the car and plopped into an empty seat. Dragonbrush then buried his throbbing head into his lap and wept bitterly.

5

11:37 a.m., Mac Arthur BART station, Pittsburg Platform,

"When I go back to Seattle It will be to get my things and get the hell up out of there." Jamilah said while reviewing her purchases. "That cow can have that room, I'm not sharing nothing!"

"If anything of Jamal's is there then I'm not going back." Omari responded with equal frustration. "I hate him, and I hate her for dealing with him."

The teens arrived at the upper platform of the outside train station in time to watch their Pittsburgh bound train depart. The two shared a graffiti covered concrete bench knowing that it would be fifteen minutes before the next one. Omari noticed that Jamilah's surly mood had returned, but the more he thought about her situation, the more he understood why she should be sullen.

"She cares more about dude then she does her own family." Jamilah lamented; her eyes fueled with pain and anger "what's wrong with her?" "You think she's on drugs or something?"

"I don't know what's wrong with her," Omari answered softly.

He once asked himself that question, but could never associate his folks with drugs addicts. "Is Dad still coming over?"

"He said he was, and when I see him, I'm telling him everything" Jamilah replied leaning over to bump into her brother.

"What do you think he is going to do?" Omari asked.

"I don't know."

A voice yelling "Catch!" interrupted their personal conversation.

Jamilah turned, and could see an object, flying in her direction. She instinctively caught the small silver drawstring pouch with bumpy items inside.

The teens looked for the pitcher of the well-tossed item and twenty feet from them stood a tall, thin, balding, dark skin, black man who looked to be in his late sixties or early seventies. There was a smile on his grizzled, white, bearded face holding 2 suitcases as he boarded a south bound train.

"Hey, it's that old guy from the airport, Vaccinator!" Jamilah called, with a start, recognizing him from a month.

"You mean Vaticinator," Omari corrected his sister. The siblings met the elder at the Oakland airport when they arrived from Seattle. He gave Omari a cross and a compact disk that changed colors with each song. The CD contained lyrics that assisted them against vampires and saving Jennifer from being taken away from master vampires, Niles and Fraiser. Omari had since stopped playing the CD once he grew tired of hearing the same song over again.

"Jamilah!" The old man called, as passengers began to flow out of the open train doors like an interrupted ant mound. "That bag will hold on to you no matter what, and you both must remember that Dragonbrush looks up to you."

"Wait!" Omari yelled, as the train horn sounded, and the train doors closed. "I want to talk to you." But it was too late the old man had stepped inside seconds before the doors closed, and the silver train darted off to the next station.

"Aw man!" Omari wailed. "There were so many things I wanted to ask him. Like how did he know about the vampires," he said turning to Jamilah who was opening up the silver bag that Vaticinator placed so much importance on.

"Eeewww!" she cried, dropping the small bag to the concrete floor. Omari watched as two dog biscuits and a pair of plastic *Elmo* from *Sesame Street* sunglasses bounced out of the bag "I don't even have a dog, and I certainly wouldn't wear those ugly, baby glasses. Why he give me some garbage like this?" She asked turning to the equally confused Omari. A few minutes later, the north bound, Pittsburg train arrived walking into the train Omari noticed that Jamilah had left the small silver bag on the ground. "You're not taking the bag he gave you?"

"I don't want that!" she replied upset that it was ever tossed to her.

"Didn't he say to hold on to it no matter what?" Omar asked, as the two boarded the train.

"Like I care," Jamilah answered, grabbing her bags.

6

11:39 a.m., Rockridge BART station, upper platform,

Dragonbrush's head throbbed. The pain from having his hair pulled was so excruciating he became nauseous and threw up in the station's smelly, public restroom. Sitting again at the far end of the station to avoid being disturbed, Dragonbrush found himself wanting his mother; his sister Gwen, and Jamilah. He adjusted his hoodie to avoid any attention, but it did very little to ease the pain. He just couldn't believe that Glock and Slimstyle had gotten away with what they had done to him, and would continue to get away with it because he would never tell. Glock was crazy and Dragonbrush knew what he was capable of doing.

Dragonbrush remembered the summer when he was eight years of age. Glock pulled him from the Malcolm X recreational play yard to make a drug delivery for him. On the way Glock noticed a parked police car, in the rear seat of the vehicle was a German shepherd who growled at them. On the car windshield there was a decal that read, "Caution do not approach or play with dog."

Glock hated the police and he didn't like dogs. Even more, he hated police dogs in squad cars with warning signs. Dragonbrush remembered watching Glock pull two packs of Black Cat firecrackers from his blue puffy jacket, lighting and slipping them through the slight gap that was left in the window in order for the dog to get proper ventilation when the packs hit the floor of the car. The snarling dog that made every effort to intimidate Glock instantly investigated the sizzling packs, stepping back from the sparks.

"Hey! What are you doing over there?" Dragonbrush remembered the Chinese officer that had gone into a coffee shop yelling as he rushed toward them, "Get away from there!" Dragonbrush remembered Glock's large arm sweeping him off his feet then dashing away from the car, down the street, and around the corner. Dragonbrush could see the shock on the officer's face as the firecrackers went off, horrifying him and the yelping German shepherd that was trapped in the back seat with the popping firecrackers.

Dragonbrush remembered peering from behind a building with Glock watching the quick thinking officer using his car key to open the rear door and getting the frightened dog out unscathed.

After making the drug delivery, Glock took Dragonbrush back to the X play yard. Dragonbrush remembered his words "if you ever told anyone what happened, I will kill your family." Later, Glock was caught and sent back to Youth Authorities, and Dragonbrush wouldn't see him for another three years. But he never told anyone about what happened with the dog because he truly believed Glock then, and that he would do it now. Just as he knew if he told Omari about what happened earlier, he would want to get involved. Dragonbrush knew that if Omari crossed Glock or Slimstyle he would end up on a slab in the morgue. Dragonbrush resolved that the best thing to do was to regain his composure, and keep what happened today a secret. Dragonbrush checked to see if he still had his parent's money and patted his jacket to see if his sketch book was also there. Assured that everything was where it was suppose, to be, he closed his eyes hoping a few minutes of sleep would ease the throbbing at the top of his crown before meeting Omari and Jamilah downstairs at the agreed time.

7

11:49 a.m., Rockridge BART station lower platform,

"I said, excuse me!" the terse words brought Dragonbrush back to consciousness, the BART station and a throbbing headache.

"Huh?" Dragonbrush responded to the female standing in front of him. Looking at his watch he discovered he had been asleep for ten minutes. Soon he would have to meet the Omari and Jamilah at the front entrance downstairs.

"I said, is anyone sitting in the seats next to you?" the female pressed.

Dragonbrush painfully turned his head from left to right, the adjacent seats were vacant. He then turned his attention to the female standing in front of him and found himself in awe of the cute, rust colored African American with bleached blonde hair worn in a bob that partly covered the left side of her face. She sported half a dozen gold chains around her neck and large gold hoop earrings dangled from each ear. She wore a green form fitting cami that displayed the Jamaican flag and black, Capri pants that were slightly tighter than her top. Gold bracelets and anklets showered her arms and sandal covered feet leaving Dragonbrush to wonder, how was she able to approach me without being heard?

To her left was a Latin beauty; her dark, shoulder length hair worn under a white, Nike bicycle cap. Oversized Versace sunglasses prevented Dragonbrush from seeing her eyes. Around her neck, she wore a Coach dog collar that Dragonbrush found unique. She wore a white tank top with the image of Odie from Garfield slobbering that was just long enough to reveal a belly button ring on her rippled stomach, light gray, baggy tech pants and white K Swiss's completed her look. The confidence the two possessed rivaled Sereena and Venus Williams, they were awesome and knew it.

"No," the Filipino answered nervously, "have a seat." The dynamic duo stood over Dragonbrush with a triumphant look which made him all the more ill at ease. They both smiled and took a seat beside him "My name is Lexus McDonald," the dark girl said introducing herself. My friend here is Maria Juaez".

"Nice to meet you," Dragonbrush answered weakly, wondering what sort of scam the two were running. "My name is.."

"We already know your name," Maria's soft voice interrupted. "Mr. Joseph Madayag Jr. I'm sorry, I meant Dragonbrush," she said with a broad grin revealing gorgeous teeth, with canines that seemed longer than usual.

Dragonbrush ignored his head "Do I know you?"

"You were really hard to find" Lexus continued ignoring his question. "The only info we were able to Google on you was that you once lived on 2235 Chase Street in West Oakland. We get there and the place was leveled after a fire and is now part of a new housing development."

"It's been years since I've lived there," Dragonbrush replied, thinking that maybe they were from the old neighborhood, but he would have remembered females that looked liked these two. "Who did you say you were again," he asked.

"Lexus and Maria," Maria responded with a polite smile. "So we get to the house and there's nothing there. We were able to isolate five scents from the house that closely matched yours." She explained to the confused Dragonbrush.

"We figured if we followed the strongest human scent that would lead us to you." Lexus picked up from where Maria left off. "Even after the new construction, the fire left a charred scent everywhere which made finding your scents hard." Dragonbrush noticed from the way the two females stared upward as they spoke, that the teens were not so much talking to him or even each other as much as reviewing a process they had practiced.

"We followed the strongest scent to the city of Alameda, to a Safeway store that scent belonged to your father" Lexus added catching

Dragonbrush's attention.

"That's where he works," The curious Filipino agreed, noticing Maria rising from her seat.

"We followed him back to Oakland to your home on Hillside Street and were able to locate only two of the original scents, and there were more people there" Maria continued.

Duh! Dragonbrush thought to himself, fascinated by the conversation, only the folks who moved into my room after I was kicked out.

"Two of the original scents had disappeared from the area," Maria continued" confused by this knowledge. Dragonbrush knew that his brother had relocated to L.A. to go to school, and he didn't want to think about his sister.

"Then we realized we were focusing too hard on the wrong scent." Lexus said also standing "and it was funny," She said now slowly pacing back and forth. Dragonbrush compared her movements to a large cat. "Once we started tracking your scent."

"It was everywhere you had tagged!" Maria added excitedly "you have tagged all over the city, it was easy to trace to you here and here we are," she said with a sense of accomplishment in her voice.

"So let me get this straight," Dragonbrush asked thinking the two needed to see a shrink more than he did. "You have been looking all over the city trying to find me by my scent?"

Lexus leaned over Dragonbrush, her nose inches from his. "That is exactly how we found you, by just following our noses." Before Dragonbrush could respond to the uncomfortable position, he was in the scene was interrupted by a male voice. "Hey sister, why don't you try sharing some of that action you're using on that zero, on a hero."

The three turned and could see five white males and one Asian all in their early twenties, all sporting caps worn backward, and except for one, they all wore dark glasses.

Two of the males wore knee length short pants, the others in jeans and khakis. Except for the shirtless male with the mouth who stuck his white t-shirt in the back pocket of his jeans they all wore t-shirts and jerseys with the San Francisco Giants insignia. It was obvious they were going to a Giants game and had started their tailgate party early by having too many beers before even getting to the stadium.

"Why don't you two bring those money makers over here and lap dance for the fella's" no shirt continued.

"Yeah we got big tips for you," another one howled.

"Lexus looked over to Maria and said "Ignore them, we're not here for this," and they both took their original seats.

It's going to happen again, Dragonbrush worried, feeling himself becoming gripped by fear.

"Calm down, nothing going to happen to you" Maria assured him. Dragonbrush turned to his side and could see Maria muscles start to tense and ripple.

"Hey bring the guy also, Jake likes doing it with dudes anyway," the laughter became even louder

The three remained silent.

"Then don't say nothin ya bitches!" No Shirt yelled with anger in his words.

"Yeah, ya skanky ho's," another one chimed in.

"We had to be bitches," Lexus said to Maria with a familiar dryness in her voice.

"We had to be ho's," Maria returned, her voice registering the same weary passion. The two stood up. "Be right back," Lexus said turning to a silent Dragonbrush. He watched the two walked towards the six loud males shoulder to shoulder their body movements, muscular and assured. Dragonbrush could tell that without even looking the two were aware of everything that was going on around them. He noticed that when they were a yard of the still teasing males they split up, each walked on the opposite end of the knuckleheads who were still jeering as if they were trying to avoid walking through the crowd. The males continued to berate the females, but Dragonbrush could not hear the insults, his focus was solely on Maria and Lexus their movement similar to a National Geographic special on the wolf. The special featured a pack of wolves chasing a clumsy, yet powerful moose. Once the wolves caught up to the great beast, they started to attack it from the sides and hindquarters quickly bringing the moose down for an easy kill. This scene was so similar to what he saw on the special because Lexus and Maria were now on both sides of the drunken group who did not realize that when the duo split, it put the group off guard by splitting their attention as to who they wanted to harass. Then the females struck with the same precision that the wolves used on the television special, only instead of pulling the beast down with the their teeth, the two females shoved the males into each other with such force that Dragonbrush could see a capped tooth fly in the air and onto the train tracks. Several of the males tried to fight back. But Maria and Lexus's speed and strength was fearsome tossing several of the belligerent males into the closed elevator door and slapping another down the stairs. The males quickly assembled and dashed down the stairs like whipped mongrels. The bystanders on the platform stood in amazement, others applauded and laughed, but none approached them. The two turned their attention back to Dragonbrush and walked toward him shoulder to shoulder with silly grins on their faces.

"Wow!" Was the word that slipped from Dragonbrush's mouth as the teens approached him, he could not believe they dispatched six guys so fast. What were they vampires? But the sun was shining, and it was just the afternoon. But more importantly what did they want from him? He wondered. Whatever it was he certainly wasn't going to say "no."

The two sat beside the Pinoy teen, each placing a kiss on his cheek, instantly embarrassing him. "We are going to a full moon party tonight and we want you to come," Lexus shared with the red faced tagger.

"Oh really," Dragonbrush answered. "Where is this party going to be?" his hoodie starting to move across his face indicating another train was approaching.

"We can't tell you that, but its going to be unworldly," Maria answered

"We'll pick you up," Lexus added "and you have to come alone." She looked at Maria as the doors to the train opened as passengers began to file out before those waiting to board could enter.

"Sure, give me your number, and I will call you," Dragonbrush responded, thinking this pair was more than he could handle, he wasn't going anywhere with them.

"Don't worry, we'll find you," Lexus remarked with a bright smile as she boarded the train. The two giggled and waved to him as the train departed.

"What was that all about?" Dragonbrush asked himself, disturbed by the two females that came through the BART station, kicked butt, kissed then cut out. The bloody tooth lying between the train tracks reminded Dragonbrush that what happened was very real. Maria and Lexus had left the teen shaken, not frightened as he was with Glock and his crew instead he was disturbed. What did they want from him? It was if they had been sent after him. How were they able to find him through his scent? He didn't smell that bad. And why would they want him to go alone to a party with them? Dragonbrush's thoughts went back to the television special on wolves they had a great sense of smell, but also ways of marking their territory. By urinating on a particular territory, rubbing their necks, or licking a trees branches to make it known to strangers that they were on somebody else's turf. Could the kisses he received be Lexus and Maria's way of marking him? "C'mon man," Dragonbrush concluded his conversation with himself. "They were not wolves," but like Glock, he planned to avoid them. The throbbing pain in Dragonbrush's head was too great to ignore any longer. He felt himself becoming nauseous and wrapped his arms around his stomach, and doubled over to keep from puking. The brown teen felt what he thought was sweat running down the side of his face when he wiped it his fingers were covered with blood. His head was bleeding, and without looking Dragonbrush knew his hoodie was soaked in blood. Worst of all Dragonbrush knew that Omari, and Jamilah would arrive any minute, to find him beaten and sick.

"I'm in deep doo doo," he said aloud as his empty stomach searched frantically for anything to violently launch upward. Dragonbrush felt a hand on his head and then a sensation throughout his body that left him momentarily stunned. He looked up to see who had touched him and could see an elderly African American male. He was tall, dark, with a white beard and a white semi, bald afro walking toward the second Pittsburgh bound train that had just arrived. "The grizzled, old man turned to face Dragonbrush and said' "I left something for you. Remember in the days ahead to use logic and love to control your actions, not primal instincts."

"Huh, what are you talking about?" Dragonbrush asked, thinking that he had run into his third crazy person today. He looked down at his side and saw a CD that was similar to Omari's. While observing the CD, Dragonbrush realized that his head was no longer hurting nor was he nauseous. When the old man touched him, he healed him. "How did you do that?" Dragonbrush shouted, but it was too late. The train doors had closed, and Dragonbrush's words fell on deaf ears. The teen touched the top of his head and then looked at his fingers. There was no blood. He then patted it. Dragonbrush didn't know how, but the pain was gone. He couldn't believe it. Then realizing that the top of his hoodie was probably soaked with blood, he quickly removed it, before Omari and Jamilah arrived with questions. When he pulled it off, there was not a drop of blood anywhere. "Am I loosing it?" he asked aloud, placing the hoodie back on, and finger combing his hair.

"Hey! Stop playing with yourself and let's go!" Omari's voice snapped Dragonbrush from his train of thought. Omari and Jamilah had departed the same train the old man had boarded. Knowing that he was finally around people he could trust and would look after his best interest, he suddenly felt very tired. The day had been tremendously stressful and incredibly weird.

"That hair-style supposed to be some sort of statement?" Jamilah asked, acknowledging Dragonbrush's pulled out do. Then before he could answer, said, "Just keep the hoodie on."

"How did court go?" Omari asked.

"It was alright," Dragonbrush replied. "It's just this judge. He could let me go but he keeps giving me court dates. He acts as if he has a personal stake in my case. Dude is going to give me time. I just know it," the teen vented.

"When do you go back? Jamilah asked, aware that something was bothering him.

"Next month," he answered. "Omari, do you have your old Sony Discman with you?" Dragonbrush asked, "This old guy gave me a CD that looked like yours."

"Did you say an old guy?" Jamilah asked with intense interest. "What did he look like?"

"He was tall, had a Bozo haircut and had a white beard," Dragonbrush confirmed. "But it was strange. I had a headache, and dude touched me and-"

"That was Vaticinator," Jamilah interrupted before Dragonbrush could finish his statement.

"How did he manage to get here? Wasn't he on the train going the other way?" Omari asked, handing Dragonbrush his vintage player that he kept to play CD's.

Dragonbrush inserted the CD into the player then placed the headphones on and listened. Dog howls and the syncopated beat of heavy drums were somber, yet catchy, immediately seizing Dragonbrush's attention.

Dog in, dogged out
You foaming at the mouth,
Your logic's off its route,
Your brain gone south,
You're chasing your tail trying to work it all out

Giving up your sanity,
Losing your humanity,
Everything you had can be taking away instantly

Your hate grows your will and dreams will cease
When your rage reveals your true inner beast

Death and self destruction is what will be unleashed
Unless you use your logic as compass and a leash

dogs run deep, creep, appear while you sleep
Packs attack the weak while running the streets,
Bared fangs and hard hearts is how they greet,

Refusing to believe that their choices are theirs to make alone,
Better learn to accept that dawgs that run in packs can be wrong.

Dragonbrush continued to listen, confused by the lyrics. The bounce was danceable but he knew there was a message. After sharing the song with Omari and Jamilah they were as perplexed Dragonbrush, "I don't know what the song means," Omari spoke as the three headed downstairs. Dragonbrush noticed that three officers were heading to the top of the platform followed by the guys that had caused the incident. If Lexus and Maria were still there Dragonbrush was sure they would be arrested. *Apparently that's how the BART police work,* Dragonbrush thought, glad to be finally leaving the BART station.

9

9:21p.m., Madayag *Residence, Fairmont Street*

For the price of one movie the teens watched three. Aunt Ayanna and uncle Uhuru picked them up, dropping Omari off at the Old Skool Café where he would meet Justin, before taking Dragonbrush to his home.

"The additional penalty was most unfortunate," Uhuru said after Dragonbrush shared the outcome from the morning's court appearance.

"That's why he should spend the night with us tonight," Jamilah advocated taking Dragonbrush home with them. "You know his parents are going to be pissed!"

"And he certainly can, after he sees his parents," Ayanna responded. "Dragonbrush has to take responsibility for his actions," Uhuru interjected. "His parents tags are not up on the walls, his are, and he has to face them and try to make things right. If things don't work out, I will gladly come and pick him up."

"We would be derelict as parents if we didn't support them," Ayanna added as the Prius pulled up in front of the single story house. Dragonbrush exited and stared at the two-bedroom house that he used to call home. Fully aware that Uhuru would not leave until he was inside, Dragonbrush walked to the back door. After several raps on the screened back door, his Cousin Tony answered the door still wearing his United Parcel Services uniform. The long time UPS Package Sorter has finally made Driver, Dragonbrush thought. Tony was twenty-four years of age but acted like a much older man. He had a close cut haircut that seemed to be the style of many Pinoy's, and one Dragonbrush was considering.

"Man, I heard what happened," Tony said to Dragonbrush, informing him that what took place in court was now common knowledge. "When your old man came in he looked like his head was about to explode."

"Thanks for the heads up," Dragonbrush replied, thinking, *that was the last thing I wanted to hear.* He entered the kitchen, hearing Uhuru's Prius drive off and was greeted by the humidity created by a large pot of boiling water on the gas stove. He watched Tony go back to the kitchen table that was covered with plastic bowls, filled with thinly sliced pork, chopped yellow and green onions, cabbage and eggs on one side and Tony's laptop computer and baby toys on the other. Tony sat and resumed his chat room session on his laptop.

"Hi Joey, Jr.," Lisa, Tony's twenty year old wife greeted Dragonbrush. Lisa sat at the kitchen table breastfeeding her four-month-old son Bayanai, while on the phone and preparing a meal of Pancit noodles. Lisa was round and petite and able to do everything while talking on the phone. Dragonbrush wondered what there was to talk about all day. But she was nice enough.

"Hi Lisa," Dragonbrush answered, annoyed at the sight of his young cousin breastfeeding *Yuck!* Dragonbrush thought to himself. Natural or not, breastfeeding still looked nasty even if he also did it as a child. The teen made his way past the nursing mother smiling casually, trying to ignore yet fascinated by the site, wondering, *were women part cow?* That was an idea he would have to sketch in his bible. Dragonbrush made his way instinctively to the refrigerator after seeing nothing of interested, grabbed a handful of cookies from the Ms. Piggy cookie jar that sat atop the frig. Dragonbrush dad was a baker for Safeway, so there were always home made cookies in the cookie jar "Anybody want one?" Dragonbrush offered before placing the lid on the cookie jar Tony and Lisa nodded no. The three were never really comfortable with each other, especially, after Dragonbrush's father threw him out the house and let Tony and his wife move into his bedroom, until they were able to save up enough money to afford their own place in addition to helping share the burden of the Madayag's monthly household expenses. No one was comfortable with the conditions in which they moved in. It was obvious that they didn't feel good about how the situation went down. But Dragonbrush knew part of it was his fault and didn't blame Tony and his family, biting into the chocolate chip cookie Dragonbrush continued into the living room where his parents sat watching the Channel 2 news.

Dragonbrush observed his father Joseph Madayag Sr. sitting in his favorite, brown, leather wingback recliner spellbound by his favorite television show, Cops, and instantly a felt fear and loathing for the portly man. Joseph Madayag Sr. stood 5 feet and 10 inches tall. His hair was black with heavy streaks of gray, his face was always clean-shaven. He and Dragonbrush had the darkest complexions of the family of five. Joseph was a quiet man who rarely argued, most of the time it was hard to tell what he was thinking, because he kept most of his thoughts to himself. Those who knew him well could decipher his thoughts through his body language that articulated everything that his mouth did not. Dragonbrush could tell by the wrinkles on his father's brow, his left hand placed over his face, how tense his shoulders were as he sat in his chair, the additional fines couldn't have come at worse time. Tony was right, Dragonbrush's pop was in a foul mood and whenever he was like this, Dragonbrush fretted, because his old man could go from calm and quiet to loud and ugly in a matter of seconds.

Sitting across from Joseph stroking his hand was Esmeralda Madayag; Dragonbrush's mother who was 7 months pregnant. Dragonbrush was still taken aback at how large his pregnant mother was, the woman that had always been thin had become the fat mama that Dragonbrush and his peers joked about. Everything else about her was the same. Her hair was still styled in a pageboy, and she still had that sweet face and disposition that could calm a beast, not just her husband but anyone, which was why she was made Assistant Manager at Walgreen's drug store. Like his dad Dragonbrush's mother had a look of concern on her face.

"Oh, Joey," Dragonbrush's mother spoke, acknowledging her son as he entered the living room "Hey guys," he spoke weakly taking several steps into the room then stopping.

"We didn't hear you come in, are you hungry? Lisa is preparing some noodles?"

"This cookie is cool," he replied his stomach still feeling the pain of bad popcorn and greasy butter from the theatre.

"You sure you don't want anything to eat?" Esmeralda pressed, sensing something askew about her son.

"He said he wasn't hungry," his Joseph Sr. said in a solemn tone, never taking his eyes off the television.

Your father's still upset," she explained, while adjusting her position in her chair to accommodate the life she was carrying. "It hasn't been a good day for any of us. In addition to the bad news today at your court hearing the doctor tells me I have to give up work a month earlier than I expected. He prescribed bed rest. To make matters worst, the store also reduced your father's hours to 30 hours a week until the store completes it's remodeling," she added.

"He doesn't need to the know all of that," his father grumbled.

"He does. He's your son, and he needs to know," Esmeralda continued, "Your father's also upset that he didn't get the position that he applied for at the post office, but they said that he's eligible for others when a slot becomes available."

Dragonbrush looked at his grumpy father and thought, Good! That's what you get for being such a butt head.

"It just hasn't been a day of good news." Esmeralda sighed." But it will turn around because we have faith."

Dragonbrush thought about the fine that his family would be forced to pay, and the amount it hit him like a ton of bricks. How could something that brought him so much pleasure, bring so much pain? Why were folks tripping so hard over graffiti?

"We know you didn't mean to bring this on us," His mother added, looking at the pain it was causing her already hurting son.

"No we don't know that," Joseph, Sr. grumbled, as he stood up to go into the kitchen. "What we know is that he continues to spray walls despite what it's costing us."

Dragonbrush turned his lip up at his father, rather than make a snide comment. "Here's your money," he stated as he handed his mother a ball of paper route money from his pocket.

"Don't mind your father," his mom apologized, as she unfolded the seven crunched twenties and single ten dollar bill and laid them flat on the armrest of her husband's chair. "He's working less hours, but everything seems to be costing more. He has an interview tomorrow at a security firm. Hopefully, he can work evenings a few nights a week in order to continue to send money to Steven."

His mother's words, though not intentioned, pulled at Dragonbrush harder than Glock did his hair.

"Steven!" Dragonbrush shouted, referring to his older brother, a business major attending UCLA. "Then it occurred to Dragonbrush that if his father hadn't gotten so pissed at him at court, he could have been dropped off, and he would have never run into Glock. "All he ever thinks about is Steven!" Dragonbrush vented, "He never does anything for me but give me a hard time. He doesn't even want to talk about Gwen!" Shock registered in his mother's eyes. They were not focused on Dragonbrush, but behind him at his father whose expression was that of pure rage. Dragonbrush turned around and could see that his red faced father was shaking.

"Get out of my house before I throw you out!" He shouted so loudly that it brought Tony and Lisa (who was still on her phone,) out of the kitchen. Dragonbrush looked at the four and walked out of the front door hearing it slam before he reached the street. Dragonbrush reached into his pocket for his phone, fealing only cookies. He realized then, that he had left it on his bed. Taking his father's homemade cookies from his pocket Dragonbrush threw them at the house and headed for nearest telephone booth to call Uhuru.

10

9:28 p.m., Night Crawler Event. Emeryville

Omari stood at the side of Justin, the DJ Jedi and watched in amazement as he controlled the movement of the 1200 square foot space. His mind, soul and body completely in sync with the patrons on the dance floor, the bass in the industrial space pumped so loud, that from the outside the building appeared to have a heart beat. Using eclectic beats ranging from industrial Goth, to television theme songs to spin the crowd into frenzy on the dusty light stick covered floor. The patrons were further fueled by the knowledge that at anytime the police could enter the illegally occupied space and cart everyone off to jail.

This was a Night Crawler production. Night Crawler was a group of guys who staged illegal parties, also known as raves. Raves were outlawed by Oakland and its neighboring cities. Night Crawler hosted raves normally in industrial settings in the Bay Area. Attendees were notified of the party's location by text message, and once the doors closed there was no getting in unless you personally knew the doorman.

After Omari was dropped off at the Old Skool Café he was taken to the designated Night Crawler location by Justin and Tyrone.

"Hey dude, want a drink?" A pink boa covered female in her mid twenties offered Omari a bottle of Crystal Geyser as she danced around the DJ booth.

"Naw, I'm cool," Omari answered pulling his own bottle from his messenger bag and showing it to the partier.

"Cool, a man that keeps his own supply," the dancer spun to the other side of the booth and made the same offer to Reggie who informed her that the area in front of the DJ booth had to stay clear. The dancer grooved back into the crowd offering the bottle to another male.

Omari didn't understand Reggie's role for being at the party until

Justin started performing. It was obvious to Omari that Reggie was not only Justin's friend, but also his personal bodyguard.

Omari eyes followed the boa covered dancer who finally found a dance partner. Omari declined anything that was offered to him at the Night Crawler events for fear of coming home too high. The freckled face teen convinced his uncle and aunt that Justin was a popular DJ with a high demand for his taped performances. Justin needed someone that could help burn CD's and upload his performances to his website for downloading. This did not involve being in club around questionable people and substances, but at the DJ's apartment.

Aunt Ayanna was against Omari being Justin's assistant, but his uncle convinced her. He was quite clear when he told him not take anything or hesitate to call if he needed a ride home. He didn't have a problem checking Omari's breath for alcohol or observing his behavior to see if he had taken any mood-altering drug. "I'm sticking my neck out for you," he would say, "But it's yours that will be wrung if I learned that you used any drugs," Uncle Uhuru threatened on each occasion he tested him. There were reasons why this wasn't a problem for Omari, the first being that he was there to learn which he couldn't do high. Omari's goal was to spend just enough time with Justin until he learned techniques that Dragonbrush and he could do at their own functions. Omari was developing his skills by watching Justin at the turntables, not from Justin actually teaching Omari anything.

Secondly Omari primary job was to move, set up and take down equipment, burn and deliver his mixed tapes of his gigs which was very hard to do when you're under the influence. At their first party, while explaining what his job duties would be, Justin turned Omari on to some Durban Poison, an herb he longed to try. When the party was over, Omari could barely function. He was grateful to finally make it home. He promised himself that would never happen again.

Lastly, the behavior of partiers too high, drunk or both to function at the Night Crawler event's was enough to keep the Omari sober. Stepping over partiers passed out in the make shift restrooms, watching them throw up on the dance floor then others slipping in it, was too crazy for the disgusted teen. Justin's drug use only added to the insanity. Most nights he was cool. Other nights Justin would be so high and unglued that he could barely function. But high or not, Justin always burned all of his music that same morning and delivered his CD's later that day. Omari made it a point to drug free while at work, Once Omari was at Justin's apartment, then he felt free to light up whatever Justin was offering and Justin offered a lot.

"Snap out of it red!" Justin called, pulling Omari from his thoughts. "We want to start taking some of this stuff down and out to the truck. Also, I have a couple of stops to make before dropping you off." Omari pushed back his Oakland Raider beanie allowing his red locks to breathe. He began to break down some of the equipment aware that if the police ever raided a Night Crawler event, DJ's like Justin, who provided their own equipment would have their property seized, so it was important that their stuff was out before the end of each function.

11

9:30 p.m. International Blvd,

"Staying cool until Omari's uncle had come to pick me up would have been the smart thing to do," Dragonbrush groaned, regretting losing it at his folks as he walked down International Boulevard, looking for a phone booth or a bus stop on the nearly empty street. "Why was everything always about Steven?" Dragonbrush fretted. Just because Steven was the oldest and first in the family to go to college, didn't mean that he didn't need support from my family.

Dragonbrush stood off the sidewalk and into the street looking to see if any buses were coming and saw nothing but on coming cars filled with people that he didn't know. Another thing about his old man that pissed him off was why didn't he want anyone to talk about Gwen? His father acted as if she never existed. But that was his father, a butthole and hard to figure out. Concluding that it would be best to think about subjects that were less upsetting, Dragonbrush's attention went back to the CD in his side pant pocket still inside the Sony Discman Omari lent him. He placed the headphones on and listened.

Memories of the deceased have you bound on leash
Learn to love and let go or your own future will cease.
They don't understand that you understand
But don't you understand why they don't understand
Why they can't comprehend, why they choose to reprimand
Rather see that their circumstances are out of hand
And that they need you to take command and be the man
And explain, that we are all losing time like grains of sands
Don't let memories be the only thing that guides your soul
You'll lose control and your body will fold

Heart turns cold and fears become bold
If freedom is your goal then logic you must hold
Adding the recipe of love to your soul
The winds will come and the winds will go
Their threats will shake and threaten as they blow.
But stay rooted like the mighty tree hold your position looking inwards
not responding to that which you hear or see

"Lost control is exactly what I did," Dragonbrush reflected on the lyrics of the song. Even leaving was a dumb idea. His family would at least let him use the phone and wait on the porch until he got picked up. They weren't that bad. Dragonbrush decided to head back to his parents house when a sleek, black, hummer limousine pulled in front of him. He looked at the gleaming vehicle seeing his reflection on the limo's polished exterior. The rear window rolled down a few inches and Dragonbrush heard a female ask. "Need a ride?"

"Naw I'm cool," Dragonbrush answered, beginning to walk away, wondering why these people were trying to get their jollies by bothering him. He started to break into a run in the opposite direction of the limo, when the rear window rolled all the way down and Maria's cheery face appeared. "Hey," Dragonbrush she smiled.

"Wow," Dragonbrush answered, startled by the fact that she had indeed found him.

"You want a ride?" She cooed. Dragonbrush looked at her and remembered the eerie feeling they gave him earlier and how he promised himself he would have nothing to do with them. "Who else is in the limo with you?" He asked suspiciously.

Maria leaned back and Lexus leaned forward waiving to him "If you join us, it will be just you, me, Maria and the driver." Maria opened the door and the two statuesque beauties stepped out and stood next to him. Maria wore a short form fitting purple dress and an equally tight black dress clung to Lexus.

"I don't know." Dragonbrush said hesitantly, "I was planning on going straight home."

"Aw c'mon it'll be fun." Lexus pressed with an enticing smile, "Just cruise around with us for a little while, then we'll take you home"

"We promise to have you home before daybreak," Maria added.

Dragonbrush looked up at the full moon. His gut told him to just say "no," when he heard a familiar voice from up the street

"Is that young Dragon getting into a stretch limo with two fine honeys?"

Dragonbrush looked across the street and it was Clem, Luscious and Jermaine walking out of an apartment building. They were drunk and loud as usual. "I didn't know that boy had that kind of game!" Clem yelled his voice echoing off the buildings on the empty street. "I'm going to tell everybody bout this."

Hey Dragon! You got room in there for one more?" Luscious shouted, forcing others to look out of their windows to see what was going on outside.

"Can you run me to the store to get some cigarettes," a woman shouted from a window.

"He's a straight playa!" Jermaine yelled, followed by an even louder laugh. Embarrassed by the unwanted attention, Dragonbrush turned and waived at the guys that were sending him praise. He reluctantly got into the limo sticking his hand out of the window letting all watching see what a player he was.

12

9:35 p.m., Bancroft Avenue

Jennifer listened to Tioni with both eyes closed, knowing that she would be asleep long before her chatty friend on the other end of line was aware it.

"Why do boys have to be so childish?" Tioni asked, before going on another tirade.

"Good question" Jennifer uttered. Jennifer liked Tioni a lot because she would really do sweet things like telling the child care director at the church where her father was the pastor that Jennifer's little sister Sophia, (who they all referred to a "Soapy") really needed childcare which resulted in Soapy being enrolled in the center. This was a major benefit to the Twan family, but like most girls, Toni's conversation seemed only limited to boys. Jennifer thought that was cool, but it did get old when she was tired.

"And why do you think Jamilah is always hanging out with Dragonbrush?" Tioni asked.

"I think it's the other way around" Jennifer answered between yarns knowing that she fading away. "Besides, Jamilah would never be interested in someone younger. With Dragonbrush, she got a slave. That's all."

"It just seems so suspicious," Tioni pressed.

"I wouldn't worry about it," Jennifer reassured her before surrendering to unconsciousness.

"Boys always want to be players. You know what? I'm going to start being a player," Tioni fumed. After several seconds of no response and hearing only heavy breathing, Tioni asked, "Hello?"

13

11:02 p.m., Skyline Blvd, Full moon

The limo careened through the Oakland hills, the full moon peering through the blackened tree lined road, reflecting the lines of the hummer as its headlights shined the only light on the blackened road. For Dragonbrush, this was a wonderful ending to an extremely trying day. The three laughed and giggled as the limo drove across town, allowing them to tease and make fun of the people outside the limos reflective windows. At one point they even took turns Mooning people. It was then, that Dragonbrush realized how cool Maria and Lexus were. They told him about running away from the group home in Tulsa and about Josephine who they didn't really like, but thought she was cool for letting them stay at her house.

"You got all that by agreeing to be werewolves?" Dragonbrush asked.

"The Union changed our lives," Lexus echoed. "And it can change yours, too."

Dragonbrush turned to the blonde haired, black girl and asked, "But did the Union change it for the better?" The two looked at Dragonbrush without answering the question. Seizing the silence Dragonbrush added, "It's time that I get back to the crib."

"Before we take you back," Maria responded compliantly, "we would like for you to meet Sandia."

Dragonbrush knew it was time to go uncle Uhuru to talk about the fallout with his family. "I've got to get home," Dragonbrush insisted, "But I would like to meet this Sandia some other time, so if you all would drop me off now, I would appreciate it," he said suddenly, feeling an urgency to get home.

The limousine stopped, and even in the dark Dragonbrush recognized the area. They were atop of the Oakland hills just above Knowland Park Zoo. The small window that separated the limo's passengers from the driver slid back, and a pair of piercing eyes met Dragonbrush's and drew him in.

"I promise you this won't take long," the driver, a large Native American with a smooth, burnt red complexion, and dark piercing eyes spoke. "I am Sandia, you have been selected to be part of the Union. Do you accept this invitation?" The Native American's offer sent a slight chill up Dragonbrush's spine.

"The Union?" Dragonbrush asked, noticing that the roomy air-conditioned car was starting to take on a pungent smell that reminded him of the inside of a dog house.

"The Union is a unique association of like minded spirits I can provided your more details only once your have been initiated."

The stench in the car was becoming stronger, and even though the air conditioner was on the temperature in the car was rising at such a phenomenal degree, the tinted windows were foggy.

"The Union thing sounds real cool," Dragonbrush answered nervously, placing his hand over his nose as he spoke while trying not to offend the owner of the piercing eyes. "But I would like to think about it first, so I'll call you tomorrow because I really need to get home." Dragonbrush rubbed his eyes. Then his eyes again fixed on the rear view mirror, and it disturbed him as Sandia's eyes were moving further apart. The color of his skin was becoming grayer and hairier. Dragonbrush felt a manicured hand on his left thigh that briefly took his attention from Sandia.

"Once you join, then you can spend all your time with us, and we'll have someone with us that's our age," Lexus added. Dragonbrush did not hear Lexus, as he was mesmerized by the changing image of Sandia. The Native American's nose was becoming broader and longer as the smell in the limousine was becoming increasingly overwhelming. Before Dragonbrush eyes, the Native American had transformed into a massive wolf.

I will need your answer immediately," the wolf snarled.

"Sure," the stunned Filipino answered overwhelmed by fear.

"Can I please go home now?"

Sandia erupted into a heavy laugh that made Dragonbrush nervous before bursting into a howl so loud that it shattered the sun roof top above them and reduced the windshields to small cubes of glass. Dragonbrush covered his ringing ears and lowered his head as the sunroof crumbled atop his head when he looked at the legs of Maria and Lexus. He could see them changing from smooth and brown to hairy and dark. He gawked in amazement as their well-manicured nails began to transform into dark hardened nails, their svelte hands becoming hairier. He watched in shock as their fingers shortened, and merged into smoking paws.

The nauseous Pinoy began to vomit over himself. Then he was struck by a blow to the chest, as Maria and Lexus, began rolling on the floor of the limo thrashing violently about as they ripped their clothes from their hairy bodies. A hysterical Dragonbrush sat atop the seats pressing vainly against the doors in the secluded space nervously trying to avoid contact with the morphing females as they twisted, kicked and screamed leaving no room for escape as a surreal smoke clouded the car flowing out the shattered car windows like exhaust from a thousand bad mufflers. Dragonbrush watched in awe as Maria and Lexus's faces began to pull and contort. Their faces jutting painfully forward and their limbs began to constrict. Their screams became howls. One of the feet of the writhing females caught Dragonbrush on the chin, instantly knocking him unconscious.

14

11:27 p.m., Skyline Blvd

Dragonbrush painfully woke up and noticed that his face and hair were covered in vomit and glass fragments. He lifted his head to get out of the vehicle then realized that a great weight pressed against his back preventing his movement. Surrounding him on the floor of limousine was the shredded clothing worn by Maria and Lexus. He felt a warm pungent breeze in his face then lifted his head coming face to face with an enormous golden, American Pit Bull Terrier, twice the size and thickness of an average one. The drooling pit gazed at Dragonbrush with knowing eyes. Dragonbrush returned it's staring with pure terror, wanting nothing more than to escape. He made another effort to rise, but again was unable to. Then he realized that there were paws pressing into his back, by looking in a corner mirror of the once luxurious limo, Dragonbrush's burning eyes could see an Alaskan malamute larger than a Saint Bernard sitting atop him.

The window that separated the driver from the passenger was suddenly destroyed in a fury of noise, flying glass and plastic, and Dragonbrush could see a gray wolf so large that Dragonbrush wondered, how was it able to fit in the front of the limo?

"Tonight you accepted to become a member of the Union of the Wolf" the wolf spoke calmly, "You will find your canine spirit and you will be one with a pack that is as old as mankind, and as agreed, we will take you home."

Dragonbrush's heart pounded as he could see the wolf approaching him with bared fangs. This is going to hurt really bad, he mused. Dragonbrush could feel the wolf's teeth penetrating his flesh and rapidly began losing consciousness. "Dragonbrush no longer felt the pain as his body had gone into shock his last thoughts were on Omari, Yes, Jamilah, and Gwen, he would miss them all very much.

15

1:57 a.m., South Hill Court,

"No!" Dragonbrush cried, sitting up in his bed with both his hands around his throat.

"What's the matter?" Omari called, turning on the television to add light to the room.

"Oh man!" Dragonbrush spoke noticing his body was covered with sweat. "Where am I?" he asked, nervously.

"Home, in your bed,"

"Oh man, something really bad happened." Dragonbrush spoke stroking his neck.

"What?"

Dragonbrush looked around the dark room, trying to piece together all that had happened. "I went to my folk's house, as always. Pops blew a fuse and threw me out. I was on my way here when this Hummer limousine came by with these two girls that I met at the BART station"

"Player, player," Omari said with a sly smile.

"So I thought, but they took me up to the hills, and then they, and the driver turned into dogs and attacked me."

"Dude, what have you been smoking?" Omari asked, "And is there any left?"

"I'm serious," Dragonbrush argued. "The last thing I remember is them attacking me, I thought I was dead. "I don't even know how I got here."

"Then nobody does," Omari added, "I was finishing up the Night Crawler gig when my uncle he learned about your family argument and called to see if you were with me? When I said no, he then said that he would be by to pick me up, so we could go by the places you hung out. Justin rushed me back to Old Skool café just before he arrived.

We went everyplace I thought you might be. We come home, and there you are in bed." Omari paused, then asked his roommate, "if you got attacked like you say you did then where are the bite marks and cuts?"

"I don't know," he answered, wondering if maybe it was all a dream.

The late night repeat of Lost was interrupted by a news flash. "This is Lisa Chow standing atop the Oakland hills where it appears another full moon tragedy has occurred, although the police are not sure what has actually happened. Not too far from Knowland Park Zoo an abandoned, stretched hummer limousine has been found. The vehicle was thoroughly destroyed, its back seat covered with shredded clothes, vomit and blood. Police suspect this to be signs of foul play. Oddly enough, there are no signs of a struggle or apparent clues outside of the vehicle.

If anyone out there has any information, please call the number on the bottom of the screen."

"That was you in that limo?" Omari asked Dragonbrush, who nodded gently. "And you say that the girls and the driver turned into dogs then ripped your throat out?" His words were met with another nod. "Then how are you still alive?"

"I don't know," Dragonbrush answered. "The worst part," he added slumping under his comforter "is that the song I got from the old man tried to warn me."

Part 3

Barks Marks

*Memories of the deceased have you bound on a leash
As on your mind they creep
Learn to love and let go or your own future will cease.
They don't understand that you understand
But don't you understand why they don't understand
Why they can't comprehend, why they choose to reprimand
Rather see that their circumstances are out of hand
And that they need you to take command and be the man
And explain, that we are all losing time like grains of sands
Don't let memories be the only thing that guides your soul
You'll lose control and your body will fold
Heart turns cold and fears become bold
If freedom is your goal then logic you must hold
Adding the ingredient of love to infuse your soul*

1

July 19th 8:48 a.m., International Blvd

With every step they took toward the childcare center located in the House of Faith church. Jennifer and Tioni had to endure Soapy's heartbreaking renditions of such childhood favorites, "I don't want to go. Why do I have to go?" And the all time classic, "I want to go home to my mommy!" Unfortunately for the five year old, her whining fell on deaf ears, as Tioni was on her cell phone lost in conversation with a friend, and Jennifer simply turned up the volume of her iPod, drowning out most of her younger sisters, cries. When the three arrived at the center, they were pleasantly surprised that instead of the anticipated drama of screaming, kicking and howling. Soapy spotted three friends and, without so much as a goodbye, the three-foot, three inch bundle of energy dashed off leaving only the tracks of her pink Fila tennis shoes.

"What happened to Jamilah?" Tioni asked after ending her cell phone conversation. "She was supposed to hang with us."

"She called her aunt needed her and Dragonbrush to do something." Jennifer explained, adjusting her yellow, Trader Joe, Hawaiian print shirt. Anticipating Tioni's response she added, "It's not like she had a choice in the matter."

"Jamilah is interested in him; you can't tell me she's not," The caramel colored teen responded defensively, her gray eyes revealing her insecurities.

"Like I said, she cares about him, I care about him, but I don't want him as a boyfriend." Jennifer explained, trying to put Jamilah's and Dragonbrush relationship in context.

"I know," Tioni jabbed seeing an opening. "You only feel that way about Omari."

"We're not talking about Omari and me," Jennifer answered, deftly avoiding getting caught in the attractive teen's web of unhappiness. "We're talking about you and Dragon."

"I don't care about Dragonbrush," Tioni replied.

"Stop lying!" Jennifer fired back, her patience at an end. "Admit you do."

"I do not!"

"Do too!"

A 1970, Buick Skylark with an unfinished exterior and dark tinted windows pulled along the side of the sparring teens, halting their conversation. "Say, what's your name?" A raspy voice along with smoke emanated from the slightly rolled down passenger side window.

"Who's asking?" Tioni mouth answered before her brain could react.

The dark tinted window was lowered revealing the face of a dark colored male in his early twenty's with red eyes, a shaved head and a mouth covered by a gold grill. "I'm Coffy, you know, just like the drink, only better, and this is my dawg Bitter." "How you doing Jennifer? Long time no see in the day time." The older male, smiled also revealing a grill.

Jennifer ignored his comment, "I see you still a stuck up, bit-" Shady caught himself, then asked, "You bitches need a ride?"

"No, but we'll take your numbers," Tioni responded flirtatiously to Jennifer's surprise.

"Sure," Coffy lowered the window and pulled out a one hundred dollar bill from his top pocket. He wrote his name and number on it. "Now, if I give you my digits, you know I'm going to want something in return,' He stated with a bright yet devious smile.

"I know," Tioni answered. Coffy balled up the bill and tossed it to her, Tioni caught it with one hand "Do you want my number too?" Coffy asked Jennifer.

"No" Jennifer replied coldly, knowing about Coffy's ties with the Cobalt gang. Coffy looked at Tioni and with a smile as the car drove off, "I will talk to you later then."

"Do you know how stupid that was?" Jennifer scolded her naïve friend. "They are Cobalt gang bangers."

"He just gave me a hundred dollars!" Tioni responded excitedly, looking at the money.

"Yeah, he also called you a bitch, and for that chump change he will think that he owns you," Jennifer continued with deep concern.

"You wanted me to take my mind off Dragonbrush. Now I have," she spoke trying to make out the telephone number on the crumpled bill. When Tioni glanced over in Jennifer's direction, she had walked away leaving the teen with the elegant braids standing alone.

2

12:03 p.m., Omari's Bedroom, South Hill Court

"Aarrgh!" Dragonbrush cried immediately sitting up as the icy cold water shocked him awake and back into the world of the living. After another hour of talking with Omari, Dragonbrush went soundly back to sleep soundly forgetting about the activities of the night before. A cold splash of water quickly brought those events back to the forefront.

"That's for having us worry about you and then ruining my day" Jamilah stood over Dragonbrush holding an empty glass.

"What I do?" Dragonbrush cried, reeling from the shock of the ice water.

"Last night when your parents called to say you left, we had no idea where you were. Then you just appear in bed and don't bother to tell anyone." Jamilah answered pouring the last few drops of water on him, "You're guys are too stupid to even talk to," she then barged out of the room.

Dragonbrush watched Jamilah's butt as she slammed the door behind her. How do I tell her what happened when I don't know? Dragonbrush asked himself. Hearing a knock on the door, "Come in," he called knowing that it was either Uncle Uhuru or Aunt Ayanna.

"I figured you would be up after hurricane Milah came through." Ayanna spoke, picking up one of Dragonbrush's many t-shirts that cluttered the room, tossing it to him so he could dry off. The cashew, colored Ayanna stood five feet and six inches tall and could be recognized in a crowd by her distinctive, African flair, short rustic brown locks, and squared granny glasses.

"She's pretty mad" Dragonbrush commented, rubbing the shirt over his face.

"Before she was mad, she was pretty worried," Ayanna commented adjusting her glasses. "I understand things did not go well last night" Ayanna stated.

"I knew that was going to happen," he affirmed.

You, Jamilah and I will talk about it what we can do to help at lunch," she added

"What happened to Omari?" Dragonbrush asked wondering where he was.

"Out doing your paper route," she answered.

"Oh God!" Dragonbrush cringed, covering his face with the shirt "I overslept. I'm going to owe Omari big time!"

"Probably," she responded. "He said after last night you needed a break," Ayanna explained. "When Omari is done with your route, he is meeting Justin for something. We will see him tonight." Ayanna looked at Dragonbrush with a smiled and said "We can't leave until you get up" then she walked out. Dragonbrush watched the door close. He was still confused about what happened last night, but it was good to be where he was wanted.

3

12:27 p.m., Omari's Bedroom, South Hill Court

After showering, Dragonbrush trampled through the cluttered bedroom to find a clean shirt to wear to lunch. The bedroom had been reduced to a wasteland of piled clothes, crumpled comic books, Graffiti magazines, burned video games and cans of Krylon spray paint that were supposed to be hidden, but because of laziness, now sat out in the open. Dragonbrush rummaged through the pile of clothes for his white vintage Invisible Skratch Piklz t-shirt. Finding it, Justin came to mind. Folks thought Justin was a great DJ, but compared to any member of The Invisibl Skratch Piklz, the Bay Area group of Filipino hip hop DJs, Justin was nothing. DJ Q-Bert, Mix Master Mike, D-Styles, Yoga Frog, DJ Disk and Shortkut were the real DJ phenomena's of the Bay Area, creating musical pieces using multiple, turntables as instruments. They even invented the term, "Turntabilsm," The Invisibl Skratch Piklz has won every scratch competition around the country, and if they hadn't broken up, they still would. What had Justin won? Dragonbrush asked. If Omari and he were to hang around anyone, it should be one of the Piklz. After getting dressed, Dragonbrush could feel something crumbling under his foot. He looked down and saw a small booklet with a Rottweiler puppy on the cover. He picked up the booklet and read the cover Your Rottweiler and how to care for them. Was Omari was planning on getting a Rot? He wondered.   He began flipping through the booklet reading the captions underneath the photos.

"The Rottweiler is a sensitive, intelligent and loyal animal and usually wants to please its owner. The Rottweiler is a robust, powerful and loyal breed with pronounced protective instincts. The Rottweiler is not a breed that fits into every home. The Rottweiler is very strong for its size. It has been used in Europe to pull carts and retains the compact musculature desirable in a draft animal.

"See that's the animal to be," Dragonbrush mused. "If I believed in reincarnation, I would come back as a Rot, a dog that instantly gets respect. The Filipino teen then remembered what Sandia had told him about selecting a canine spirit and realized that unwittingly he had done just that.

4

12:29 p.m., Justin's Apartment. Lake Shore Avenue,

Omari opened his eyes, and one look at the room filled with large music speakers, mixing equipment and floor to ceiling with bookshelves crammed with albums and memorabilia from countless parties, and the bi-racial teen remembered that he was in Justin's apartment, in the second bedroom that he converted into a music room/office.

After hearing about Dragonbrush's disturbing misfortune, Omari decided to do his paper route allowing his shaken friend to sleep. When Omari arrived at Justin's apartment later, Justin and Edwin had been up all night editing the mixes from the Night Crawler gig. Omari did not know where the two got their energy, nor did he want to, Afterward, he made music deliveries. Although Dragonbrush's paper route consisted of delivering newspaper to almost every home over a ten block radius, dealing with inserts, dogs and crazy drivers, Omari thought it still preferable to the deliveries he made for Justin. Omari delivered CD's and cassettes to very questionable locations in San Francisco's Bay View Hunter's Point and Visitacion Valley. His local deliveries were in the deepest of East Oakland, and the very bottom of West Oakland. South Berkeley and parts of Norf Richmond completed his route. What was odd was that the folks he delivered music to and collected payments from did not look like the types that would listen to the music Justin produced. Adding to the weirdness, Justin would drop Omari several blocks from the delivery locations claiming it would hurt his image to be seen delivering his own music. Justin informed Omari that now that Edwin, *(a person he liked less and less)* was back he would be doing all the driving. To Omari, it didn't make sense, and his gut told him not to trust Justin, but he was getting paid and learning how to DJ, so he would put up with it for a little while. At the apartment, Omari was given the duty of shrink wrapping the mix tapes and CDs while Justin and Edwin were out running to get more blank tapes and CDs. Omari completed the CDs then fell asleep.

Moving his rusty locks from his freckled face, Omari stood up from the wooden desk, standing up to stretch his lean frame and to slightly pull up sagging pants. As he walked into the living room of the stylishly furnished apartment overlooking Lake Merritt, Omari wrestled with the details of Dragonbrush's ordeal. Even if he thought Dragonbrush had gotten high, and had imagined the whole thing, how did he explain the news report about the stolen Hummer Limousine?

Exhausted from the lack of sleep the teen plopped on the comfortable leather couch and spied a color piece of paper on the glass coffee table and read it.

Top 10 Signs That You've Been Hanging Out with DJ's Too Long

10. You have sleeping patterns that would kill normal human beings.
9. It doesn't even phase you to hear, "Yeah, I ordered $300 of records this week."
8. Words like Chicago, Orlando, and L.A. are descriptions of sounds, not cities.
7. You're expected to know the difference between a 606 and a 909.
6. You know that mixing isn't what you do to a cake, a board isn't used to build a house, and tables aren't for eating.
5. When traveling, one of the first things you do is look for a store that sells vinyl.

4. You can identify a track within the first 5 seconds of play, even when it's being mixed with another track.
3. You start calling songs "tracks".
2. A constant thought is, "Need more bass."
1. You can't remember your own telephone number, but you can clearly recall the title, artist, and vocals of an obscure song you only heard 3 times back in 1993.

"Yeah, that's about right." Omari muttered, fighting the desire to go back to sleep. He decided since no one was there to look inside Justin's closet to see his wardrobe. When Omari opened Justin's bedroom door, he was expecting to see a cluttered room that mirrored his own. He was surprised at how immaculate Justin's bedroom was. Several circular mirrors adorned the otherwise empty walls. A Sony entertainment center with a flat screen television sat across his unmade queen size bed. Omari opened the first of his two closets and found a walk in closet that was lined with the latest fashions. Not knowing how long before Justin would return, Omari quickly opened the second walk in closet and noticed a small piece of red paper fall to the cream colored carpet. Inside were more clothes neatly organized stacks of shoeboxes and small dressers in the back of the closet. Then he noticed affixed to the wall above the dresser a post it that read, *"Get more strawberry for Robbie."* Knowing that strawberry was a street name for LSD, Omari peeped inside the bottom left dresser drawer and found it filled with sandwich bags of marijuana, all neatly stacked. Dude never have to buy weed, Omari thought knowing that every bag was probably accounted for. Looking in the bottom right drawer Omari found a metal case. He opened it and saw an assortment of pills and what appeared to be fragments of mushrooms all neatly placed in small baggies. "Damn!" Omari said aloud, "He never have to buy anything!" Knowing that the contents of the box could only bring him trouble Omari quickly placed the case back, closed the closet door and went back into the Justin's music room and continued shrink wrapping the cassettes. Then it occurred to Omari that the red piece of paper was Justin's way of knowing if someone was snooping around. Omari rushed back into the room and quickly placed the red shred of paper inside the door jam of the closet. Minutes later after he had finished the last cassette, Omari could hear Edwin laughing from outside and knew they were back.

"Check it out man," Edwin entered the room loudly, unaware of his own obnoxiousness "Which of your parents is black and white?"

Ignoring the question and looking past Edwin to Justin, Omari explained, "All the tapes are ready."

"Cool, Justin responded, noticing that Edwin was upset at being slighted.

"Hey man, you just going to dismiss my question like that?" Edwin asked clearly offended.

"I don't owe you an explanation about myself, or my family." Omari replied with venom.

Omari's statement caught Edwin off guard, "A brother just wanted to know, that's all," Edwin responded giving Omari words little thought.

"So, I'm supposed to tell you my family's ethnic history just because you want to know?" Omari challenged the larger and clearly stronger of the two.

"Bro, just ignore the village idiot," Justin said heading back to his bedroom with Edwin behind him. Omari could hear Justin whisper, "See I told you." The two returned with the red piece of paper from the door attached to Edwin's forehead

Omari acknowledged that he had a real problem with Edwin but obviously not as big as the one Edwin had with himself. Omari's eyes went back to the piece of paper still affixed to Edwin's head. He now -doubted if the deliveries was about the music and as his father would always say "When in doubt, then there is no doubt."

5

1:47 p.m., Red Robin Restaurant, San Leandro

"How did you manage to get into the house without anyone knowing?" Ayanna asked Dragonbrush while meticulously dipping *-her French fries in the small plastic container of ketchup despite having no intentions of eating them. Ayanna treated Dragonbrush and Jamilah to lunch at Red Robin restaurant at Bay Fair Mall in order to talk about what happened at his family home in civil manner.

"I just climbed the tree in the backyard into the bedroom," Dragonbrush lied. "I didn't want to talk to anyone, so I just went to bed."

"I understand," Ayanna consoled the teen, thinking that she would have to better secure her home by trimming back the trees in the backyard. "Next time, just call, and we'll pick you up okay?"

Dragonbrush nodded in agreement between bites of his cheeseburger, wondering if he could in fact get into the second story bedroom from the tree, or if that was how Lexus and Maria were able to get him inside without anyone noticing.

"I know you and your parents are upset, and you all need time to cool off," Ayanna spoke softly. "Uhuru and I have invited them to join us for dinner after your camping trip. You mother regrets what happened last night, but you have to understand they are in a very bad way financially."

"And I'm making it worse," Dragonbrush added his words garbled by a mouthful of delicious burger.

"Not you." Ayanna corrected him, "Your actions. But, your family also acknowledges your contributions. Lets give everyone time to cool down so we can look at things with fresh eyes," she smiled sincerely. Turning to Jamilah, Ayanna asked, "Don't you have something to say to Dragonbrush?"

"No. I don't think so." The attractive teen replied, recovering from a brain freeze from her virgin, strawberry Daiquiri.

"Jamilah," Ayanna clarified, sensing behavior that was both un-lady like, and rude. "I'm talking about this morning."

"I know," Jamilah responded, basking in the taste of her delicious drink.

"Jamilah"! Ayanna said in a tone her niece did not want to push. "Why are you being so difficult?"

"I'm sorry for pouring water on you this morning, Okay?" she said out of frustration. "But pothead owes me an apology, too. He could have called me. He could have called Omari." She removed some daiquiri from her tall glass and flung it at him. "I bet if his little butt had been chased by vampires, he would have called us," Dragonbrush's expression made Jamilah realize what she had said. She immediately resumed sipping her drink.

"Well if there were vampires, I'm sure he would have called you two," Ayanna responded the remark going over her head. "But Jamilah does have a point. Dragonbrush do you feel you owe Jamilah an apology also?"

"I'm sorry," he said quickly recovering from the initial shock. "Next time, I'll call you." Then he said with a wry smile, "I didn't know you cared so much."

"Why you little piece of-" Jamilah responded, angrily.

"Enough!" Ayanna cut short her niece in mid sentence before her cell phone interrupted her. After listening for several seconds she excused herself from the table and headed toward the lobby of the restaurant where she could get better reception.

"See what you almost made me do?" Jamilah charged, watching her aunt walking further away from the alley view that their window provided.

"Jamilah," Dragonbrush pleaded. "Let me tell you what happened."

"Save the drama," she spoke standing up. "I'm going to the bathroom. See, I tell you everything, and you tell me nothing," she fumed as she walked away.

Before Dragonbrush could say another word, he felt a painful sensation in his head so severe that he closed his eyes until the ache quickly subsided. When he opened his eyes the restaurant and everyone in it was in black and white and various shades of gray. Panicked by the fear that he was losing his site, the Filipino teen closed his eyes again hoping for normalcy. Before he could reopen them, his olfactory system was assaulted by the overwhelming scents of meals heavily seasoned with garlic's onions and other spices. The smell of alcohol from the adjacent bar mixed with the various high priced and cheap perfumes and colognes made Dragonbrush want to wretch. Another explosion sounded off in his head as the clanging of pots, dishes dropping to the floor and massive dishwashers competed with the countless conversations that occupied the room. Dragonbrush placed his hands tightly over his ears to drown out the sounds and could hear muffled voices that sent a chill through his body.

"Ooooooooouweeee, look at that booty!" Dragonbrush heard one hoarse voice say

"She's shakin dat azz!" another voice jeered.

"Glock, make that fool bring that freak out here to meet a playa."

Dragonbrush turned to the window three booths from his and could see Glock and two others looking in his direction with shopping bags in their hands.

"Come here!" the fro hawk wearing Glock ordered Dragonbrush, with a forceful wave. "They're talking about Jamilah," Dragonbrush gasped, realizing that Jamilah and Aunt Ayanna were in danger. Suddenly his senses were no longer overwhelmed, as his single-minded purpose was to protect his loved one. Dragonbrush stood up from the table forgetting why he was there and headed toward the window where the trio waited.

"Where you going?" Jamilah called, bringing Dragonbrush immediately back to the world of color and normalcy.

"Oh," he stumbled, stunned by the sudden return to color and muted sound, but still feeling a strong need to protect. "I see someone I need to talk to," he answered, his eyes meeting Glock's through the tinted windows.

"I'll go with you," Jamilah offered, "let me tell auntie."

"These are folks that you don't want to meet," Dragonbrush responded, not wanting her anywhere near Glock or his gang.

"Why not?" The attractive teen pressed, not accustomed to the word "*No.*"

"Jamilah please," Dragonbrush pleaded, knowing she insisted on having her way.

"Who is she?" Jamilah pressed, "And why are you so nervous about me meeting her?"

"They're lesbian bikers, and I owe them money," Dragonbrush retorted. "Do you have fifty dollars that I can borrow until payday?" He asked with his hand out.

"Get real," Jamilah snapped back. No longer interested in the conversation, "You know where I am if they don't put you in the hospital," she said as she continued to her seat. Dragonbrush turned his attention to Glock, and felt the surge of senses and sounds and the lack of color return. His eyes again made contact with Glock's and he noticed that something had startled Glock, as if he knew what Dragonbrush's intentions were. Dragonbrush's first instinct was to charge at them through the plate glass window when he heard Ayanna call, again bringing himback to the land of color and muted sound.

"Where are you off to?" she asked, still on her Blackberry.

"I was going to see some people I know," he answered nervously.

"Don't be long," she added, preoccupied with her call. "Something has come up at work. We need to cut our festivities short, so I can drop you off and get to the office."

"I won't," he assured her. Dragonbrush watched as Aunt Ayanna walked back to the booth consumed by her conversation. The increased, sounds, scents and colorless world had returned, but the long haired teen ignored it. His need to protect his loved ones was so deep, that he didn't feel the creases growing on his forehead, his eyes tightening or the drool flowing from his mouth. When he arrived outside, Glock and his associates were gone. "What happened to him," Dragonbrush questioned as his senses returned to normal. Then Dragonbrush shuttered, for a brief instant, he was willing to attack and rip apart the one person he feared more than anyone in life.

6

5:39 pm., House of Faith Childcare Center

"Why did you leave me?" Tioni asked, Jennifer, meeting her at the childcare center as she was picking up Soapy.

"It's one thing to be silly; it's another thing to be stupid." Jennifer said curtly, as she walked her sister toward the bus stop "If you want to play around with people like that fine, but you're not pulling me, my family and real friends down with you."

"I was just playing," Tioni said apologetically, crushed that Jennifer did not want her company.

"You play too much and think too little." Jennifer said to her with all seriousness. "Those guys are some of the most ruthless Cobalt's, and everyone's afraid to mess with them."

"Why didn't you tell me?" Tioni asked, not understanding how she could have done such a thing.

"I did when I told you to stop being so stupid!" "The three stood at the bus stop, Soapy dancing while still holding Jennifer's hand.

"You were a Cobalt, and it wasn't so bad," Tioni tried to minimize her indiscretion.

"It was bad," Jennifer corrected her, "I was glad when I got out because most of the folks I ran with are gone." A black Lexus stopped in front of them. The rear window rolled down and Coffy stuck his head out.

"Hey baby," he called to Tioni. "I've been thinking about you all day."

Jennifer heard Tioni gulp. Tioni reached into her purse pulling out the hundred dollar bill, 'I was wrong for taking it." She said handing him back his money.

"Is it like that now?" he asked through a Midas mouth. "Too bad. I was going to treat you like the Nubian queen that you are." Jennifer noticed Tioni starting to blush. "Well can we give you fine ladies a ride home? It's still better than waiting for the bus." He offered opening the car door to the elegant ride.

"C'mon Jen lets go," Tioni agreed, not seeing the harm. "Oowww!" she cried feeling Jennifer's fingers firmly around her neck preventing her from moving toward the car, to the dissatisfaction of the occupants in the Lexus.

"Thanks, but we're going to catch the bus." Jennifer spoke with one hand holding Soapy's and the other pulling Tioni back, before releasing her grip.

"Leave her if she doesn't want to go." A second voice called from the car.

Tioni turned to Jennifer, and reluctantly said to Coffy, "No thanks, I'll catch the bus."

"So who are you, her mother?" an enraged Coffy asked.

"Yeah I am," Jennifer said defiantly, aware that the silly Tioni, like Soapy, was also her responsibility.

"I didn't know a slant, could have a nigga for a daughter." A fourth voice came from the car.

"If the only women you met, weren't sharing the same jail cell with you, then you would," Jennifer responded with matched attitude.

"What you say?" another voice spoke, as all four windows rolled down, revealing that six guys were occupying the car.

"You ugly, stupid and deaf?" Jennifer asked defiantly.

"J-Dawg is not here to protect you, I'll beat you down!" A fair skinned black, with gold teeth and a perm threatened.

"Then come wit it!" Jennifer challenged, realizing that Soapy was clinging to her in fear.

"Damn!" the driver shouted, giving Jennifer a dirty look then driving off as its occupants rolled up the windows.

"Where was I supposed to sit?" Tioni asked, her words making Jennifer cringe. "How did you know that they were all in the car? She asked watching the Lexus turn the corner.

"Tioni, I didn't." Jennifer responded dryly. Her eyes also on the car, "I just don't get into cars with strangers."

"At least I listened," Tioni added giving the situation some consolation and wondering what made them leave.

"Yeah you did," Jennifer acknowledged with a smile. A police car drove up in front of the girls. The driver was Sergeant Norbert Bright, a local cop and a friend. Moments later he was taking them home.

"I don't know what that was about," Bright spoke referring to the Lexus incident. "But I will say this once, stay away from them! Am I clear?"

"Yep," said Soapy wearing the sergeant's hat while bouncing in the car. "I didn't like them anyway."

"I'm with the Soapster," Jennifer agreed, smirking at her happy sister.

"Me too," Tioni added, thinking, *There was something hot about a dangerous guy like Coffy.*

7

6:48 p.m., living room, South Hill Court,

Jamilah could only look at Dragonbrush sitting at the opposite end of the couch in stunned silence. Had Dragonbrush shared his werewolf experience a month ago, Jamilah would have dismissed him as crazy or on drugs, but less than a month ago she learned that her best friend, Jennifer, and a guy she was dating were vampires. If vampires existed it stood to reason that so would werewolves. *What kind of place was Oakland?* She wondered. "So the two girls who you don't know, never seen before but were able to locate you by your smell, convinced you to ride with them in a hummer limousine and after taking you up into the hills transformed into werewolves and bit you."

Jamilah asked, getting her bearings.

"No," the chauffer, Sandia, is the one that actually bit me" Dragonbrush clarified, "The others held me down"

"And after all that, you have no bite marks or anything?" Jamilah continued, looking Dragonbrush up and down.

"Right," he nodded in agreement.

"So what happens next?" Jamilah asked, resolving to accept what the tagger said on face value.

"I don't know," he answered.

"You not going to turn into a big wolf and try to eat us, are you?" Jamilah asked jokingly but with a hint of seriousness.

"No! I could never turn on you guy's, no matter what," the Filipino said with supreme conviction.

"I know," Jamilah said with certainty. I am sorry for pouring water on you, after you all you went through," Jamilah said with sincerity. "Let me make it up to you by letting you take me out. What do you want to do?" she asked.

"How about another movie at the Grand Lake Theatre?" Dragonbrush asked excitedly.

"So we can get attacked by an audience of werewolves? I don't think so," Jamilah corrected him. "Let's check out the Chabot Science Center?" Jamilah offered.

"That's fine," Dragonbrush agreed, just happy to be going out with Jamilah.

"Good. I'll call and find out their hours, and don't worry about this werewolf thing," she said while fishing for her iPhone between two couch pillows, "we're all in this together."

The two could hear the front door open. Before Omari could speak to his sister and best friend, his cell phone rang. "Hello," he answered wearily, thinking it was Justin. "Oh hey Jennifer," Jamilah and Dragonbrush noted the disappointment in his voice. "Listen. I'm about to head to work. Can I call you back? I don't always say that! I didn't forget about going to the fair tomorrow at 11:00. If you don't believe I will be on time, meet me here. Bye." Seconds later, Jamilah and Dragonbrush were joined by the exhausted Omari.

"We have another gig tonight Justin will be back in 20 minutes. Just wake me up if I'm still sleep," he said crashing on the loveseat across from them.

"Big bro, you're too tired to go anywhere," Dragonbrush stated the obvious, looking at Jamilah who looked at Omari shaking her head.

"I got it covered," Omari mumbled before passing out. Thirty five minutes later the sound of a car horn snapped Omari from his sleep.

"See you guys" Omari said as he clumsily headed outside as the other teens watched 103 and Park on BET.

"I'll be right back," Jamilah said to Dragonbrush who watched her follow her younger brother.

Omari was opening the passenger side of Justin's Jeep when the two heard Jamilah call Omari's name, stopping him in his tracks.

"Omari's not going." Jamilah spoke slamming the door of Justin's Jeep close with her Nikes.

"I'm cool." Omari dismissed her claims.

"Look at you." Jamilah said with all seriousness. "You can barely stand up. The only place You're going is to bed."

Omari looked at Jamilah with shock then weak defiance, "I got to go. I work, remember."

"Not tonight you don't." Jamilah answered, placing both hands on her brother's shoulders and pulling him away from the vehicle.

"Don't Omari get a say so in his own life?" Justin argued, ignoring Jamilah's affront to his vehicle with her foot. Justin knew females like Jamilah, a self centered beauty accustomed to having her way. Justin knew this when he first met Jamilah, and made it a point to have as little to do with her as possible.

"Yeah he does," Jamilah answered, "but right now, mine's the only one that matters." Jamilah knew that this was embarrassing for her brother, but was left with no choice. She could see that Omari's employer was going to be difficult because the Justins of the world only cared about Justin and her brother wasn't going to be mucked over so he could get ahead. She pointed the exhausted Omari back toward the house and gave him a slight bump. Omari figured the rest out on his own.

"Omari is my right hand man. I need him to help me do the show," Justin argued, desperation showing in his voice.

Jamilah smiled, "you have apparently confused me with someone who cares." The teen then headed back to the house, never bothering to turn around to see Justin's reaction.

"Omari's pretty mad," Dragonbrush shared with Jamilah as she entered the room.

"Like I care," Jamilah answered, plopping down on the couch next to him. "Omari's so fried he doesn't know which way is up. When that happens, it's my job to decide what's best for him, not care how he or anybody else feels about it. That's what family does." Jamilah then slapped Dragonbrush on the back of his head.

"Oww! What was that for?" Dragonbrush asked his feelings and head hurt.

"So you will remember to contact me the next time you're in trouble," changing the subject back to their earlier plans. "They start looking at the planets at the Chabot Science Center at 8:10 p.m. And I got to remember to tell uncle when he picks us up, that baby brother is upstairs passed out."

"You still want to go out?" Dragonbrush asked.

"Duh, yeah," She answered.

"Jamilah," Dragonbrush spoke.

"Yeah Dragon," Jamilah answered, dryly, picking up her phone from the coffee table in order to *instant message* Jennifer.

"Promise me you will live forever." Dragonbrush stated.

"I'll see what I can do," she answered, as she messaged Jennifer's

8

10:38 p.m., Kitchen, South Hill Court

"So the dead finally rises," Jamilah greeted Omari with a smile. Even after slumbering for sixteen hours, Omari still had sleep in his eyes. The back-to-back parties and the running around in between with Justin had finally caught up with the teen, and he knew it. Omari noticed that his sister was wearing a black shirt with gray and white Goth designs and thumb holes, tight fitting blue jeans draped with a studded belt and her hair down underneath a black Dolce & Gabbana newsboy hat. And thankfully nothing that belonged to him. As much as Omari wanted to be angry at his sister for pulling rank on him in front of Justin, he was thankful that he had someone that could rein him in even when he didn't feel it was necessary.

"Sup?" Omari greeted his sister with a slight bump.

Being in bed gave Omari time to think, *now that Edwin is here what did Justin need me for? The teen pondered,* it wasn't like he did anything more than carry equipment and deliver music to seedy business and even seedier individuals. Maybe if I had spent less time smoking with Justin in his apartment and more time paying attention to what was going on, then I would have noticed that something wasn't legit. After seeing all the drugs in Justin's apartment Omari figured it was probably time to put some distance between the two.

Before taking his shower, Omari checked the four messages on his phone. The first was Jennifer reminding him to be ready when she arrived. The next two were from Justin whom Omari figured was calling to tell him he was out of a job after the way Jamilah went off on him. But, to Omari's amazement, Justin's first message asked whether or not Omari was working tonight? Followed by what time should he pick him up?

Jennifer and Tioni were on their phones and Dragonbrush was intently watching an old, Lassie movie on the television in the living room

"There's been a change in plans." Jamilah spoke turning to Jennifer for confirmation. She nodded in agreement "Instead of the Pleasanton Fair, Jennifer's aunt is taking us to Wal-Mart to get last minute supplies for the camping trip this weekend."

"That's cool," Omari agreed, looking at Jennifer to see if she was alright with the decision.

"It was my aunt's idea, not mine," the slender teen spoke placing her phone to her chest. "We can go to Old Skool's or a movie after or maybe do something this evening."

Omari wanted to ask the Vietnamese beauty where did she get her clothes? Wearing a white, Krispy Kreme Donuts crew shirt altered to hug her slender form and reveal her flat belly, fitted denims and open toed sandals that brought attention to her French tips, her long, dark hair worn up in a happy ponytail with a cowlick between her eyes. The two had planned on spending the day together at the Fair leaving his evening free. Omari called Makemba yesterday asking her out. The fourth message on his phone was her confirming their date at 7:00p.m., at the Old Skool café.

"Let me check with Justin. We have something planned for later." He lied, Why don't we just hangout after Wal-Mart until six," He offered.

"Okay," Jennifer agreed, going back to her conversation.

"Cool," Dragonbrush" chimed in changing the subject. "Then you can get me tickets to Night Crawler."

"What?" Omari asked as he entered into the living room.

"Looks like we will see you in action at the big Night Crawler party," Tioni greeted Omari, her gray eyes showing her excitement.

"Really?" Omari responded, wondering how this was possible.

"Julie was able to get us tickets. She and a few of her friends are going to chaperone us." Tioni explained.

"But they didn't get me a ticket," Dragonbrush interject disappointedly, "can you believe that?"

"Julie was only able to get so many comp tickets. She said just ask Justin. It shouldn't be a problem, and if it is, she will get him in." Jennifer added.

"Justin, huh"

"Is that going to be a problem?" Jamilah asked her brother, noting a hint of skepticism.

"No, it's cool." Omari replied, thinking, it was a good thing that he didn't call Justin and call the whole thing off yet. "Just don't expect to see me do more than handing Justin albums. And, aren't you all would worried about leaving for the camping trip on time."

"Julie and her friends are also going," Jamilah clarified, "and they'll be dropping us off. How will you be getting back home?"

"It shouldn't be a problem, but if I can ride back with one of you, then I will," Omari answered, resolving he would end his association with Justin after the event. "You guys need to be real careful while you're there, and don't take nothing from nobody." Omari warned the group.

"I know the pothead is not calling the kettle crack!" Jamilah cajoled.

"Why is it whenever folks warn you about drugs they talk to you like you're stupid? Jennifer added.

"I mean they say things like don't drink anything, even water that is not sealed. Don't eat anything, and don't take stickers. I mean duh! Only an idiot would do any of that!" Jamilah continued.

"I'm tired of them telling me to not do stuff that they do," Tioni responded.

"Why? Are you saying that your parents drink, smoke and use drugs?" Dragonbrush asked, coming to Omari's defense.

"I wasn't talking about them," Tioni remarked. Wearing a purple House of Dereon sweat suit, her hair beautifully, braided in Belgian Waffle cornrows accentuated by her large hoop earrings, gave the gray eyed teen and even more exotic look.

"So you don't really know then," Dragonbrush countered. "Watching my old man stand out on the porch on a rainy day, so he can smoke is why I will never smoke."

"You must be talking about cigarettes" Jamilah chimed in. "Because you and Omari stay seriously bombed by that other form of tobacco."

"Thanks for sharing all of our business," Omari remarked with an edge, sorry he even opened his mouth.

"Like we didn't know," Tioni responded rolling her eyes at Dragonbrush.

"Jamilah told you?" Omari accused his sister,

"Jamilah ain't told us nothing. We got noses." Jennifer stepped in ending her call. "Or have you two been sniffing so many paint fumes that you don't know that others around you know what you're doing!"

"You two are pathetic," Jamilah scolded the males with a condescending tone. You're going to warn people about what to do or not to do at a party?"

"Yeah, At least I'm not up in my room experimenting with different brands of forties," Omari charged back.

"So!" Jamilah answered with insolence, "Tell them!"

"I will," Omari threatened, generating the interest of the others.

"Do it, I don't care," Jamilah fired back.

"Moms and the old man had got into another of their famous shouting matches," Omari explained. "So, pops was on the couch, and mom's was in her bedroom. Anyway, Jamilah had brought home a forty ounce can of Colt 45. So, while everyone was snoring, Jamilah was in her room pouring." Omari smirked.

"So, what happened?" Tioni asked fully engaged.

"I'm in my bed sleep when I hear someone say in a slurring voice, "You make me sick." Then I feel a slap upside my head. I sit up, and there's Jamilah stumbling out of my room. I sat there for a couple of minutes trying to figure out what was going on. So I get out of the bed to find her when I see mom's walking down the hallway saying, "I know that little hussy didn't just hit me."

"Ooooooooo" Jennifer echoed the thoughts of the others. "What did your moms do?"

"We walked into Jamilah's bedroom, and she wasn't there, that's when we heard, "You make me sick," followed by a loud slap which we quickly concluded was my pop's bald head." Then we heard him yell, "Jamilah what is wrong with you?" "So, me and mom's rush down the stairs, and there pops sitting up trying to figure out what had happened "Where did she go?" moms demanded" pops pointed to the dining room. We all followed and saw Jamilah using the Ficus tree in the dinning room for a toilet. She looked up at all of us with ruby red eyes and said, "You all make me sick." before falling off the plant to the floor." Omari's story was followed by hysterical laughter.

"What happened to her?" Dragonbrush asked as if Jamilah wasn't in the room.

"Daily inspections in my room and random breath checks," Jamilah answered sorely.

"What happened to the plant?" Jennifer asked.

"It didn't make it," Jamilah answered.

"That must have been hella embarrassing," Dragonbrush added.

"The sad part of it is that for a minute no one was yelling. Everyone was concerned about Jamilah the way our family use to be." Omari replied glumly.

"Well alcohol is still not as bad as weed," Jamilah fired back, in an effort to regain her dignity.

"Wrong again!" Omari corrected her. "Remember that report I did for science. I found out that most vehicular accident, reports of domestic abuse, liver damage and the best episodes of Cops are almost always associated with an alcohol."

"I know about that domestic abuse part," Jennifer added "My mother could be as easy going as butterfly, but when she would get to drinking with her buddies, hours later they would be tearing up things in the house."

"How is she doing?" Omari asked.

"So far she hasn't had a drop of anything other than coffee or water," Jennifer replied touched by Omari asking.

"You want to see someone change" Dragonbrush added to the conversation. "Let my father go a couple of hours without a smoke. He gets nervous, irritable and acts like he's going to lose his mind." Dragonbrush thought about his father's need to get up in the middle of the night to go out and buy cigarettes, and cringed, "Cigarettes ain't no joke."

"That's what I'm saying," Omari said using alcohol and smoking to prove his point. "Smoking and drinking are possibly worst for you than weed, but they're legal and weed is not. It's not fair."

"If they did legalize it, you would still be too young to smoke it," Jamilah chimed. "And if it was legal, what's to say it would be any less addicting?"

"It's legal in California if you have cancer or AIDS and a doctor can prescribe it." Jennifer added then looking at Omari, "Of course you have to have AIDS or Cancer."

"I don't need it that bad" Omari replied moodily, glad he was going out with Makemba.

"So if you're dying it's alright to use it?" Tioni asked thinking about how the doctor prescribed morphine for her great uncle that was dying from cancer.

"They say that marijuana helps the appetites of those with cancer and

Aids" Jennifer responded. "But I don't know what all the details are."

"So when you DJ you must smoke a lot of weed?" Tioni asked.

"No, never at work," Omari clarified. "The folks that run the Night Crawler parties don't play that."

"See there," Tioni added, "I bet drugs are not even that big a deal at raves."

"Yeah they are," Omari explained. "Just because they don't want their DJ's high, don't mean everyone else can't be."

"So there is a lot of drug use at the raves, and you get offered drugs a lot?" Jennifer asked.

"All the time," Omari replied.

"I've never seen you come home high." Dragonbrush added.

"Duuuuh!!!!! Because I don't take any of it!" Omari answered with a condescending expression.

"Why is it that, you never met a blunt you could say no to, but you won't do anything else," Jamilah asked amazed at her little brother's will power.

"Because the drugs they be doing at those parties have folk's wilding out. I'm scared of the stuff they use." Omari replied turning his attention to the living room television where the TBS colorized version of the black white classic, Lassie come Home, that was on.

"We're not going to the Night Crawler to use drugs. We're going to have fun," Jamilah explained. "Right Jennifer?"

That's right," Jennifer confirmed. "What drugs will you be doing at the Night Crawler Tioni" Jennifer asked.

"My favorite brand is no drugs," Tioni added. "What about you Dragon?" she asked, noticing that Dragonbrush attention was affixed to the television. "Earth to Dragon," she called.

The group turned to the TBS classic on the large flat screen and tried to see what had captured Dragonbrush full attention.

"It's almost like he's trying to tell us something," the man on the screen stated.

"What's that Lassie? Little Timmy is trapped in the well boy?" The man asked the well groomed Collie.

"That dog is not trying to tell you anything fool!" Dragonbrush fired back at the screen, clearly insulted by what he was watching. Turning to the others he explained, "First off, he, Lassie is a she, and all she's saying is "did I do good? Did I do well? Do I get a reward?" Duh! Smart? Lassie was a real dummy." Dragonbrush felt the eyes of the others on him. They were amazed at his conversation.

"Are you saying that you can understand what that dog is barking?" Tioni asked.

Dragonbrush, uncomfortable with the question nodded in agreement then asked, "You mean you guys didn't understand what she said?"

"Dragonbrush," Jennifer said with a deadpan face. "Just say no to drugs."

Omari and Jamilah could only look at each other and wonder, *what was happening to their friend?*

Part 4
Growls & Glow Sticks

Growls and Glow Sticks
Dog in, dogged out
You foaming at the mouth,
Your logic's off its route,
Your brain gone south,
You're chasing your tail trying to work it all out

Giving up your sanity,
Losing your humanity,
No that everything you had can be taking away instantly

Your hate grows your will and dreams will cease
Beware when your rage reveals your true inner beast
Death and self destruction is what will be unleashed
Unless you use your logic as compass and a leash

Dogs run deep, creep, appear while you sleep
Packs attack the weak while running the streets,
Bared fangs and hard hearts is how they greet,

Refusing to believe that their choices are theirs to make alone,
Better learn to accept that dawgs that run in packs can be wrong.

1

6:08 p.m., Old Skool Cafe

When Omari arrived at the busy hip-hop themed burger joint, he spied Makemba Ellington at a booth littered with the leftovers from the previous patrons completely engaged in a conversation on her cell phone. Makemba was as pretty as Omari remembered. Her face slightly hidden underneath a brown, baseball cap, her ebony tresses gracefully accentuating her face as they cascaded across her shoulders, entangling themselves in hoop earrings that were even larger than the ones worn by Tioni. Makemba wore dark blue jeans, a form fitting, chocolate Roca Wear zip up hoodie, opened to reveal a white t-shirt with Miseducation of Lauryn Hill tour printed on it, sitting sideways with her white, Chuck Taylor covered feet dangling off the edged on the seat. The dark beauty seemed oblivious to her surroundings.

The 3rd Bass old school classic, *"Pop Goes the Weasel"* flooded the café as Omari made his way to join her wondering, why is she sitting like that at a dirty table? Then he observed two males in sagging blue jeans, white t-shirts and dark baseball caps approached Makemba's booth. Placing her iPhone to her chest, she told them she was waiting for someone." Looking at the dirty plates, napkins and Styrofoam cups that occupied the other seat, the two males simply continued on to a cleaner space. Very clever Omari observed. I hope she wasn't put off by their fits. Omari mused as he was wearing the same ensemble, only instead of a plain white tee, his had the image of Damian Jr. Gong Marley emblazoned on the front and a charcoal long sleeve tee underneath. As he drew closer, it was clear to Omari that the person on the other side of Makemba's conversation was her mother. From what the dreadlocked tagger could gather, the attractive teen was reassuring her mom that the chores that she had forgotten to do would get done later. When she noticed Omari approaching her, she quickly ended her conversation and greeted him with a broad and infectious smile. Grabbing the attention of a busboy, Makemba immediately had the booth cleaned. Minutes later, Omari was occupying the formerly messy space, and the two enjoyed Old Skool burgers.

Omari noticed Makemba's sunny disposition change to one of concern and asked "is everything alright?"

"I want to say I am so sorry about that kiss remark in the note I gave you." Makemba said nervously, taking a sip of her diet coke. "My friend Nikko told me I should use that line if I wanted to get a guy to call me back," she said in between more sips. "If you planned on doing more than talking then that's Nikko, not me. If you want her number I can give it to you" she said with embarrassment

"I just came to talk." Omari explained, wondering what Nikko looked like.

"You sure?" The eye-catching teen pressed as Kurtis Blow's classic, "These are the Breaks,", followed 3rd Bass to the dismay of some patrons that wanted a more contemporary playlist.

"Are you sure?" Omari pressed back wondering where the conversation was going.

"I won't do that again," Makemba confessed with a sigh of relief. "I can't stay long," She changed the subject in between fries. "My mama, who's tripping as usual, has a rule that if I don't finish the slave duties around the house, she'll pick me up from wherever I am to finish them, I swear," she said shaking her head in frustration. "I can't wait to go off to college, get a job, or join the military anything that will get me away from her." She paused, "I was joking about the military because the U.S military is never where its supposed to be, so why be part of a regime that refuses to aid those in need?" Realizing that she was going on and on, Makemba asked, "You think I'm crazy don't you?"

"I think you are really fine," Omari answered, unaware that he had uttered his thoughts out loud."

"And so are you," Makemba easily replied before catching herself. "I have to stay focused," she whispered to herself. " Looking at Omari she said, "You're a tagger and I need your help."

"How did you know?' Omari asked, wondering which of his recent activities exposed him.

"When I saw you the other day, I noticed that your jacket was slightly discolored which happens when you spray paint a surface and the spray bounces off that surface onto you."

She was right. Omari remembered tagging a wall in Beacon Hill, Seattle and questioned if it was a good idea to spray in a new jacket.

"My cousin Chris was a tagger, and he would mess up his clothes with spray paint all the time" Makemba spoke as she extended her open hands across the table. Omari instinctively placed his hands in hers. She rubbed her soft fingertips against his and said, "Yep, the fingertips on your index fingers have calluses from constant spray can use, just like Chris. His tag was "help!" by the way."

"What happened to your cousin, he stopped doing tags?" Omari wondered.

"While tagging an overpass, he fell broke both legs, his left arm and sustained a concussion." Makemba explained, pushing her half eaten burger to the side.

"He slipped and fell?" Omari pressed.

"No. He was drunk, high, and took the song I believe I can fly literally."

"Let me guess, when he got out the hospital, he gave up writing," Omari asked.

"When he got out of rehab, he got fed up of everyone describing him as the very first fool. He and his girlfriend relocated to Las Vegas where he now works as a welder." Makemba said somberly. "He was my favorite cousin, and my mother hated me being around him."

"I'm sure she'll love me," Omari said jokingly.

"I wouldn't put you through that," Makemba reassured him. She closed her eyes and whispered to herself, "Stay focused, don't let the freckles and bronze hair take you off point."

Opening her eyes she asked, "Did you know that AIDS is wiping out Africa?"

"It is? Omari asked.

"Sub-Saharan Africa has been more severely affected by AIDS than any other part of the world. The United Nations reports that 29.4 million adults and children are infected with the HIV virus in the region, which has about 10% of the world's population, but more than 70% of the worldwide total of infected people. The overall rate of infection among adults in Africa is 8.8%, compared with 1.2% worldwide."

"I didn't know it was that bad," Omari confessed.

"Most don't, that's why I need your help." She spoke as she again reached across the table and held Omari's hands. "While folks around here are wondering who will have a better season LeBron James or Carmelo Anthony, women and children are dying everyday. We have to do something to bring attention to this cause, a mural, tags something that will get people talking and make them aware of what's going on." Marva Whitney's Tell Mama" interrupted the conversation Makemba looked at her phone with an irritated expression.

"Let me guess," Omari observed. Makemba answered, informing her mother that she was on her way. "I got to go, but will you help me, please say yes."

"When do you want to start?" Omari asked, not clear on what they would be doing but wanting to spend more time with Makemba.

"Thank you!" she said excitedly "I'll call you. No, we should meet, and I'll call to set up a meeting." She stammered as she slid out of her booth. "I better go before she comes in to get me, I'll call you tonight."

"Okay," Omari agreed, also slipping out his booth. He watched the stunning teen approach him and allowed her soft fingertips to gently caress his face and locks.

"I wanted to do that when I first saw you," Makemba said softly before walking out the door.

Omari watched his dream date walk out the door and noticed many of the other guys in the café did the same. Jennifer's ringtone interrupted his thoughts. Hello?

"I'm sorry for ruining your day" Jennifer said sadly, referring to the cancelled trip to he fair.

"Don't say that," he consoled her, "I enjoyed hanging out today"

"It wasn't the same," she moaned.

"I don't have to be at work until 11:00. You want to hang out until 10:00?"

"Sure," the Jennifer answered with enthusiasm, "You want to meet at X, or Old Skool?" "Old Skool is fine," he answered.

"I'll see you there in a few,"

Omari thought about Jennifer, then Makemba and then Jennifer again. He muttered to himself as Jay Zee's, *"Hard Knock Life,"* began, "What am I going to do?"

2

11:08 p.m., Night Crawler, Downtown.

A condo development of 20 townhouses stalled as a result of the housing market collapse of was the location of the Night Crawlers themed party, "Pajamas in the Jungle,". Rick the owner of Night Crawler cut a deal with the sites, security guards, paying the duo to allow cars onto the restricted property and for the use of two of the nearly completed units for his party. Each car would also pay the guards $2.00 for entrance and parking.

"Theme parties are just not my thing," Gustav remarked as he drove Omari and Dragonbrush to the condo development in his vintage, black, 1963 Volvo 544. "I've decided to join some friends of mine not too far from here. If you need a lift back, give me call an hour before you're ready to leave."

To Omari's surprise, not only did Justin agree to provide Dragonbrush tickets for the big event, he also invited Dragonbrush to attend tonight's party. Justin also shared that he planned to let Omari play some of his own music and to bring some vinyl. Omari called his friend Gustav and asked the poet, computer wizard if he was going to tonight's Night Crawler event. Gustav agreed to pick Omari and Dragonbrush up.

"Thanks" Omari exited the Volvo carrying his album case referred to as a Coffin filled with selected vinyl albums, wondering what Justin's reaction would be once they met.

Instead of being angry, he found Justin's mood to be almost euphoric. Justin told Omari that he needed him to make a delivery with them after the party to drop music off to some new clients. Omari hesitantly agreed then he and Dragonbrush walked around the party.

"I see what you mean," Dragonbrush spoke rubbing his nose, "I can smell drugs all over this place. How do you do it?"

"I smell some cigarettes, weed and some alcohol, but that's all," Omari replied wondering what other scents could be in the air missing.

"I guess my nose is better than yours," Dragonbrush acknowledged. "And what is Justin, a dealer or a real heavy user?"

"Why do you say that?" Omari asked.

"Because he has drugs on him and in those Jewel cases" Dragonbrush affirmed with knowingness in his voice.

"How would you know?" Omari asked, knowing that Justin's music was always wrapped in plastic.

"I can smell what's in it," Dragonbrush answered, with assuredness.

"You can smell it?" Omari asked before being interrupted by Rick who placed his hand on Omari's shoulder ending the conversation.

"I'm glad you're here," Rick spoke, unaware and unconcerned that he was interrupting their conversation. "One of the DJ's scheduled to perform in the other condo has car problems and can't make it, so I need you to fill in, but here's the real problem, I just got word that the Police may be coming through so I need you to quietly close the set out. Are you up for it?" Before Omari could respond, Rick answered, "Great! Come with me." Without a word the two followed Rick out of the first townhouse and into the equally crowded second unit.

"Had I known that "Pajamas in the Jungle" would prove so popular I would have chosen a legitimate location that was larger, advertised and charged more," Rick mumbled, walking the two to the DJ booth. "DJ Macaroon has another gig to get to, but he left his equipment. I need you to just wind it down slowly, but gradually, so folks will start to leave before the police come in and bust all of us," he said with joking seriousness. "I've informed the guard's to let no one else in, and chase any wanderers off the property" Sighing at the crowd Rick said, "The only thing harder than making partiers go home early, is making them go home early and not bad mouth you. Excel will be here in a few to take everything down. If you need anything, figure it out."

The teen's watched Rick morph into the crowd and on to the next crisis, Noticing that the DJ Tiësto remix, had only five more minutes of play time, Omari placed on driving gloves that he brought in hopes of one day using them as a DJ trademark. Omari quickly browsed his own coffin in search for the next song.

3

11:21 a.m., Night Crawler Condo 2

At first Omari was overwhelmed by the anxiety of actually being in control of the floor, if anything went wrong it would be on him and everyone would know it. Then it hit him as long as everybody's dancing then he was doing all right. This allowed he and Dragonbrush to relax and enjoy, the party laughing at the eclectically attired party goers and their herky-jerky, movements. But, another dread replaced that anxiety. Omari wanted to discuss with Dragonbrush what he should do about Makemba and Jennifer, when he realized that addressing the changes Dragonbrush was experiencing was probably more on his tagger friend's mind than Omari's dating dilemma. If Dragonbrush was really transforming into a werewolf, no one knew how to deal with it.

However, for Omari Dragonbrush the wannabe DJ was currently a bigger pain than Dragonbrush the soon to be werewolf. Omari knew Dragonbrush was passionate about music but forgot how passionate, he wanted to try techniques on mixers and offered suggestions that Omari didn't want to hear. This was Omari' big break and he wasn't going to blow it.

Rick walked by giving Omari thumbs up then motioned his hand as Omari had seen several times indicating that he was to start winding the party down in one hour and that Excel was on his way. At that point Omari realized that he actually had learned a lot from watching Justin.

"I'll be right back" Omari informed Dragonbrush before zipping to the men's room knowing that the Bananas-NYC mix, he purposely slowed down would play another 7 to10 minutes. On his return he would mix in an even slower track. This would result in partiers leaving the dance floor before announcing his last set. When Omari returned, he was shocked to see that Dragonbrush had changed his mix, replacing it with a louder and more up-tempo beat. While maneuvering back to the DJ booth the dreadlock Omari spotted Excel from across the dance floor who sternly gave him the "wind it down gesture". When Omari arrived at the booth, Dragonbrush was wearing his headphones while trying to decide which track he would mix in next. Omari recognized the look in Dragonbrush's eyes, DJ mania, the realization that others enjoyed your taste in music as much as you and the need to give them more and more. Omari knew this because he was also experiencing this rush of euphoria, which is why it was so important to do as Rick instructed, otherwise after tonight he would be to going cold turkey.

"What are you doing?" Omari spoke, removing his headphones from Dragonbrush, upset that Dragonbrush would man the DJ booth without even asking. "We need to start winding the set down so folks can go home and we can take down the equipment."

"We can't do that now." Dragonbrush contested, his hair bouncing to the beat of the music "The party is starting to pick up again"

"We have to. We need to slow the beat down." Omari insisted, thinking something from the S.U.N. Project would be more cutting edge than Sasha. "I don't have a choice okay?"

"Let me try something first?" Dragonbrush asked reaching for another album ignoring Omari's instructions.

"No! This is my gig, not yours!" Omari flared not willing to discuss the issue any longer.

"You know what?" Dragonbrush returned, "Bite me!" He walked off the DJ's booth and melted into the crowd. Omari started to go after the angry Pinoy but he wasn't leaving the turntables for an argument. He placed his headphones back on and went about integrating the slower beat into the current mix, bringing the crowd dancing down by two notches. He looked across the room at Excel who was listening to some instruction from one of electricians that was removing the last of their special effects machines who gave Omari a thumb's up. Minutes later, the sturdy, twenty-something, Irish Italian never seen without his trademark black tight fitting t-shirt or Yves Saint Laurent styled glasses. If Rick was the heart of Night Crawler, then Excel was the soul. "Hey Excel, I'm sorry for messing up the beats. He said ready to relinquish the turntable.

"No problem," Excel shouted over the music rubbing his fingers through his Caesar cut. "You saved us, and you're pretty good. We would like a favor, next Saturday is the big one and I want you to DJ in the new talent room. That is, if you're man enough to do it?"

"Yeah!" Omari answered ecstatically. "Do I have to sub for the Jedi?"

"Nope, Do whatever, and bring whoever. Just get me a MP3 or cassette sample of what you got."

"Done!" Omari said thrilled with the opportunity to perform

"Good, hold down the room while we deal with a couple of Cobalt's shaking down our patrons," Excel spoke while sticking his hand into his pocket and pulling out a wad of green bills. He then handed Omari two fifty dollar bills.

"Is it bad?" Omari asked.

"Its part of doing business," Excel replied dryly. "The Cobalt's are also throwing a party next week, that's more a drug and sex show with more music rather than a party." He smiled before taking a swig of the bottled water in his hand. "I'm just hoping ours is more music and good times, because that's what brings em back." Excel continued to scan the room with a look of concern on his face "Unfortunately, this place is becoming more a drug zone than a rave. The best thing to happen tonight was your music." Looking at Omari's gloved hands; he asked "What's with the racing gloves?"

"Oh, I wanted to see if they would handle better than just my hands" Omari responded. "They didn't."

"You were looking for a gimmick weren't you?" Excel asked with an easy smile. Omari answered with a grin of his own. Taking a slow glance at the revelers on the floor who were starting to slowly exit the building, Excel turned to Omari and said, "Hold it down for a few more minutes, and I'll have someone come by to dismantle this system. He handed Omari his card;

"Get me that playlist, and I'll see you next week." Excel smiled before slipping back into the crowd.

Wow, I got to tell Dragon! Omari thought slowing the beat half a notch. Then he remembered that he was mad at him and went back to the mixer.

4

12:29 a.m. Night Crawler Condo 1

"All the money and drugs you find on me on me you can have because you would just take it from me anyway." Justin said calmly while working the mixer, aware that he was relatively safe from harm in the crowded environment. "I haven't even been paid for this gig yet." Justin explained to the menacing, dreadlocked gang member.

Slimstyle knew that Justin was a dealer. E, Shrooms, and other hallucinogens were his specialty. He also knew that Justin had branched out from dealing exclusively at parties where he performed, to using liquor stores, bars and beauty parlors to sell his goods, so Slimstyle was sure that Justin had either profits, drugs, or both, on or near him. The gang banger was sure that the rich kid would come clean, after a couple of pimp slaps, but in the packed house the parolee also knew that he would be doing serious time for that smack. Because one thing that rich kids, had, were parents that could pressure the District Attorney into making sure you went to jail for a long time if you ever got out. Justin's partner Edwin wasn't so lucky. Slimstyle figured if they took the two out back and threatened kill Edwin and showed they meant it by slicing him a few times then the white-boy would probably give in to their demands.

"Check it out. It's that little punk Dragonbrush." Shady, the permed gang member interrupted.

The others watch Dragonbrush walked through the crowd and out the unit.

"Didn't Gat say we owed him a beat down?" Coffy asked.

"Yeah we do," Slimstyle answered. He gave Justin and Edwin a menacing glance then walked away.

"Whew, that was close!" Justin sighed, turning to Edwin who was equally shook up.

"How did they find this place?" Edwin asked, feeling his heart racing.

"I don't know," Justin confessed, "I do know that if they would have searched me they would have gotten all of tonight's take," he spoke while watching to see if the gangsters had come back. "I got to get our money out of here before they finish beating down Dragonbrush." Lifting a small brown paper bag from the litter and glow stick strewn floor, Justin stuck his hands into his jacket pocket and pulled out a thick bundle of cash, several wrapped cassettes and a plastic bag filled with pills, and mushrooms, chips, each in it's own baggie "Do you have any more E.?" He asked Edwin

"Sold out hours ago," Edwin answered proudly, "I was also able to get Robbie's strawberries."

"A sell out, selling out," Justin joked stuffing the paper bag filled hallucinogens into pocket. "I'm going to finish this set, Grab Omari head back to the crib to seal up our product and put away our stash, then take Omari to drop off the product, while you take down our things. He spoke handing Edwin the bundle of cash. "You hold on to tonight's take and I'll meet you at the house later. If those guys come back which I doubt, walk away from everything." Justin added watching the last of the Cobalt's exit the unit minutes behind Dragonbrush.

"Why are you still using him?" Edwin asked angrily, "What's up?"

"I'll tell you what's up," Justin replied annoyed at being questioned. "Mr. Redlocks is currently the only delivery boy I've have. Now, if that's okay with you, I'll go handle my business." Edwin placed the money in his pocket then watched Justin slow down the tempo.

5

12:32 a.m., Night Crawler, Outside

"Omari was a power mad prick!" Dragonbrush fumed, upset for even coming to this stupid party. "And the music he played wasn't that good," he grumbled as he wandered through the unfinished condos occasionally coming across folks sneaking in or looking for privacy. Even though he was angry at Omari, the teen knew it was short lived. He figured he would just check out the other abandoned units for the next hour then go back to see if Omari needed anything. Then it occurred to him with so many vacant units with white walls, this place was begging for some art. Pulling out a black magnum marker from his side pocket, Dragonbrush decided he would find the perfect vacant wall and do what he did best.

6

12:34 a.m. Night Crawler, Outside,

"Where did he go?" Slimstyle asked, finding the coolness of the night a refreshing contrast to the hot and humid dance space.

"I don't know. But he couldn't have gotten too far" Coffy answered, pulling up his sagging denims while looking at the vacant condominiums in various stages of completion. "Let's split up."

"Bad idea," Shady interjected, "I jes overheard somebody say that they shutting down early, cuz the police might be coming by. We best stay together, case we got to get up out of here."

"Whatever," Slimstyle agreed, unfazed by the threat of the police or the prospect of going back to jail. "Then we check everyone of these houses, but we not leaving till we find that lil punk!"

7

1:12 a.m. Night Crawler, Condo 2

Omari decided he would wait for only a few minutes longer Dragonbrush. Excell arrived, and as agreed finished up the set and would take down the music system. Omari searched the split level condo to see if Dragonbrush was still in the unit, and wasn't surprised that he didn't find him.

He called Dragonbrush several times earlier, but with the music so loud, there was no telling if he could even hear it. Irritation was setting in as Omari knew that Gustav needed an hours notice before he arrived, and things looked like they were shutting down. Looking up, Omari was surprised to see Justin in the unit.

"How did your set go?" Justin asked, browsing the still crowded condo.

"It went okay," Omari answered coolly, containing the excitement within. "Rick wants me to perform at the big Night Crawler event."

"Look at you, DJ Omari is on his way," Justin added, eliciting a grin from the freckled face teen. "Why are you waiting around?" Justin asked scanning the room. "You need a ride?"

"I'm cool, I'm just waiting for Dragonbrush," Omari answered, thinking a ride now would be better than waiting in the dark for another hour.

"Dragonbrush is gone" Justin replied. "He and some his Cobalt friends left about 20 minutes ago."

"What?" Omari flashed with shock. He then composed himself, and said to Justin. "Let me get that ride".

"Cool," Justin smiled, "I hope you don't mind us making a stop on the way?

8

1:14 a.m., Night Crawler Condo 2 Upstairs

"This werewolf thing wasn't half bad," Dragonbrush said to himself, not knowing what to make of his newfound abilities. It was terrifying when he lost the ability to see color. And as much as he was enjoying the music inside, the volume had giving him a terrible headache. He could feel the very vibrations in the air as if they were waves of water. Any aspirations he had of being the next Q-bert were over. Worse still his olfactory senses were bombarded with odors and stench. Even the scent from the black *Mark-A-lot* marker he was using to tag a wall inside the unfinished condo was nauseating. The flipside was, he never felt stronger. Any apprehensions he about heights were gone, as his ability to leap were like something from a comic book. In a single bound he could leap from the ground to the roof of the vacant townhouses. Surprising himself the first time, he did it again, and again. When he found the right wall, Dragonbrush became so engrossed with his tag that he lost track of time. After realizing that his phone was dead in need of charging. Dragonbrush rushed back at condo 2, expecting Omari to still be mixing, but was surprised to see that the DJ station dismantled and many of the partiers were gone. "What happened to the DJ with the red locks?" Dragonbrush asked a partier that he had seen earlier.

"He left with the other DJ," the partier responded.

I can't believe he left me, Dragonbrush thought to himself, *how did he figure I was going to get home?* Turning again to the stranger Dragonbrush asked, "Can I borrow your phone to call my ride?"

"Sure," the stranger replied handing Dragonbrush his fur covered cell phone. The Pinoy teen immediately dialed Omari.

9

1:33 a.m., Embarcadero Blvd, Northbound

"I thought I was the one driving?" Justin joked, commenting on Omari's gloves.

"Oh, I tried them hoping they would provide a better grip on the vinyl," Omari confessed. Omari could not believe that Dragonbrush would get so angry that he would leave without saying anything. He felt his phone vibrate in his side pant pocket, "Hello? Where you at? I'm on my way." Turning to Justin, "take me back," Omari insisted.

"He's still there?" Justin answered, surprised that the Cobalt's hadn't found him. "I know I saw him and his friend leave together," Justin explained. "Listen, my bad, let me make this quick stop a couple of minutes from here, and then we go get him."

"The best thing you can do is take me back now." Omari spoke through gritted teeth, unbuckling his seatbelt ready to begin firing on Justin's face if he didn't immediately comply.

"I can't do that," Justin answered his eyes on what was in the rear view mirror. "Because-" Omari looked behind him and could see the red flashing light.

"Quick, hold this!" Justin reached into his pocket and handed his brown paper bag to Omari.

Without thinking Omari complied, placing the paper bag on the floor between his feet never questioning "why," as Justin pulled the car to the side of the road.

10

1:34 a.m., Embarcadero, Northbound.

"Get out of the car slowly and place your hands on the top of the vehicle where I can see them." The loud speaker squawked, seeing that they had no choice the two complied, A bright flashlight hit them in the face preventing them from seeing the officer. Justin squinted as he watched the unidentified officer walk behind Omari, cuff him, and walk him to the squad car.

"What did I do?" What's your badge number?" Omari asked. The shadowed policeman ignored his questions placing him into the back seat of the squad car, slamming the door behind him. The walking flashlight then approached Justin who had not moved.

"If I checked your car what will I find?" The officer asked his flashlight now in Justin's face.

"Sir, feel free to check my car from top to bottom," Justin answered compliantly, "If you wish to impound my vehicle, you have my permission," he continued as the officer patted him down "I have a hundred dollars and some change, that I earned from DJ-ing." He added as the officer looked at his identification.

"What about your friend?" The officer asked not certain of Justin's sincerity.

"Omari is just a friend. I hooked up with him at the Rave. I was taking him home," his voice dropped in volume "I will never testify to this, " Justin confessed to the bright light "but back in Seattle where he is from he is a known dealer."

"But is he a dealer here?" the grim face three striped officer asked,

"If he knew, I told you, he would kill me," Justin answered with fear in his voice.

"We will protect you" the officer offered "Just spit it out."

"If you search the passenger's side seat where he was sitting you will see." He whispered.

"That's all I needed to hear," the officer replied. "Are you still at this address?" He asked writing down the address on a note pad.

"Yes I am," Justin replied compliantly.

"Then if I have any further questions I know where to find you" he added handing him back his license before pulling the paper bag from Justin's car "You're free to go," the officer said before walking back to his car and after his third step he could hear the Jeep speed off.

The car door opened in the back seat of the police car and the flashlight again was in Omari's face who had just watched Justin drive off

"Why are you keeping me?" He asked in a panicked voice. "I didn't do anything!"

The officer opened up the paper bag and a roll of small baggies filled with small vials and cassettes fell into Omari's lap, then breaking open one of the cassette revealed mushroom chips.

"Those are not mine!" Omari cried, knowing instantly Justin would never admit that the drugs his, which is why he gave them to him.

"I need to call my mama," he cried and then it occurred to him, she was too far away to help him, "I need to call my uncle, honest to God, this stuff is not mine!"

The officer removed the flashlight from Omari face, and he recognized that it was Sergeant Bright

"Man this not what it looks like," Omari pleaded.

"It's not?" The sergeant responded, removing the handcuffs from the teen. "You mean I catch you with drugs and it's not what it appears to be?"

"I swear to God it's not," Omari pleaded.

"I believe you," he said, "and you know why?" Omari looked at him without an answer. "Because I have to, I have to believe you are a good person, not the type of person that would poison even an idiot that is willing to pay to be poisoned."

"I wouldn't. We saw the flashing headlights behind us, and Justin told me to hold the bag for him." He said shamefully. "I didn't even trip."

"You should know he denied having any drugs and stated that you were dealing."

"He set me up just like that," Omari said aloud, "And was going to let me take the fall. I thought we were dawgs."

"Speaking of dogs, where's Dragonbrush?" Bright asked, knowing that the two were rarely separated.

"I need to go back to the party to get him," Omari answered quietly, realizing Dragonbrush warned him about what Justin was carrying.

"Tell me how to get there," Bright responded turning the car around and sped up the road

"I'm not sure what your friendship with Justin will be like after this," Bright spoke to the demoralized teen, never taking his eyes off the road. "But you should know that, Justin is a suspected low level drug dealer who hasn't been caught because he's smart, and his rich daddy is a city Councilman with lawyers. His associates have not been so lucky. I suspected as much when I saw you in the car with him. Had I been another officer you would be on your way to jail right now."

I've learned a lot from Justin, Omari thought. When they arrived at the construction site, Omari convinced the sergeant to allow him to go into the now nearly vacant site to get Dragonbrush as it would have been impossible for him to explain his relationship with the officer and not raise suspicions.

"I'll give you ten minutes then I'm coming in behind you" the officer shouted as Omari ran past the nervous security guard and toward the Townhouses.

11

1:36 a.m. Night Crawler

"Dragonbrush is gone and so should we," Shady voiced his frustration as the crowd was disappearing and their opportunity to rob anyone of money or drugs.

"Word, He's not here." Coffy agreed. "I'm rolling," he spoke heading to his vehicle several yards away before he felt Slimstyle's tap on his shoulder.

"Look up there," Slimstyle pointed to the second floor window of the townhouse where they first shook down Justin.

Coffy spotted Dragonbrush in a lighted space using a magic marker to tag the bedroom wall.

"That's why I'm running things, and you all just take orders" Slimstyle replied his voice filled with superiority.

"I be damned," Shady uttered, "lil punk must have double back. How he get by us?"

"Let's go ask," Coffy led the way.

12

1:39 a.m. Night Crawler Condo 2 Upstairs

For Dragonbrush, deciding to tag another wall in the upstairs master bedroom while waiting on Omari was a big mistake. He had barely finished his piece before the fumes were too much for his buzzing head. Woozy from the fumes, Dragonbrush sat underneath an open window and admired his work while clearing his head of the vaporous toxins. He looked at the Magnum marker in his hand then tossed it out the window. Until Omari arrived Dragonbrush decided he would close his eyes and clear his head. While he drifted off, he could pick up four distinctive scents that grew stronger. Dragonbrush's senses told him to open his eyes but he ignored it. The feeling persisted. When he did, he was immediately gripped with terror. Slimstyle, Shady and Coffy were standing over him.

13

1:45 a.m., Night Crawler condo 2, upstairs

"Don't take this ass whupping personally," Slimstyle smiled, launching his right fist directly at Dragonbrush's face. "It's just business."

Years ago, Dragonbrush remembered watching the brutal Slimstyle punch out his parole officer with what he called a *"One-hitter-quitter."* That same punch was now coming toward the young Filipino, but Dragonbrush knew Slimstyle had to be toying with him because Slimstyle was moving in slow motion, and Dragonbrush easily avoided his effort. When Slimstyle swung again, Dragonbrush also it. Coffy and Shady also tried and failed as their target sidestepped their blows with very little difficulty. That's when Dragonbrush realized that his attackers were not pretending. He was that much faster. When Slimstyle threw another punch Dragonbrush quickly side stepped the punch and delivered a blow to Slimstyle's jaw that dropped him where he stood. Quickly recovering, Slimstyle was back on his feet reaching inside his jacket for his gun.

"Yeah you fast," Slimstyle acknowledged, as he pointed his Browning semiautomatic at Dragonbrush "But do you think you're faster than a bullet?" Dragonbrush felt the vice of fear again controlling his body and froze not knowing what to do. Then he watched the right side of Slimstyle's face go chalk white as he was struck with a chunk of broken sheetrock, his arm went awry dropping his gun to the floor.

"Run stupid!" Dragonbrush heard Omari yell, as he threw whatever was available at the two other thugs.

Seeing his opportunity to escape, Dragonbrush leapt over Slimstyle with an effort that caught the attention of everyone, as he landed on the other side of Omari. Having nothing else to throw, Omari charged the remaining two gang members allowing Dragonbrush to run to safety.

Outside Dragonbrush breathed a sigh of relief. He had escaped. His relief was short lived when he realized Omari was still inside. That realization was followed by an onslaught of sounds, smells and vibrations rushing throughout his being, turning his world black and white. He swiftly returned to the unit to find Coffy with Omari in a headlock as Shady was reaching for his gun. Dragonbrush felt a gurgling in his stomach wanting to roar, but instead lunged into Shady slamming him into the door, and into unconsciousness. Coffy released Omari to attack Dragonbrush, only to be dropped by Dragonbrush's "*One-hitter-quitter.*"

Slimstyle had regained consciousness and reached for his fallen gun, but Omari reached the piece first and struck the larger Slimstyle with the butt of the gun.

"You better kill me now, cuz if you don't, you dead!" Slimstyle cried through a bleeding mouth. "You don't know who are fucking with!"

"Don't care either," Omari responded before savagely kicking his downed opponent right between the eyes, sending him painfully back into unconsciousness.

He turned and saw Dragonbrush standing behind him, grateful for the assistance. "Who are these fools?"

"Cobalts, " Dragonbrush sadly replied.

"You got beef with the Cobalts?" Omari asked.

"Not the gang, just them and a few more. They might try to kill me and now they may try to kill you," he said with concern. Omari slapped Dragonbrush against the back of his head "Then we die together. Nobody smacks my little brother but me," he fumed. The two headed toward the parked police car, constantly looking over their shoulders

"I'm sorry," Dragonbrush grumbled.

"No worries," He replied. "But it wasn't all bad tonight" Omari added with a smile, "I got a big gig next week, and I want you to do back up."

"I don't know," Dragonbrush replied, "not knowing how to explain what a painful experience the night was. "Tonight gave me a serious headache."

"That's tonight, next week will be better" Omari replied.

No, next week will be worse, Dragonbrush thought. The two spotted Sergeant Bright on the radio in his squad car. Seeing them he signed off and opened the passenger side of the door.

"Bright?" Dragonbrush exclaimed, looking at the squad car.

"If it wasn't for Bright, I would be behind bars right now" Omari responded.

"What?" Dragonbrush asked.

"I'll tell you about it later," Omari said as they greeted the sergeant.

"You took longer than ten minutes," Bright said with a smile, as the two got in the car not offering an explanation, nor were they asked.

"Are you going to raid the place?" Omari asked

"It appears most of the partiers are gone" the sergeant replied, "But I will send a couple of squads to check it out."

"There going to find some Cobalt's in there," Dragonbrush acknowledged.

"Then they will be going to jail." Bright responded without a hint of emotion

"Are you going to arrest Justin now that you know that the drugs and the money are his?" Omari asked as a clueless Dragonbrush listened.

"Nope," the officer responded dryly.

"Why not?" Omari asked, sure that if he hadn't known the officer, he would be in lock down right now.

"Do you want to go to jail?" Bright asked, getting the two's attention. "Because if I arrest Justin, the first thing he would do is implicate you, and we don't want that do we?" he stared at the nodding Omari."

"So what do we do?" he snapped back, wanting justice.

"When you see Justin again and you will, he's going to want to know why you are walking the street. When he asks, tell him that the policeman took the bag and left you on the street to walk home. If you do that, then you won't have to walk around town with a snitch jacket on you."

"Yeah, what are they going to do when it happens?" Dragonbrush interjected. "Call the police?"

"What about the drugs?" Omari asked.

"I'll take care of them," Norbert said driving toward the freeway.

14

1:44 a.m., Tioni's Bedroom, College Avenue

Tioni pulled the cover of her comforter over her head, careful not to disturb her head wrap and called Coffy.

What?" the deep gruff voice answered.

"Hi Coffy," Tioni said gleefully.

"What kind of games are you playing little girl?" The thug's asked his voice revealing his annoyance. He and a few others were able to get out of the condo before the police arrived, but Slimstyle wasn't as lucky. He was sore and pissed.

"I'll have to explain it to you later," she said coyly.

"There might not be a later," he said with assurance. "You play games like a child I only deal with women you understand? That why I had this ladies Rolex for you."

"You do?" Tioni said excitedly.

"I did. But, I'm about business and you're about childishness. I don't have time for that" He smirked, "But if you want it, it's yours."

"I don't know if I can take a gift like that, but I want to see you again," she said trying to sound more mature.

"Well if I don't see you this week, then next week we are having a big party. We're going to have some big time rappers and producers there, and I want you to be my guest, you know what I'm saying? But, you got to be real and you got to be a woman, are you?"

"Yeah"

"And you know what I want, don't you?"

"Yeah," Tioni answered nervously.

"Well, I got diamonds and rings and a mansion waiting for you if you do that. Now the question is will you do that?"

Tioni could hear her parents talking outside her door, "I got to go," and clicked the phone off. The door opened, and she heard her mother say to her father "Honey, you're hearing things in your old age, that girl is sleep."

Minutes later, Tioni was dreaming of Rolex's and diamonds and how jealous the others would be when they saw them on her.

15

4:25 a.m., South Hill Court

From his bed Dragonbrush listened to the sounds of the house. It was as if the house had let him in on its secrets, revealing all the creaking and sounds that echoed throughout. Taking in the distinct scent that the house possessed. Dragonbrush was keenly aware that everything and everyone had its own unique scent that followed them everywhere. A distinctive smell that could not be washed away, covered over with lotions or expensive perfumes. He understood how Maria and Lexus found him. Once they locked onto his scent there was no shaking it unless the area had overwhelming, masking scents there was no sneaking up him. Most surprising, was the strength and speed that came with his adrenalin rush. He felt like he could do anything. Dragonbrush's mind drifted to the earlier events at the condo with Slimstyle and the others. *Why did he run from Slimstyle and the others only to dispatch them with ease?* Fear had paralyzed him from knowing his own strengths. *What was he afraid of?* He sat up feeling his hair brush against his shoulders and found himself becoming angry, *they were not going to continue to push him around they were not going to threaten his family.* He could feel his heart pounding and his mouth beginning to drool and growls growing in volume and bass, and then he was struck with a pair of pants, followed by shirts and jackets.

"Fool, stop making all those sounds, and go to sleep!" Omari yelled as he rolled back over.

"Oh yeah? If you stop snoring then I could go to sleep," Dragonbrush returned.

"At least I don't have to be out delivering papers in a few minutes." Omari said, burying his head under his pillow and ignoring the clothes that were thrown back at him.

"Oh my God!" Dragonbrush looked at the clothes covered clock. Grabbing some underwear and Nike sweats he headed to the bathroom. When he peered into the mirror the center of his shoulder length hair was standing on end like that of an angry dog. Dragonbrush smiled, his tongue rubbing against his canine teeth. He would protect his family and himself, his days of running scared were over.

Part 5
Barks & Bites

If someone's bark is worse than their bite, they are not as unpleasant as they seem, and their actions are not as bad as their threats.
thefreedictionary.com

1

9:04 a.m., South Hill Court, Jamilah's bedroom

"Hello," Jamilah said weakly answering her phone on the second ring, never bothering to open her eyes.

"Good morning," Shayla greeted her daughter. After a second of silence she asked, "Jamilah are you going to say something?"

"I'm not going back to Seattle," Jamilah answered flatly, now wide awake and as angry as ever. "So if you are trying to convince me, you can forget it," she replied sitting up in her bed.

"I want us to try to talk to each other with a little civility and respect." Shayla urged.

"You mean the same kind of respect you showed when you told me your dog friend's daughter would be moving into our house and into my room? Jamilah fumed. "Now I'm supposed to show you respect? Please, let me get off this phone."

"No please don't," Shayla implored.

"I told daddy about what happened, and he said that if I didn't want to go back to Seattle and live under those stressful conditions, he would see you in court," Jamilah lied, feeling her pain and her rage build.

"None of that is going to happen," Shayla interrupted. "And I'm not going to force either of you to come back any sooner than planned."

"I'm not coming back, ever."

"Fine, if that's what you want, but there will be no one in your room while you and Omari are gone"

"She's not moving in?" Jamilah asked her curiosity aroused, "What happened?"

"I had no right to try to create the Brady Bunch without your permission," She confessed. "I had to hear it the hard way from your aunt, No one is infringing on you or your brother. The funniest thing about all this," Shayla sighed, "is that a month ago neither you nor Omari wanted to leave home, and now you're fighting equally as hard to stay away."

"Omari would go back in a minute." Jamilah conceded.

"Omari is very much a mama's boy" Shayla said with love, "And you will always be a daddy's girl. Your father and I always knew whose side you two would take in an argument."

Jamilah smiled. "I just called to say that I am sorry for putting you through all that, I was selfish and wrong and when you are not so mad at me we'll talk longer."

"Mama?" Jamilah asked.

"Yes."

"Get rid of Jamal," she pleaded.

"I'll see what I can do," Shayla answered quietly.

2

4:49 pm., 19th Street BART Station

Dragonbrush patiently sketched ideas into his bible knowing that soon the empty blue, tiled station would be flooded with home bound commuters. After completing his paper route, Dragonbrush worked on the mural at the Malcolm X Youth Center, where he and Yes, his Puerto Rican buddy painted the stairwell wall of the four story building as a condition of their community service. Unable to tolerate the fumes of the aerosol cans, Dragonbrush found filling in the outlines created by Yes with acrylic paint was slow going. Yes, currently out of town, had created the concept for the wall and had yet to complete all the illustrations. The mural was filled with warring, angels, evil looking black blobs, ferocious dogs, zombies and vampires. In the middle of the piece was four yet to be completed figures holding what looked like a horns. That was as far as the piece went, and Dragonbrush had no idea where the piece was going. Starting a new sketch, Dragonbrush thought about how as a result of his heightened sense of smell the Chlora-flora-carbons emitted from Krylon paint cans and magic markers made him nauseous. He lamented that now he would never be like his graffiti hero's Mike *the Dream* Francisco, whose inspiring work brought the drab walls in the most desolated parts of Oakland to life, or even create startling works like *Neckface*. "Oh well," he whispered to himself. There was always slap tagging, or putting up posters like Shepherd Fairey, the world's most famous street artist, best known for his red, white and blue poster of Barack Obama. It was just hard out here for a tagger. One of Dragonbrush's online buddies emailed him a news article about legendary New York taggers, *Cost* and *Rev* whose work could also be seen on many city roof tops. Cost and Revs were so prolific in the 80's, that then New York Mayor Rudy Giuliani knew the two by their first names. When the police caught Cost, whose real name is Adam Cole tagging a mailbox, in court, the judge estimated that Cost had done over 100 million in damages but only fined him $2,126, which was far less than what Dragonbrush had to pay. Cost's partner Revs disappeared from the graffiti scene and was rumored to be writing his thoughts on the subway tunnels of New York City. Looking down the dark hollow passageway that was the BART tunnel filled Dragonbrush with dread. Cost's incarceration and Dragonbrush's interactions with law made him ponder the question *If tagger's had to go to jail and pay fines for their work then, why couldn't it stay up?* Dragonbrush's thoughts were interrupted by two distinctive scents, scents that brought him to the station. Dragonbrush put away his bible, then stood up and allowed BART officers Malcolm Walker and Edward Stansfield who were patrolling the stations to see him.

When the two officers spotted the teen, they remembered him from the incident at the Lake Merritt station Walker pointed at him and laughed, "Hey the hair is still long. I guess you won't be pressing charges."

Dragonbrush ignored the officers as they walked toward him. He pulled a piece of adhesive paper from his backpack and slap tagged on the tiled wall "*BART Police Blow!*"

Malcolm looked at Edward and said "You see now we have something to arrest this little tagger for, and we can make it stick." Malcolm cut a glance back his partner as they cautiously approached the motionless youth and said, "Remember when we had to chase this little hardhead though the San Francisco station? I think we may have to rough this one up a little."

"After all the trouble he put us through, oh he's going to hurt, I guarantee you," Stansfield replied.

Dragonbrush glared at the two with knowing eyes. Many police hated taggers as much as they did hardened criminals, and it just wasn't in Oakland. When Dragonbrush went online to graffiti chat rooms he constantly read about how some pork chop brutalized a tagger. Dragonbrush instincts told him the two approaching him were especially vicious.

Dragonbrush looked at the officers holstered guns. Malcolm was left handed, and Edward right handed. Their pistols faced each other. Dragonbrush felt the world go black and white, and his senses could pick up the vibration of the thousands of people on the street level above leaving at five o'clock. He felt a growl in his stomach and fought an urge to go for both of the officers throats. The officers noticed the crouching teen's hair begin to stand on end and paused to observe him. Then before they could respond, Dragonbrush somersaulted between them, snatching their guns from their holsters. The awestruck officers turned behind them and could see the Filipino tagger nine feet away. Seconds later he was between them again, this time snatching off their belts sending both officers pants down to their knees. Instinctively, Malcolm and Edward reached for their downed pant and could hear a clicking sound and the cold steel on their wrist and ankles as the teen was faster than their eyes could follow. Dragonbrush had used the officer's handcuffs to cuff their hands and their feet. Unable to comprehend what had happened, the two veteran policemen toppled over cursing as they struggled to get up. Turning away from the clumsy duo, Dragonbrush looked down the BART tunnel that had caused him pause earlier, and raced into the darkness. Passengers and trains began to flood the station in time to see the two humiliated officers of the law, lying on the cold station floor, with their pants literally down.

3

7:09 p.m., Copy's 4 U

"This is lot more fun then painting and a whole lot cleaner," Makemba acknowledged as she and Omari used the Copy Shop's paper cutters to slice the 8x10 sheets of adhesive paper into fours. Omari had designed a slap tag about preventing the spread of AIDS in Africa. The two planned to pass out the tags to friends and place them in public places throughout the city.

"But it won't get attention like the banner," Omari replied, stacking the slap tags into neat stacks to be rubber banded once they were completed. Earlier Makemba met Omari at Malcolm X Recreational Center with two king sized sheets she brought from home. The duo spent the day painting both sides of the sheets with white, latex paint that was used to paint the walls of the stairwell. They then painted their message in black and red and green paint once the sheets were dry.

"I still don't know how you're going to hang the banner when the freeway over pass is fenced in." Makemba asked. "You really should let me help you."

"Why is this Africa thing so important to you?" Omari asked, flipping his locks over his shoulder side stepping the question.

"It started as a class project where we had to find a social cause to champion," Makemba answered, keeping an eye on the cutter to avoid ruining her cut. Some chose the environment, animal rights, poverty and AIDS among women in the U.S. While googling, I came across what was happening in Africa and couldn't figure out why it wasn't in the news more or why the government wasn't doing more to help."

"What do you want your banners to do?" Omari asked as he began to band the stacks together.

"For people to write and call their Congressman and Senator demand they help." She looked at Omari and asked with a smirk, "Do you care, or are you just trying to get next to me? I'm sorry." Makemba added thinking about her words. "We need to stay focused".

"Can I do both?" Omari replied revealing his pearly whites.

"You mean cut and stay focused?" She asked slicing and stacking more stickers.

"I mean care about getting the message out while trying to get next to you?"

"Your graffiti is really good" Makemba acknowledged Omari's art work, changing the subject. "Why do you put it on walls where it's only going to get painted over?" she asked, determined to stay on track.

Why can every corporation tell me what to buy, smoke, and do on every building, bus and flat surface available, but if I write something on a wall or bus shelter, I'm committing a crime? Why? Because I don't have big bucks to pay for it," Omari argued his expression revealing passion. "I thought speech was supposed to be free."

So, it's not about the art, it's about freedom of speech?" Makemba acknowledged, grasping the gist of Omari's argument.

"Well the art should look cool," Omari pointed out.

"Your banner is cool," Makemba offered, "and it looks really good."

"And so do you," Omari said with a smile, then added, "I know, stay focused."

4

8:13 p.m., Parking lot, Pearl Harbor Liquors

Glock, Beamon and Coffy stood in the glass littered parking lot of the liquor store openly sharing a fifth of Jim Bean. Because of the drug dealing, the violence, the selling of alcohol and cigarettes to minors and public intoxication that took place in the front and the parking lot of the troublesome store, the police and the City Council considered Pearl Harbor Liquors blight to the community. Yet, the store and the problems associated with it continued.

"You know who the biggest crooks are? Glock waxed philosophically. "I mean bigger than the mafia and all of them." He asked as he poured out a small amount of the bourbon in memory of all the fallen homies.

"Who?" Beamon asked.

"Them damn lawyers," Glock exclaimed extending the bottle to Coffy. "You going to pay a lawyer no matter what side of the law you on; they the biggest pimps," He bemoaned having to pay thirty-five hundred dollars to bail Slimstyle caught trespassing on private property. When Beamon called their attorney Leo Lieberman, he was out of town and would send one of his assistants as soon as one was available.

"Leo said any of us could have went in and posted bail," Beamon spoke, reiterating what the vacationing attorney told him, watching Coffy take a long sip of the bourbon.

"Man, that is the reason why you will never even make Lieutenant in the Cobalts!" Coffy scolded Beamon handing him the bottle as Glock shook his head. "You let your mouth piece go into the jail because the police won't jam him up about where the money came from, or try to associate him with another crime. He just walks in and walks out."

"You remember Cedric?" Glock shared. "That fool and his old lady got into it about him cheating on her.

She pulled a gun on him, some neighbors saw it, called the police, and they took her in. Cedric decided he would bail her out and took the money that he stashed with his weed. The police smelled the weed on the money and arrested him. His parole was violated. She did three days, and he's still in jail. I wouldn't bail my mama out."

"Yeah, but you have in the past," Beamon added.

"That was then." Glock replied, taking a long sip on the bottle, followed by another.

"This is now even she would be on her own if I couldn't get someone else to do it."

"When are we going to talk about what we're going to do about making that lil, punk Dragonbrush and his freckle face friend pay for what they did?" Beamon changed the subject. "They attack one of ours, we need to bring some Cobalt justice to they ass"

"I'm waiting for the word," Coffy answered looking at Glock taking and even longer sip, aware of Glock's and Dragonbrush's history.

Glock looked at the bottle, his thoughts on the last time he had seen Dragonbrush at Red Robins. Dragonbrush was not the same; it seemed as if he had developed a killer instinct.

"I say we place their bodies where the world can see Cobalt justice," Beamon offered, bringing Glock's attention back.

"That all sounds good", Glock added throwing the nearly empty bottle into the street nearly missing a bus, "But whatever you do, make sure I'm not around. I don't want to be implicated in any of this and you already know that Bright is going to come looking for me when it happens" Glock said heading toward his Impala.

As Coffy and Beamon followed, Coffy's thoughts went to the gray eyed teen Tioni. He first noticed her with fellow Cobalt Tyrone before he, J-Dawg and the other gang members disappeared. He wanted Tioni in the worse way and would tell her anything she wanted to hear if it meant him getting her alone. He would call her later and say what needed to be said. As far as Dragonbrush was concerned, he and whoever helped him the other night were good as dead.

5

July 26th 10:07 p.m., College Avenue, Tioni's bedroom.

"All I want you to do is just come to the party, and introduce you to everyone. It shouldn't take longer than a minute," Coffy pleaded on the phone. A week had gone by now Tioni was again having second thoughts after agreeing to attend the Cobalt party with him.

"I don't think so," Tioni answered. Coffy's call caught her off guard. She planned to text him to cancel their date. Second thoughts, and pressure from Jennifer were getting to the better of her, and Toni wasn't sure if she was interested in Coffy because of his b-boy image, or if she was trying to make Dragon and the others jealous which clearly wasn't working.

"Why do you keep doing this to me, Coffy pressed with seductive charm. "All I want to do is give you things and shower you with affection, and all I get in return is pain."

"It's just that my friends all want me to go to another party" Tioni struggled, not knowing she would be faced with this type of resistance.

"You can still go to the party" Coffy pressed. "I'll just swing by, swoop you up, take you to the party that my folks are throwing, you show your face, I give you your watch and ring and zoom you back."

"Well the other thing is that I am not ready for that," Tioni mustered the courage to say

"Ready for what?" Coffy asked, feigning ignorance.

"To be showered with affection," Tioni added without wanting to address details

"Cool if you don't want to go there that's fine," Coffy agreed.

"And, I'm not playing any games," she stressed.

"No means no," he reassured her. "If you're not ready, then you're not ready. Nobody's going to make you do anything you don't want to do."

"Good" she cheered. "Do you know where the big Night Crawler party is going to be?"

"Yeah, I know."

"Then I will meet you at the main entrance at one, but I will have to be back by two okay?"

"I will have you back by one fifty nine," Coffy agreed. "Better still, one forty-five"

"Okay then, I will see you next week," she said hanging up the phone then heading toward the kitchen. Underneath that b-boy exterior, Coffy was a nice guy, Tioni mused.

6

July 27th, 1:04 a.m., 580 Overpass Northbound

When Omari asked Gustav if he would be interested in spreading information about AIDS prevention in Africa, not only was he willing to support bringing attention to the continents plight, he was quite knowledgeable about the issue.

"I can't wait here." Gustav explained stopping at the overpass to allow Omari and Dragonbrush to get out. "If anyone makes out my plates I'm in big trouble. When you are finished" I will be parked around the corner" He said before driving off.

"So who is this Makemba that got us all out here hanging banners in the middle of the night?" Dragonbrush asked.

"Someone who wants to stop people from dying from AIDS in Africa," Omari answered trying to figure out how they would get around the fence that guarded the overpass. The barrier was nine feet tall and arched inward. This design prevented pedestrians from climbing up the fence, preventing suicides, and items being tossed onto the freeway. It would also prevent anyone from hanging a banner for the early morning commuters.

"You mean someone you like a lot?" Dragonbrush added.

"She's good people," Omari said with a smile, checking the sturdyness of the fence before attempting to climb it.

"I thought Jennifer was good people?" Dragonbrush asked.

"She is," Omari replied as he could see that climbing the arching barrier would prove a challenge.

"So who is gooder?" Dragonbrush asked watching Omari unsuccessfully scale the fence.

"I don't know," Omari answered clearly frustrated, "I don't think we can do this," he said.

"Sure we can," Dragonbrush said, Omari watched in amazement as Dragonbrush grabbed the rolled up banner then leapt effortlessly atop the barrier, then nimbly slid down the outside of the fence and tied the banner to the outside of the overpass fence in less than 2 minutes. 2 minutes later he had affixed the second banner to the south side of the overpass, and the duo were headed toward Gustav.

"How did you do that?" Omari asked completely dumbfounded.

"I don't know" Dragonbrush answered calmly. "I just knew I could."

7

2:17 a.m., Brentford Street, Jennifer's bedroom

Jennifer sat up in her bed nervously, it was the middle of the night, there were no lights on, yet she could see everything in her bedroom clearly. Leaping from her bed and pulling back the drapes, the empty street appeared as bright as day. Then it occurred to her that she had made it across her bedroom in less than a second. Her speed and abilities had come back, but how, why? Did this also mean that her dependency on blood and the harmful effects of the sun also had returned?

"Giving up your life as a vampire will not be as easy as you think." The words of Niles the vampire came back to haunt the teen. It was obvious that Niles knew more about vampirism than he was sharing. Jennifer also recalled the words of Tioni's father, *"that vampirism was like an addiction."* Jennifer knew first hand from watching her mother go weeks of attending 12 step meetings and not taking a drink, the negative effects of one

beer. Maybe like being an alcoholic or addict one remained a vampire the rest of their lives.

"No, this can't be happening," Jennifer said, refusing to go back to fearing the sunrise. Then as if covered by a dark cloak, the world went black, her heighten senses dulled. She was normal again.

Did I imagine the whole thing? The nervous teen thought getting back under her covers. Jennifer resolved she would ask Dr. Flora when they met.

8

3:55 a.m., South Hill Court

Dragonbrush listened to the world from the rooftop. He could hear the fat squirrel resting on a fragile branch until it broke sending it scurrying to a more secure branch. Dragonbrush was aware that all birds did not sleep at night, many even active, and every now and then he noticed the sound of a cat quietly stalking a scampering rodent, each making a distinctive sound as they moved over dry, crumpled leaves.

But, it was the dogs that held the Filipino's fascination. He could hear their barking from near and far, some making it known to anyone on foot or vehicle that they were guarding their territory and anything near it was in danger. While roaming canines were encouraging the guard dogs to relax, leave their post to go out for some adventure. Many were looking for companions and many more were just looking for trouble. There were dogs not from the area that decided to visit a new environment. Dragonbrush could even pick up the whining of dogs trapped inside their caretaker's homes and chained to their backyards wanting to get out and be part of the activities. In the wee hours of the morning, dogs were a lot like their human caretakers. Dragonbrush could understand what the canines were saying from the long haired Sheppard howling because he was too hot, the short tempered Pitt Bull that threatened, he would figure out a way out his chains and would terrorize anyone around;

to the pack of house dogs that all escaped their yards challenging the Pitt to "come with it!"

Dragonbrush leaned back on the roof allowing his legs to dangle, impressed by the fact that dogs knew all the secrets to the city and with their exceptional abilities could probably accomplish anything if they would just communicate to one another about issues other than territory and domination. Back inside the bedroom, Dragonbrush could hear Omari stirring. Omari had been practicing non stop preparing for tonight's performance, earlier Omari crept behind the garage and lit up. When he staggered back in, Dragonbrush knew he was down for the count. Thinking about the others, Dragonbrush entered back inside to a walk through of the house. After browsing the first floor and the refrigerator, the teen walked to the bathroom. Looking at the toilet bowl, Dragonbrush suddenly felt very thirsty, and was tempted to get on fours and drink from the toilet bowl, but chose the kitchen instead. Back upstairs and outside the window, the teen ran nimbly across the roof stopping above the bedroom window of Uhuru and Ayanna. They were both light sleepers and he had to be careful not to disturb them, with the exception of the annoying dripping of their shower faucet in their bathroom everything was fine. He quietly entered Jamilah's room through her window that was always open. Ever since Jamilah' followed Dr. Flora instructions she hadn't complained about her stomach. He watched her breathing and realized that he loved everything about her, but as a girl friend, or was it more? Jamilah treated him like his sister Gwen used to. He loved Jamilah like he loved his sister, he could come to her and she would be there for him. Dragonbrush leaned over and softly kissed her on the forehead and exited the window with memories of Gwen flooding his mind. Back in his room he laid on his bed and felt himself overcome with loss, his mind flooding with the memories of his older sister, his eyes becoming heavy.

9

3:59 a.m., South Hill Court

"Are you certain the ones selected are even worthy?" Rabies snarled as the three Dobermans observed Dragonbrush's behavior from another rooftop several houses away.

"I see nothing noteworthy of the one who calls himself Dragonbrush, other than immaturity and weakness," Remus the blue Doberman agreed.

"He has no clue that he is even being watched. Even primal fury can be tapped and harnessed I see none in him. I would have thought that this Dragonbrush would be more."

"Do I sense frustration or insecurity?" Josephine asked. "And when were your thoughts a consideration? The criteria for who the selected members are was created by the elders, if your existence means as little to you as it does me, then challenge one of the selected ones and if you should defeat them, then you can explain to the Unions their err in judgment."

"Maybe I will." Rabies the red Pinscher snarled.

"Maybe is a coward's answer," Josephine replied, knowing that the elder wolf would be eager to challenge Dragonbrush. "But not today, as there is other business that needs to be set in order."

Part 6
Night Crawlers

How To Spot A Raver
Ravers know where all the best toy stores are. Ravers are the only people who don't have their age calculated in months, yet still wear and use pacifiers. Ravers always consider every new place they go to as a possible location for a party. Ravers hug EVERYONE. Ravers can DANCE. Ravers can be found dancing everywhere EXCEPT the main dance floor. Ravers understand the art of the bathroom conversation. Ravers choose their clothes by texture, color, and size. Ravers always order water when they go out to clubs. Ravers realize that "Evian" spells "naivE" backwards. Ravers never know the name of their favorite tracks. Ravers always choose "e" on multiple-choice questions. Ravers are good at playing "guess what he's on". Ravers will say "hi" to those people they don't know, yet always see on the bus. Ravers define the style of music they listen to as "good".

Ravers know what to do with a dead glow stick.

1

7:10 a.m. Omari's bedroom, South Hill Court

"Oh my God!" Makemba screamed seconds after Omari said hello. Her piercing voice instantly waking up Omari and Dragonbrush, "Quick, turn to channel 2!" she urged. Omari flicked the TV remote on and could see traffic on 580 at a stand still with horns blaring before the camera panned to a banner that read

Over 12 million children in sub-Saharan Africa
have been orphaned by AIDS
Honk if you want to Help!!!!
Support UNICEF
Call your Senator
Tell them to take Action!

"I can assure you that many of the honkers are honking because of the gridlock" reporter Lisa Chow explained. Banners mysteriously hung from the north and south bound 580 overpass had resulted in at least ten fender benders, now two lanes have been shut down as the banners are being removed, which has only added to the congestion."

The banners do call to attention the health crisis in Africa and the need for support which tonight this station will be doing a special report, but right now I think commuters are more concerned with getting to their destination than they are with reading the banner. This is Lisa Chow back to you, Matt."

"Do you think they would be doing a special episode on AIDS in Africa if that banner hadn't been place there?" Omari asked.

"You did it," Makemba said with gratitude in her voice. "How did you do it?" Makemba asked with excitement.

"With a lot of help from my little brother Dragonbrush," Omari answered giving Dragonbrush a thumbs up.

"What time did you want to get together?" she asked, "I wish you were here now. I am so excited," she said, her voice filled with mirth.

"Today is really jacked up," Omari said knowing that he would be disappointing Makemba and himself. "But, I have to prepare for tonight's gig and get ready for camping," he replied, realizing it would be a week before they saw each other again, "That's why we rushed to get your banner up".

"But I was hoping that we would at least go slap tagging together," She said sadly. "Can we still talk?" she asked.

"Of course," Omari agreed.

"Are you still going to help me out with my campaign?" Makemba pressed.

"Of course," Omari reassured her.

"Then I will see you when you get back," she resolved.

"I will talk to you then," Omari looked across the room at Dragonbrush who was also enthralled by the news on the television, but knew overheard the conversation. "Okay, say what you got to say."

I hope you know what you're doing." Dragonbrush said never taking his eyes off the news broadcast.

"Me too," Omari said with concern in his voice.

2

8:43 p.m. Omari's bedroom South Hill Court

"What do you mean you changed your mind?" Omari asked Dragonbrush. After spending the better part of the day practicing and preparing for tonight, Omari did not expect Dragonbrush to bail out on him.

"I can't take the loud music," Dragonbrush answered reflecting on his last rave experience. "My head is starting to hurt just thinking about it."

"It's that bad?" Omari pressed.

"You know how you feel the beats? Well, I literally feel the beats!" Dragonbrush explained.

Uhuru walked into the room and sensed tension, "Is everyone ready? He inquired.

"Dragon is sick and wants to stay home tonight," Omari explained, twisting one of his errant locks.

"You alright?" He asked.

"Yeah" Dragonbrush replied, "I just have a headache. I think I need to just stay in and chill."

"With Ayanna and I leaving in a few hours on a four day cruise and you all leaving for Yosemite National Park in the morning, maybe attending a party the night before is not a real sound idea." Looking at the stacks of dirty clothes, the level of garbage the two allowed occupy in the place they slept. "Maybe cleaning up this place is a better idea." He said thinking outloud.

"But my gig is tonight. I got to be there," Omari pleaded to his uncle before he could respond. "We'll clean it all up when we get back, I promise." Hearing Omari's panicked voice, Jamilah entered to see what the commotion was all about.

"What's the matter?" She asked.

"Because Dragon doesn't want to go tonight, Uncle is saying none of us can go!" Omari complained.

"Why don't you want to go?" Jamilah demanded.

"I have a headache," Dragonbrush answered.

"Then take a Midol and let's go!" she insisted.

"I don't want to go," The Pinoy held his ground.

"This is not fair," Jamilah erupted bringing Ayanna into the picture

"Why is everyone in an uproar?" she asked.

"Dragonbrush is faking a headache, now uncle is saying we can't go to party and I've already got my costume!" Jamilah pouted.

"My headache is not fake!" Dragonbrush fought back.

"It's not more important than my gig!" Omari fired.

"Honey?" Ayanna questioned her husband for an explanation.

"Will you people calm down," Uhuru spoke lifting his hand to get everyone's attention. "Jamilah, Julie is still chaperoning tonight and picking you all up tomorrow as planned?" He acknowledged his nieces, nodding head. "Good," looking at the group he said, "Omari go, Dragonbrush stay, Jamilah please go." Taking his wife's arm, he said, "honey, lets go." The two left the room.

"See what you almost did?" Jamilah fired at Dragonbrush.

"You know," Omari said with embarrassment, "Maybe I overreacted."

"You think?" Dragonbrush asked.

3

10:03 p.m. Claremont Avenue, Home of Julie Kieltch

When Julie's Dad, Jim Kieltch opened his door, he could only shake his head at the three gaudy dressed males that entered. The lean, eighteen year old, Ted Chakiris, better known as "Rainbow," entered first. Wearing, skinny, tight fitting plaid pants, white studded belt, a tight, black t-shirt displaying the cover of Michael Jackson's Thriller worn underneath a purple, zip up hoodie with various political buttons all accentuated by a black, blazer. He wore red, leather, low top, Chuck Taylors and his very straight platinum, blonde hair, with electric blue highlights flocked his face covering his blue eyes and Greek tan. The muscular, nineteen years old, Italian American, Emirel Guccini, better known as "Issues" followed. Issues long, black, scene hair was layered in the front and spiked in the back. His lip featured a labret piercing and snake bites featured prominently under his lips and large black, plugs occupied his ear lobes. The rugged, teen's attire consisted of tight, charcoal gray, flat front, Gap chinos, black, studded, belt. A black t-shirt, featuring, Shirley Temple and Bill Bojangles Robinson, dancing on stair steps revealed arms and a neck that were muscular and fully tattooed. Draped around his waist was a black vintage track jacket and Black, Saucony's covered his sockless feet. A giggling Robert George, also known as "Toyz" raced up the steps behind Rainbow and Issues. The lean, seventeen year old, wore a form fitting, black, long sleeve t-shirt with the word "Emo Millionaire" printed in white letters. Like the others, he sported skinny, black, jeans and black studded belt. Unlike the others, the attractive teens, dark, auburn brown hair flocked underneath a black and white Zildjian trucker cap that hid his pierced ears. A black and white Afghan, scarf draped around his neck. Black finger nail polish and white hi-top Chuck Taylors completed Toyz's look.

"Where's the last one? Jim asked, looking beyond the three and could see the always-sleepy looking Gustav Klein attired in his customary monochromatically black, flat front pants black pea coat, black, t-shirt and bowler hat running from his black Volvo, while completing a text on his Blackberry. Jim had grown accustomed to visits from the four gay gentlemen. They had arrived to take his daughter, Julie out partying.

4

10:07 p.m., Julie's bedroom, Claremont Avenue,

Julie struck a pose in her mirror admiring her shimmering black, full-length dress and favorite silver tiara that sat on her purpled colored coif. The full figured, 17 year old gave her-self a large healthy grin, then let out a sigh, the kind of sigh that she hated. The same sigh she sighed when she gave up the cello for the key boards. It was that sound that led her to give up four years of karate, for five years of Tai –chi and another sigh led her current fascination with Tai-Bo. That painful sigh pulled her from New Age to Hip Hop and now Goth. Julie knew the sigh meant she was tired of the rave scene. The party jumping, attired in flashy clothes, toys and happy attitude had lost its thrill. She wanted to slow down and reflect on the world and its current state

Julie blamed her short attention span on her parents. As visual artist and former Dead Heads, Julies life had been a bombardment of creative people and projects one more interesting than the next. "Oh well," she sighed. She would have to tell her friends who more than likely knew. Her recent penchant for black, anything and everything by or about DJ Sepulcher indicated that her interest were taking her in a new direction. Some of her current friends like Gustav would stick with her. The others would do their own separate thing, and they would join up again when their interests matched, as it was with Issues and Toyz and martial arts. Looking in the mirror and checking her teeth as she could hear the guys coming up the stairs, tonight she was chaperoning Jamilah, Jennifer and Tioni to a blockbuster rave. She didn't care so much about having a good time, as she was concerned with getting them back safely. Raves were a lot of fun but also potentially dangerous. Of the three, Julie wasn't particularly worried about the streetwise, Jennifer. She always resorted to common sense. Jamilah and Tioni, Julie wondered if she would have to go through hell and high water to make sure they made it home okay.

Julie heard the knock on the door, checked her flawless make up and was ready. She opened the door to the "ooh's", and "ahhs," of her worshippers. "Its show time" she smiled.

5

11:03 p.m., Night Crawler, Hegenberger Road

Omari followed Excel through the large warehouse filled to half capacity. The former Home Builders Express went out of business when Home Depot opened a few miles north. The former building supply company's loss however was Night Crawlers gain, as the city of Oakland allowed large parties and other venues to occupy the massive space located in the city's desolate industrial hub. Walking through the party that started several hours earlier made Omari's stomach drop, suspended from the rafters were fifty enormous sheets of Styrofoam painted in fluorescent pink, yellow, orange and green, each 12 feet in height and 1 foot in diameter, held by black nylon ropes giving the appearance they were hovering in mid air dividing the large space into five areas. Excel explained the logic of the colored room dividers. Pink was for Night Crawlers staple sound Progressive Trance, commanding ten of the building's twenty five thousand square feet. The DJ booth sat, on an elevated platform, ten feet above the floor, behind the DJ booth was two movie screens featuring a montage of visual delights. Directly opposite the DJ booth was the light technician, displaying a laser light show that promised to get better as the night progressed.

Against the wall, was a roped off VIP lounge, and one thousand feet long bar offering mixed drinks, juice, water and free oranges that required a staff of twenty. Orange was the color of the eight thousand square foot section devoted to House music, the second, and to many the most popular music space. The room was identical the slightly larger trance room, only instead of one long bar there were two that sat on opposite walls. The 2 popular rooms promised to be studded with celebrities and celebrity DJ's. Goa and Psy split the four thousand square foot yellow section. A storage facility upstairs was converted into a Chill room. The only carpeted area in the warehouse filled with hundreds of pillows of assorted shapes, sizes patterns and colors. Ten, six foot tables stocked with the fruit primarily oranges energy bars, large bowls of baby carrots and chopped celery sat against the wall for free consumption. A brightly dressed male, struggled to move around the perimeters of the area with an ice cream pushcart, selling chilled and frozen bottled water and frozen sponges. Experimental, Jungle, and Drum & Bass and New Talent occupied the green space, the smaller space featured plastic plants that surround the stage and roped off VIP session that sat on a platform with table and chairs and waiters allowing "A" list visitors a place to relax and view the party in luxury. Thousands of white helium balloons congested the ceiling. Spot, fluorescent and strobe lights were all well positioned to further articulate the configuration of the rooms. The layout of the building was perfect except, as always there were too few restrooms.

"I see you got rid of the gloves," Excel commented on Omari's hands

"Yeah, it was a stupid idea," he responded lugging his coffin filled with albums.

"Most great ideas often are," Excel added, looking around the grand space for areas that would need his attention next.

"Did Night Crawler go legit for this event?" Omari asked, impressed with the layout.

"Our big events are always legit," Excel answered never looking back.

"Too many things can go wrong, we even hired off duty officers for security and traffic. All of our smaller venues are on the under because we need the money to pay for events like this," Excel laughed. "We did go somewhat overboard with this one, because some folks are here shooting a documentary, and folks from URB magazine are also here, and we can always use good press." The two continued, the energetic law student bursting through the thickening crowd vanishing, when Omari caught up, Excel was giving instructions to several men running wires followed by a man with a large roll of electrical tape. You need to keep up," Excel explained, "Otherwise, I might lose you."

"I'll find you." Omari yelled over the blaring music. Of course it was easy for Excel to move through the crowd he wasn't carrying a 35 pound coffin filled with vinyl albums Omari prayed would be good enough, that the audience wouldn't stop dancing and start booing.

"If you say so," Excel replied continuing to move through the waves of people. "I have a lot of things to do, so stay up."

Leaving Dragonbrush home was even more painful than Omari imagined. *Why would he change his mind about wanting to be a DJ now?* He really needed Dragon for back up. Every DJ needed back up from the Jungle Brothers to the Invisibl Skratch Picklz, and even though Jamilah, Jennifer and Tioni said they were there to support him, they were really there to have a good time, Omari fretted.

"Did you have a hard time finding the place?" Excel asked realizing the weight that Omari was carrying but not enough to offer help.

"Gustav dropped me off," Omari replied, his words catching Excel's ear.

"Gustav, is he here now?" Excel inquired, leading Omari up two flights of stairs to where he would be performing.

"No, He had to go pick up some others," Omari replied. "Gustav's cool," he added, acknowledging his appreciation for his ride to the site.

"Totally, he is like one of the true good ones" Excel added, "And his car, my girl and I want to use it in our wedding. It's a classic and he keeps it in such good shape. He lets nothing happen to it."

"It looks like a Hearst for midgets," Omari replied dryly, failing to see anything special about the prehistoric automobile.

"Can a vehicle be more perfect than that?" Excel questioned. He led Omari behind the stage of the Green walled area and up a small flight of stairs to a curtained off space. Inside three other DJ's, two males and a female, were observing the current DJ performing on the main stage, a flight above them, a tall, female wearing a man's red suit, matching shirt, and tie with flowing, bleached, blonde hair. Omari placed his coffin between his legs and sat in one of the available chairs, he also watched the scarlet starlet. She looked great, but sounded awful Omari mused. *No wonder she was first.*

Rick entered the room with two of his staff vying for his attention regarding their concerns. The waiting four DJ's immediately giving him their attention. Rick explained to his staff he would address their needs momentarily. He gazed out at the DJ performing and shook his head, his dirty blond hair falling in front of his face before pushing it back with one motion of his neck. "That's my wife's niece, DJ Crimzone, the things I do to keep peace in the house," he sighed. "As a way of giving back to the music community," Rick continued, turning his attention back to the four, "Night Crawler gives up and coming local talent the opportunity to showcase their work. You will each perform for an hour and later you will have the opportunity to watch some of the heavy hitters perform. Hopefully, you will learn something that will better your craft." Rick began to pace back and forth like a military general inspiring his troops before they went off to war. "I have to say that even though this is the smallest space, it's definitely the one with the greatest promise. Those who are interested in new sounds will be here. And who's to say, your future may be in the hands of someone in the audience that likes your product. So, while you may be the opening acts, go out there like you will be closing the show because the next time you're here it could be as a headliner." He turned to Excel who handed them each a pair of Sennheiser headphones. "This is a small token of our gratitude. He shook each of the DJ's hands, who were astonished to be receiving the Rolls Royce of headphones then wished them luck. He quickly left the space followed by the questioning, concerned staff.

Excel walked before them and gave further instructions, "You each will have one hour, but use the last ten minutes of your set for winding down, allowing the next DJ five minutes to set up and roll. No matter how into the groove you are in when your set is up, it is up and if necessary, we will have security pull you from the booth. We are that serious. We are on a tight timetable. We want everyone to able to perform and not conflict with DJ Marky who will be closing out the show." He pulled a list from his pocket and began to read it.

"Okay this will be the order of performers" He paused looking at the group, "First of all, Rick did the line up, so please don't argue with me. DJJZ you are up next, followed by DJ Dizzy Dacey then DJ Omari, DJ Kumar you're up last. It's a good idea to have a spare stylus in case yours break. Also keep your old headphones nearby, as headphones have a tendency to break when you most need them. You are responsible for your own slip mats if they get lost, we are not liable. If there are any technical problems, have someone get me immediately. I will try to be around at the start and end of each set, good luck." Seeing terror in some of the DJ's eyes, Excel smiled then raced down the stairs.

The four watched DJJZ walk to the DJ booth and started cranking. The female known as DJ Dizzy looked at the others and said, "Hi my name is DJ Dizzy, and I'm a nervous DJ." The others smiled and introduced themselves.

6

11:47 p.m., Night Crawler

"Welcome to the spectacle!" Julie shouted seconds before Tioni, Jamilah and Jennifer entered the building. Their senses bombarded with the sights and sounds of a party in full tilt. Tioni's gray eyes were the size of midget moons, wearing an Oakland Raiders uniform made up of a black and silver baseball cap worn backwards, her single braids cascading to her shoulders as if they had a life of their own. Shiny, silver Capri pants and black mid-drift top with a silver #1 on the front, and silver Converse high tops; she had never seen anything like the near capacity crowd even at the church's gala. The exotic looking teen scanned the enormous dance floor filled with frenetic, partygoers bathed in disco globes, strobe lights, and dancing lasers, all accentuating their uniqueness. Nothing and no one appeared out of place, like an enormous collage of happiness everyone fit.

Jamilah dressed in a shimmering gold, cheerleader uniform wearing a form fitting top with glittering, puffy wings attached to the back and short pleated skirt and that accentuated her long dark, legs. Her appealing face covered by heavy makeup, glossy gold lipstick and a brilliant, gold wig in a bob cut was immediately in sync with the vibe of the place, moving with the crowd that gyrated in as many forms of dance styles as there were colors and dresses. Some of the dancers were visibly talented, and their movements proved their professionalism. Others could barely hold a beat, dancing awkwardly with movements both strained and painful to watch, but skill didn't matter, merriment was the only prerequisite for the evening. The fun was as contagious as a virus, and Jamilah, like the rest, was clearly infected.

Jennifer wearing a florescent pink surgeon cap and mask, white physician's jacket that covered her hot pink medical scrubs, looked at the crowd of good timers, many shaking their bodies while swinging multicolored lights sticks of various lengths and shapes into the air and thought to herself, this is the biggest dork fest I've ever seen in my life. But she quickly concluded the folks on the opposite spectrum of cool clearly knew how to have a good time.

Julie navigated the three through a barrage of assorted scents associated with a hodgepodge of personalities. From alcohol to incense, from marijuana to the funk of sweaty un-bathed bodies to an area that was more compassionate to their nostrils. Julie waved at a group of brightly dressed males then turned to her girlfriends, "What do you guys want to do?" She screamed over the blaring music. "You can hang with me, or you can dance, and mingle on your own which I don't recommend, or you can fly as a trio. Either way you will have a good time. But whatever you do," she said even louder over the introduction of a mix that was all bass. "Don't take any drinks from anyone, don't drink open bottles of water, and for Christ don't let anyone place a sticker or patch on you."

"Alright, mother, we understand," Jamilah spoke on the behalf of the others tired of hearing warnings. "How about we meet here in two hours?" She then looked at Julie and reassured her, "Go ahead. We will see you in two hours." They watched their larger friend disappear into an ocean of costumed dancers.

"So where do you want to start?" Jennifer asked.

"Lets find out where Omari's is performing," Jamilah answered, "We can start there and work our way around."

7

11:49 p.m., Omari's room, South Hill Court

Dragonbrush deeply regretted letting Omari down, but his newfound sensitivity to sounds and scents had grown even stronger. Earlier he slipped out the window carrying all of the spray cans and magic markers placing them in the garage. The idea of being trapped in a space with loud partiers all with their own signature scent and even louder music a was not too appealing.

"Knock, knock," Uhuru spoke as he entered. "Ayanna and I are leaving. Our contact numbers are on the refrigerator, and you have the cell phone number, so we will see you when you all return"

Dragonbrush walked the couple to the door. "You keep everyone safe until we get back okay," Ayanna said as the teen closed the door. When he heard the hybrid drive off, Dragonbrush had to fight the overwhelming desire to whimper and throw a tantrum, like a puppy left alone in the house.

8

12:53 a.m., Night Crawler

Omari gave high fives to JalAl Zangeneh, whose professional name was DJJZ, after ending his set and to DJ Dizzy Dacey, whose real name was Dacey McLaughlin. She told Omari before taking controls of the DJ booth "anyone born with freckles, red hair, worn in locks should know that the creator wanted you to be a DJ." In the brief time he had been around the other DJ's Omari had already formed opinions of them. Like Omari, this was Dizzy Dacey's and DJJZ's first time performing to a crowd this size. They were happy just to be there. On the other hand, Raj Kumar, DJ Kumar the twenty one year old Punjabi, was an arrogant prick. He had seen it all and done it all. Nothing anyone did was interesting or fresh. The word that Omari's mother used to describe individuals like Raj Kumar was *"toxic,"* being around him only upset you.

"How'd I do?" the 17 year old, olive colored Iranian, with a glowing orange crew cut, plaid, yellow short sleeve shirt and tattered blue jeans, asked Omari, hyped and exhausted from the rush of performing.

"You were great man!" Omari responded. "I feel bad for DJ Dizzy cuz she has to follow you." DJJZ looked at Omari who was speaking the words he was afraid he would not hear and couldn't stop smiling. "You don't believe me?" Omari continued. "Look at the room." DJJZ looked out at the crowd, there was barely room to stand, let alone dance. With a broad grin, DJJZ gave Omari another high five and said, "I'm going to get something to mellow me out. What's your pleasure?"

"Just water for me," Omari replied.

"I'm cool," DJ Kumar answered.

"You guys watch my stuff, I'll be right back." He jumped off the platform onto the floor dancing and moving through the crowd.

"Why did you lie to him?" DJ Kumar asked Omari just above the raging sound of DJ Dizzy Daisy set.

"What do you mean?" Omari asked the heavily gelled East Asian, wearing a black sleeveless t-shirt, green camouflage cargo shorts and open toe sandals, wondering what he was talking about.

"JZ's set was worst than a trip on bad shrooms. It left me nauseas and wanting my money back," Kumar snarled pulling out a cigarette from his back pant pocket, lighting it and blowing Unions in the air.

"I thought he played a good set, and the crowd like him," Omari said defending a person he had just met.

"Oh grow up," Kumar retorted with a chastising tone. "The set was whacked; there is a reason why we were placed in the order we are in," he spoke with a hand motion that demanded that your eyes followed the cancer stick in his hand. Omari paused when he saw a pair of copper colored hands cover Kumar eyes. Kumar removed them and turned around to see Reggie and Justin standing behind him. "Reggie!" Kumar laughed, "I knew you and Justin the DJ Jedi would be here."

There was a moment of tension when Omari saw Justin that Kumar quickly picked up. "You guys know each other?" He asked.

"Man that's Justin, he knows everyone" Reggie intervened defusing the scene. "You got time to sample some primo product with me?"

"Always," Kumar answered gleefully. "Jedi are you joining us?" He asked as he followed Reggie.

"I'm right behind you." He reassured the curious DJ.

Omari turned toward DJ Dizzy who was having the time of her life at the controls.

"I swear the folks Steve picks keep getting worse ever year," Justin commented at Dacey's performance.

"What?" Omari asked though teeth clinched as tight as his fist. Omari knew that if he swung at Justin, he would not be performing.

"I just came by to wish you good luck man, and give you these, that's all," Justin explained. Omari noticed that in Justin hands was a tall can of *Rock Star* and an empty gallon jug. Justin noticed Omari's eyes scanning the can and jug with a suspicious eye.

"This one is for energy, because you can get real tired up there" he explained lifting up the chilled can and this empty bottle is for when you can't leave the turntable," Justin said with a wry smile that had probably succeeded in getting him back into the good graces after a many of betrayals. Omari continued to look at him with an apprehensive eye. "Look, the other reason why I came by was to say that I was sorry. I shouldn't have left you holding my product." He looked over at DJ Dizzy and grimaced at her Ganja Kru mix "But you have to understand, I really didn't have a choice."

"What do you mean you didn't have a choice?" Omari asked his disbelief obvious.

"My father is a City Councilman, his voice zinging with a sincerity that Omari wasn't buying, "and I can't do anything to embarrass him".

"Even if that mean's having me take a drug rap for you?" Omari argued.

"I can't do anything to embarrass him. Do you understand?"

"How about not sell drugs?" Omari snarled, noticing Excel walking their way.

"Look, Justin!" Excel said in frustration as he walked up the small flight of stairs, "If doing what you're asked to do is too much of a bother, I have someone else who will."

"Oh no, I'm there," He commented handing the bottles to Omari

"I don't want your stuff, keep it," a sullen Omari answered turning back to join DJ Dizzy at DJ station as Justin followed Excel down the steps of the platform. Omari scanned the growing crowd looking for his sister, Jennifer or Tioni. He was next, and no one would know. Omari regretted that Dragonbrush was not there. Then it occurred to him that tomorrow was a full moon. *What would happen to him?* Omari wondered.

"Did I miss any exciting conversation?" DJJZ asked as he bounced in front of Omari offering him a cold bottle of Evian water bringing Omari thoughts back to the here and now.

"Not a thing," Omari replied downing the bottle of refreshing water. "Not a thing."

9

1:13 a.m., Night Crawler

Coffy, Beamon, Shady, and Curfew, and Soul Boy entered the den of humidity, their objective: to shake down smalltime drug dealers selling hallucinogenic drugs for their money and product and to woo females from the Night Crawler to their own private party several miles away. The grouped moved through the sweltering building in a predatory manner, looking for familiar and interested faces.

"How long before we head back?" Soul Boy asked, not wanting to forsake the party that the Cobalt's were throwing.

"Just long enough," Coffy answered, finding Tioni was on his personal agenda as he scoured the crowd bouncing to the massive sounds. "But, while we're here, let's see what kind of trouble we can get into."

10

1:27 a.m., Goa Room,

Learning that it would be a while before Omari was to perform, Jamilah, Jennifer and Tioni sampled the musical sounds from each massive space before agreeing on the Goa room. The trio danced among themselves, giggling, flirting and rejecting all request to join them. Jamilah initially thought the idea of wearing a costume was stupid, found it less so in an environment where the majority was also fully clad in outlandish attire that ranged from cellophane diapers to fluorescent kilts. Jamilah felt for the first time in a longtime she could be someone else. Not someone whose father disappears or whose mother was willing to trade her daughter in for her boyfriends, Jamilah was just like most of the females in the room, no problems, no cares.

"Can we all pair up?" a guy asked wearing a Darth Vader mask accompanied by a Storm Trooper and Jar Jar Blink.

"No this is sort of private," Jamilah responded smiling at her giggling friends while continuing to dance. Jamilah was not completely opposed to dancing with someone else. She had noticed the extremely talented and gorgeous dancer across the room trying to make eye contact with her. She would look the other way to avoid contact, but found herself every so often glancing to see if he was doing the same. He was older than she; maybe in his mid twenties with skin the color of golden sand, his dark brown hair in a tight wavy, ponytail. He wore black cargo pants stuffed in his shiny black military boots. His muscular upper torso stuffed in a tight silver body shirt. Wiping the sweat from her brow as it continued to run under her hot wig and down the side of her made up face Jamilah thought to herself, *if he asked, I would dance with him.*

11

1:30 a.m., Goa Room

Jennifer removed her brilliant pink colored, surgeon cap, allowing her dark silken tresses to drape her white doctor's smock. When she conceived the Beat Doctor's costume, wearing a medical cap and mask seemed like a good idea, but having her face completely covered in a humid environment had become "*icky.*" She resolved that the surgeons, mask and stereoscope would have to do. Jennifer observed Jamilah dancing with a smile on her face and thought, *what a total role reversal*. Initially, only she and Tioni were gung ho about going out dancing in costume. Jamilah was hesitant and not sure if she wanted to participate; now it appeared that Jamilah was having a great time, and Jennifer wished she had remained home.

A strong sense of dread similar to what Jennifer felt at the old Montgomery Ward building had engulfed her. It seemed the nightmare of vampirism was back, and the teen didn't know what to do.

Just then, Jennifer felt Jamilah's hand embrace hers, shouting, "Girl, don't just stand there; shake what yo' mama gave ya!"

12

1:33 a.m., Goa room

The party was everything Tioni thought it would be great music, great fun and more. However, as much as she enjoyed being with Jennifer and Jamilah, she had to figure out a way to get away from them to meet Coffy. He had to know that she was not a flake, and she would prove it.

13

1:36 a.m., Green Room

Omari wondered how he allowed himself to get into another argument with Kumar, who was not only condescending, but downright mean.

"If you want to call that crap they play on the radio hip hop, then hip hop is as dead as *Nas's* career or worse, it's like that garbage Dizzy is playing out there." DJ Kumar argued.

"Hip hop is not the stuff you hear on the radio. The heart of hip hop is, and will always be underground." Omari fumed back, looking to see if Jennifer and the others had come back. He could really use their support about now.

"I'm so tired of hearing that line about underground music. If you ask me, it's just a cop out to say that what is known not to exist does." Kumar retorted.

"You know, you seem to hate every body's music." Omari said bringing this discussion to an end before it went another level.

"I haven't heard yours, yet." He replied with a devious grin.

"I haven't heard yours, or of you" Omari countered.

"No, but what we do know is that I'm here because of my talent," Kumar smiled, "You're here because Rick is committed to helping at-risk minorities in the community. That's why you are the youngest here. Rick does this stunt every year."

Omari wished he had followed DJJZ's lead. After ten minutes of listening to Kumar noxious, rant, he decided to take a walk around to see what the other artist was doing. Omari looked over his shoulder, and could see the orange, haired Iranian, had returned with three, bottles of Crystal Geyser water. He handed Omari one, but the bottle he handed Kumar slipped from his hand the cracked plastic, immediately springing a leak upon impact on the wooden stage floor.

"I'm sorry." DJJZ apologized at his own clumsiness, watching the water flow down the make shift stage floor. "You can have mine," He offered the annoyed Asian "its open but, I never drank from it." Kumar took the water shaking his head at DJJZ's ineptness and began to swig. Omari fed up with the conversation looked at his watch and knew he had to find Jamilah and crew to let them know he was about to perform. He walked over to DJJZ who had picked up the fallen bottle and was dumping it in a trashcan and said in his ear, "you should know talking to him is like drinking poison. It will only make you sick."

"I know" JZ responded with a wily look in his eyes, "I know." He then watched Omari blend into the crowd to find his family and friends before his set started.

14

1:39 a.m. Trance Room,

The crowd responded to the Tiesto remix by bouncing, twisting and grinding into frenzy, so enticing was the hypnotic beat that Jamilah and friends loosened their dance clique, allowing them the opportunity to dance with others. The handsome dancer that exchanged glances with Jamilah from across the room used that opportunity to skillfully waltz his way to the golden angel impressing her with fancy moves and flashes of pearly white teeth. By the song's end, the dancer had completely captured Jamilah's attention, from her friends. The dancer told Jamilah his name was Marc Morrison, a dancer and an actor visiting family from L.A.

"You all want to dance over toward the stairs where we can at least get a breeze?" Marc asked acknowledging the warmth of the room.

"I do." Jamilah said wanting to continue dancing with her new partner.

"You can't go!" Jennifer admonished Jamilah, "Omari's set is coming up and we said we would not split up."

"I'm just moving to the other side of the building, not leaving. I'll be there before Omari begins" Jamilah argued, "He's my brother," she explained to Marc. "You and Tioni go on," she said dismissively.

"I was going to head over there now; don't you want to see him?" Jennifer pressed, trying to verbally pull her friend away from the guy she had so quickly fallen head over heels for in a matter of minutes.

"I'll be there," Jamilah responded trying to keep her composure, "after the song is over."

Tioni realizing that she would also have to come up with an excuse, added, "We didn't say we would treat each other like babies. If one of us wants to walk around alone for a few minutes, what's the big deal? I'm going over to one of the other rooms and will meet you at Omari's,"

Jennifer began to feel a strange sensation come over her. So powerful, that she didn't want to argue. She simply walked away not noticing that Tioni was no longer behind her.

15

1:44 a.m., Green Room

The night was proving unprofitable for the Cobalt gang. They had yet to shake down anyone for drugs or money. The Transactions taking place, were either so blatant that they would have to take on all the occupants at the party, or so covert, that they couldn't locate who was doing the heavy scoring. They had been reduced to simply passing out invitations to their party. Soul boy and Curfew met females and escorted them to the Cobalt party. Only Coffy, Beamon and Shady, remained

"Man this is whack!" Shady bemoaned wondering why he was standing around at the Night Crawler like a gangbanging wallflower when he could be treated like royalty at the Cobalt's function, "I'm out of here!"

"Check it out," Coffy spoke, something or someone from across the room catching his attention. "I need a couple of roofies."

Curfew reached into his jacket pocket then handed Coffy several Ruphynols in a plastic baggy.

"Wait here while I go check something out." Coffy spoke placing the date rape drug in his back pant pocket.

"How long will you be gone?" Beamon asked, with little patience.

"If I'm not back in ten minutes, bounce without me," he said wading through into the crowd

"That's just enough time to get me a drink and come back," Soldier said to Shady as he headed toward the bar.

16

1:46 a.m. The Goa Room

Marc Morrison was an exceptional dancer, taking the time to teach the impressed Jamilah new dance steps. With very little effort, the charismatic dancer convinced the wide eyed teen to put off seeing her brother perform to join him in the Goa room. Jamilah thought the music blend of techno and East Indian sounds were weird, but Marc was enthralled by it, telling her stories about the legendary Pagan parties in London during the early '90's and meeting DJ's Mark Allen and Chrisbo, who ran the popular events.

None of this meant anything to Jamilah who wondered *how old was her dance partner?*

As they moved to the music, dancing toward the exit, Marc placed his hand into his side pocket. "Care for one?" Marc offered, pulling out a can of Altoids mints and offering it to her

"Sure," Jamilah answered, taking the can open can and popping several of the pills in her mouth. When they landed in her mouth, the stunned teen quickly realized that they were not mints and instinctively spit the first one out.

"Don't spit them out, just try it," Marc assured her picking up the falling tablet. Jamilah looked at him, smiled and swallowed. "Let's go to the Chill room and then the roof," Marc said while spinning Jamilah around to the music.

"The roof?" Jamilah questioned.

"Yeah the roof," Marc smiled.

"Sure, why not," Jamilah agreed hesitantly, wondering if she should have swallow something she knew nothing about.

Marc led Jamilah to a side room occupied with throw carpets, assorted pillows and individuals in various stages of consciousness, through a door that led to a dark hallway. Using a small glow stick from his pocket, Marc led Jamilah up four flights through a metal door where she was bathed with the cool night air. She quickly noticed the countless couples on the roof, enjoying the view of the planes landing and departing from the Oakland airport several miles away. Others sat on the edge of the building, their feet dangling as their bodies felt the vibration from the sound below.

"You've been here before?" Jamilah asked, curious how Marc knew to come here.

"Yeah, quite a few events are thrown in this space. We're not supposed to be up here, but as you can see it's too nice a place to obey the rules."

"Has anyone ever fallen off this building? "Jamilah asked

"I'm sure it's happened," Marc replied his words sending a chill through the teen.

Jamilah found her self-moving toward the center of the roof where it was safer, when an eerie sensation hit her. Jamilah began to feel overwhelmed by a creepy sensation that was making her uncomfortable and agitated. "What did you give me?" she asked on the verge of panic, wondering which way was back to the exit.

"Oh wow, sorry' Marc apologized taking Jamilah's hand, "I didn't know that this was your first time dropping "E."

"E?" Jamilah asked.

"Yeah, Ecstasy," Marc said with an easy smile.

"I am so stupid!" Jamilah confessed. She had done what she had been warned against over and over. Then she felt her breathing becoming strained as she began to hyperventilate.

"You're not stupid, you're beautiful," Marc reassured her sitting her down on the tar mat as he rubbed her winged back. "Just relax and take slow breath's; it will be over in a minute."

"A newbie?" Jamilah heard someone speak to Marc, apparently referring to her.

"Yeah, her first time," Marc said reassuring the stranger that things were under control.

"Here's some Evian. It hasn't been opened," the stranger placed the water in front of Jamilah who could slowly feeling herself snapping out of her panic. *What had been done to her?*

17

1:47 a.m. The Green Room

Making his way back to the Green Room through to the ever-thickening crowd, Omari couldn't believe that Jamilah and company were nowhere to be found. Dragonbrush would have been at my side the whole time, Omari fumed. Even calling Jamilah and Jennifer in such a loud, vibrating place was useless. Omari really needed them at his side to counter DJ Kumar's negative comments about his set. Unfortunately, his time to perform was soon, and he had to get to the stage. "Sorry," Omari said to the two guys he bumped into while making his way back to the stage. Giving DJJZ a high five, he joined DJ Dizzy Dacey on stage, quickly searched through his coffin to find a lead in song that matched the speed and complimented Dacey's final track. Placing his lucky Pioneer headphones over his red locs and the vinyl LP on the second turntable, the excited teen began to slowly fade out Dacey's mix while slowly bringing his own brand of Drum & Bass to the forefront without the crowd ever missing a dance step. Giving Omari and DJ JZ high fives, DJ Dizzy Dacey ended her set with the crowd dancing in a sweat filled fury. Omari looked out into the crowd and saw no familiar faces. He turned to the left and could see DJ Dizzy Dacey on the floor doing a rapturous dance with her partner in celebration of her successful set. Looking further left, he could see a smiling DJ JZ pointing to DJ Kumar who was sitting with a queasy look on his face before leaving. Omari smiled at the other two

DJ's, then turned the volume up slightly. Family or no, he was now in control of the floor. Then it all made sense. He understood what it meant to be a DJ. He was in sync with it all, from the glow sticks that flowed in a blurred motion throughout the space, to the waves of light bathing the bodies of the crowd with multicolored luminosity. There were no bad or good dancer's only partiers enraptured by his sound. The music covered all flaws and ambiguities', synchronizing everyone wonderfully. No individual stood out. The entire floor was one body and Omari, he was the heartbeat.

18

1:48 a.m., Green Room

Jennifer heart was racing. Everything was as bright as day, which could only mean that her vampirism had returned. Disturbingly, Jennifer could also see from their crimson eyes, that at least a dozen vampires were at the rave, many dancing, one even a DJ. All acknowledging her, aware that their presence was only known by others like themselves. Remembering that Tioni was behind her Jennifer looked over her shoulder and Tioni was nowhere in sight. *This is good,* Jennifer thought, not wanting to further expose her friend to danger as she followed a forceful call emanating from the VIP session reserved for celebrities, music industry big wigs and the rich and powerful. Two large body guards secured the roped off area that had tables with lighted candles. In the midst of this group were the master vampires, Niles and Fraiser, beckoning Jennifer to join them.

19

1:48 a.m. The Trance Room

Tioni looked at her silver and black Swatch. It was well past the time she was supposed to meet Coffy. After several walks throughout the building, she concluded that she best find Jamilah and Jennifer, so they could all report back to Julie.

"Going somewhere?" She heard a voice from behind. Tioni turned to see Coffy standing behind her holding a two small Styrofoam cups in his hands. "I thought you weren't going to show," he said extending one of the small cups to her.

"What is this?" Tioni asked, fully aware that she was being given champagne.

"It's to celebrate our finally getting together," he said with a charming smile that exposed his gold dental wear. Coffy wondered, if Tioni was able to see that he had spiked her drink with Ruphynol.

Tioni looked at the bubbles ascend from the bottom of the small white cup to the surface. "I don't drink," Tioni replied meekly, trying not to sound dorkish.

"Aww c'mon," he chided her, "Is tonight ladies night, or no one under seventeen admitted without a parent night?" Coffy pressed, tapping his cup against her before saying "here's a toast to an unforgettable night."

Tioni thought why not? Smiled and began to take one of many small sips of the champagne.

20

1:49 a.m. Yellow Room

Tired of waiting for Coffy, Shady and Beamon were leaving when Beamon said, "That was him!"

"Who was him?" Beamon asked.

"Wasn't that the dude from the other night? Shady briefly recollected. The half black, red dreadlocks and freckles?" he said in reference to Omari bumping into them on his way to the DJ stand.

"Where he go?" Beamon asked, finishing his drink, letting the empty plastic cup drop to the floor as he scanned the place trying to sort Omari from the hundreds of other red heads in the building.

"I believe he went that way." Shady pointed toward the Green Room. "Let's find that lil, punk and put him down Cobalt style."

21

1:50 a.m. The Green Room, VIP Section

The burly, but professionally dressed bouncer, pulled back the purple, velvet rope allowing Jennifer into the exclusive area decorated with a massive purple rug that accommodated ten circular tables covered with purple table cloths and candles, surrounded by white padded deck chairs. Jennifer ignored the comments and stares of the others that sat at the surrounding tables, her focus on the vampires, each more attractive than the next. Niles dark brown tresses were topped by a black pork pie hat. His white gaunt features hidden by lightly tinted squared Yves Saint Laurent tortoise shell glasses, which Jennifer knew was for show as vampires did not have vision problems. He wore an elegant black double breasted suit that cascaded elegantly over his lithe form and black wife beater. Fraiser sat at Niles right, his long golden blonde mane flowing over his Dolce & Gabbana, black, leather blazer that covered a brilliant, red, silk shirt all highlighted by a single platinum hoop earring that dangled from his left ear and half inch thick platinum rope that drooped around his neck. At Frasier's right, was an elegant Japanese man, wearing a black silk shirt with thin, metallic pinstripes unbuttoned to his navel, revealing an intricate tattoo on his chest, black linen slacks, covered by a Versace, full black, full length ramie coat. He had a thin manicured beard and his short, black spiked hair designed so every strand was in place. Even though Jennifer could not see through his dark Armani sunglasses, his lustful eyes made her uncomfortable. The woman to his right, also Japanese and in Jennifer's opinion was stunning, with creamy skin and ruby lips, except for a long thick braid that started at the top of her head and continued to the floor, her head was bald, large 'Burmese jade earrings dangled from her ears and jade necklaces adorned her neck. She wore a meshed metal mid drift top and long leather skirt with a deep slit that revealed her ivory legs and spiked black boots. The elegant woman also noticed her tablemate's devious glances and placing her leather-gloved hands on his jaws, she engulfed him in a full mouth kissed revealing fangs that startled Jennifer.

"It's good to see you again," Fraiser greeted the nervous teen, ignoring the couple. "We didn't know you did the Night Crawler haunts."

"Not as surprised as I am to see you," she responded, finding her courage.

"Why is that?" the Asian male spoke with a lustful tone, still embraced in his lover's arms.

"I didn't know that vampires came to places like this to find their victims."

"Oh we don't," Niles quipped, "We leave the preying on victims to all the drug dealers, undercover cops, murderers, drug addicts, rapist, and gang bangers that frequent establishments such as this to exhibit such antisocial behavior," he said with a grin. "No, we are just here for a night out."

"Please forgive my manners, we've never been properly introduced,"

Fraiser said extending his hand to introduce those at the table. "At my far right is Itoe, her companion Michiyo, this is Niles and I'm Fraiser. "One of the curses of being a vampire is that you believe everyone knows as much as you do, and as you know, that's just not true, is it Ms. Jennifer Twan?"

Jennifer did not know how to respond, but she knew they knew that also.

"It appears that our recent addition to the Circle is straddling the fence between us and them." Niles teased, "Maybe leaving the vampires, life is not as easy as you thought."

Niles words hit hard, Jennifer found herself clinching her fist in anger.

"You keep that up pretty one and you will be one of us in no time." Michiyo spoke making Jennifer aware that she was being enticed into using the powers she had retained.

"I made my decision, and I haven't changed my mind," she answered.

"I don't know" Fraiser added with smirk. "Maybe she would be more content running with the Union." The others at the table laughed heartedly. Jennifer had no idea who or what the Union was.

"What's that?" she asked not ashamed to show her ignorance.

"The Union little one," the lone female at the table spoke,

"Is what you all refer to as "werewolves", they are not as bountiful as the humans that walk the earth, but their number is nearly equal that of the Circle of the vampires."

The Union and the Circle, they're just gangs like the Crimsons and Cobalts." Jennifer acknowledged, "Only for vampires and werewolves"

Michiyo looked at Fraiser with a smile that only accentuated her beauty, "this one is divine."

"Well there's a fresh sound," Fraiser interrupted the conversation bringing everyone's attention back to the music. Jennifer turned toward the DJ booth and spotted Omari. She then turned back to the vampires and noticed a devious smile on Itoe's face that sent a shiver up her spine.

The vampires knew that Jennifer was protective of Omari, and now she was worried for him.

22

2:00 a.m. The Rooftop

Panic was replaced with elation, the need to flee, replaced by the desire to rumba. Shortly after taking the mood altering drug, Jamilah was able to get over the fact that she was not herself, but clearly under the influence of what she did not know. Whatever it was left her feeling relaxed in a way that not even chronic had ever done. The stresses over family had disappeared, replaced by an eerie sense of serenity, and a need to dance in the moment and throw abandon to the wind.

23

2:09 a.m. The Red Room

Exhausted from dancing Julie leaned against the wall to catch her breath and pulled from her purse one of the five diapers she dyed black. Wiping the perspiration from her face and neck, Julie looked at her Skull & Crossbones watch. Her charges were late. She knew they would not meet her at 1:45a.m., but expected to see them at 2:00 a.m. As a precaution she sent her friends to go out and corral them in. It was a shame that in a place that argues so strongly for love, harmony and balance, there had to be such negative activity that always followed raves. The media further distorted raves, as places where everyone was a drug addict doing ridiculous amounts of ecstasy, which couldn't be further from the truth, she fretted as she continued dabbing the diaper on her face so not to ruin her make up. Julie didn't drop E and neither did her associates. She looked up and Rainbow approaching her "We split up to cover more ground" he expressed, and tell other we know to be on the look out."

Clevant, a mutual friend, joined them. The tall, anthropology major had recently came out to his parents who, to his surprise, took his admission of being gay better than he expected. His flamboyance had since grown. "Any luck?" Rainbow asked.

"You know, I was having such a great time," he said while catching his breath from dancing with furious abandon. "Then I see Marc Morrison, and I got sick all over again"

"He's here?" Rainbow asked, "I thought he was in jail for solicitation of a minor?"

"Apparently, he's out on bail." Julie chimed in.

"He's also HIV positive and has promised to take as many with him as he could."

"What does that have to do with me finding my group?" Julie asked, afraid of the answer.

"He was dancing with some underage cutie with bright gold hair and wings"

"Where did you see her?" Julie demanded, turning to Rainbow. "Get the others," She instructed.

24

2:11 a.m. The Trance Room

"Tioni was giggly and dizzy from the champagne, moving in what seemed like slow motion. She and Coffy had stopped briefly to look for Coffy's friends, then taking the teen by the waist, the sweaty gangster made his way through the ever increasing crowd toward the exit.

"The sooner we leave, the sooner I can get you back," he said to the anxious teen over the noisy crowd. Ignoring her attempts to break free of his tight grip and pleas of "let me tell my friends that I'm leaving!"

"I can't hear you, tell me outside," was his response. Feeling more and more lightheaded, Tioni could feel the cool outside breeze on her face as they approached the exit. She was leaving the Night Crawler, and no one knew.

25

2:11 a.m. The Green Room

"There he is right over there." Shady pointed out Omari at the DJ booth. After circling the party, the two found the person they were looking for in plain sight. "Cap him and get," Beamon said with urgency.

"Man slow yo roll!" Shady argued, "let's make sure he's the right one. I'll get Coffy to make sure fo we start a riot up in this place. Don't do nothing, til we get back," the gangster stressed, rushing back into the crowd toward the Yellow Room.

"Forget make sure," Beamon snarled as he pulled out his glistening, nickel plated 45, with a silencer made from plastic, PVC pipe attached. "I'll handle it, and explain later." He walked behind a set of speakers surrounded by large plants, so when the shot was fired no one would see him. Lifting his jacket hood over his head, Beamon aimed his gun toward Omari's head.

26

2:12 a.m., The Green Room

Omari's performance entertained the group of vampires, which greatly disturbed Jennifer. From what she could see, he was just playing albums and turning knobs. She was so bothered by the table that she didn't notice that Jamilah or Tioni were nowhere to be found.

"He's has a raw unique sound," Niles said commenting on Omari's set.

"He has a talent that could be developed," Frasier acknowledged.

"He's clearly no DJ Craze," Michiyo smirked.

"What do you know about music?" Jennifer asked defending the music of Omari even though she wasn't impressed by it either.

"What do I know about music?" Michiyo asked with a sensuous, smile. "You believe vampires spend their time secluded in dark and drab castles in the middle of nowhere surrounded by a bunch of frightened peasants? There are very few trends that we are not involved in."

"From Bach to Kitaro, from Jacopo Peri to Cab Calloway to Afrika Bambata, "Itoe added. "If its cutting edge, vampires will have some involvement. For us, Techno music is just another way to pass our time, not much different than the disco crowd of the seventies or the prohibition parties of the roaring twenties."

"Although I had very little to do with the grunge movement out of Seattle," Niles interjected, "Sweat jackets and flannel shirts, much too tacky for my taste."

"As a vampire your options are broad, and your choices are many" Itoe added. "Think of all the things you could do as a member of the Circle and know that you have an eternity to do it."

"You could ask your friend to join us also, and with centuries to practice, he could create a sound never heard before" Michiyo added.

"Why am I so important? What is so special about me?" Jennifer asked, "I made my decision."

You should know that the days for your human compatriots are more limited than you think, and it is important that the Circle is fully organized." Fraiser added with seriousness in his voice.

"Look, someone is trying to kill the deejay" Niles interrupted the conversation. The group could clearly see a hooded figure hiding behind a large plant firing shots in Omari's direction, amidst the loud music, and the smell of incense no one would ever react to the gun fire or even see smoke.

With her vampire powers, Jennifer, eyes were able to follow the four bullets soaring toward Omari's head in slow motion. Unable to move, she could only watch as her dear friends beautiful, freckled, face and life about to be destroyed in hail of bullets. She then witnessed Niles leave his seat in blur, traveling across the room with incalculable speed, his hand plucking each of the four slugs in mid air inches before contact, causing a slight breeze that altered the DJ's locs. Niles returned to the table as quickly as he left, and the table observed a puzzled Beamon, who wondered, what happened to the shots I fired.

"Everyone's a music critic." Fraiser smirked, unimpressed with Niles' unparalleled feat.

"I happen to like drum & bass music," Niles interjected. Before Beamon could fire again, Itoe blew his breath across the room, and Jennifer could see the impact of his focused breath making an indentation in Deep's forehead, cracking his skull, and sending him reeling behind speakers and plants where no one would see his body.

"Good thing your friend has talents," Fraiser said standing up. "Of course if you join us you could make sure your friends are safe all the time, and don't worry, someone will remove the body."

"We're tidy that way," Niles added with a gleeful smile.

Turning to the others at the table Fraiser asked "Who's for another round on the dance floor?" The group left the baffled Jennifer staring at the four smoking metal slugs left on the table.

27

2:15 p.m. The Roof Top

When Julie and her friends arrived at the roof top, they could see among others, Jamilah dancing with Marc, twirling, wildly in place, with her eyes closed.

In a euphoric state that she could not describe, Jamilah stopped her spinning and opened her eyes to see her dance partner. only instead of Marc dancing beside her in her spinning world, he was lying on the ground, surrounded by three males, their feet pressed atop him, and an angry Julie approaching her.

"Did you do anything with him?" Julie demanded.

"What?" Jamilah asked, wondering why Julie was spinning around.

"Did you do anything with Marc!" Julie screamed.

"No! We didn't do anything!" a terrified Jamilah shouted back. "I promise!"

Julie grabbed Jamilah and hugged her. "Thank God," she whispered.

"You guys going to let me get up?" Marc asked Toyz and Issues.

"Nope," Issues answered, looking toward the exit like the others.

"What if I spit in the mouth or eye of one of you, would you be afraid then," Marc threatened,

"You even try and you're getting tossed from this roof" Rainbow fired back. Steve arrived on the roof followed by four large tuxedo attired men all wearing gas masks.

"I told you, you were not welcome at any Night crawler event" Rick said with anger in his voice. "Now get out, before I personally call the police and send you back to jail."

Marc stood up and left the rooftop without a conflict, the tuxedo squad right behind him.

Before Jamilah could ask what was going on, Rick walked over to Jamilah and said, "You should be more careful of the guys you're going to put out to!"

Before an insulted Jamilah could respond, Julie grabbed her hand and said, "Let's find the others and take them home before anything else happens."

28

2:20 a.m., The Green Room

"Okay here's the deal," Excel said to Omari as his set was coming to an end. Omari noticed that DJ JZ and Dizzy Dacey were standing right behind him, yet DJ Kumar was nowhere to be found. "Do you have enough music for another hour or until DJ Marky arrives?"

"Sure," Omari nodded, "What happened to Kumar?" he asked.

"I don't know," Excel answered dryly, "Maybe he dropped the wrong pill. "So, what do you want to do?"

"Can I tag team with the fellas?" Omari asked, watching the other two giving each other hi-fives.

"I don't care if you spin nude, just keep the crowd dancing," Excel answered, racing downstairs to the next emergency.

"Let's keep the same order, and we spin twenty minutes each." DJJZ the orange haired Iranian spoke while searching frantically through his black coffin to find a beat as frantic as Omari's to fade in.

"What happened to Kumar?" Omari asked disappointed that he was not going to hear what the braggart's sound was like.

"Oh, I happened to DJ Kumar," DJJZ answered finding and kissing the album that he was searching for and placing it on the mixing table. "I listened to how he was berating everyone's set, and I knew that mine was weaker than the both of yours. So, I added polyethylene glycol into his water

"What's that?" Omari asked, rubbing his sweaty, locs from his face.

"It causes all the water that Kumar drank to be retained in his bowels; which softens his stool, increasing the number of his bowel movements. In short, diarrhea, or the squirts," he smiled.

"You just walk around with meds that give you diarrhea?" Dizzy Dacey asked,

"Yeah, one thing that most folks don't know is that allot of the drugs the folks around here are taking leave you constipated big time. When it does, I can name my price for the diarrheic that will relieve a cramping stomach"

"Man!" Omari said in awe. "I didn't know it was that deep at these parties"

"My dad calls it "Nitch Marketing," DJJZ responded as he began to fade out Omari's music.

"Your dad sells drugs?" Omari asked.

"Worse, he's in advertising," DJJZ answered with a smirk.

Omari looked across the room and saw Jennifer and gave her a broad smile then waved. He was happy that she waved back even if it was weakly. DJ JZ tripped into Omari trying to get by in the cramped quarters and caught Omari's attention.

When he looked up, Jennifer was gone. Then it occurred to him maybe she didn't like his set. *Oh well,* he thought, *it was not like his music saved lives.* Then he left to go to the restroom thinking about what he would play during his next set.

29

2:21 a.m., The Exit

Jennifer pressed her way through the crowd toward the exit in a daze. Had it not been for the vampire Niles, four bullets would have ripped through Omari's body, killing him instantly and senselessly while all she could do was stand by. *What sort of world was this?* She continued out of the building, numb from the experience. The vampires had to be wrong. Jennifer had done the right thing by choosing not to join them. But a vampire saved Omari. *If they were so evil why help? Could the vampire life be better?* The cool night air offered Jennifer only one solution, *maybe she should go back and joins the vampires.* Jennifer's dilemma was interrupted by a familiar voice calling her name, the confused and exhausted teen could see Yes, Omari's and Dragonbrush's friend approaching her. The 15 year old Puerto Rican tagger with thick eyebrows that gave away his emotions, wore a large black, paint splattered tee shirt with the image of a white dove on his chest, sagging black cargo shorts and Allen Iverson's on his sockless feet, covering his wildly curly afro, he word a dark blue Tiger Wood's floppy golf hat. Even at a crowded event, the skateboarding enthusiast had his board.

"Hey Jennifer" the affable teen greeted, "you're leaving too? I have a cab waiting for me; you can ride along." Yes could see that Jennifer was lost in thought, so he made the offer again

"I don't know, Yes," Jennifer responded trying to make up her mind. "I was sort of thinking about going back in."

Yes placed his arm around the Jennifer's waist and escorted her away from the crowd and toward the waiting cab. "You really want to come with me," he explained. "There's nothing in that place that will do you any good."

30

2:28 a.m., Parking Lot, outside

"Why are you tripping like this," Coffy asked with frustration. "We're going to a special party. I'm going to introduce you to a few friends and then bring you back, honest." He said forcing Tioni into the back seat of his unfinished Buick Skylark, then closing the door behind her.

"I want to go home," Tioni whined, as Coffy started the ignition feeling her words beginning to slur.

"Then I will take you home after." He explained, his attention focused on quickly getting the car moving before Tioni tried to get out.

"I don't feel good," Tioni ached.

Coffy reached under his seat, pulled out a bottle of Gibley's gin and handed it to her. "Try some of this. It will knock out whatever is bothering you."

She took a sip from the bottle as the car took off and coughed spilling the alcohol on her pants. "It didn't help, it made me feel worse." Tioni's head was spinning, the car was moving faster and faster out of the parking lot. Tioni knew she had made a major mistake.

31

2:32 a.m., The Green Room

"So, where he at?" Shady drawled, as he looked around the green room. Unable to find Coffy, the seventeen year old Atlanta transplant returned to the Green Room to tell Beamon that shooting the red head DJ was a bad idea. Only now he could find neither Beamon, nor the red head DJ. *Did Beamon take red outside and shoot him?* Shady wondered, knowing the depth of Beamon's ruthlessness. *No telling*, he concluded, quickly walking past the speakers where the dead body of his fellow gang banger had been recently moved.

32

2:45 a.m. The Red Room

"Well it looks likes she wants to dance, to me," the stringy haired male continued. Julie was finally able to get the jubilant Jamilah to remain with her against the wall even if she was still too high to stop dancing, when a stranger approached the smiling and bopping Jamilah requesting a dance.

"Trust me when I say she doesn't," Julie replied perturbed by the man's persistence.

"Pretty lady," the man asked Jamilah ignoring the already annoyed Julie "Would you like to dance with me?"

"Yep," Jamilah answered bobbing her head.

"What'd I tell you!" The man said extending his arm for Jamilah to accept it.

"Tell toothpick dick to take a hike, and that I'm not going to say it nice again," Julie instructed Jamilah, her tone resonating controlled anger.

"Take a hike toothpick dick, she's not going to say it nice again" Jamilah said still grooving to the music.

"You just want her for yourself," The man accused Julie with contempt in his eyes.

Julie grabbed the man and pulled him forward by his wrinkled white shirt, his buttons jumping from his shirt like fleas. "Do you want to fight for her, right here, right now?" She said loud enough to draw attention from some of the dancing crowd.

"Hey, I just wanted to dance, that's all," the man stuttered. "I'm gone!" When she released him, the man faded into the crowd.

Julie turned to Jamilah and said, "You must attract every weirdo in the solar system. No wonder Omari's always pissed." Jamilah scooted next to Julie, the effects of the Ecstasy still in full swing and said, "You know, you are like a big sister to me, you know that?" she asked placing her full weight on Julie.

"Yeah, Jamilah, I know that," she echoed.

"I love you big sister, you know that don't you?" Jamilah cooed with a routine that always worked on her father and brother.

"Yeah, I know that too," Julie answered dryly.

"So can I dance for a little while?" Jamilah asked, hoping for a happy response.

"Not a chance, little sister," Julie responded pressing her back against the wall, looking up at Toyz and Gustav who were making their way back.

"You're not like a sister," Jamilah pouted, "you're like my mother."

"I know Jamilah." Julie sighed as she mumbled the words of Tori Amos *"Give me life, give me pain, Give me myself again."*

When Toyz and Gustav arrived Julie asked, "Where are they?"

"I received a text message from a "Yes," saying that he ran into Jennifer, she was sick and he was taking her to Jamilah's" Gustav explained. We've searched the Green Room twice for Tioni. We now have a squad out looking for her."

"Why would he text you about Jennifer and not me? And how did he get your number?" Julie questioned her friend.

"I have no answer to either of your questions." Gustav said flatly.

"You think Omari might know where they are?" Toyz asked, watching Omari preoccupied with the turntables.

"Let's ask him last because if he doesn't know, it's certainly going to show in his music." Julie responded. "I'll call Jennifer to confirm that she's actually there and not God knows where. You, keep looking, Tioni's got to be here somewhere."

"Tioni's got to be here somewhere," Jamilah repeated.

"Please hurry", Julie explained, "I really want to take Ms. Groove home because she's clearly not rave material."

Part 8

Werewolves the Mix Tape

"If you call one wolf, you invite the pack"
Bulgarian Proverb.

1

2:55 a.m. Old U.S Army base, The Old G

Coffy drove Tioni to the former Oakland Army base, now thirty acres of series of desolate buildings, one of twelve California military bases decommissioned. Coffy continued through a cluster of dark buildings and parked in an area occupied by other vehicles.

"Does anyone live in this place?" The drugged teen asked, as Coffy led her into a darkened building where blaring music could be heard.

"Why, you looking for a place to stay?" Coffy asked dryly, leading her through a long darkened hallway, with a calmness that could only come from being familiar with the environment.

"No!" Tioni replied nervously, stepping over syringes and used condoms this place has rats."

"Rats prefer to stay outside," the thug explained. "They don't come inside unless something scares them, so don't worry about them." Coffy led Tioni into the three story building that once housed servicemen. The Cobalt's renamed it the "Old G club." Others called it what it was, *a big old crack house* located in a place most folk avoided.

Tioni imagined the club would be glamorous and elegant much like in the shows and music videos on television. The Old G was neither. It was completely ghetto. The walls of the two thousand square feet common area were completely covered with graffiti tags, bullet holes, but mostly black mildew. The vibrant and fluorescent colors used on the tags added to the room giving it an early nineties music video look. A fifteen foot bar sat against the wall. Behind it four inoperable refrigerators and a couple of freezers with the doors removed that held melting ice and forty ounce beers. The hard drinks were apparently gone as the floor was cluttered with hundreds of empty Styrofoam and Dixie cups, and several garbage cans were filled to the brim with empty bottles and cans.

The chairs ranged from bar stools to thrones, and the tables ranged from poker to board room, and the hierarchy of an individuals importance could be immediately determined by who sat at which table and at what chair, which also explained why so many chose to stand.

The sound system was the only thing in the building that was sophisticated. The DJ was mixing familiar tunes that sounded better from the outside because inside, those who did not like the DJ's "choice of music," placed their own boom boxes on their tables and played what they wanted creating the sound of chaos. Tioni's eyes hurt and watered from thick cloud of cigarettes, cannabis, mildew, funky gangbangers and crack that filled the air of the dimly lit space.

"Who are you? What do I got to do, to do you?" Glock said stepping directly in front of Coffy, slightly shoving him back. Tioni saw the shove and automatically feared Glock. There was also something about him that made her sick, possibly the smell of expensive cologne on a funky body.

"She may be young," Glock spoke to the others as if she weren't there, "but look at the *doo doo maker* on her. Oh, we going to celebrate tonight!"

Through her fogged brain, Tioni thought about everything Jennifer had said about Coffy and his company and wished she had listened.

2

2:56 a.m., South Hill Court

Unable to sleep longer than thirty minutes at a time, Dragonbrush walked throughout the empty house in only his navy blue Joe boxer shorts resolved that he would be up until the last person made it home. When the phone rang startling him, Dragonbrush released a loud bark that startled him. He raced up the steps where he had left the phone, wondering if it were Uhuru, who promised he would check in, "Hello?"

"Dragonbrush," It was Julie, and there was concern in her voice. "Have you heard from Tioni?"

"No, I thought she was with you, Jamilah and Jennifer?" Dragonbrush answered now equally concerned.

"Unfortunately, everyone split up. Jamilah is with me, and we just found out that Jennifer fell ill, and called to say that she was on her way there. But, I have no idea as to where Tioni might be."

Dragonbrush nose picked up familiar scents outside. "I hear Jennifer at the door," Dragonbrush reassured Julie "What do you want me to tell Tioni if she calls?"

"Tell her I'm in the Green Room with Omari, if I find her I will call."

After hanging up Dragonbrush ran downstairs to meet Jennifer at the door. He could still smell the distinctive CK cologne on her, but it was slightly different. He opened the door and when the Vietnamese teen saw him, her eyes immediately went red. Dragonbrush felt the hair stand up and bared his teeth defensively.

"You are of the Union," Jennifer said with fangs also bared, her skin had changed to a leathery green and her nails, like his had grown.

"And you are of the Circle," Dragonbrush responded his fury matching hers. Dragonbrush felt something painfully strike his ankle, momentarily taking his attention off Jennifer. He looked down, and it was a skateboard with the image of a wing on it. The board bounced off his ankle and landed on the left foot of Jennifer. The board striking him cleared his thinking, "I'm sorry Jennifer," he whispered, not knowing what came over him, when his eyes met Jennifer's, she was also back to her old self.

"I need help," she whispered, before collapsing into his arms. Dragonbrush moved her into the living room when he heard a voice say. "Let me help," Without having seen him, Dragonbrush knew it was Yes. Turning to his good friend he asked. "What just happened?"

3

3:00 a.m., The Red Room

"I have bad news," Issues expressed to Julie. "Toyz just found out that someone saw a member of the Cobalt gang walk out with a girl that fit Tioni's description."

"I remember Jennifer telling me Tioni had a thing for a Cobalt piece of garbage, Ooooh!" Julie grimaced trying to contain her anger. "Wait until I get my hands on her!"

"The Cobalt's are also throwing a party," Gustav added. "I know where they are and how to get there."

"Does this mean we're going?" Issues asked.

"Duuhh!" Julie answered, leading the way, dragging Jamilah along.

4

3:03 a.m., South Hill Court

Jennifer soundly passed out as soon as her head touched the soft couch. Dragonbrush sat on the edge of the couch unaware that he was only in his boxer shorts. "When did you arrive back in town?" Dragonbrush asked his good friend as he plopped his lean frame onto the love seat. It had been several weeks since the two last spoke.

"Tonight," he answered, looking at the slumbering Jennifer. "I was in New York and will be leaving for New Orleans in about six hours. I heard you all were going to the Night Crawler, so I went straight their hoping to find you guys. That's when I saw Jennifer who was pretty stressed and I told her I would drop her off. She told me you were here, and agreed to join me." Looking around the room admiringly, he asked, "Is this you? It's nice. Omari and his family must be treating you pretty well."

"Omari, Jamilah and their uncle and aunt are like one of the best things that ever happened to me." His demeanor became quiet as he spoke. "Let me tell about the worst," Dragonbrush spoke, handing Yes his skateboard, sure he would leave shortly after hearing his story.

"What?" Yes asked, his left eyebrow arching, telling Dragonbrush that he was prepared for the worst.

"Do you believe in werewolves?" Dragonbrush asked.

"Yeah, I do, why? You telling me you're one now?" He asked in a non judgmental tone that surprised his friend.

Dragonbrush shook his head shamefully.

"Cool," Yes answered taking the news as nothing serious. "Now you can use that to help folks who need it."

"Man, you don't understand," Dragonbrush argued, "It's not as simple as that."

"What's there to understand?" Yes asked calmly. "You told me you were a werewolf. I said cool; now you can help people. What's the problem?"

"I don't know, I just never looked at it that way," Dragonbrush answered with confusion in his voice and on his face.

"And speaking of helping," Yes spoke giving Dragonbrush a knowing look. "Shouldn't you be doing something about Tioni?"

Before Dragonbrush could respond, the telephone rang. "Hello," Dragonbrush answered, it was Julie. "Dragonbrush listen," Julie spoke with controlled concern. "We believe Tioni went to another club with some thug called Coffy. If she calls, tell her to stay put. We are on our way there." She then hung up.

The name Coffy sent a shockwave throughout Dragonbrush's system. Coffy would hurt Tioni. Dragonbrush turned to Yes and said, "I have to go, but you have to stay here and watch Jennifer, okay?"

"I'll stay until someone comes," Yes agreed placing his skateboard on the side of the couch. He began surfing the television wondering what was in the refrigerator?

"Thanks man," Dragonbrush said rushing up the stairs. "I gotta go."

"I know," Yes whispered under his breath, before heading to the kitchen, "I know."

5

3:06 a.m., Parking lot

Ten minutes into DJ Marky set, the Brazilian superstar demonstrated to Omari, DJ JZ and Dizzy Dacey how a professional's worked, with a mix that electrified the audience. The room jumped giving the congested area even less space for dancing. Excel paid and thanked the up and coming DJ's, and an exhausted Omari who did not see Jamilah, Jennifer, Julie or anyone assumed they had gone home. When an equally tired DJJZ offered to drop him off, Omari willingly accepted the ride. The two had reached DJJZ's silver 2006 Honda Civic and were preparing to place their heavy coffins in the backseat when Omari could hear Edwin running toward them, calling his name.

"The Jedi wants to talk to you." Edwin explained to Omari, turning to DJJZ he said, "We'll drop him off."

"Justin ain't running nothing!" Omari responded, giving Edwin an incredulous look and continued toward the silver car.

"If it wasn't for him, you wouldn't have even gotten this gig. You owe him a cut," Edwin charged.

"Are you his slave or something?" Omari shouted, wondering what part of no did not sink into this fool's baldhead.

"I'm nobody's slave," Edwin charged, walking up on Omari and pointing his finger in his face "You're going back if I have to drag you by those dreads!"

DJJZ looked at Edwin, who face was directly in Omari's. He could see that Edwin was large enough and strong enough to make good on his word. Omari was in trouble.

"Alright man," Omari answered, dropping the heavy coffin he was carrying on both of Edwin's feet. When the metal case filled with albums bounced to the ground, Edwin followed grabbing both of his feet in pain before eating the dust Omari kicked in his face.

"Let me tell you something!" Omari shouted while picking up his coffin. "The next time you walk up on me, I'll kill you, Ya hear me?" He then placed his coffin in the back of his new friends car.

"That was pretty smooth." DJJZ commented, placing his music in the backseat of his car, ignoring Edwin's cries of pain.

"Thanks." Omari replied, as he got into the passenger side.

"Of course it wouldn't have been worth it if a single vinyl is chipped," DJJZ added as he drove off leaving the bald bully writhing on the ground.

Spoken like a true DJ, Omari thought to himself as he rolled down the window to feel the breeze of the early morning air on his face before checking his collection of albums. *Spoken like a true DJ.*

6

3:07 a.m. South Hill Court

Dragonbrush quickly placed on sweats, a hoodie and Adidas. He slipped out the second story bedroom window. The night winds blew forcefully through Dragonbrush's hair, as if its intentions were to pull it from his head. Dragonbrush ignored the wind as he nimbly scaled the roof, his mind focused on one thing. That he couldn't, and wouldn't let anything happen to Tioni. Dragonbrush knew Tioni was at the Old G's, the spot where the Cobalt's threw all of their functions, but worried if he would get there in time. He needed help and instinctively knew what to do. He leapt from the roof landing gracefully on both hands and feet in Pluto and Zeus's backyard and was immediately greeted by the two Rottweilers.

"You've turned into one of them," Pluto said to Dragonbrush acknowledging his transformation

"What does that mean?" Dragonbrush asked the middle age dog.

"Werewolves kill the people we protect and werewolves would seek to destroy our way of living."

"But you descended from the wolves," Dragonbrush replied.

"But dogs and werewolves both want different things," Pluto explained.

"I respect that?" Dragonbrush acknowledged Pluto's point.

"Most wolves don't see that, you are different, unless you are here to kill our human friend," Pluto argued.

"I am not here to hurt your human friend, I am here to ask that you help me, help my human friend Tioni," Dragonbrush spoke still on his hands and knees at eye level with the Rotts. "She is at a party at the Army base and I need someone to interrupt it until I get there."

"Who's Tioni?" Zeus asked looking at Pluto.

"You know, the female that was throwing us those mushrooms and anchovies from her pizza that time," Pluto said refreshing Zeus's memory.

"Oh her," Zeus answered. "I was going to bite her first chance I got, throwing us that crap when she was eating pepperoni."

"No one is biting Tioni," Dragonbrush spoke with the authority of an Alpha male. "But I want you to call all your friends and tell them I need them to interrupt that party" The music is loud and there are a lot of people dancing and smoking.

"We don't know anyone on that side of town" Pluto replied. "I don't see how we can help"

"Call your friends and ask them to spread the word, someone will," Dragonbrush ordered.

"Does Tioni have a cat?" Zeus asked.

"Call your friends now, because Tioni is in danger!" Dragonbrush growled, both dogs placed their heads into the air and began to howl their loud calls instantly picked up by the dogs down the hill, up the hill around the block.

"Pluto, Zeus!" the male voice called the howling pair, "get in here!" the dogs ignored their master and continued.

"I said now!" the owner demanded, Dragonbrush gave them a permissive nod

"Thanks guys," the hidden Dragonbrush said as they trotted by.

"All you had to do was ask" Zeus replied before running back to their angry master.

With a powerful leap Dragonbrush was back on the roof of his house, amazed at his own abilities, then leaping off the building headed down the hill toward the freeway at an incredible speed, leaping over the overpass he dashed onto the 580 freeway passing cars, trucks and motorcycles.

7

3:16 a.m., The Old G

What was keeping Coffy so long and how am I getting home? Toni thought, Coffy and the others had left Tioni at a table with a group of older women who were frankly scary. They were loud, drunk, and bragged of using drugs, abortions, inflicting violence on others and being in and out of jail. Tioni also painfully realized that she really didn't know if she could trust Coffy, but she trusted him more than the terrifying Glock. Even in her drugged state, Tioni knew she had to get out of there. Glock rejoined the table, causing Tioni's heart to skip a beat. He motioned to the female that sat between her and Tioni to "*move.*" He placed six cigar-sized joints on the table before them, "These puppies normally go for fifty a pop, but since we celebrating the arrival of my new friend Tioni, I'm treating every one at the table tonight."

"Where's Coffy?" Tioni asked nervously.

"He around here somewhere," Glock answered nonchalantly, "But you need to know I run all that you see around here, what's everyone's, is mine, but what's mine is mine, and tonight" Glock said grabbing the leg of Tioni's chair, pulling it toward him, "You're mine." He removed the frightened teens, Raiders cap and was impressed by Tioni's beautifully, designed braids. The thug lit up the first joint, took a long drag from it then handed it to Tioni who could feel a blind panic starting to come over her; the other females at the table looked at her with giggles and jealousy.

Tioni took a nervous hit on the joint and Glock leaned over and began to whisper then nibble on her ear. Tioni simultaneously leaned her head toward Glock pushing his face from her ear, simultaneously using her right hand to remove his hand from her breast. "Stop, later, okay!"

"It won't be too damn much longer." Glock retorted clearly frustrated before he heard his name called. "What do those fools want now?" He said standing up and walking away. He said "Don't go away." He looked at the others at the table and said, "You keep my friend here company and don't let her do nothing stupid," then left the table.

"I have to get out of here," Tioni in slurred words standing to her feet before a heavy hand forced her tired body back into her seat

"You heard the man," a large white woman with a green wig and gold teeth said with intense attitude "You ain't going nowhere!"

"Didn't nobody tell you to be coming up in here in the first place," another added, "So now that you here, you just going to have to give the man what he wants."

Tioni could feel the warm tears begin to roll down her face. She had to figure a way out.

8

3:19 a.m., Outside the Old G

"Well, this is the place," Issues commented pointing out the scores of cars parked outside the noisy building. "What are we going to do now?"

"Were going in," Julie asserted, pulling off her tiara as she stepped out of Gustav's gleaming Volvo along with the others.

"Gustav, you need to stay and watch Jamilah," Julie spoke getting out of the car, "And be ready to drive off in case we really need to get out of here. The rest of you, come on." Smiling to lift the mood of her friends as they walked toward the fenced off building, Julie joked, "Just think of this as another party to crash."

"I don't think so," Rainbow echoed the thoughts of the others as the three continued behind her. "This is the type of party your mama tells you to avoid."

9

3:20 a.m. 580, Freeway, West bound

Dragonbrush raced down the side of the freeway like a brown streak. While listening to the sounds of dogs howling his speed grew faster with every step, his body hunching over until he was using both his hands and feet to obtain and maintain a maximum speed. To the public the sound of so many canines howling at one time was unnerving, causing countless house lights to turn on, its occupants peering through their windows, and even more stepping outside willing to face the fear that something beyond normal was happening. Throughout the city, Dog spoke to dog, their communication, a cacophony of howls that sent birds flying, and setting off car alarms. The hissing and shrieking of cats frightened by the wave of howls added to the maddening sound, joined by panicked, pet owners, dog lovers and haters yelling and cursing to the top of their lungs for the aggravating sound to stop.

The dogs were effectively communicating, but not as Dragonbrush expected. He had no idea so many parties were being thrown at this hour. He quickly learned that a canine's interpretation of a large party differed from dog to dog; creating more problems than it was solving. Dogs were requesting permission to raid parties, and a few packs did so without permission before Dragonbrush commanded them to leave. The situation was getting out of hand. Dragonbrush stopped on the side of the freeway, and thought. The army base was in a large desolate area. He had to articulate that the area he was looking for was not in a place where there were a lot of humans, no grass, trees, houses or apartments. Dragonbrush added to the concert with a howl of his own. Seconds later the howling elevated to a degree that the police were called for their assistance, they in turn contacted Animal control who could offer no solution. Howling continued throughout the four corners of the city, instilling dread and fear in psyches, thieves and the homeless. Some even stood in the middle of the street proclaiming that the "end of the world had come!" For three minutes, Oakland and its neighboring cities was shut down by the concert of noise. When Dragonbrush heard of the party at old U.S Army base, he sent out a mighty howl that frightened a driver who was caught off guard as she drove by on the freeway. Then the howling ceased, Dragonbrush's dawgs had done their job.

10

3:35 a.m. South Hill Court

"Thank God the dogs finally shut up," Omari acknowledged as he entered his home, inside he was surprised to find Yes sitting in his living room eating a bowl of Captain Crunch, while watching reruns, of the Boondocks, "When did you get back in Oakland?" Omari asked, noticing Jennifer sleeping on the couch across from him. "Where is everyone?"

Yes placed his finger over his mouth, and motioned Omari to meet him in the kitchen. Omari placed his coffin down and complied

"I heard you guys were all at the Night Crawler and ran into Jennifer on the way back. She passed out once we got here. Dragon got a call from Julie a few minutes ago saying, that Tioni was missing. He went out to find her and asked me to wait here with Jennifer until someone arrived, not knowing what to do for I found her home number on her phone and called her aunt. She's on her way."

"Is she okay?" Omari asked, concerned about the slumbering teen.

"I don't think she's up for this trip," Yes observed.

"Why do you say that?" Omari asked.

"When I ran into her, she seemed really disoriented. It may be better if she just chilled," the Puerto Rican answered as the two walked back into the living room.

Omari sat beside Jennifer and looked at the dark, shiny hair of his sleeping friend. "Dragonbrush is turning into a werewolf" Omari confessed to Yes, his words soft and filled with concern.

"I know," Yes replied picking up his bowl of cereal, "He told me."

"Vampires and werewolves," Omari sighed moving his locs from his face. "Man, I honestly don't know if I can deal with this." he confessed, his face revealing how much this situation was weighing him down.

"It will work out," Yes reassured Omari.

"How can you say that?" Omari asked, "Or can you say that because it's not happening to you?"

"Dragonbrush is a knucklehead, but his heart is in the right place, and Jennifer fell in with the wrong crowd, but she's out now. You've helped both of them" Yes explained.

"But I don't know how to help a vampire and a werewolf" Omari confessed, admitting his fear.

"Omari your friends know your heart," Yes reassured him. "And just as you are looking out for them, they are looking out for you. Besides what could be better then having a werewolf and vampire covering your back?"

"Omari smiled, "I never thought of it that way."

11

3:38 a.m., The Old G

Tioni heard the females at the table laughing then noticed they were throwing her Raider cap from person to person. That's when she realized that she had dozed off again. She watched a shorthaired white girl with needle marks on her overly exposed chest placing on her Raiders cap. "Give me back my cap!" Tioni wanted to say, but the words would not come out of her mouth. It was as if she was aware of what was going on, but didn't have the strength to do anything about it. All she could think was that Jennifer had warned her. Smoke from the nearly self-consumed joint given to her irritated her already red eyes as she laid her head back on the table and passed out. Tioni woke up when she could feel her body being lifted. Glock was carrying her in arms, and she was too weak to even fight back or even struggle. Tioni heard him say to the others at the table, "I'm going upstairs to take care of some business, and I don't want to be disturbed." Tioni wanted to scream, but fell unconscious instead.

12

3:39 a.m. The Old G

Issues, Toyz and Rainbow circulated separately through the crowded party, enduring the jeers and insults of some of the regulars. Julie walked around the smoke filled common area politely turning down offers for drinks, drugs and sex. The four had managed to cover the large densely populated space in a short time. Toyz spotted Glock carrying Tioni away from an occupied table, across the room and through a door. He quickly joined Issues and Rainbow and the trio followed. Julie spied the group from across the room and did likewise.

The door led to a hallway where two large, Mexican bouncers stood sharing a blunt, blocking a closing door. Taking the lead, Rainbow immediately approached the brute's capturing their attention. Noticing Julie peeking through the hallway door, Toyz and Issues followed Rainbow lead, ready to create a diversion that would allow Julie through the blocked door.

"Where you going?" The larger of the two bouncers asked the trio, in a tone that was purposely intimidating. "This area is off limits."

"Look, I was told the toilet was through there," Rainbow argued "and after paying twelve dollars to get in, I should be able to take a piss without an argument."

"The toilet's not in there," the second brute charged. "So why don't you go screw yourselves somewhere else."

"No, he didn't!" Issues said clearly offended, "Just because, unlike you, we're all having a good time, don't talk down to us, because if you want to talk smart, then why don't you say that to me outside" Issues said challenging the man that was a foot taller and at least sixty pounds heavier.

"Get out of here, the party's over," The larger bouncer said trying not to lose his cool, even though he knew he would.

"I know you don't mean us; we are the party." Issues postured knowing he was infuriating the bouncer. "What's the matter? You scared I will whup yo ass, like a little beeotch?" Issue challenged, the brute, rolling his head and his eyes before saying, "No homo."

"Oh, lets do this," the large man raged, as he grabbed Issues and Rainbow and rushed them through a door that led to an alley with Toyz and the other bouncer right behind them. Julie saw the opportunity her friends had created and rushed through the empty door.

13

3:40 a.m. The Old G

Many of the party goers could hear the barking outside, clearly audible over the musical chaos inside but ignored it largely preoccupied with their own personal excesses. That all changed when the dance floor was flooded with mice and wood rats the size of cats, the rodents, more terrified of what was outside than the screaming and stumping occupants inside the dance hall. In a matter of seconds, the rodents sent the hysterical partiers leaping and stumbling over each other, in their attempt to get atop chairs, tables and any objects that stood off the floor, as the frightened rodents covered the floor like a grey wave, racing up the legs and backs of partiers, tripping and fighting each other in order to escape contact with the disgusting critters. A tidal wave of nearly seventy cats followed the rodents, all black, all feral, and willing to risk being trampled, rather than face what was outside. Instead of scattering across the floor, the agile felines crossed the room by leaping atop the bars, chairs, and the heads and shoulders of hysterical partiers, whose cries followed them as they flowed out the building. Minutes later, many of the hardened gangbangers and partiers raced back into the rodent and feline infested building there screams and cries revealing a state beyond hysterics as the space was flooded by a tsunami of growling dogs of all breeds, shapes, and colors, numbering in the hundreds, forcing open the doors and shattering every window with such intensity, that their sheer volume destroyed everything in site and forced the panic and sobered party goers that could not escape the building to stand against the wall as the canines chased rodents and cats, snapping at panicked, partiers whose manic gestures could only be interpreted as hostile. Then suddenly, the pack lost interest in being in the former serviceman hall and fought with partiers to exit the building, leaping through windows and any exit available as mysteriously as they arrived.

Coffy in the pandemonium had forgotten about Tioni or being pissed at Glock for humiliating him by taking Tioni away. He watched as a lit cigar that dropped from the mouth of a fleeing partier hit the alcohol covered floor. The flame followed the pattern of the spilled drinks giving the impression that the flames had joined the chaotic dance, chasing patrons, rodents, felines and canines, adding to the urgency to leave the building.

"Put that fire out!" Coffy yelled. His equally intoxicated peers without thinking proceeded to throw their drinks at the fire spreading it even faster. Realizing the seriousness of what they had done, Coffy headed for the exit, his associates close behind as the flames quickly spread throughout the building.

14

3:40 a.m., South Hill Court

Jennifer's Aunt Nana arrived still in robe and pajamas; she followed Yes to the living room where Omari and Jennifer watched TV.

"Are you okay?" Nana asked.

"I'm just tired and want to go home," Jennifer answered wearily, rising from her spot.

"No trip?" The manicurist and shop owner asked, with curious compassion.

"No trip," Jennifer answered with finality in her tone.

Omari and Yes walked behind them to the car, Omari carrying the bags Jennifer's was to use for camping.

"I'm sure the rest of your friends can't sleep in anticipation of the next few hours." Nana said smiling, wearily and driving off.

15

3:41 a.m., The Old G

The rodents running through the halls reminded Julie of the time she and her activist friend released caged mice at a bio-tech lab in Emeryville. She stood against the wall and rodents ran by oblivious to her as well as the dogs that followed. The screaming, barking and smoke from the main hall had her wondering, **what is going on in there?** But she kept her focus ignoring everything, trying to figure out which of the many doors down the long corridor held Tioni. A bald male covering his face with a handful of paper napkins ran past Julie and banged on the center door yelling, "There's a fire yo! You got to get out!" The male entered the room and minutes later, five males ran out holding a suitcase and bags as smoke flooded the closed hallway. "He's where? "Damn!" Julie heard the same bald male shout then watched as he ran to the hall and up a flight of stairs. Julie followed keeping her distance. The smoke trailing, smoking growing ever darker with every step she took upstairs. After ascending two flights, she over heard someone banging on a door.

"Glock! It's me Money," he yelled banging even louder. "Man, the whole place is on fire we got to go!" Julie peered from the corner of the darkened hallway and could see the male waiting impatiently outside a door.

"I'll be there in a minute!" Julie could hear Glock yell through the hall that was becoming less visible.

Throwing up his hands, Money ran toward the hall, seeing Julie he yelled, "Get out my way!" Julie leaned against the wall to let the male go by. Her heart was gripped by fear as she watched Money make his way downstairs and hopefully to safety as the sound of wood popping and bottles of alcohol exploding was growing louder.

"Oh no," Julie whispered, knowing that the fire downstairs had become a real problem. She ran to the door where the male was standing and found that the key was still in the door. Julie swung opened the door and what she saw caused her to scream.

16

3:43 a.m., Alleyway outside

"There's nothing's worse than fighting a gay with a 3rd degree black belt," Issues said to the two bouncers that lay sprawled on the ground, too hurt to move. "No homo," he high fived his peers.

"You mean yes homo" Rainbow added. As the three were about to re-enter the building, they were overwhelmed by an exodus of fleeing rodents, patrons, cats and barking canines. When the flurry subsided, they rushed in,but the fury of dark smoke that assailed them, forced them to retreat.

"We can't go back in there!" Rainbow said between coughs, his words were followed by a loud explosion that sent bits of debris through the smoke, forcing them to run from the rain of rubbish. They grabbed the downed bouncers and moved to a safer distance, concerned about their friend inside.

17

3:43 a.m., The Old G

"Get away from her!" Julie screamed at the top of her lunges, stunning Glock, as he was removing Tioni's pant, as she lay unconscious on a wooden desk. Julie grabbed the startled Glock and shoved him to the other side of the small office. She quickly stood between him and Tioni pulling her pants back up.

"Bitch!" The angry Glock responded by delivering Julie a viscous slap that sent the large teen flailing atop a fog headed Tioni who was aware of the smoke in the room but couldn't reply.

"Yeah, and you hit like one." Julie replied, returning the physical favor with a massive right jab that stunned Glock and a left cross that sent the bully reeling out of the office against the wall before dropping to the floor.

"Tioni, wake up!" Julie cried, happy that she arrived when she did. She stood her drugged friend up, then heard the door slam shut and a metal sound against the door. Julie ran to the door and tried the knob, but Glock had locked the door from the outside. Julie struggled against the door as the room quickly filled with thick, black smoke.

18

3:44 a.m. Outside, The Old G

Dragonbrush was amazed at his own abilities. He had run over 10 miles and felt no signs of fatigue. His Adidas, however, were ruined. From miles away, the teen's sensitive nostrils picked up the scent of the burning building, growing thicker and more pungent as he drew nearer. The fire of course would be at the one place he hoped it wouldn't, and the situation was worse than he imagined. Stopping at the parking lot Dragonbrush witnessed the exodus of people, canines, felines, and rodents all rushing out of the flaming building and wondered, was the fire the dogs doing? He picked up many familiar scents, Gustav and Jamilah were nearby, but inside the burning building, through the ever thickening smoke he could make out the scents of Julie and Tioni. As he marveled at the growing blaze, Dragonbrush's ears began to ring at the sound of fire trucks approaching minutes away. The teen raced toward the blaze like a brown blur. He leapt headlong into a second story window and into the inferno, despite his lupine and common sense telling him to do otherwise.

19

3:45 a.m. South Hill Court

You're leaving already?" Omari asked Yes, who informed him that it was time for him to go. "Can't you at least wait until everybody show's up?"

"I have to leave town in a couple of hours," Yes answered apologetically.

"Cool," Omari said dryly and went back to watching television with his cell phone in hand.

"Yes could see the concern on Omari's face. He looked at his watch, then slumped back down in the love seat and said, "Trust me everything is going to be fine."

"How do you know?" Omari asked, reassured by Yes's certainty.

"Same way I know anything," the Puerto Rican answered, adjusting his mound of afro underneath his hat, before walking back to the kitchen.

20

3:45 a.m., Outside, The Old G

The building had been transformed into an enormous matchbox with the last remaining patrons leaving the space in a coughing fury. Most of the occupants drove away from the site for fear of implication, but others remained watching the building being reduced into a searing piece of Oakland's history, in a matter of minutes.

Gustav sat impatiently in his car tapping feverishly on his steering wheel asking through gritted teeth, "What is taking them so long? C'mon get the hell out of there!"

His attention was snatched away by the sound of the fire trucks rushing in and patrons rushing out when he spotted Issues, Rainbow and Toyz rushing toward the car.

"Did she make it back?" Issues asked between gasps.

"No, I thought she was with you" Gustav asked in desperation.

"Then she must still be in there!" Toyz cried.

Jamilah still groggy from her "E" experience could see the flames, and her fogged mind started to quickly sober up when she noticed that the others around the car were crying and demanding that the firemen unload their trucks in a hurry. She then realized that two of her best friends were in the blazing building.

21

3:46 a.m., Outside The Old G

"Man, I knew you would make it." A worried, Money exclaimed, as he saw the coughing Glock run toward them between two fire trucks.

"Did you hit it?" Money asked referring to his planned assault on Tioni.

"Man, I waxed it in the smoke!" Glock lied holding his sore jaw. "And I made sure that nobody else get any of what she had to offer," he said looking coldly at Coffy. "Now let's get out of here before the police put the blames on us."

22

3:46 a.m. The Old G

Julie's futile struggle to open the door, coupled with the rapidly rising smoke left her exhausted. The office and her world were becoming black, filled with the sound of crackling wood. Julie finally resolved that she and Tioni would not be able to escape. With her last efforts, she cradled the drugged teen in her arms. "I knew I would die from something stupid," she said, kissing her friend on the cheek. "I just didn't know it would be from trying to save your silly hide." She laid her head on top of Tioni's and surrendered to the smoke.

23

3:47 a.m., The Old G

A roar so loud that it shook the walls of the smoke filled coffin brought Julie back to consciousness. Looking through smarting eyes, Julie could see something or someone above her tearing away at the roof. She was showered with falling debris and dust, as the smoke ascended from the office like it sought freedom from the small room as much as she did. Her smoke filled eyes could only make out the silhouette of a small figure that descended from the heavens, landing next to her. The figure grabbed Julie's massive frame with no effort at all, and secured the unconscious Tioni in the other. That's when the floor beneath them caved in, and the three fell through the floor landing in what looked like a corner in hell.

Unable able to open her smoked filled eyes, Julie felt the figure crouch, her body dropping to the floor as she could feel the mighty growl growing inside her mysterious savior and with a deafening roar she felt herself heading skyward followed by the sound of a massive explosion.

24

3:48 a.m., Old G

"Oh my God, no!" Gustav screamed as he could see the magnificent explosion that sent debris and cinders skyward. The others sat in the car and sobbed bitterly at the loss of a great and gentle friend who died trying to save another. But their grief was interrupted when a heavy object landed atop Gustav's vehicle, denting his roof in considerably.

"What now?" Issues asked. He opened the passenger side door and a hand dropped down. After several hysterical screams, Gustav quickly stepped out of the car and could see a stunned Julie and an unconscious Tioni lying atop of his dented car" "Everybody quick you have to see this!" Gustav shouted excitedly, kissing his large, groggy, friend.

"How did you get here?" Rainbow asked Julie, the rest wanting to know the same thing.

"Something grabbed us and flew us here." Julie answered between coughs, as clueless about what happened as her friends."I kid you not."

"We can talk about this later, we're out of here," Gustav stated getting everyone back into the car and driving off.

25

4:19 a.m., South Hill Court

"Wow," Omari sighed, hanging up his cell phone. "That was Gustav. He said some weird stuff happened but everyone is okay. They will try to explain it later, and they are on their way here, with Jamilah and Tioni."

Hearing his cue, Yes grabbed his skateboard and headed for the door. Omari followed him to the curb outside. "How are you going to get home? Are you going to fly?" Omari joked.

"Actually, I had planned on skating down the hill then flying. But then maybe I won't wait that long," Yes replied with a smile.

"Why don't you just stay the night?" Omari insisted, wanting Yes to be there when everyone arrived.

"Honestly, if I could, I really would, but I really have to go to New Orleans for a few day. Tell everyone especially my dawg Dragonbrush, I said, what's up? I'm ghost," Yes said skating down the hill. Omari walked back into the house and then said to himself, go back and look, he ran to the corner and looked down the hill. Yes was nowhere in sight.

26

4:20 a.m., Omari's bedroom

When Omari re-entered the house and went upstairs to his bedroom, he spied Dragonbrush slipping through the window. Dragonbrush's body was covered with soot, and his sweats were charred and barely holding together. He looked at his wild looking friend stunned by his appearance.

"Let me tell you what happened," Dragonbrush said, ready to tell Omari everything.

"You saved the day didn't you? Everyone is just fine." Omari responded with a smile filled with exhaustion, Dragonbrush affirmed Omari's statement with a smile. "Good. Now take a shower, and I'm putting those clothes in the trash outside."

27

4:40 a.m., Tunnel Road

After being assured that both Julie and Tioni were alright and needed no medical attention, Issues and Rainbow drove Julie home. Gustav and Toyz took Jamilah and Tioni to Jamilah's.

"Is there a God or what?" Toyz asked Gustav still mesmerized at how Julie and Tioni were dropped atop Gustav's car.

"There's no God," Gustav replied drolly, "there's probably a dozen reasons why the two survived," he explained even though he was also at a lost as to how Julie and Tioni were delivered from the explosion.

"Even Julie said an angel saved her," Toyz challenged.

"Julie was suffering slightly from smoke inhalation and shock," Gustav parried.

"Well, I'm sure of two things tonight," Toyz added looking at the two unconscious teens in the back seat

"What's that?" Gustav asked.

"There is a God, and he doesn't like your car," he added trying to press up the large dent in the car.

"Don't be ridiculous," Gustav responded still smarting from the dent in his vehicle.

The two in the front heard a gurgling sound, the two looked back, and Tioni had vomited on the cars carpeted floor.

"Don't say a thing," Gustav cut Toyz off before he could open his mouth. "At least they're safe, if not in better condition than my car," he said with a sigh and continued toward their home.

Minutes later, he could again hear the sound of someone hurling. This time it was Jamilah vomiting on his vinyl seat.

"We are too close to their home to stop," Gustav said with frustration as they rolled the remaining windows down. "We'll just drop them off then hose the car out at the car wash, and please don't say that was an act of God!" Gustav groaned, pulling up to the Jackson's driveway.

"I don't have to," Toyz smirked, "God made it pretty clear, himself."

28

7:51 a.m., Jamilah's bedroom

After washing out the car, a few hours of sleep, some Red Bull and Peets coffee, Rainbow drove Gustav and Julie to South Hill Court. Issues followed in his own car. They would squeeze everyone into the two vehicles until they arrived at the trips meeting spot, the Malcolm X Youth Center. Toyz, who would not be attending the week long camping trip, would make sure that Gustav's prized possession would be as good as new when he returned. When Julie and Gustav arrived, Omari and Dragonbrush did not know what to say to the grim faced, black attired pair. They simply allowed them in and followed the two up the stairs into Jamilah's bedroom where a restless Jamilah was awake and Tioni was still asleep.

No one had spoken of the events from earlier that morning, but as she entered the bedroom, it was obvious that the exhausted, red eyed Julie was there to change that. Everyone present only partially knew what actually happened, but knew Tioni was central to a nearly fatal morning. The attractive teen awoke finding her friends standing over her.

"What are all of you looking at?" Tioni asked, "Oh, I have to get dressed!" she said excitedly then realized that her head and body ached. "Oooh," she said falling back on the bed. What happened?"

"You mean you don't remember anything about last night?" Julie asked.

"I remember leaving for another party with Coffy," Tioni thought aloud with an aching head. "But it was only supposed to be for a few minutes. And, I'm here so I guess it wasn't such a big deal," she said with little concern. Dragonbrush sensed the tension in the air growing.

"No big deal? Let me update you all on what happened last night." Julie trying to keep her temper in check. "You," she said staring at Jamilah, "Hooked up with a guy infected with AIDS who wants to use his remaining time on this planet infecting as many dummies as he can. And last night they didn't come much dumber than you." Jamilah started to make a comment to her massive friend when Julie said "What!" in a tone most intimidating.

"Nothing," Jamilah answered meekly.

Dragonbrush body began to tense at Julie's threatening tone and gestures toward Jamilah, his instincts were to protect her, but his logic told him to walk away.

"Where you going?" Omari whispered.

"I'll be back," the Pinoy answered, leaving the room.

"You walked out of your house then turned stupid," Julie continued at Jamilah. "Your fatal attraction last night could have changed your life in the worst way, and what were you doing dropping "E?" Weren't you told not to take anything from anyone! Are you so stupid now that you can't understand English?"

Jamilah turned to Omari, hoping he would say something in her defense, but Omari looked the other way.

"You can't talk to me like that!" Jamilah defended herself, standing up to the larger female.

"Yeah I can, and you're going to listen!" Julie said pushing Jamilah back on the bed with ease, "Now stay there and shut up!" She turned her attention to Tioni. "Jennifer told me that you were told over and over again to stay away from that sleazoid, Coffy and you left the club with him without telling anyone anyway?" Her volume had risen. "Let me tell you what happened, He drugged you, he took you to one of the most dangerous places in Oakland, and then his gang boss Glock tried to rape you. A fire broke out. To keep him from violating you, I got into a fight with him." Julie turned to the others and showed them her red bruise on her face. "Don't worry this will be gone in a few hours, his won't. But he did manage to trap the two of us in a small room where if it wasn't for some angel, we would have died in that fire. I certainly thought we would," she paused, "all because you had to go out with this loser!"

"Is that true?" she asked the shaken Jamilah before feeling the painful impact of Julie's open hand slap and instantly broke into tears. Omari looked over his shoulder, and Dragonbrush had returned.

"Don't do nothing," Omari whispered through gritted teeth.

"I'm not," he whispered back, with attitude.

"You don't ask her! You believe me!" Julie shouted. She leaned over the red face teen, Tioni's gray eyes filled with tears and hurt "And I'm telling you it happened. I am sick of you two! You have friends who love and care about you, willing to tell you what's right, and what do you do? You ignore them, so you can follow some cockroach who means you nothing but harm." She looked at her two red faced friends "I almost lost my life for you all, and I would do it again in a minute. But you better start acting like you have some sense, or I'll be the one to end it." She leaned over Tioni, "You pick the partner you will be with on this trip and you better stay in their sight the entire trip. Who will it be?" She demanded.

"Omari!" she said, sobbing louder.

"Then you better do what he says the whole time, now go take your shower and let's go have a good time." As she reached the door she turned to them and said "It's called tough love and sometimes we all need it," then stormed downstairs.

"You guys need to know she really cares about you." Gustav said apologizing for his friend

"Naw, don't even go there," Omari said interrupting Gustav. "Julie told the truth and she was right. Don't apologize for her, she didn't do wrong, she saved lives." Omari turned to the sobbing two, "We'll take your stuff downstairs."

29

7:53 a.m, Jamilah's bedroom, South Hill Court

Jamilah looked at Tioni, both humbled and hurt in front of their friends and family.

"Will you wait for me to get dressed" Tioni asked Jamilah.

"Sure," Jamilah nodded, feeling the shivers from her near brush with a monstrous disease.

Part 8

Lycanthrophy

The word "werewolf" comes from the word "were" meaning man.
The word literally means man-wolf. A word commonly used to describe werewolves is lycanthrope.
The word lycanthrope has a similar meaning (wolf-man) from two Greek words: lykos (wolf) and anthropos (man).

Source
http://www.dragon-warrior.com/Bestiary/werewolf.shtml

1

11:45 a.m., Yosemite National Park

"This is a first," Mildred Marshall, one of the four mini bus drivers and chaperones, commented on her snoozing passengers. "I've never had a van full of teens where everyone slept the entire 4 hour trip." Minutes inside the mini bus the teens were sound asleep, missing the opportunity to see some of the 250 awe-inspiring Giant Sequoias, the largest trees in the world, many, nearly 3,000 years old, standing more than 200 feet tall and 15 or more feet in diameter.

"My understanding is they all went out last night and arrived home only a few hours before we departed," Steven Wilkens head counselor who led the city sponsored trip for the past five years explained.

"Now I see why they all fought to ride in the same bus." Marshall observed.

Once the teens arrived at their cabins, they unpacked their things and went back to sleep.

2

1:02 p.m., Los Amore Vineyard, Home of Dr. Flora Rodriguez,

When Jennifer opened her eyes, she was realized that she was not home, nor was she at Jamilah's or Tioni's. Then she remembered arriving at home and calling Flora who picked her up at 7:00 a.m. and brought her to her house. Once Jennifer was escorted to her guest room, she immediately crashed. She remembered watching haplessly as bullets almost claimed Omari's life, only to be saved by a vampire. If Yes hadn't intervened, Jennifer wondered if she would have joined the vampires. That thought created an avalanche of questions, *how did Yes find me? How did he know we would be at the Night Crawler event? How did he know to bump*

Dragonbrush and me with his skateboard? What happened with Dragonbrush and me? If I'm associated with vampires, is Dragonbrush now associated with werewolves? Then she realized that everyone had left for camp and would be gone for a week. Jennifer then questioned if calling Flora was a good idea. *What does a doctor for vampires do?* There were many questions that Jennifer knew needed answers to. She resolved the best way to immediately address them, was not to. With that, she slammed her head back into the pillow and went back to sleep.

3

2:02 p.m., Housekeeping Camp, Yosemite Valley

Dragonbrush's nose wrinkled again, picking up the faint scent of a bear, miles away, and several squirrels and a possum in the vicinity watching him. A lone wolf had marked the territory where he stood, but it was Dragonbrush's now. The teen hiked several miles from the campsite, the further he journeyed, the greater he enjoyed it. For Dragonbrush, the woods felt so right, No cars or reminders of civilization, only the sweet sounds and smells of nature. The Filipino teen untied his braid, and his hair dropped to his shoulders. He removed his shoes and socks and let his toenails scratch the soil. His clothing felt heavy and burdensome, and he felt a great need to remove them in order to hunt. But his inner voice told him otherwise. This was the same inner voice that told him to jump into a burning building to save his friends when his instincts told him otherwise. The voice was smart, and he trusted it. It was now telling him to join the others before they became worried. He would go back, but first, he had to mark his territory.

4

5:02 p.m., Housekeeping Camp, Yosemite Valley

It was early evening when Jamilah raised from her bunk looking at the dark clouds above; it was obvious that it would rain at any second. Despite the weather, the teens at the campsite were actively engaged in activities, archery, baseball, swimming and hiking. Each activity seemed interesting but Jamilah didn't feel like participating in any.

It wasn't the dark clouds that overshadowed Jamilah's mood, or even feeling out of sorts after taking the drug *Ectasy,* but the morning's events. Even though Jamilah was deeply hurt and angered at how Julie had humiliated her and Tioni in front of the others, she had to accept that it was their actions that brought about Julie's reaction. Jamilah painfully acknowledged that she chose to separate herself from her friends at the party in order slip off with a stranger. She took drugs offered to her and was open to a one night stand with a sick and angry man who wanted to dole out death sentences. Julie saved them and was angry that she had to do it. Despite her current feelings, Jamilah was grateful to have Julie as a friend. She had to find Julie and set things right. She spotted Mildred Marshall, and asked, "Have you seen, Julie?"

"They went up the hill," she said noticing that global warming was producing unseasonable rain fall. "They were all going to cook tofu burgers for any vegetarian interested, though with this weather I don't see them staying out too long."

"Oh." Jamilah responded, feeling the heavy drops of rain beginning to tap her on the head while wondering what she should do.

5

5:17p.m., Housekeeping Camp, Yosemite Valley

"Can you believe this, Rain in late July?" Tioni noted to Omari as the two sat on the porch of the old rustic cabin watching the campers run for cover from the sudden rain. The campground was quickly becoming wet and muddy.

Normally, Omari found Tioni annoying, but knew that he needed to be supportive. Even if she was stupid and decided to run with the worst folks in the hood, Tioni didn't deserve what happened to her. It was obvious she was beating herself up for allowing it to happen, even if she couldn't remember much of it. But Omari didn't know how many more of her crying spells he could take. The rain began falling harder, and even those who endured the light rainfall were now running for cover. Omari felt Tioni's braided head lean against his shoulder. He instinctively placed his arm around her.

"I'm really sorry for what I did. You know that don't you?" her voice crackling.

"You need to tell that to Julie and Jennifer" Omari assured her in a comforting voice thinking he should text Jennifer and Makemba.

"I can't because they hate me, especially Julie. She almost died trying to save me." Pausing she asked, "If I would have died, do you think I would have gone to hell? I mean, I drank, I lied and I was out with the wrong crowd. I did everything everyone told me to not do. Plus I would have been responsible for killing Julie." She became emotional, "I would have burned in hell forever."

"Tioni, look at me," Omari said, seeing where Tioni's emotions were leading. "God didn't want you to go to hell. If he did, then you wouldn't be here talking about it. Okay?"

"You're right," she said astounded by the revelation, "Why is that?"

"Because you are a good person, you didn't try to hurt anyone. You need to remember it was your prayers that helped us save Jennifer from the vampires. God knows that."

Tears began to trickle down her eyes after hearing Omari's words, "Thank you Omari." She said with gratitude, placing both of her arms around him, "I really needed to hear that."

"Of course God doesn't want you to be stupid anymore either." Omari added.

"I know that," she said acknowledging her rash decision. "Why isn't Jennifer here?"

"She got really sick at the party last night" Omari responded seeing no need to upset Tioni further. "But she's alright."

"Was it my fault that she got sick?" Tioni asked tears slipping down her face.

"No, it wasn't your fault," Omari reassured her. Placing his arm around her, Omari looked out into the rain and thought to himself, *this is so not the camping trip that I planned.*

6

5:19 p.m. Housekeeping Camp, Yosemite Valley

"Who looks silly in a pea coat in the woods now?" Gustav mocked the group, his trade mark black pea coat allowing him to grill undauntedly in the rain. Refusing to allow the rain to ruin their meatless barbeque, Julie, Gustav, Rainbow and Issues stretched a plastic poncho between two heavily branched trees and commenced to start a fire on the grill under the dry shelter

"Gussie, you never look silly and you know that." Julie cajoled.

Gustav watched the front that Julie was putting up, but it was obvious to those who knew her, that she was still upset from the events earlier that day. They could all take solace that with the exception of the years that were taken from Gustav's life when he saw the enormous dent on his roof. No one was seriously hurt. Still, the most disturbing part of the morning could not be explained. It was like a splinter in his mind, *how did Julie and Tioni escape the inferno?* Julie maintains that someone or something grabbed them, and flew them from the room where they were trapped, landing atop his car. Julie said it happened as fast as her first ride on a rollercoaster. When she woke up this morning, the hardest part was realizing that what happened was not a dream. Unfortunately, Julie felt responsible for what happened, and that was for bringing Jamilah and Tioni in the first place. But Jamilah and Tioni also had to own up to their part in what happened if the friendship between the three was going to last. Gustav also knew that despite Julie's outburst earlier, she was hurt and would sulk and suffer in silence. Gustav looked at his black clad friend and smiled. She tries to be tough, but on the inside she was fluff.

"Why is it, that no matter what campsite you go to, the toilets is disgusting." Rainbow added still not fully wake. In well worn jeans and a khaki colored shirt, the thin male with the flock of dark blonde hair looked less his street name and more like *Joe Average*.

"I don't know," Julie said smiling as the coals on the grill were warm enough to cook the first round of tofu patties and dogs. "Maybe when people get out in the woods how clean the toilets are isn't one of the priorities that determine whether or not they camp."

"I bet it is when its time for them to go." Gustav added flipping the patties, while getting soaked.

"When you have to go bad enough, you'll be glad just to see the little shed with a crescent moon on the door" Julie said lifting a sizzling dog from the grill then quickly placing it in a bun.

"I was googling *Outhouses*," Issues added to the conversation also looking out of place in Khaki shorts and a white Rasputin, t-shirt, his dark blue parka doing little to protect his heavily moussed, black, hair from the rain.

"What's the matter? You don't know the codes to remove the parental block on your computer?" Rainbow jested.

"Oh be quiet," Issued responded "Anyway this guy named *Bruce Carlson* wrote a book called *Iowa's Vanishing Outhouse* In the book he says, "The history of the quarter-moon on the door of the outhouse goes way back. Most serious historians who are students of the subject are of the opinion that the custom started in Europe in the 1500s or the 1600s. It was common practice, back then, to identify which outhouse was which, by means of a circular symbol on the door of the men's and a quarter-moon on the ladies. The use of symbols rather than words was necessary due to the widespread illiteracy of the times. When a *feller* can't read and is headed for the outhouse, he sure doesn't need some incomprehensible hieroglyphics on the door to figure out. The circular symbol and the quarter-moon were Europe's version of the Chinese Yin and Yang. The Union was representative of the sun, which symbolized masculinity. The more subdued and submissive moon, on the other hand, represented femininity. The use of the Union and quarter-moon was especially common at inns and houses for lodging. Not only was illiteracy a problem, but also the clientele of such places were more likely to be travelers from another country and spoke another language. These universal signs were easy to make and easy to "read", so most places had the little houses out back designated, one with a circular sign, and one with the quarter-moon. So why is the quarter-moon applied in more recent times to outhouses in general? The answer, to that apparently lies in the economics of maintaining outhouses, if one of the outhouses at an inn, were to have fallen into a state of disrepair".

"What's disrepair?" Rainbow asked, "When the pit finally fills up?"

"Don't even dignify that with a response," Julie added rolling her eyes at Rainbow.

"As I was saying before I was so grossly interrupted, when a *crapper* fell into a state of disrepair, the inn's keepers rationale was that a man could always just find a tree but, for females, that was not an option.

"And it's still not," Julie added.

"So whichever outhouse left standing received the door with the quarter-moon on it.

This practice became so widespread that in many cases, only a women's outhouse would be available to those who frequented such public places. Since those carried the quarter-moon, that symbol soon evolved into the sign for any outhouse in general, rather than one for ladies only."

"You know why?" Gustav added, "Because guys started using it anyway." The conversation was interrupted by the sound of a familiar voice cursing as they slipped in the mud. They all looked up and could see a poncho covered, Jamilah making her way toward them.

Gustav noticed Julie tense up as she came closer, "You want a tofu dog?" he offered.

"I like real hotdogs," she said walking toward Julie who turned away from her. Jamilah stood by her larger friend then bumped into her. Julie ignored it. The others were fascinated by the interaction between the two and what it promised. Jamilah stood next to her for a few more seconds and bumped into her again. Julie maintained her stoic visage. Then Jamilah leaned over and kissed her on the cheek. "Thanks for everything. I'm glad you worry about me." Jamilah then bumped into her again which was met by a bump of Julie's.

"Are you smarter now than you were then?" Julie asked.

"I'm here saying I'm sorry, what do you think?" She answered with a typical smirk.

"Far as we know," Rainbow added, "You could be here trying to steal one of our tofu dogs."

Jamilah opened her backpack and pulled out a plastic bag, "I just happen to have stolen some real meat hot dogs from the freezer." Taking them out of the plastic bag she proclaimed, "This is going to be cool." When Jamilah placed her two hotdogs on the steaming grill, her hot dogs rolled and knocked one of the tofu dogs into the fire and the other onto the muddy ground. "Oops" she said witnessing the loss of two tofu dogs. "Sorry guys," she said with embarrassment.

"Don't worry Jamilah," Julie said with a laugh, as the rain continued to soak the group "They're only tofu dogs, nothing to lose a good friendship over."

7

6:02 p.m., Highway 41 from Fresno, CA

"John you need to slow down. This road is too slippery," Officer Anthony Meadows warned his partner Officer John Towner of the rain, the narrow roads and the sharp turns.

The two had driven to Fresno to bring Telma Simmons and Louisa Fletcher back to Hayward to be arraigned for the kidnap and murder of a local Hayward businessman.

"Stop your whining," John replied, his words filled with confidence as he careened around the blind curves, ten miles faster than the posted twenty-five mile speed limit. "This baby is handling like a dream" he referenced the police issued Crown Victoria that seemed to move with his every thought. "How are you gals doing in the back?" He asked fully aware that ever sharp turn tossed his handcuffed prisoners from the seat to the floor.

"You and your gay lover can both go to hell!" the stocky brunette shouted as she was tossed over her partner in crime. Telma Simmons and Louisa Fletcher met in Fontera State Prison a year ago even though the name had been changed to the California Institute for Women. The two found they had three things in common: a history of violence, theft, and a bitter hatred for the law and its representatives. Co-incidentally, they were released during the same month, when they joined up they went on a crime spree robbing banks from L.A. to Silicon Valley.

In the City of Hayward, the two, kidnapped a Silicon Valley Software Executive, demanding one hundred thousand dollars. When the executive's family contacted the authorities instead of negotiating with the kidnappers, Telma and Louisa executed the businessman and left for Reno where they were apprehended at a Burger King drive through shortly after America's Most Wanted did a feature on them.

"You first" John responded accelerating the police car, sending the two females painfully face first into the bullet proof partition that separated the driver from the passengers.

"Slow this car down right now!" Anthony demanded, no longer amused by his partner's recklessness. Anthony looked at the partition and could see blood on it, and didn't know if it was from a bloody lip or a busted nose. "See what you did!" Anthony shouted, taking John's attention from the road to windshield, just when the car should have turned. The police car missed a sharp turn, sending it down a slippery hill, crashing into young trees, and ancient rocks, flipping over three times until it forcefully crashed on the road below.

When the car came to a complete halt, Louisa lifted her foot and painfully kicked the glass that separated the prisoners from the officers, "You dumb ass, hick! You could have killed us!" Louisa shouted as her foot slammed against the cracked window. She noticed the blood on the windshield and realized that both of the officers were unconscious or dead. She turned to Telma and asked, "Are you alive?"

"Yeah, why don't you try kicking the door instead of the window?" Telma answered, bringing Louisa attention to the lower part of her side door car that had greatly broke open as it slammed into trees and rocks. With several solid kicks, Louisa and Telma were able to force the pried door wide enough to escape. After a struggle, they were able to obtain the keys to their handcuffs from the unconscious officers, and their guns. When the duo was twenty feet away from the accident, Telma looked at Louisa and said, "Watch this." She fired a bullet into John's unconscious head.

"That ain't nuthin," Louisa replied, firing her stolen gun into the gas tank watching the car lift from the ground after its explosion.

"I guess we'll be walking," Telma smirked, looking around the familiar area.

"Yeah, but we're still in better shape than them." Louisa laughed.

8

6:02 p.m., Los Amore Vineyard

The day had gone by when Jennifer finally got out of bed. The Vietnamese teen expected her stay to be restrictive with Flora keeping her under lock and key, constantly bombarding her with difficult and personal questions. On the contrary, Jennifer was allowed to walk freely throughout the large eight room house without question. Jennifer found the doctor in her office placing papers in her file cabinet. Flora asked Jennifer was she ready to talk? Jennifer wasn't.

"When you're ready, I'm ready." Flora replied and went about her daily activities of seeing clients without disturbing the teen. The only time Flora approached Jennifer was to ask if she "wanted to eat dinner in or out." The two went out for gourmet pizza.

9

6:04 p.m., Oakland City Jail

"So Leo Lieberman finally got up off his ass and showed up so a brother could get out of jail," Slimstyle smiled as Glock gripped his hand followed by Coffy.

"I hate them damn lawyers," Glock grimaced.

"So what up now?" Slimstyle followed Glock and Coffy outside to the parking lot where a shiny Black Ford Ranger waited.

"The punks that put you in jail and hurt a couple of our folks all went camping," Coffy spoke. "We know where they are, and how to get them." Glock opened the back door of the vehicle, and there were rifles with scopes and night goggles. He looked at Slimstyle and said, "Go home and get yourself together. Tomorrow we're going hunting for Dragon."

10

9:02 p.m., Housekeeping Camp, Yosemite Valley

With the exception of water dropping from rain soaked trees landing lightly on the moist soil and the occasional sound of a lone wolf howling in the distance outside was eerily silent. The sudden rain had come and gone, but dark clouds remained threatening to throw another of nature's curveball, in the form of more summertime rain. The end of the first day was celebrated with a traditional evening campfire, s'mores, veggie kabobs and ghost stories. Camp leader, Steven Wilkens with his deep, aching, voice was a master storyteller. Wilkens could spin tales that were hard to tell if they were truth, fiction or both. In the damp darkness a scary story made for great entertainment.

Moving his illuminated arms dramatically, the animated speaker held the teens and chaperones captive, as bits of firewood snapped, crackled and popped before them. The ground was wet and slippery from the rains, so everyone sat on plastic squares cut from an unused tarp.

"Did you hear that?" Steven shouted, startling both staff and teens. "It's so easy for the mind to say, oh that's just a dumb ole' wolf. But in the woods, on a damp, sinister night like this, one evening shy of the full moon, who really knows if it is indeed just a wolf or perhaps something more! The myth of a human that transforms into a terrifying beast is found in most cultures. Usually the animal is the most fearsome of the local predators: Africans change into leopards; Peruvian natives turn into jaguars; in India one becomes a tiger; Russians shift into bears; the Chinese have both were-foxes and were-tigers. Our Western disposition to fearing the wolf is derived from the folklore of Scandinavia and southern and eastern Europe, where the wolf was a threat particularly to the poor."

As if on cue, the wolf howled again followed by the sound of another further in the distance, causing the group to huddle closer together

"In folklore and superstition, a human being that has changed or been changed into a wolf, or is capable of assuming the form of a wolf, while retaining human intelligence are referred to as werewolves. In mythology werewolves are entities that are human, but they shape shift into animal form during certain lunar aspects, which affects their DNA. As rulers of the wilds, the werewolf has no peers. The bear, cougar and wolverine the great eagle, and hawks are nothing more than a meal for them, even in the Artic, it is rumored that the werewolf hunts polar bears and killer whales to sate its hunger." Looking at the group of teens with fingers sticky from s'mores Steven whispered, "You folks would be nothing but a snack for a ravenous werewolf." There was another howl in the clearing and other counselors were starting to wonder.

"I hope no one has to got to the outhouse," Steven said with large grin his wide eyes reflecting the flames from the fire. "There are three classifications of werewolf.' The first is Lycanthropic Disorder, Lycanthropic Disorder is the clinical term for most cases of supposed werewolfry, the victims suffer a mental disorder and nothing more," Steven explained. The person suffering from this malady believing they're werewolves will respond to the full moon in different ways, howling at the moon, exhibiting aggressive and sometimes dangerous behavior. Hospital workers dread the full moon because as a result of it, they have to deal with a lot of people who believe that they are not themselves, but animals.

"Is jail another name for the kennel that holds folks that act out on the full moon?" Issues asked, to the giggles of many. Steven was tempted to add a humorous comment to Issue's, but with tongue in cheek chose not to. "The second type of werewolf is a Genetic Mutation".

"Like the X-men?" one of the younger teens asked.

"Yeah, just like the X-men," Steven responded trying to bring the spirit of the macabre back to his story,

"In Guadalajara, Mexico, at the Center of Biomedical Research, Dr. Luis Figuera a geneticist is studying a Mexican family with a rare genetic mutation that causes fur like hair to grow all over their bodies. This werewolf disorder has mysteriously resurfaced for the first time since the middle ages.

"Are you saying that during the middle ages everyone was covered with hair," Gustav asked

"No." Steven answered Gustav, "But the disorder was first recognized during that period which may have contributed to the werewolf legend. The gene that causes the mutation lay dormant for centuries. It can be passed through either parent in the "X" chromosome. This is known as the "Werewolf Disorder."

"Hey Gustav?" Rainbow cracked, "doesn't your mama have that disorder?" Gustav lifted his kabob between his middle fingers and showed it to his friend.

Ignoring the two, Steven continued, "The third and best known is when the physical change to wolf form does occur. The change can be voluntary or can be forced by certain cycles of the moon, like the full moon tomorrow," He laughed in an unnerving way.

There are several ways to become a werewolf. The most common is being bitten by one. The victim's blood becomes tainted or cursed, and undergoes a complete transformation from a civilized human, to a beast that reacts only to its own primal urges." The howling continued in the background, as if the wolf was aware of the conversation.

"It is a rarity that you will find werewolves in the city because it does not provide the space for them to move about freely," Dragonbrush felt uncomfortable with the tone of story and hoped Steven would get around to telling regular ghost stories. The group's eyes followed Steven's head as he searched around through the clouded darkness as if he was looking for something in particular. "You know, they could be watching us and plotting against us as we speak." Steven said in a muffled voice that forced the group to lower their heads to clearly hear him.

"Who?" One of the younger teens asked.

"The werewolves," He answered speaking louder and more clearly, "A werewolf is not just a true wolf while in wolf form. There is some proof that the werewolf retains enough knowledge to assist his killing. Recognition of victims, evasion of traps and human cunning is all documented in werewolf cases. Werewolves are immune from aging and from most physical diseases due to the constant regeneration of their physical tissue. They can therefore, be virtually immortal. It is hard to imagine that a dog so old would not have picked up a few new tricks along the way."

"They could be brilliant!" Julie added, not familiar with werewolf lore, but fascinated by the information.

"Like real wolves, werewolves can live alone for many years, yet the instinct for a pack often leads them away from their secretive lifestyle, into confessing their nature to a priest or close associate. This is when the otherwise cagey werewolf opens himself to detection."

Omari looked across the bonfire and could see that Steven's words were hitting Dragonbrush like silver bullets. Another howl interrupted Steven.

"Werewolf packs cause immense destruction. A pack consists of one werewolf who became a werewolf through sorcery, birth, or curse - in other words; his is the original tainted blood. This werewolf is called the Alpha werewolf.

The remaining werewolves in the pack are called Beta werewolves because they became werewolves through the bite of the Alpha, and they carry the Alpha's tainted blood.

"How do you kill a werewolf?" One youth asked. Jamilah noticed Dragonbrush tense up. She walked over and sat beside him, causing Tioni to roll her eyes.

"Some common myths on destroying a werewolf are that they can be killed by any wound that destroys the heart or the brain, or any form of death that causes brain or heart damage such as hanging."

"Great, they only hang werewolves and black people" Omari scoffed.

"Some folks get no love," Steven smiled "But hanging or a blow to the head or heart of a werewolf may be all myths. The only sure way to slay a werewolf is with silver, but research indicate that the best way to destroy a werewolf is while it's in human form and noticing changes in the would be werewolf's personality. Therefore, look for symptoms in your human suspects that include increased violence, increasing aggression, unprovoked rages, insomnia, restlessness, and other bizarre behavior."

"How do you know that the person that exhibiting that behavior is not mentally ill?" Gustav asked.

"Or on crack? Issues asked.

"Or suffering from PMS?" Rainbow offered.

"Or a bad hair day?" another added.

"You don't!" Steven answered, with a maniacal laugh. The wolf howl in the background made his exaggerated amusement all the more disturbing.

"Anyone that confesses to killing a werewolf will spend the rest of their lives in an insane asylum, and anyone that mistakenly kills the wrong person will spend the rest of their lives in jail looking over their shoulder wondering when the werewolves will seek revenge." Steven said with a grim expression. "Getting bitten by a werewolf is the worst thing that could happen to a person, because once you are bitten, then your fate is set forever" Steven let the howl in the night, and the crackling of the burning wood to allow his words to seep into the minds of teens gathered around him.

Omari walked from his spot and sat on the other side of Dragonbrush. Without looking at Jamilah and Omari on both sides of him, Dragonbrush relaxed and felt safe.

"I've told you what I have researched, now let me tell you all what I believe." Steven said, looking gravely, "I believe life deals you the hand you are given, but it's your choices that determine how you will play the game. Every life has to face some unspeakable evil, some greater than others, some more often that others and some longer than others. In life there are also things which we cannot explain. But, we must be assured that there is a greater good to address that great evil, and staying true to it will save us from that evil and lead us out of the unknown.

"You make it sound like a werewolf doesn't have to be a werewolf," Jamilah stated.

"I'm saying that human spirit is a greater force than can ever be imagined," Steven said flatly wanting his words to sink in. "We all have primal urges, but we are not bound to them, we have the power of choice and an independent will to ensure that our decisions are carried out. Choosing to do evil is an individual's choice, and it won't happen if the individual doesn't want it to." Steven stood up before the crowd stretching his limbs "Never forget how powerful you are. Ever!" He turned to his left, whistled and another counselor stepped out of the darkness with a boom box wrapped in plastic. When the group looked at him, he pressed the play button on the box and the sound of a wolf howling emitted from the speakers.

"Awww man, you was messing with us," Omari echoed the sentiment of the others.

" Yeah, me and Paul came out here a couple of weeks ago and were able to record these wolves to add to the sound effect," Steven said with a smile that was emblazoned by the fire. "But, I hope you all got the gist of my story. Now let's gets some sleep because tomorrow is the big hike.

11

9:32 p.m. Housekeeping Camp, Yosemite Valley

"I thought you could understand what dogs were saying when they barked?" Omari asked Dragonbrush as they headed back to their cabin.

"I can," Dragonbrush answered.

"Then why didn't you know that Steven was just playing a boom box with recorded sounds of wolves howling?" Omari pressed.

"I did," he answered nervously.

"Then why were you tripping? For a minute, I was getting nervous." Omari confessed.

"Because I was scared," Dragonbrush fired back.

"Scared of what?" Omari asked beginning to feel nervous by Dragonbrush's behavior.

"Steven didn't know it, but what were recorded were actual werewolves, and they were talking" he said in a disturbed tone.

"What were they saying?" Omari asked, spooked by Dragonbrush's response.

"Join us," he answered.

"What does that mean?" Omari asked.

"I don't know," Dragonbrush answered with concern. "But, there are a lot of werewolves out here, and I don't know what to do."

12

9:39 p.m., Housekeeping Camp, Yosemite Valley

"You knew he would be here?" Lexus asked Sandia impressed by his fore-knowledge as they stood on a ridge overlooking the camp ground, able to pick up the scents of all of the campers but Dragonbrush's in particular, even after the fresh rain.

"Some things are meant to be. You must accept that, and soon, so will he." The large, wolf answered, before joining the others in the pack leaving Maria and Lexus. The two continued to watch with sad hearts, having given up their home, clothing, music and other belongings. Their future would be spent roaming in the woods with the other wolves and everything about their lives would be forgotten.

Until this point, the two had been unwilling to accept their fate, but now they had to come to grips that their wants and desires really didn't matter, The dye had been cast, and their fates as werewolves had been sealed, but maybe the words of the campfire leader was possible, Lexus hoped.

13

Sunday, July 28th, 1:39 a.m., Unknown, Yosemite Valley

The two convicts moved deeper into the woods, slipping every so often from the mud and moist leaves, rarely speaking, instead listening closely for the sounds of sirens, dogs and helicopters. A manhunt that would begin once the two Hayward officers failed to arrived with the convicts. The rain and muddy ground worked to their advantage making it harder for the dogs to track them. When the two felt they were relatively safe, they built a shelter underneath thick trees with fallen branches and built a fire. Shortly after, Telma lucked out and killed a slow moving possum.

"How do you know so much about this area?" Louisa asked, asked as they prepared to eat their dinner on a tribal rotisserie. Louisa Mixon, a stocky thirty-seven year old woman standing 5 feet and 7 inches tall, her face worn from hard drinking and drug use, she lost her two front teeth in a bar fight and kept her dark blond hair cut short. Despite living in California for the past 17 years, her Missouri drawl remained.

"My folks were in the militia. They believed that one day when the Government went to hell that it would be smart to retreat to the woods where the battle could be even," Telma explained turning over the skinned rodent. Telma Richards had spent 14 of her forty-three years of life behind bars for crimes ranging from forgery, identity theft, to bank robberies. Her longest stretch was getting caught in a sting set up by *Alcohol and Tobacco and Firearms* trying to purchase military issued guns.

Telma stood at 5 feet 6 inches tall but her swagger made her seem larger. She was lean, mean and resourceful. Telma's petite frame was primarily muscle from countless sit ups and push ups. Her face was drawn, her steal blue eyes extremely observant, and her dark stringy hair was heavily laced with gray streaks   "I know this area like the back of my hand. We will need to lay low down here for a couple of days until the media is no longer hyped about the death of two pork bellied officers. Then we're home free."

14

7:37 a.m., Housekeeping Camp, Yosemite Valley, Full moon

What!" Omari yelled defiantly before opening his sleep filled eyes at Dragonbrush's relentless shaking,

"I want to carve some tags on a few trees and need you to come with me," Dragonbrush insisted, excited about getting back out into the woods.

"It's wet outside." Omari moaned, placing the pillow over his head trying to block the sun out his eyes and Dragonbrush out his mind.

"I know, that means it will be easier to tag the trees." He said with a cheery voice. He looked at Omari who was returning to sleep and said glumly, playing on Omari's sympathetic heart, "I can't be out there with no one covering my back."

"Do you guys ever think about me?" Omari stressed as he threw off the covers revealing the black hoodie and sweat he slept in. He walked over and looked through his shoe bag for his Timberland boots.

"I am thinking about you," Dragonbrush smiled pulling out two hammers and chisels.

15

8:15 a.m., Unknown, Highway 41, Yosemite Valley

Telma led the city bred Louisa from the thick of the woods, closer to the road. They knew the police would be looking for them, but there was always the chance that they would be able to carjack their way out of the area before the authorities became the wiser. So, they wandered, trying to stay out of sight, waiting for the opportunity to pounce on an unwary driver.

16

8:32 a.m., Unknown, Yosemite Valley

Dog in, dogged out
Foaming at the mouth because your logic's off its route
And you're scratching your tail trying to figure it all out
Giving up your sanity, losing your humanity, amazing how what you had so long can be taking away instantly
Rage reveal your true beast
Death and self destruction is what you unleash
Master yourself using logic as a leash.
Or hate will cause your will and dreams to cease

Hoping the lyrics could provide some insight into Dragonbrush's plight, Omari and Dragonbrush listened to the lyrics on their iPods as they used their hammers, chisels and carving tools to chip away the bark from a fallen thirty-foot pine, in order to carve their imprints.

After carving into two standing and one fallen tree, Omari and Dragonbrush hiked further up the trail to a large rock that provided an arresting view of the forest

"Man doing rocks are even harder than trees. When we finish this, we're heading back." Omari said to the nodding Dragonbrush, "Now I see why taggers just Krylon rocks, all of this carving is hard."

"I didn't know how bad Krylon was for the environment just smelling it makes me sick." Dragonbrush responded becoming nauseous just thinking about it, "but its funny, even animals tag." Dragonbrush said to the clueless Omari. "I know you can't smell it, but every animal leaves its scent on rocks trees and bushes so other animals will know that they were there."

"I guess even animals want to be remembered." Omari responded understanding that animals marked their trails. Omari looked at the natural arrangement of the great outdoors and agreed the forest was no place for statements made from shiny cans with small metal balls inside them.

"What do you think is going to happen tonight?" Dragonbrush asked hoping the older teen could offer some insights.

"I don't know, but tonight is the full moon, I guess we'll see." Omari answered unsure if a werewolf transformation was even possible. "How do you feel?"

"You know out here it smells and feels right." Dragonbrush answered looking for the words to describe his excitement about being outdoors. "Out here I do what I want to do and not have to worry about the police fining my parents for tagging," "There are no gangs out here that are fighting for no reason, nor are there parents stressing you." Omari watched as Dragonbrush removed his shoes and socks and stood unfettered by the pine needles, pebbles, twigs and branches underneath his feet. "Here I am free,"

"What are you doing?" Omari asked Dragonbrush who seemed suddenly pre-occupied by something Omari could not see.

"This!" Dragonbrush shouted, then leapt from the rock and dashed down the hill where a great buck suddenly appeared and was startled by Dragonbrush. Instead of fleeing the massive deer charged headlong at Dragonbrush its antlers capable of rending him into small pieces if they impaled him. Grabbing the buck's antlers Dragonbrush forced the great beast, head down and deftly leaped across its back. The great beast fought savagely to throw the teen off before dashing into the woods with Dragonbrush still atop its back. Omari could only watch stupefied.

17

8:37 a.m. Housekeeping Camp, Yosemite Valley

After a late breakfast, Tioni and a listless Jamilah sat outside of their cabin back to back atop a camping table, talking on their phones and listening to their iPods. Electronic devices were not allowed on camping trips primarily for liability issues, but the rule was rarely enforced.

"What do you think ever happened to Tyrone?" Tioni asked out of the blue, about the vampire she dated and whom she suspected Jamilah was dating also.

"You know, I don't know." Jamilah answered, giving Tioni's question minimal consideration as she looked at her phone "I hope he's alright." She turned to Tioni and changed the subject. "Girl friend, I could see you being sprung on Tyrone, but what was the big deal with Coffy?"

"I was so stupid," Tioni confessed. "When I met him at the party, I didn't plan to leave without telling you all. It all got to moving too fast when I was scared for my life at the other party. I know one thing," she paused looking at the baby oil in her purse. I never want to see him again".

"Why did you ask about Tyrone out of the blue" Jamilah asked, bringing the subject back.

"It just seems to me that taking things that belong to others doesn't' bother you."

"Did I take something of yours?" Jamilah asked, knowing this moment would arrive.

"I think you know the answer to that better than I do," Tioni replied with equal edge.

"If I did anything to hurt you, I'm sorry, okay."

"Okay," Tioni answered thankful for the breakthrough.

"But I resent you saying I don't care about anyone's feelings because it's not true." Jamilah said irritably.

"It is true," Tioni insisted. "You took Tyrone and Dragonbrush from me."

"I'll admit I did talk to Tyrone. I was wrong for doing it and apologize for it, but Dragonbrush, give me a break. He's like Omari's little brother; he's like my little brother. That's it, that's all."

"Then why are you keeping him from me?" Tioni demanded.

"You are so full of it!" Jamilah turned and matched her fury. "You don't call or come by like you used to, but you want to blame me because things are the way they are."

"That's because he only wants to be around you," Tioni replied with tears welling in her eyes

"No, you said that I was keeping him away from you. There's not one place I've gone with that squirt that you couldn't have joined if you would have just asked. You know why you haven't asked? Because you were too busy hating me for being with him,"

"That's not true!" Tioni argued knowing otherwise.

"More bull! As of the last couple of weeks, all you've been doing is walking around giving attitude. Have you once said anything to me about Dragon? Have you?" Jamilah charged her silent friend "Not one word! In fact, I bet that the only reason why you were interested in that glob of snot Coffy was because you thought it might piss us off?"

Tioni turned to Jamilah with her mouth open, "My God you are so right!" she said to the revelation.

"Girlfriend, you talk about everyone. But are you talking to them?"

"I guess not." Tioni answered, thinking of the weeks that she had spent resenting Jamilah, but never actually talking to her. "But, it's something that I'm going to start doing."

"Good," Jamilah answered, happy for the breakthrough.

18

8:45 a.m., Unknown, Yosemite Valley

After seeing Dragonbrush's new found abilities first hand, Omari never questioned the outcome of Dragonbrush's challenge to the buck. While waiting for him to return, Omari parked himself on the tree where he and Dragonbrush carved their tags and fired up a joint. In between puffs, Omari wondered how much Dragonbrush would continue to change. "Whoa," Omari coughed, Dragonbrush rode the buck back from the clearing toward him. Omari was mesmerized as Dragonbrush leaned forward near the beast's ear, and seemed to talk to it, as they rode closer and closer until they stood in front of Omari.

"I know you don't want to walk back," Dragonbrush said looking down at Omari.

"You want me to get on that?" Omari asked, his head buzzing from the weed.

"Yeah and hurry, it's fighting me," he said restraining the beast by applying pressure to its neck and antlers.

"Then why am I trying to get on it?" Omari questioned his own actions as he mounted the buck and it begrudgingly, carried them off.

19

9:32 a.m., 63rd and Foothill Blvd, Oakland

"This is straight harassment, ya heard?" Glock vented as he, Slimstyle, Coffy and Shady assumed the position on the side of the Sergeant Bight's squad car.

"Yeah, some brothers want to drive around town trying to stay out of trouble and the police bring it to them." Slimstyle voiced, echoing Glock's sentiment.

"This is just a driving while Black thang," Coffy argued.

"As long as your name is Glock, Slimstyle and Coffy, you getting my love, ya understand?" Sergeant Bright said in dirty south slang. "It wouldn't matter if you were white, Catholic and female. I would still harass you."

"Ha hah" Glock fired back "Well you ain't going to find nothing, so I will be expecting an apology."

"I don't find anything I will be one happy camper." Bright responded, looking under the seats of the vehicle "So far, so good, You fella's are restoring my faith in mankind," he said with a smile, "I heard there was a three alarm fire at Old G Club the other night, you wouldn't have been anywhere near there?" he asked.

"We were on this side of town the other night, right? Glock answered, the others nodded in agreement.

"You trying to link us to a fire at our own place?" Shady asked with feigned anger.

"That's the investigators job, not mine." Bright answered calmly. "Personally, I bet a match fell to an alcohol covered floor and some of you geniuses tried to put it out by throwng more alcoholic drinks on it and set the place ablaze."

"You must think we stupid? Slimstyle asked unaware of how right the Sergeant was.

Bright noticed Justin and Edwin driving by in the same car he stopped Justin in the other night, and remembered what he had to do. He turned to the three and said, "You stay out of trouble, and I'm calling your parole officers. So, you better check in with him," he got into his car and sped off.

"My P.O. is with your Mama, white boy!" Glock yelled, aware that Bright couldn't hear him.

"I'm surprised he didn't say anything about finding any bodies in the building?" Glock asked, aware that he left Tioni and Jennifer trapped in a room with no way out. "Sometime, they wait before they reveal anything." Glock answered his own question.

"Man where's all the hardware?" Slimstyle asked assured that Bright would find their weapons, resulting in them going back downtown for weapons possession.

"Strapped to the bottom of the truck, my man" Coffy smirked.

"Good." Glock said heading for the freeway entrance. "Let's get out of Oakland for a minute and handle our business."

20

9:37 a.m., Housekeeping Camp, Yosemite Valley

Jamilah noticed Tioni tense up when they saw Julie, Gustav and Issues leaving their cabin with Rainbow close behind. Gustav was carrying his hand held video camera and laptop, two more items the campers were instructed not to bring.

"Hey guys!" Jamilah called, "Where you going?"

"We figured if *Oren Peli,* could make *"Paranromal Activity"* and get rich off nothing more than a held hand video camera, then we owed it to ourselves to give it a shot." Julie responded holding up her own video camera. She then glanced at Tioni and said. "Good morning Tioni."

Tioni realized at that moment that she was supposed to be with Omari and responded with "Omari left this morning without telling me where he was going."

"Okay," Julie responded forgetting about telling her that she should stay near Omari at all times. "How are you?"

"I'm alright," she answered "How are you?"

Julie placed her items on the nearest picnic table and walked over to where Tioni stood. "I'm sorry for yelling and hitting you. I had no right," she said exhaling the words that had apparently been a heavy burden.

"I'm sorry for making you hate me," Tioni said happy to be talking to her friend.

"I don't hate you," Julie responded. "It's just something about a near death situation that brings out the worst in me." Julie could hear snickers in the background.

"Yeah, it's funny how that happens." Tioni added to the levity and the snickers. "I'm serious when I say I only remember parts of what happened"

"That's the other reason why I'm sorry. Rainbow told me that you were probably drugged with roofies," Julie explained.

"Roofies?" Jamilah asked.

"That's the street name for Rohypnol, or the date rape, drug. It's placed in its intended victims, drink. They pass out, then assailant can do whatever they choose, and the victims can sometimes have no idea who committed the crime against them.

"Coffy gave me a cup of champagne. I remember that," Tioni said struggling to remember what happened. Then, like wading through fog then recognizing where she was, Tioni began to recall some of the events from earlier that morning. She remembered being trapped in a small room with Glock, who was laughing as he was trying to remove her pants. Tioni remembered being unable to defend herself. Then Julie appeared and forced him to leave. "You saved me," she said to her large friend.

"Yeah, she got into a fight with the guy who was trying to assault you," Issues chimed in.

That realization sent shivers through Tioni's system, "Excuse me," she said weakly before running to the nearest tree to puke.

21

9:38 a.m., Rose Avenue Apartments, Union City, CA

Janet Azzara couldn't believe the good news, as she hurried through the house trying to find her keys. The hospital called to inform her that they had located a liver for her six-year-old daughter, Lauren. For two years Lauren had been on the waiting list, she was told that it was possible that it could happen, and now with the blessing of God it had.

Janet finally found the keys by her purse on the end table near the door. She then rushed to the bathroom door, "Lauren, you make sure you scrub. Don't just sit in the tub and play!"

The liver was on its way, and when it arrived, she would have to be at the hospital to be prepped for immediate surgery. She kept the phone in her sweaty hand because when the call came, she and Lauren would be on their way.

22

9:39 a.m., Yosemite Valley

Anticipating that the defiant buck would attempt to kick him as he dismounted, Omari leapt far enough from the deer to avoid a potentially crippling injury. The huge animal galloped away as soon as Dragonbrush released his grip from the buck's antlers.

"Helluva ride wasn't it?" Dragonbrush asked after the exhilarating experience.

"Next time, I'll take Greyhound," Omari cracked, understanding why deer were never chosen as a mode of transportation. He tossed Dragonbrush his tennis shoes. "You need to put those on before we head back to the camp."

"I'm not going back" Dragonbrush answered, the Adidas hitting him square in the chest before falling to the ground.

"What do you mean you are not going back?" Omari asked.

"There is nothing back in Oakland for me. I feel like I belong here; everything is so right here" Dragonbrush argued.

"You don't live out here; you live in Oakland." Omari countered.

"Omari, I can't go back." Dragonbrush pleaded, rubbing his fingers through his hair, "I'm turning into a wolf. I don't know if I can even control myself! You and Jamilah might be in danger. I won't do that to any of you. I won't!" Dragonbrush regained his composure and continued. "I brought you here because you are more my brother than my own brother, and I need you to tell everyone."

"No." Omari responded. "You are not leaving, Jamilah, and I need you more than the woods, so you have to stay." His words caught Dragonbrush off guard. He expected Omari to put up a fight, but not be so commanding. It was almost as if his words had to be obeyed.

"But why?" Dragonbrush asked, his tone filled with bewilderment.

"The lyrics make sense now," Omari explained. *Foaming at the mouth, that's you. Giving up your sanity, losing your humanity, amazing how what you had so long can be taken away instantly.* So what? You're going to run around the woods like Tarzan of the forest?" Omari charged. "Your family is in Oakland. Your friends are in Oakland. Everything is there including you. Put your shoes on, we're going back, together!"

"What about me turning into a werewolf?" Dragonbrush argued.

"Good, then you can protect us from all the other werewolves that you say are out there." Omari countered using Yes's tactic.

Dragonbrush's inner voice told him that Omari was right. It was then that Dragonbrush realized his inner voice was his humanity fighting his growing wolf, like desires. Omari's cool and commanding voice forced Dragonbrush's loyalty as a friend and canine.

As they headed back, Dragonbrush could not read if Omari's silence was a result of his behavior or the all the weed he inhaled.

"I'm sorry," Dragonbrush expressed. "It's this werewolf thing in me. I just don't want to do anything to hurt you all. I'm not going anywhere, promise."

"Man you need to know that folks care about you," Omari reassured him.

"I just hope you all still care after tonight," Dragonbrush added, feeling the growing presence of the full moon and the growing changes inside him.

23

10:02 a.m., Yosemite Valley

As a courier, Weldon Cooper has delivered some truly unique items. Once he delivered a skull for a science vs. religeon testimony, blood samples for a rock star paternity suit, and even the sperm of a thoroughbred horse. But, it was deliveries like today's that made his job worthwhile, a liver for a little girl. An organ could stay incubated for up to eighteen hours. This would be delivered in four to the Children Hospital despite the police road blocks for the two escape convicts, or in four and a half hours tops.

Weldon looked ahead and immediately slammed on the brakes. A woman was lying on the the road just ahead of him. The car skidded, and when it had come to a complete stop, he ran to the woman to learn of her condition. When he knelt over her, she was holding a gun to his stomach.

"Okay fat boy," Louisa said, standing to her feet. "We are taking your car, and you are getting some much over due exercise," she said walking to the courier van where Telma was already behind the wheel.

Weldon wanted to tell them that a little girl's life depended on getting that organ to the hospital, but at the moment, he was grateful just to have his, he thought as he took the first step of the long walk back to the police check point.

24

1:57 p.m., Los Amore Vineyard,

Strolling barefoot through Flora's house allowed Jennifer the opportunity to think about her future. When her mother who sufferers from Bi-Polar disorder stopped taking her medication. Jennifer dropped out of school to take care of her. Now that she, her mother and sister had moved in with their aunt, they were all doing so much better. Jennifer could resume her interest in school. She set aside time once a week to study for her school admissions test. Once she passed the test, and she would, come September, she would be allowed into her rightful grade and back on the track team. Jennifer always knew she wanted to run track. She just never thought about what she would do beyond it. Looking at Flora's spacious house sitting on three acres of land, and able to help folks like her, Jennifer wondered if she should become a doctor of psychiatry like Flora.

Jennifer entered into Flora's office. Her desk was covered with small stacks of paper and folders. Two file cabinets sat behind her; both also had stacks of folders. Jennifer noted that the rest of her house was orderly, but her office showed where she did her real work. She also wore thick reading glasses and glanced between her folders and her laptop.

"You don't mind being in this big place by yourself do you?" Jennifer asked interrupting the doctor's concentration.

"I'm normally so busy I forget that it's a big place" she replied never looking up.

"You must trust people a lot." Jennifer stated doing a pirouette, taking in the room as she spun,

"Why do you say that?" Flora asked, looking up in time to catch the slim teen spinning, her long hair catching up with her seconds later and wrapping itself around her face once she had completed her spin.

"You let me walk around the house and never say anything."

"I don't trust everybody, I trust you." She said looking back at the case study she was adding notes to.

"Why do you trust me?" Jennifer asked.

"Because my little track star, you are special," Flora asserted and went back to the forms inside the folder.

"I am?" Jennifer asked, the doctor's comments catching her off gaurd.

"You are," the doctor continued, adjusting her glasses.

"I hate Omari," she confessed, leaning against the wall before dropping to the floor. Looking under the desk, Jennifer could see that Flora wasn't wearing shoes either.

"Okay," the doctor replied, turning her attention to the laptop.

"He plays too much, he acts like a big baby. All he wants to do is smoke weed and run around in the middle of the night, spray painting walls, which is stupid because Dragon butt's parents owe a lot of money because of his tagging," she pouted."

"Doesn't sound wise to me," the doctor agreed tapping at the keyboards.

"Of course, he is younger than me."

"Yeah by one year, he's a baby," the doctor added dryly. "You should know better."

"You really mean that?" Jennifer asked, surprised at Flora's response.

"No."

"What I hate about him the most," Jennifer finally confessed, "Is that he acts like he likes me, then the next minute he acts like he don't even know me." She sighed, "Is he retarded or something?"

"No." Flora explained, "Just a male."

"All of them are like that?"

"Many of them grow out of it, some never."

"What's wrong with them?"

"It's called play."

"Like what little kids do?"

Flora sighed, "Yeah, like what little kids do."

"So what am I supposed to do?"

"You need to find out if he feels the same way as you, and the only way you can is by talking to him."

"I've got nothing to say to him," she blurted.

"Well you might want to concentrate on your own interests, and the things you like."

"Oh, like buying clothes and running track?"

"Those are perfect examples of you doing things for you that make you happy."

"Flora?" Jennifer asked cautiously. "The vampires came back, they asked me to join them, and I almost did." Jennifer spoke the statement that had brought her into the room, "I wanted to be a vampire"

"What caused that?" Flora asked, giving Jennifer her full attention.

"They were at the party, and they stopped a guy who shot at Omari."

"The vampires saved Omari?" the Latina asked.

"Yeah, I could see the bullet heading toward Omari's face," Jennifer explained with a cringe.

"You could see the bullet?" the therapist asked, "then you had the speed, why couldn't you save him?"

"I just froze." Jennifer explained with helplessness in her voice. "I couldn't move."

"That's interesting," Flora observed. "Most track runners don't freeze up."

"I normally don't, wait!" Jennifer responded giving thought to what the doctor had said. "Are you saying that the vampires prevented me from moving?"

"I'm asking if the vampires wanted to encourage you to return to their undead existence, would they care what method they used to convince you to join?"

"They played me," Jennifer acknowledged with knowingness. "And if Yes hadn't shown up I would have."

"Who is Yes?" Flora asked.

"Another of Omari and Dragonbrush's tagger friend; that did me a big favor," Jennifer realized as she headed for the door. She stopped in the hallway and said to Flora, "You know what? I bet they even lied when they said they liked Omari's music."

25

6: 02 p.m., Highway 41 from Fresno, 2 miles outside Yosemite Valley.

After a quick vehicle inspection along with a question and answer session with the officers at the checkpoint, Glock and his traveling companions were allowed to enter the park. Several miles past the check point, Glock instructed Coffy to pull over. Glock then crawled under the black Range Rover and tossed out four rifles, silencers, handguns, night goggles and several packs of ammo.

"Where did you get all of this stuff?" Coffy asked, placing on the goggles before taking a sip from one of the three bottles of *Hennessy V.S* they brought for the trip.

"There is this dude who sells his stuff out of his truck whenever there is a gun show. I stashed these away for a day like today," Glock added before taking a sip of brandy.

"Are you sure we are going the right way?" An anxious Slimstyle asked.

"Oh yeah," Coffy pointed with a malevolent grin to the sign that said Yosemite Valley, 2 miles.

26

6:52 p.m., Mist Trail, Yosemite Valley

"If you're coming, then come on!" Steven shouted at the stragglers as he and two other counselors led the group of fifteen teens. The goal of the predawn hike was to hike to the top of Mist Trail to see the magnificent Vernal Falls, and then back to camp before the setting sun. The Mist Trail ascended the canyon below and alongside the falls. Steven led the group climbing the hundreds of huge stone steps up the steep hill as the spray from the falls lashed across the upper part of the trail, drenching the hikers, as the thunder of the falling water, just a hundred yards away deafened them. The group, had taken in the incredible scenery, and now raced the setting sun back. Steven told the group, normally they would have made it back to the camp by now, but the rain had made the trail twice as slippery. This was evident by the muddied knees and hands of eight of the fifteen that took the challenge of the trek. Steven's concern with getting back was compounded by the uncommon fog that was rapidly setting in. Hopefully he would have the last child in their cabin before visibility was zero. As they descended the trail that overlooked part of the 28-mile river that originated from Yosemite National Park on the crest of Sierra Nevada at an elevation of 11,000 feet, the teens watched the intimidating river beneath the falls as the waters raced impressively down steep rapids that looked like smaller waterfalls. The river was great for white river rafting, but because of the fog, no one was in sight and because of the fog, Steven was pushing his team even harder.

"Come on, you guys, double time!" He yelled, knowing that the group was half way to camp. They would make it back in time.

27

6:55 p.m., Mist Trail, Yosemite Valley

"Omari, you should be ashamed of yourself!" Jamilah ribbed her brother from the front of the pack, where she and Dragonbrush had remained from the beginning of the trip. "You've been the booty on this hike since we started!" Dragonbrush was able to stay in the lead with Jamilah then walked back to where Omari and Tioni brought up the rear and back to the front again.

"I told you that my legs are hurting from the hike this morning," he groaned with aching limbs from the ride on the buck that he would tell her about later.

"Yeah, and I'm sure that chronic that you were probably out smoking didn't help," she teased. "And what's your excuse, Ms Tioni?" Jamilah challenged the one person that was dragging behind Omari.

"I'm not supposed to let him out of my sight, remember?" She said with a flushed complexion.

"You two are too much" Jamilah said with a broad smile, as Dragonbrush made his way back to the two laggers.

"I think next time we should do like Julie, Issues and Gustav did, go on a short hike that doesn't have a time frame," Tioni smiled as she caught up and maintained a pace with Omari.

"You know what? Tioni, you are really cool" Omari spoke with appreciation.

"Thanks," she replied, her gray eyes illuminated from the rays of the setting sun as they shone through the thick treetops as Dragonbrush waited for them.

"Dragon," Omari blurted out. "What's up with you and Tioni?" He spoke, openly embarrassing the two.

"Why you putting me on full blast like that?" Dragonbrush blurted.

"Yeah, that was so unnecessary?" Tioni agreed.

"Don't talk to me, talk to each other," Omari added.

"Omari, don't be doing this to me" Tioni spoke trying to side step the conversation.

"Oh, it only works when you're jamming someone else up?" He continued.

"Don't do this to me big brother," Dragonbrush said equally embarrassed.

"Too bad, you two walk around ignoring each other like you are not even friends, and yet you are around each other constantly."

"Tioni, are you mad at Dragonbrush?" Omari pressed.

"Dragonbrush hasn't done anything to me," she asserted, noticing that Dragonbrush was concerned with what she had to say.

"Do you hate him?"

"I don't hate anyone."

"So you like him?"

"Yeah, I like him, so there." Tioni confessed. "I like him a lot. He just doesn't like me all he cares about is Jamilah." She began to sob, as Dragonbrush stood dumbfounded. "He doesn't call me. He doesn't ask me to go anywhere. He just spends all of his time with Jamilah."

Dragonbrush looked at the crying teen and said, "I'm sorry, I didn't know," reaching to touch her only to watch her turn from his touch toward Omari.

"You know it was Dragon that saved you and Julie from the fire?" Omari informed her. Tioni stood back and looked at him in disbelief. "He was home," Omari continued, "and when he heard that you had disappeared, he freaked, left the house, found you, saved you and stood over you until he knew that you were alright."

"That's impossible!" She responded still sustained by disbelief "He was across town. How could he have gotten there?" Then she was hit with another revelation that by passed her earlier yesterday. "Oh my God!"

Tioni answered, with her hand over her mouth as they fell even further behind the group in front of them.

"What you said happened, I can remember some of it" Then it hit her, "Dragon how were you able to get there so fast? Are you a vampire? " Tioni asked reflecting on Tioni's abilities.

"I am not a vampire," Dragonbrush answered, sounding slightly insulted.

"Then what are you?" she asked.

Before he could answer, they heard Jamilah scream. Catching up with the group, they could see Jamilah slipping rapidly down the muddied hill into the rapids before being taken down river at tremendous speed.

"Jamilah!" Omari shouted, as he raced down the hill to her aid, only to be grabbed by Steven.

"Omari!" he said holding the twisting teen. "If you go, then we'll have to rescue the two of you. Let's rush to the edge and try to meet her at the path. The rest of you head back to camp report to the others what happened and be ready to assist when called upon." He instructed the other counselors.

As the group was heading back one of the teens yelled, "Steven look!" The counselor turned and could see Dragonbrush leaping from one of the higher points of the hill and diving head first into the raging water, Omari looked at Dragonbrush swimming strongly through the water, his focus straight ahead and Omari knew it would be all right.

"Let's go!" Steven shouted, and Omari followed him down the hill with an uninvited Tioni close behind as the fog quickly settled in.

28

6:58 p.m., Merced River, Yosemite Valley

Jamilah struggled to keep her head above water and her hand reaching out for anything that could prevent her from being pulled further into the currents. Several attempts to grab a hold of a rock proved fruitless as the stones were too slippery to hold. Things were moving too fast to think or even be scared. It was all she could do to keep her head above water, as she felt herself sliding down the largest of the three rapids and her world being consumed by water.

29

7:02 p.m., Mist Trail, Yosemite Valley

The visibility on the road had become near impossible. Glock and crew found the night goggles they brought a saving grace. The group had driven around for hours, coming across several campgrounds but none with their intended target. The group continued to drive, trying to avoid crossing any police checkpoints, but determined not to return home until they did what they came there for.

"I have to take a leak," Glock groaned, the sound of the river below painfully reminding him of what alcohol does to the bladder when you're driving. He pulled the Range Rover over and stood at the edge of an embankment overlooking the foggy river to relieve himself. The others waited in the Rover when they heard him call.

"Is that who I think it is caught up in the rapids?" Glock asked pointing at a figure flowing down the river through his goggles.

"I'll be damned!" Slimstyle shouted, running back and retrieving the rifles.

"Sometimes, you don't have to hunt." Glock laughed, "Sometimes the prey comes to you." He took the rifle placed the silencer on and adjusted the sites.

30

7:03 p.m., Merced River, Yosemite Valley

The sounds of the crashing rapids roared loudly in Dragonbrush's ears. The water burnt his nose as it savagely slapped his face and familiar scents nearby warned him of trouble. Dragonbrush ignored them all, his attention focused on finding Jamilah as her scent became stronger, his swimming pattern changed from strokes to more powerful dog paddling.

Then Dragonbrush felt a stinging in his left arm. The pain became greater by the second. He ignored it and continued forward. Then he felt a piercing through his stomach that stopped him mid motion. He instinctively struggled out of the water forcing his bleeding body to shore where he witnessed three more bullets exit through his chest, the final one through his heart. The teen collapsed to the ground as his blood mixed with the water that had washed to the shore. He had failed his sister and now Jamilah. On his pained lips he whispered, "I'm sorry," then felt his world go blank.

31

7:04 p.m., Mist Trail, Yosemite Valley

"Halt!" the Park Ranger demanded. "Freeze where you are, or I will shoot!" The Rangers repeated stopping Steven, Omari and Tioni in their efforts to follow the murky path that Jamilah and Dragonbrush had gone.

"Two of my kids fell in the river!" Steven shouted. "Either help or start shooting!" He stared at the dumbfounded officer who was ten years younger than Steven, but ten years older than the Omari. "Well, what are you going to do?" Steven challenged, sweat flowing freely down his face.

"The officer walked toward the rivers edge then immediately radioed in, "We have another problem; two kids have fallen into the river." He turned to Steven, "How long ago?"

"Minutes ago," Tioni spoke before Steven or Omari could get a word out. "You received the call," the officer said to the radio. "Well dispatch, you should have notified us immediately." He looked at the three with apologetic eyes then turned back to his radio. "I understand, but I want someone at the river at every half mile, for the next two miles from Echo Park to Daniels view, or there will be a problem." The officer turned to Steven, "I apologize for the gun. Last night two officers transporting two murder suspects were killed and their vehicle destroyed. Earlier this morning a courier carrying a liver for a transplant was robbed of his vehicle, by two women fitting their description. We suspect that the same women committed the double homicide. This place has been swarming with rangers, and the FBI has taken over our switchboard, which is why we didn't know about your kids. I'll drive you the rest of the way, and hopefully we will find them. But, it's getting dark, and the fog is making visibility a bear. If we don't find them within the next hour, we will have to continue first thing in the morning," he spoke leading the three to his vehicle.

"Did you say that the murderers are ladies?" Tioni asked.

"I said women; the two that escaped are not ladies. They are more like scary monsters," the Ranger explained while opening the door of his squad car and they raced down the road.

32

7:05 p.m., Above Mist Trail, Yosemite Valley

"Ha Ha Ha! We got him!" Glock laughed. "Those bullets ripped through that fool," his words filled with mirth.

"Yeah that was easier than I thought it would be," Slimstyle added.

"Why do you think he was in the water?" Coffy wondered.

"Who cares?" Glock smirked. "We got him, now let's go, make sure that he's dead, and then find red," he added, leading the group down to the embankment.

33

7:05 p.m., Above Mist Trail, Yosemite Valley

Turning off the headlights of their stolen vehicle every few yards as they drove through the fog, Telma and Louisa came across an empty, black, Range Rover and to their surprise could see the keys inside.

"This must be our lucky day," Louisa smiled getting out, her gun ready to convince the trucks owners that they were taking the vehicle. "I'll take the truck, and you follow in the car. We'll ditch it a little ways up and drive the truck out of the park."

"Wait!" Louisa called, carrying the heavy case that was in the courier's car to the Rover. "This may be something of value." Placing the case in the Rover, they quickly drove off.

34

7:23 p.m., Merced River, Yosemite Valley

Jamilah washed ashore exhausted and battered. She was cold, wet, it was foggy and dark. She walked a few feet before sitting on a large stump. She reached into her left pant pocket for her phone and realized that it was also soaked and useless. She reached into her other pant pocket and pulled out the small sack that held the dog bones and Elmo sunglasses.

"Why does this thing keep popping up?" She asked herself placing, it back into her pocket, thinking she may have to eat the dog biscuits if she didn't find anything else. Not knowing which way to go. Jamilah decided to remain where she was. Hoping someone would find her.

35

7:25 p.m., Merced River, Yosemite Valley

"I know this is where he was!" Coffy argued, staring at the spot where they saw Dragonbrush fall.

"Then what happened to him?" Slim Style asked, seeing that the spot was covered with blood.

"Adjust your night visors y'all," Glock said checking his forty-four Magnum for rounds. He looked up and could see the full moon peaking slightly through the foggy night. "I want Dragonbrush's head cut from his body, and we're not leaving till I do it!"

36

7:30p.m., Rose Avenue Apartments,

"Hello?" Janet Azzara spoke through the phone excitedly. It was Doctor Collins from Children's Hospital. "We can be there in twenty minutes," she assured the doctor.

"I'm sorry ma-am. It appears someone has car jacked the vehicle that the donor liver was in." The doctor explained with heartfelt sympathy.

"How could that have happened?" She asked, feeling as if she had just received a heavy blow to her chest.

"I do not know. But the authorities are doing everything within their power." He assured her.

"What does this mean? Is everything going to be okay? What can we do?" she asked overwhelmed by the bad news.

"We can only hope and pray."

37

7:50p.m., Los Amore Vineyard

The two watched, Flora's Guilty Pleasure, *Oprah*, a show she recorded then watched a week of episodes back to back.

"Am I getting worse? Am I a danger to my friends?" Jennifer asked Flora the question that brought her to Napa Valley as she walked to the kitchen to get a bottle of water.

"I suspected the same," the doctor responded. "That your hormones and your emotions coupled with your latent vampire desires were overwhelming, but that's not the case, Flora said fast forwarding through the commercials. "The truth is you are a well adjusted teen, and the things that you like and dislike and your love, hate relationship with Omari is normal."

"It is?" Jennifer responded between sips of water. "But, ain't I dangerous?"

"After evaluating you, you coming here was a mistake," the doctor responded. "It appears to me your friends are keeping you healthy and grounded. As for dangerous, no, not really," the doctor added. "Your desire to join the vampires is there, just like the desire to try drugs, steal money from a cash register or throw your sister down an elevator shaft." Flora watched Jennifer smile, "But you have a healthy conscience and great friends, which would prevent that from happening."

"Really? I've done some really bad things," Jennifer confessed.

Flora asked, "As a gang member or as a vampire?"

"Both."

"Do you remember what you did as a vampire?"

"I vaguely remember fighting other vampires, but it's like a fading dream." Jennifer answered, searching her mind for details of the events.

"We will have to continue our talks."

"If everything is alright, then when can I see my friends?" She asked excitedly.

"As soon as they get back," Flora replied.

"But, I can get there on my own," Jennifer argued knowing her own speed.

"Using your powers is not always a good idea, and it can also backfire," Flora added.

"Why do you say that?" Jennifer asked.

"To quote Stevie Wonder, *when you believe in things that you don't understand then you suffer*. Everything is not as perfect as we would like to believe." Flora explained, "You don't fully understand why you still have your abilities. I personally believe, it's an indication of some really big problems for this world in the very near future, and we must prepare for it." Flora spoke with a seriousness that concerned Jennifer.

"How?" Jennifer asked.

"That's a question I can't answer yet," she said turning her attention back to Oprah.

38

7:53p.m., Vernal Falls, Yosemite Valley

The two stood silhouetted against the dramatic falls. "Sandia," Lazarus spoke with grave concern. "Humans are congregating on the outer edges of the forest in search of one of their own that has been lost. Should we reconsider the passing for another time?"

"Has fear clouded your mind?" Sandia asked, his voice filled with almost contempt for his cautious age-old friend. "Tonight we continue a tradition we have practiced when man was in a cave hiding from his own shadow. And any one who interferes with the business of the Union," he said with fangs bared, "will sorely regret it."

Part 9

Union of the Werewolves

"Wolves are not our brothers; they are not our subordinates, either. They are another nation, caught up just like us in the complex web of time and life."
~ Henry Beston

1

8:00 p.m., Children's Hospital

"This is Lisa Chow standing in front of the entrance of Oakllands Children's Hospital Where a little girl's life hangs in the balance; a courier transporting a liver to be used for the small child transplant was carjacked and there is no word as to its whereabouts. A private donor is offering a reward of $25.000 for the safe return of the organ inside the 13 hours needed to keep it vital. If you have any information, please call the number on the screen below."

2

8:02 p.m., Housekeeping Camp, Yosemite Valley

Omari wasn't worried, despite what had happened. He knew what Dragonbrush could do, and how he felt about Jamilah. Dragonbrush would find Jamilah and bring her back safe, as he had done with Tioni and Julie. Tioni joined him on the cabin porch, Omari felt her arms wrap around him, as she laid her braided head on his shoulder.

"They'll be back, I know they will," she said, wanting to believe her own words.

"I know they will," Omari assured her placing his hand on hers. "Dragon will take care of it."

"Has anyone heard anything yet?" Gustav questioned, as he, Issues, and Julie joined them.

"Have you called your uncle and aunt yet?" Julie asked.

"Yeah, no one was home, so I left a message." Actually, Omari hadn't bothered to call his uncle and aunt nor give the Counselors their cell phone because he knew they would panic, and being unable to get there, meant harassing him every few minutes.

"I'm going back to see if Steven needs any additional help" Gustav added, unable to sit around and do nothing. "I'm right behind you," Issues followed, placing his hand on Omari's shoulder as he walked out of the cabin.

"You know, I am not surprised that it was Dragonbrush that dived in the river after Jamilah," Julie added.

"Why is that?" Omari asked, wondering if she also knew of Dragonbrush's' Lycantrophy.

"I guess you all wouldn't know because it's been a while" Julie added. "Dragonbrush had an older sister name Gwen. She was like his second Mom. She was always taking care of him, drawing pictures for him and stuff like that. About eight years ago, she passed away from a rare form of leukemia, and the Madayag's didn't take it well. In fact, Dragonbrush's brother once told me that they were not to even mention Gwen's name around the house because it hurt the father so bad."

So, who were they supposed to talk to about it?" Tioni asked, seeing the ridiculousness of that logic.

"That's sort of when Dragon and his dad started having problems because he loved and missed his older sister. In fact, the only other person that he seems to be truly happy with is his new big sister Jamilah. That's why he can't stop hanging around her and taking her abuse," Julie smiled, waving her hand through the fog. Omari and Tioni looked at each other, Jamilah's and Dragonbrush's relationship now made so much sense.

"I would hate to be the person that tried to come between Dragonbrush and his big sister," Julie added.

3

8:32 p.m., Unknown, Yosemite Valley

After an hour of waiting in the dark, Jamilah decided to walk, hoping to come across a campground rather than remain in one spot in the freezing cold. She soon found walking to be an even greater challenge; the thick fog prevented her from seeing her own footsteps, resulting in the teens stumbling to the ground every few steps. Nor was she sure if she was making progress or going in circles. Walking with her hands outstretched Jamilah's hands pressed against the trunk of a tree. Pulling on the branches, she realized that she was able to climb, thinking about the snakes, bears, and wolves that hunted at night. Jamilah found herself using the dim moonlight to guide her hands and feet until she climbed high enough to feel safe, cold, but safe.

4

8: 49 p.m., Highway 41, Yosemite Valley

"You really do know all the roads around here," Telma commented, impressed at Louisa's resourcefulness. The two had dumped the courier's car and shared one of the five joints Telma had found in the glove compartment of the Range Rover.

"Some things have changed, but not much." Louisa commented, as she sipped from the brandy bottle that they had also found in the truck along with the guns and ammo.

"But we're going to have to park and sit tight until the morning." Louisa explained knowing the vehicle' headlights would instantly give their position away if helicopters were deployed. Their only chance was to park and use branches to cover the vehicles, shiny finish, making it impossible to find in the night.

5

8:55 p.m., Mist Trail, Yosemite Valley

"Man these glasses are too much!" Coffy commented on the night goggles that displayed the forest in an odd bright green, allowing them to see animals scamper and birds flying ahead. Occasionally one of the four would remove their goggles to compare the emerald view with the white wall that the fog had created.

"Yeah, they cool and all that" Glock commented as they made their way through the woods rifles, "but what happened to Dragonbrush? I saw him take four bullets."

"Where could he have gone?" Slimstyle added, with annoyance as he began to tire of the search.

"Let's head back." Glock told the group, realizing that in his rush to shoot Dragonbrush, he inadvertently left the keys in the ignition of the sport utility vehicle and his cell phone.

"Word," Coffy agreed. "Which way is back?" He asked, depending on the others to know the way back to the SUV. The group stood in their tracks and argued on which way they had come when Glock declared. "Shit! We're lost!"

6

9:02 p.m., Unknown, Yosemite Valley

"Stop!" Dragonbrush barked, clearly irritated at the licking at his face. "I said stop!" He snarled, understanding how Omari felt being disturbed by him, when he was trying to sleep, but Dragonbrush would continue to annoy him anyway. "Lexus stop licking on me!" he growled.

"Then get up!" the pit bull barked back, "We have to go!"

"Go where?" He asked, also recognizing Maria's scent, but not the others with them.

"Sandia said, and I quote, *'It is crucial that you three are at the Gathering.' Whatever that means,*" the Malamute added. Dragonbrush moved his head, but didn't feel his hair draping his shoulder, then he remembered being wet, but now he was warm, even though the fog had become even thicker. *What had happened to him?* He couldn't remember. He felt his mouth opening wide and his tongue dropping from the side of his sharp teeth, as he tried figure our how he got there.

"Look Lexus, the bullet holes are all gone." Maria spoke, admiring Dragonbrush's trunk.

"It's like they was never there." Lexus commented. "How does it feel?" she asked Dragonbrush.

"It doesn't hurt anymore," he replied. Then the memories of the gun shots that left him bleeding on the banks of the river while he was trying to save Jamilah began to flood his thoughts. Suddenly, his thick, black nose had picked up her scent again. He stood up on all four of his legs and dashed in the direction of the scent.

"Where are you going?" Maria growled running behind him. "We have to get to the Gathering."

"I'm not doing anything until I find Jamilah," Dragonbrush snarled, "I'll get with y'all later." He continued hastily toward a gap between two trees that would lead him back on the trail only to have the path blocked by a Saint Bernard, two German shepherds, and 4 larger wolves.

"You do not understand," the larger of the wolves spoke with a black scar over his left eye

"You were not asked to participate in the Gathering. You were told. All other matters must wait."

Dragonbrush stopped, as the canines in his path all lowered their heads ready to subdue him. Dragonbrush ignored their canine posturing, all he knew was that he would save Jamilah, and no Gathering would stop him. He rushed toward the growling canines, well aware that he would have to fight when he felt his back legs becoming wider and stronger. Suddenly, he felt himself no longer on four legs, but on two.

The canines looked at the transformed Dragonbrush with awe, as he leaped above them, landing in the trees and with tremendous speed, leaping from branch to branch before landing back on the ground, heading toward Jamilah with the hounds howling far behind.

7

9:12 p.m., Unknown, Yosemite Valley

"You sure we didn't go this way before?" A frustrated Glock asked.

"With these glasses on, everything looks the same, green." Coffy added.

"See that fat tree over there," Coffy commented, disenchanted with what he had just learned. "We passed that tree when we first got here. We've been walking in a circle."

The four continued walking aimlessly through the woods cursing, threatening and blaming each other for their predicament.

"Man look up there," Coffy called motioning to everyone to look at a tree several hundred yards ahead. The group focused their goggles and saw what Coffy was referring to. The outline of a figure in a tree, moving closer, they could see it was the outline of a female.

"I guess they grow freaks out in this part of the woods," Slim Style said with a lascivious grin as they walked toward the unsuspecting Jamilah.

8

9:14 p.m., Unknown, Yosemite Valley

The howling of wolves snapped Jamilah from her sleep bringing her back from the dreary situation that was her reality, sitting on a branch staring at the great sea of foggy nothingness. Jamilah could hear birds and squirrels scrambling in the background, but was far more concerned with that which she could not see down below as she continued to cling to her base of security. Unfortunately, being awake reminded Jamilah of how wet, cold and hungry she was. Jamilah thought about the dog biscuits in the small sack that Vaticinator had given her, and remembered eating dog biscuits when she was little. They didn't kill her then, a couple of more biscuits wouldn't make a difference now. Besides no one could see her and no one would know.

Jamilah reached into the bag and pulled out a biscuit with the pair of plastic Elmo sunglasses entangled in them. She placed the biscuit and the glasses near her eye to get a good look at what she was about to eat when she noticed that she could see through the glasses as if it was day. After a double take, Jamilah realized that she could in fact, see through the glasses. After quickly placing them on, it was as if it was mid-day, no darkness, no fog, just rustic trees with majestic branches adorned by colorful weeping leaves

"I should be able to find my way back to the camp," she smiled. Then she looked ahead and could see four men trotting her way and felt fear grip her heart.

9

9:16 p.m., Unknown, Yosemite Valley

Dragonbrush could hear wolves howl. Their calls both compelling and enticing.

"What are you doing?" A wolf questioned.

"Listen to your instincts!'" A dog barked.

"You're one of us now. Forget about the humans." A fox snarled.

"Stop being stupid," Another voice howled.

"We will not allow you to leave us!" Another joined.

Despite their efforts, Dragonbrush's resolve had not diminished. Jamilah was nearby, and he would find her. The others would not stop him, they were fast, but he was faster. Then there was a howl that was louder than all of the others, shaking the forest, demanding that all cease what they were doing and to return to the center of the woods.

The howl forced Dragonbrush to stop. He looked around, and the others had already retreated, following the direction of the call.

"No!" He barked, ignoring his instinctual need to participate in the Gathering and continued toward Jamilah.

10

9:17 p.m., Unknown, Yosemite Valley

Jamilah quickly descended the tree, she knew that the four approaching her were up to no good, and didn't question her own common sense. The four were aware that she was planning to run and picked up their pace calling, "Hey we're lost, too. We need your help."

Jamilah grimaced as her wet shoes landed squarely on the flat ground, sending a stinging sensation up her legs. Her feet had also gone to sleep while they dangled idly in the tree. Ignoring the pain she stumbled off into the woods with the four close behind.

11

9:19 p.m., Above, Yosemite Valley

"This is Chopper ten reporting zero visibility in the perimeter." Helicopter pilot Broderick Page and his co-pilot who preferred to be called *Ace* radioed in as he carefully navigated the copter over the forest. "I will make one more circle of the area before heading in, we'll have better visibility in the morning."

"Roger that," the heavy voice spoke through the radio.

Because there were lost children, a lost organ and escaped killers all in the same vicinity, Broderick and his partner risked flying in near zero visibility, but the only thing his spotlight had picked up was an occasional wolf. If they were lucky, he would find the kids, the notion of finding all three was improbable at best. He prepared to make his final circle and wondered, *what else was going on down there?*

12

9:20 p.m., Unknown, Yosemite Valley

"The one who calls himself Dragonbrush refused our call." Lazarus commented to Sandia "That has never happened before."

"The evening is not over, he may yet appear."

"And if he doesn't, what does that mean?"

"We will participate in the Gathering as always, Sandia snarled, "Our reluctant addition will appear."

13

9:25 p.m., Unknown, Yosemite Valley

Try as she could, the wet and tired teen could not outrun her pursuers for long. Eventually they caught up and surrounded her.

"Damn baby, did you fall in the lake?" Coffy asked, stunned to see that the person they were chasing was drenched from head to toe

"Shut up fool!" Glock checked Coffy. "Look, we are lost and need your help," Glock said with sincerity "We are going to rest here for a while, and then we will all leave together." He looked at the others that surrounded her and said, "Right fellas?"

"Yeah baby, yeah," Slimstyle mocked.

Jamilah looked at the group clearly through her glasses, and had resolved that she would fight kick and punch until she got away.

"Check it out," Glock spoke. "We don't know nothing about this area. All we need you to do is lead us out of here, and we're ghost, and with four players like us around, you don't have to worry about anything happening to you. You're safe."

"Especially the with all those damn wolves howling around here," Coffy added.

Jamilah backed up slowly, but could sense the others behind her, their night visors allowed them to see what she saw. If she could manage to remove them from their faces she would have the advantage and could escape.

"I don't know what happened to you, but I see you're wet and must be cold," Glock added. "Somebody, give her a jacket." He commanded the others. Slimstyle removed his short, blue, *North Face* down jacket and tossed it to her. Jamilah grabbed the jacket and held it while scanning the ground for a stone a stick anything that could be used as a weapon.

"Alright bitch, now tell us how to get our asses out of here," Glock spoke the mock compassion gone from his voice.

"I don't know," Jamilah replied weakly, "I'm lost, too."

Glock pulled out his gun and pointed at Jamilah, "Then you just been wasting my time."

Just then the sound of helicopter roared through the forest shaking the trees and the blasting dirt into the air. Glock, Slimstyle, Coffy and Shady instantly looked into the direction of the sound and the copters spotlight cut through the fog directly into their night visors. The four screamed in agony as the light seared their eyes, blinding them.

14

9:26 p.m., Above, Yosemite Valley

"This is chopper ten reporting," Ace radioed, unable to hear the screams below. "We've done a second sweep of the perimeter with no success. We will try again first thing in the morning."

"We will be waiting," The heavy voice spoke through the radio.

15

9:27 p.m., Unknown, Yosemite Valley

Jamilah kicked, stomped, and spat on the blinded four. Her fear turned to rage, and she had released it at its source. Noticing that Glock was reaching for his gun, the teen kick the gang member in his face; grabbed the jacket that Slimstyle had placed on the ground and ran deeper into the woods.

16

9:30 p.m., Unknown, Yosemite Valley

Telma was awakened by the sound of her own snoring, when she sat up the radio and the heater was on, and Louisa was intently listening to it.

"You know there is no way we will get out of the woods," Louisa said gravely.

"I know you are not talking about turning yourself in." Telma said in an incredulous tone. "Like I said, we can hide out here for weeks, until the heat dies down and then make our escape

"I don't want to hide out, I want to make history," Louisa added. "Tomorrow I want to start my day off by driving through the park killing everything in sight." She looked at Telma, "It will be glorious."

"Telma looked at her partner on the lam and said, "I wasn't planning on doing anything better tomorrow," she said before going back to sleep.

17

9:30 p.m., Unknown, Yosemite Valley

"Get up!" Glock shouted in the crisp fog, "No slut is going to do this to us! I want her dead! Ya heard?" He said spitting blood on the ground where she had kicked one of his eyeteeth in, "Remember this spot, Split up. We will meet back in here in ten minutes. Don't kill her because I want to put the bullet between her eyes myself." He said walking into the woods while the others did the same.

18

9:37 p.m., Unknown, Yosemite Valley

In the foggy night it was impossible to see, but because Jamilah's mystical glasses allowed her to see in the night as if it was day, Jamilah clearly spotted the outline of the black Range Rover covered by bushes and branches. Her guess was that the vehicle was empty, and no one was in it and with four angry thugs behind her, it was worth a try to get in it and pray that there was a cell phone inside. Jamilah ran so hard that when she reached the vehicle she bumped into it. When she looked inside, there were two sleeping females inside.

"Let me in! You've got to help me!" Jamilah pleaded, as she pounded on the side windshield. Then Jamilah could see the startled pair reaching for their guns.

"Oh shi-,"Jamilah cried, running back the way she had come, before the two in the truck could get a good look at her. Jamilah ran back up the hill looking over her shoulders to see if the two with the guns were behind her. When she finally turned to look ahead of her, she saw Glock pointing his gun at her, and with a sneer he fired three shots at her.

Jamilah braced for the impact, then checked herself, there were no bullet holes in her. She looked at Glock who couldn't believe he missed at point blank range. He fired again, and again no bullet landed. Jamilah picked up a rock and threw it at him it landing squarely in his face toppling him over in pain.

"What happened?" Glock cried, unable to comprehend why Jamilah was still alive.

"I happened" a third voice spoke.

The two turned their right and was startled by what they thought was a bear, a second glance revealed the beast to be a massive Rottweiler, standing at nearly five feet, weighing more than six hundred pounds.

The two stood in terror of the muscular canine unable to process its ability to speak. The beast turned toward the frightened Glock and spat the bullet heads at his feet.

"You picked the wrong place, the wrong night and the wrong person to hunt." The dog spoke in a merciless tone.

"Did you just speak?" Glock asked, in sheer unbelief.

"You're not deaf," the Rottweiler with blazing eyes answered.

"Dragon?" Jamilah called recognizing the voice.

"What?" he answered.

"That you?" she asked with unbelief. "A dog?"

"I'll explain later, okay?"

"Dude you a dog, I mean a talking dog, Does Omari know and didn't tell me?" She pressed.

"I said, I will explain it to you later, man!" He snarled to himself, "why is everything with her always so hard."

Jamilah walked over to the large beast and wrapped her arms around Dragonbrush's massive body all her fears gone. She looked at the terrified Glock and said with a malevolent grin. "Yo ass is in big trouble now."

19

9:39p.m., Unknown, Yosemite Valley

"Did you see who that was?" Louisa asked, as she was jerked back into her seat when the SUV roared into the night.

"No I didn't. If I had, I would have put a bullet in his head." Telma spoke as she drove afraid to turn on the SUV's headlights for fear they would instantly reveal their location.

"You cant' keep driving like this without the lights on" Louisa screamed, reaching across Louisa for the lights

"Leave it alone, I know where I'm going," Telma said, pushing Louisa's hand aside, minutes before the SUV drove over a steep hill, tipped over and slid down on its side. When the vehicle finally stopped, Telma and Louisa crawled out of the shattered windshield and stumbled into the fog.

20

9:44 p.m., Unknown, Yosemite Valley

It happened faster than Jamilah's eyes could track. Dragonbrush went from an enormous four legged Rottweiler to a werewolf standing on two. His massive arms scooped her up, instantly warming her with his fur covered body and with a mighty leap, soared twelve feet into the air of forest, placing Jamilah on a solid branch of a mighty redwood.

What are you doing?" Jamilah asked Dragonbrush, grabbing hold of trunk of the as she looked down

"I need you to wait here until I come back, okay?" Dragonbrush explained turning to leap.

"But I can't stay up here." Jamilah exerted, noticing the stench of the Dragonbrush's dog breath.

"Jamilah please, just this one time, do what I say. Stay here until I get back." Dragonbrush dropped to the ground to track down Glock who had run away. After dealing with him Dragonbrush would then figure out what to do about the other werewolves in the area.

"You knothead!" Jamilah shouted, "I have to pee!" She looked at the ground and realized that she could climb down and could probably climb partly back up. She carefully scaled down the tree.

After she finished her business, she agreed that the smartest thing to do was to remain where Dragonbrush told her to stay. She proceeded to climb the tree when she sensed eyes on her, she turned and hundreds of wolves and assorted dogs suddenly appeared, all staring at her.

"Oh man," Jamilah whispered to herself.

21

9:49p.m. Unknown, Yosemite Valley

As he stumbled through the woods, struggling to catch his breath, Glock couldn't remember where he told the others to meet him. Heavy perspiration fueled by panic fogged up his night goggles, making it impossible to see. He stopped and dried the visors with his t-shirt, all the while listening in the dark for anything approaching him. Wiping the heavy sweat from his face. Glock dropped to the ground. He could not comprehend what he had seen, some how Dragonbrush had turned into a Rottweiler. He was now a dog that was faster than a bullet and could talk. This was not possible, yet it had happened. When he placed on his night goggles the out of his element gangbanger saw standing before him a cloth less Dragonbrush oblivious to the icy elements.

"Man, you don't know how stupid you look?" Glock said with a nervous smile to the slightly framed, teen that hardly appeared menacing. "You're wondering why I've bothered you over all these years." Glock spoke the nervousness still in his voice. "Now you're asking yourself how did I know that, Isn't it obvious?" He spoke while wiping the sweat from his over heated face "ESP, I can read some peoples thoughts." Glock's confession caught Dragonbrush off guard.

"What? You thought only white, pointed head geeks that watch the Syfy Channel can have *Extra Sensory Perception?*" He asked the silent Filipino. "My Grandmother had it and two grandmothers before her" he said catching his breath. "People used to pay my Grandmother to tell them their future. When she could, she would just tell people what was on their minds and what they wanted to hear. In many case, she was just lying to them. My mother never had it and doesn't know that I have it. That's right, I read people's thoughts." He said with a sly grin. "Like knowing who to rob, who just got paid and who's carrying drugs. It all comes in handy. But of all the people I could read, your thoughts are the clearest, and I always knew you were soft with no fight in you. All I had to do was threaten somebody you cared about, and you would do whatever I wanted. I realized I could read your thoughts the first time we jacked you, and your brother and made him rob that store." I knew about you and your family." He continued, watching tears flow freely down Dragonbrush's eyes, "And I knew how scared you were of me and that you were not going to cross me because you had no heart."

"Then you knew about my sister Gwen being sick, and how she wanted to see me while she was dying in the hospital, and you knew how bad I wanted to see to be with her, but I had to deliver drugs for you anyway." Dragonbrush's spoke, his voice choking and his eyes burning from the teary memories.

"You didn't say anything." Glock remarked with arrogance.

"You said you would kill my family and my sister last," Dragonbrush spoke his muscles tightening.

"Listen man," Glock responded defensively. "That was about business. If I hadn't gotten those drugs to that dirty cop Parnell, he would have arrested me, and I wasn't going back to jail, and that was it."

"I walked into the middle of a sting, and you went to jail anyway," Dragonbrush charged. "If your powers so great, why didn't you know that?"

"Like I said, it doesn't work on everybody, and if your thoughts wouldn't have been whining, then I might have been able to pick up the thoughts of others." Glock fired back, forgetting his current situation.

"All I wanted to do was see my sister who wanted to see me in the hospital. If any other officer other than Sergeant Bright, would have picked me up I would have went straight to juvie." Dragonbrush argued, his voice growing deeper, his appearance darker. "When Sergeant Bright took me to the hospital, that was the first time I ever saw my father cry, and he never forgave me for that."

"Your sister didn't die that day" Glock spoke using what he thought were words of compassion. "You got to spend another three weeks with her, so why you tripping?"

"Why? Because you knew how scared I was, and it didn't matter to you how it affected me. All of the nightmares, all of the fear and my love for my sister, you knew all of it." Dragonbrush lowered his head, his hair dropping in front of his face and asked, "Glock, can you read my thoughts now?"

"Naw, I can't," he responded nervously. "It's like there are two things going on in your head at the same time." Glock's mouth opened with fear as he watched Dragonbrush transform from his small frail self into a massive, menacing, seven foot part man, and part Rottweiler.

"Is that better?" Dragonbrush asked malevolently.

"No," he whispered as the Cobalt leader that instilled fear in so many shrunk back from the horror that stood before him.

"Is this better?" Dragonbrush asked, as his final transformation was that of an enormous Rottweiler, whose heart was completely free of human compassion or guilt.

"Yes," Glock whispered with pure cowardice, further humbled by the realization that he had defecated in his own pants.

"Good," Dragonbrush spoke with his full fangs bared. "You should take your goggles off because you don't want to see what's going to happen next."

Dragonbrush's world was no longer black and white, his fury was completely red, and Glock's screams filled the night.

22

9:54 p.m., Unknown, Yosemite Valley

It was a moment of awkward silence, hundreds of dogs of varying sizes, shapes, colors, and breeds surrounded Jamilah. Knowing that trying to scale the tree before being ripped apart would be a waste of effort. She decided to remain still, and did so, even after hearing the sound of a screaming man far off in the woods. Whoever it was, he was the least of Jamilah's concerns. The dogs that surrounded her seemed perplexed by her, as if not knowing what they should do, not growling, barking or even approaching her. They just remained in place their eyes glowing in the deep fog. "Why are there so many dogs out here?" Jamilah asked out loud as the hundreds of canines continued to stare at her.

"We are here for the Gathering," a rusty brown Afghan spoke, surprising Jamilah.

"You can talk just like Dragon can?" Jamilah asked, wondering if it was possible that Omari and her other friends had somehow been transformed like Dragonbrush.

"We all can," the long haired dog answered.

"Omari are you out there?" asked.

"There's no Omari here" a German shepherd answered.

"You're all werewolves," Jamilah asked, remembering Steven's story wondering if he knew how much truth there was to it.

"You could say that," the Afghan answered.

"Even the Chihuahua? Jamilah questioned.

"Yeah, even the Chihuahua." The small dog spoke with a surprisingly deep Brooklyn accent.

"Really?" Jamilah pressed with disbelief speaking directly to the Chihuahua.

"You got a problem with small hairless dogs, little girl?" The Chihuahua responded with mega attitude.

"I got your little girl," Jamilah responded with attitude "And I'm sorry for insulting you, I don't meet talking dogs every night."

"And if you weren't in possession of lamb's meat, this would be your last." The Chihuahua responded.

"I don't understand," Jamilah spoke, baffled about the lambs meat.

"No human is allowed to witness the Gathering without being destroyed, unless, they have aged lamb meat."

"Meat?" Jamilah questioned. All she had on her were the dog bones that she couldn't get rid of. "My God!" she said out loud. If Vaticinator hadn't given her the dog treats the hounds in front of her would have ripped her apart. "And to think I threw them away." She fretted,

"My name is Lazarus," a gray wolf spoke, "and you are welcomed to the Gathering."

Dragonbrush, still in his canine form leapt between Jamilah and the canines. "You all stay away from my friend!" He spoke, excitedly. The pack began to laugh in both human and canines voices.

"What's so funny?" Dragonbrush asked sensing that Jamilah was in no danger.

"They just invited me to observe the Gathering.

"They did?" Dragonbrush acknowledged, "Cool, What's the Gathering?" He asked.

"I don't know," Jamilah answered, "I guess it's a werewolf thing."

"It's time;" Napoleon called from inside the forest. "Let the Gathering begin."

"Jamilah rode on Dragonbrush's back and said, "I guess we're about to find out."

23

10:05 p.m., Unknown, Yosemite Valley

Jamilah and Dragonbrush sat on a large rock in the heavily wooded area. Although Jamilah was assured that she was would not be harmed, being the only human in the midst of thousands of wolves and dogs was nevertheless unsettling. A Pitbull and Malamute named Lexus and Maria whom Dragonbrush seemed to know joined them. To Jamilah they seemed as pleasant as two werewolves could be. Like she and Dragonbrush, they had no idea why they were there or what to expect. Jamilah noticed that in addition to the barking and growling, numerous werewolves communicated in foreign dialects in addition to English indicating that many had traveled great distances.

There was also a fascination with Dragonbrush whom they referred to as the *"New One"* Jamilah overheard Lexus share with Maria. The other canines spoke of Dragonbrush's ability to change his form from hound to human and in between at will, something no other werewolf was able to do. This ability caused interest, jealousy, fear and in some, even anger. This made Jamilah nervous, but not as nervous as it made her Rottweiler friend.

Jamilah stood up to stretch and felt a small dog land on her shoulder. She turned and noticed the small dog struggling to maintain its balance. It was the Chihuahua that she had argued with earlier. Jamilah placed her hand on the small dog, adjusting its balance so it wouldn't fall off her shoulders.

"Thanks toots, I knew you humans were good for something."

"What do you want?" Jamilah asked annoyed.

"All the best spots have been taken, so we figured that you would be willing to lend us your height" the Chihuahua said in his husky voice. Jamilah looked at Dragonbrush who replied, "I don't know what's he's talking about."

"Hey, Steel Nose wants to see, too." Jamilah felt a pair of paws on her wet feet looking down she saw dachshund on its hind legs and carefully picked up the wiener dog, careful not to knock the hairless off her shoulder.

"Careful lady, watch the hands." The dog said in a deep gruff voice.

"How about I drop your little ass to the ground you oversized weenie." Jamilah replied offended.

"Hey, did your mother breast feed that dirty mouth of yours?" The dachshund replied, braced to feel the impact of the ground when the human dropped him, but was surprised when Jamilah said, "Just shut up and enjoy the view."

"Hey Faheem," the dachshund called, "this human's alright."

"What are you trying to see?" Dragonbrush asked, entering into the conversation.

"Don't look, feel." The dachshund whispered. Jamilah felt a chill run up her spine that turned to a sickening dread. Her first response was to run from the area as fast as she could. Something was approaching, and without seeing it, she knew it was a fearsome site and felt herself wanting to scream out of sheer terror.

"It's okay, you're okay," Faheem and Steel Nose consoled her. "Relax, take a deep breath then slowly let it out." Faheem whispered in Jamilah's ear.

"And, don't drop me for Pete's sake," Steel Nose pleaded. Jamilah felt something large push against her, it was Dragonbrush; he was as much a mix of emotions as she. Jamilah remembered on a field trip to the Seattle Zoo years ago a docent explaining to her how animals were more attuned to nature than man. She realized that whatever was spooking her Dragonbrush was feeling with even greater intensity, so were Lexus and Maria. Not knowing what else to do, Jamilah found herself slightly bumping back into her Filipino friend now in the shape of a massive Rottweiler reassuring him that she was there.

The ground in front of them began to illuminate in a soft glowing yellow, revealing the majestic trees that towered over them and the countless canines that had gathered. A hush and awe fell on all as the giant redwoods that sat on the glowing earth disappeared, leaving a glowing path that led from the forest and ended in a newly created clearing in the once heavily wooded area. The canines including Dragonbrush, immediately responded to the phenomenon by howling with such intensity that it shook the earth. Jamilah clasped her ears, and screamed in pain, dropping Steel Nose and knocking Faheem to ground. Then stillness returned, and the attention of all turned to the edge of the woods where in a blinding flash a pack of wolves appeared at the edge of the path. The first wolf Jamilah cast her eyes on was the size of a Hummer. The enormous, dark, wolf looked similar to a timber wolf only its fur was longer, its head larger and broader, and its legs much thicker than any canine present. The most frightening part of the wolf was his massive mouth, filled with teeth both sharp and intimidating. The terrifying wolf's fearful presence was undeniable. There was no question in Jamilah's mind about it, he was the leader, a fact confirmed by all the other canines present lowering their heads in humble submission to the awesome beast. A slightly smaller version of the same wolf trailed, who Jamilah deduced was a female, as females tended to be smaller than males. *Wow,* Jamilah thought to herself, the time spent in Ms. Mawson's science class was actually worth something. Then it occurred to her, if the others are bowing their heads, she should do the same. She lowered her head but continued to look. The two towering wolves walked to the center of the clearing and sat.

"Who are they?" An equally terrified Dragonbrush whispered after the pair had walked past them.

"That is Anubis," Faheem whispered back, as he again leapt on Jamilah's shoulder. "The father of all werewolves, he is a fearsome site. Oh, and by the way sorry for howling in your ear." He apologized to Jamilah.

"Sorry for dropping you guys," Jamilah added, picking up Steel Nose.

"Next time warn a sistah."

"Anubis is the undisputed leader of the werewolves" Steel Nose added. "He created the Union; he and his wife alone rule it."

"What is the Union?" Dragonbrush asked the question that was also on the minds of Maria Lexus and Jamilah.

"The Union is the partnership of werewolves," Steel Nose answered. We are unique creations that prefer our autonomy, but we come together to recognize that we are all part of a larger pack."

"It's also a time to discuss business and to remember our shared enemy," Faheem added.

"Would that be the vampires," Jamilah asked.

"That would be anyone that is not a werewolf," Faheem answered, "But primarily the vampires."

"Shhh!" A black, Labrador retriever whispered, "You guys are talking too much." The dog spoke in a nasal, female voice, bringing their attention back to the procession.

"Stuck up Lab!" Steel Nose whispered, getting a snicker out of Jamilah.

"Steel Nose!" The Labrador whispered, calling him on his comment, "Why do you have to wait until there's human around to act stupid?" She scolded him.

"Sorry," he replied.

"That's Tasha, his old lady," Faheem whispered in Jamilah's ear.

"A lab and a weenie dog?" Jamilah remarked.

"Yeah, Go figure, But hey, they're werewolves," Faheem explained.

Jamilah observed how the other canines watched the procession in awe and knew that Anubis was either held in high esteem or great fear. She also realized that among the werewolves there was a hierarchy. The wolves in the front row of the luminous ground stood undisturbed while the viewing canines in the back fought amongst each other snapping and growling at who would stand where. This explained why Faheem was on her shoulder and Steel Nose was in her hands.

"It's a mind blower, isn't it?" Steel Nose commented.

"I've never seen anything like it," Maria added.

"And to think you wanted to miss this" the dachshund said to Dragonbrush

"I did what I had to," Dragonbrush said slightly leaning his weight against Jamilah. "I would've missed this if I had to." He looked up and could see Jamilah looking down on him with a loving smile.

"See them?" Steel Nose spoke, ignoring Tasha's shushing in order to comment on the seven assorted canines that trailed the gigantic wolves, side by side, "They are the seven territorial leaders of the Union."

Jamilah and the others took their eyes off the larger beast and placed their attention on the five ordinary looking canines. "Abyssinia," Steel Nose pointed out the Ethiopian wolf that led the pack, "represents the African continent."

"So, what's the big deal with them?" Lexus asked, seeing the wolf that bit her in the line.

"Only territorial leaders can enroll a human into the Union," Faheem answered. "They are given the ability to transform a human into a werewolf by Anubis himself."

"You mean none of the werewolves here can bite and turn somebody into a werewolf?" Jamilah asked with surprise.

"In traditional wolf packs only the alpha male and the alpha female can bear offspring," Faheem explained. "The same principals apply to the werewolf community. Instead of Anubis and his wife Anput enrolling everyone into the Union, they have delegated this ability to the territorial leaders." The group looked at the seven canine that followed Anubis and Anput with renewed respect.

"The Dingo beside him," Faheem added to the conversation, "is Corroboree from Australia and Jade. The gray wolf at his left side represents all of Asia."

"The Maned wolf is Lima" Tasha interjected describing the canine that looked like a mix between a wolf and a fox. "He leads the werewolves of South America."

"Shush," Steel Nose teased her.

"Big mouth Daushund," Tasha retorted.

Touché` girlfriend, Jamilah thought to herself.

"The white wolf next to him with the thick coat of fur is Alexander from Antarctica" Tasha continued.

"Antarctica?" Jamilah asked, remembering her school teacher Ms. Mawson saying that *there was very little life in coldest part of the world*. "What do they do? What do they eat? I mean there's nothing there but ice?"

"Werewolves are not like vampires. We do not to eat to survive." Tasha answered. "We are a spiritual force of nature.

"However, we are hunters," Faheem added, if we eat it's for the sport, not hunger, and in Antarctica, they hunt whales, seals, penguins and any explorers that spot them."

"See the Timberwolf over to the far left," Steel Nose spoke bringing everyone's attention back to the seven canines. "The large black wolf is Napoleon, the leader of Europe."

"You mean it's not Josephine?" Lexus asked with surprise.

"No, she is with the Wolfen," Faheem explained. "They will be along shortly."

"To hear her talk, you'd think she was Anubis," Maria snarled.

"That's why Josephine had no clue as to why we were selected," Maria whispered to Lexus. "She apparently doesn't have the power to turn a human into a werewolf."

"Why are you whispering?" Dragonbrush asked, "Everyone can hear you."

"Everyone here has super hearing, but everyone can't hear everything at the same time," Tasha explained. "When you sense that the wrong person is overhearing your conversation, then you change the subjects immediately, no questions asked."

"Last, but not least," Steel Nose continued, "the Timber wolf in the middle is Sandia, the leader of the free world of werewolves," he joked, "or the United States."

"Yeah, the President *Obama* of werewolves," Faheem added.

"Why you punking him?" Dragonbrush asked, aware that Sandia was the wolf that transformed him.

"Punking him?" Steel Nose challenged. "We deeply admire Sandia."

He has led us werewolves in peace for six thousand years." Faheem added, "Peace that others don't want."

"You guys were at war with the vampires?" Jamilah asked thinking about her friend Jennifer.

"Millions of year ago the Union and the Circle fought side by side and successfully gained dominion of the land mass called earth," Tasha explained. "Allowing others dominion of the air, the sea, the earths core and other dimensions. As the centuries have gone by, the two have become natural enemies, as we each seek more dominion of the earth.

"After a bloody war that lasted a thousand years," Steel Nose said with a solemn voice. "Sandia was able to negotiate territories that both werewolf and vampire have honored."

"But, everyone doesn't feel the same way Sandia does. Some werewolves feel that we should have more territories, and force is the way to attain it," Tasha added.

"Who wouldn't want peace?" Dragonbrush asked.

"Look at them over there," Faheem interjected changing the subject.

"Who are they?" Jamilah asked, following the dogs lead, pointing to the seven werewolves that also walked side by side in a line behind the territorial leaders.

"Let me guess," Maria answered, "The wives of the leaders?"

"You are right," Tasha acknowledged.

"That must mean that the pack following are all the second's in command." Dragonbrush added, to the agreement of Tasha and Steel Nose.

"You may call them second in command," Faheem sneered, "but I refer to them as tipping points."

"Why is that?" Jamilah asked, knowing that the conversation was again in an area that no human had heard.

"Tonight the second in command, can challenge the pack leaders for leadership;" Faheem answered. "The new leader can change the course of their pack which could impact the entire Union. All of the second in command agree with the philosophies of their leader, Corroboree. Lima and Ruaha all want greater territories; the others are not interested in going to war for it. The tipping point is Sandia's second, Judas the Saint Bernard." The group watched the Saint Bernard, Judas, and six the other canines at his side.

"You mean the Saint Bernard?" Jamilah asked, "I thought they were loving dogs, uh, I mean werewolves."

"He may be a werewolf that looks like a Saint Bernard, but inside Judas is nothing but a snake that cannot be trusted" Steel Nose agreed. "And what Sandia sees in him is beyond all of us."

"I don't trust him and neither should Sandia," Faheem added, "Judas is *Dick Cheney* on a leash. If he should challenge Sandia and win, then our next leader could lead us to destruction."

"Judas, has no chance of defeating Sandia," Steel Nose offered

"I still believe Apisi the Coyote, who maintains that he was spiritually attacked the night before he fought Judas at the last Union gathering," Tasha offered.

"I believed him also," Faheem added, "Judas is capable of anything."

"Which means behind them are their wives," Lexus noted, aware that it was time to change the subject as the group could feel the attention of Judas on them. "Always one step behind."

"There's Josephine." Maria used her nose to point out the forty-nineDoberman Pinchers trailing behind the second in command. "So, what is the big deal with this Wolfen?" she asked.

"The Wolfen, are the guards that protect the leaders of the Union," Tasha explained. "each leader has seven guards, they are extremely fierce."

"I'm sure they couldn't wait to go to war," Dragonbrush muttered.

Trust me, they welcome any opportunity to cause destruction," Steel Nose added.

"What are Anubis' thoughts on going to war?" Maria asked.

"Anubis is the Hound of War, destruction is his domain." Tasha whispered softly, "But he and Akhenaton, the lord of the vampires have an agreement not to sanction a war, but would not interfere if a conflict escalated between the Union and the Circle."

"So if Sandia was to lose to Judas or if Judas was able to convince Sandia to go to war, how bad would it be?" Lexus asked, wondering what the ramification would be.

"When they are in human form, many of our pact brothers are world leaders, politicians and nuclear arms dealers," Faheem answered gravely. "The conflict would have global implications for werewolves, vampires and humans."

A disturbing silence fell on the group as they watched the rest of the procession.

24

10:52 p.m., Unknown, Yosemite Valley

When the procession ended, Jamilah and the pack turned their attention to the fearsome sight that was Anubis. When his eyes passed Jamilah's way, the urge to run away screaming returned. Looking at the quivering Dragonbrush, Lexus and Maria who had huddled near him Jamilah got the impression that had she run, they would be right behind her.

Jamilah could see nothing in Anubis or his mate's eyes that resembled love, compassion, or even empathy. Faheem told Jamilah that werewolves ruled by force; weakness was punished. The social structure of the wolf pack changed every one hundred years. Werewolves in the pack could move up or down the pecking order only by combat. A werewolf one rung below could challenge the werewolf above them for their position. If the leading werewolf loses he and his mate would likely go to another pack where he would have to start from the bottom rung or operate outside of a pack. Many werewolves remained where they were rather than risk being at the bottom. Finally, Anubis was never challenged, as everyone knew that in addition to losing the battle, the loser's physical form would be destroyed thus banning their spirit from the Earth to never be seen again.

"Ours is a kind that rules by might." Anubis spoke in a deep, dark and authoritative tone. "Tonight with your might, those who would challenge the current leaders are given the opportunity to change how the Union is governed." Then with a devious snarl he challenged, "For those of you who would dare, let the battles begin!"

Jamilah watched as ambitious werewolves that aspired to rise in status and former losers reduced to a lowly station all fought to ascend the hierarchy of the Union. The battles were faster than her eyes could follow lasting in most cases seconds, but witnessing the combatants after, left no question that the fights were savage and brutal. When the time came for the seconds in command to challenge the pack leaders, there were no challengers. And as always, no one dared challenge Anubis.

"Why didn't Judas challenge Sandia?" Lexus asked.

"Because he could never best Sandia one on one," Steel Nose responded.

"I still wouldn't trust him," Tasha added.

Jamilah could tell that the even though there was no challenge the issue was not as resolved as she imagined. The seven pack leaders joined Anubis and Anput as they addressed the pack.

Dragonbrush was stunned when he, Lexus, Maria and seven others from the other continents were asked to stand before Anubis, as he cautiously approached the fearsome creature with Lexus and Maria close behind, Dragonbrush could hear some of the comments being said about him and Lexus and Maria adding to his discomfort.

Why are there only ten?" Jamilah asked, "If the U.S has three werewolves shouldn't that mean that there should be a total of twenty-one?"

"It's up to each pack leader to choose as many or as few wolves to join they're pack," Tasha responded. "They only select who they believe will be of benefit to their pack, apparently Corroboree, Jade, and Alexander felt that there were none worthy to part of their packs."

"Werewolves are not indiscriminant like vampires in whom they allow into the Circle, the pack leaders only select those that can be of great service to the pack," Faheem added.

"You were selected by your pack leaders to be part of the Union of the werewolves" Anubis deep voice echoed. "Your might will serve us well as we consider the future of the humans and our agreements with the vampires." The great wolf looked beyond the ten before him and asked, "Are there any that would disagree?" Acknowledging the consent given by silence, Anubis turned his attention back to new recruits and snarled, "This is the time when old traditions must make way for new ideas. You must choose your own path, whether you will join the pack that is the Union or take the path of the lone wolf. There will be those who will support it and those who openly reject it, but the choice is solely yours."

"Understand, that if you choose not be a part of the Union we will offer no protection." Anput the mate of Anubis spoke her voice softer but no less authoritative than her husband's. "Should you choose to join, you must earn the respect of your pack, something that will only come with time."

"Those who will join the Union step forward," Anubis ordered, he watched as two Gray Wolves, a Jackal, two Red Foxes, a German shepherd and a Coyote approach the ginormous Dire Wolf.

Dragonbrush remained as did Maria and Lexus who chose to not follow the pack when they noticed that Dragonbrush wasn't moving.

"Aahh, Vaticinators pick," Anubis said to Dragonbrush with amusement, "why am I not surprised, and it appears that you have started your own pack."

"I had no idea that Vaticinator was involved in this." Sandia spoke to his own defense.

"There is no way that you could have known," Anubis answered. "I know of his plans and they do not conflict with us but he did send us a guest;" he continued, turning his massive head toward Jamilah. "Approach human bearing lamb's meat from the Curse of the Firstborn," The Dire wolf commanded, Jamilah nervously walked toward Anubis stopping at Dragonbrush's side, bumping into him.

"Have no fear," Anput reassured Jamilah "as Vaticinator knew, the meat protects you from harm and allows you several requests."

"Like wishes?" Jamilah asked.

"Requests," Anput answered firmly.

"With all due respect," Dragonbrush spoke mustering all the courage he could in front of the frightening pair, "we just want to go home. I didn't want to be here, but I wasn't given a choice. But we don't want to piss off anything or anybody"

"That's what we want too" Lexus added with Maria nodding in agreement.

"That's what I'm requesting," Jamilah spoke knowing what she had to say, "that we can all leave with no bad feeling."

"Very well," Anubis agreed, "Upon completion of the ceremony you may leave. Sandia will offer you the opportunity to again join the Union when he feels that it is appropriate."

"Can I ask one last question?" Jamilah said knowing that she would get the proper answer

"Speak," Anubis ordered.

"Did you guys have anything to do with that family in South America that all have hair growing over their bodies?"

"No we did not select that family in South America plagued with rampant hair growth." Lima the leader of the South American Union answered. "Their situation is unique, but has nothing to do with us. The Union would never allow any of its pack to be so obvious and unprotected."

"Now if you all would step back," Sandia instructed, "we will proceed with the ceremony."

"You have chosen wisely," Anubis spoke to the remaining seven "As members of the Union it is time that you reveal your original form."

With a mighty growl from Anubis every canine was transformed back to their human form. That's when Jamilah, realized that she was the only clothed person in a sea of nakedness, and quickly removed her glasses as an embarrassed Dragonbrush, Lexus and Maria hid behind rocks and trees.

"Thanks God for the fog." Jamilah mumbled as the thick fog prevented her from viewing the various body types, color, age and ethnicity of all present.

As Dragonbrush struggled to cover his nakedness, he could see amongst them well known athletes, celebrities and politicians. At one point, he thought he saw *Roberto del Rosario* the inventor of the *Karaoke* machine but was mistaken. *Wow, there are lot werewolves out there*, he thought.

"Now in the body that you were born in pledge your fealty to the-cause of the Union," Anubis demanded which was followed by the howls of all present as everyone was transformed back into the canine forms to the relief of Dragonbrush and friends.

"I welcome you to the Union," with another howl, Anubis and Anput disappeared and the glow died and the trees and large stones returned in their place.

"Is it over?" Maria asked.

"It's time for the hunt," Tasha said excitedly.

"Hunt?" Jamilah asked.

"Yeah the new members of the Union have to now commit a kill" Steel Nose added.

"Come on guys it is time for us to have fun," Faheem said to Dragonbrush and the others.

"Who are you going to hunt?" Jamilah asked, concerned about her safety.

"Those who have death in there heart." Steel Nose replied, as he took off into the brush followed by Tasha.

"Are they talking about our folks, the just regular campers?" Jamilah continued now "thinking about her family and friends."

"No" Faheem replied. "Only predators, what fun is there in killing something hapless? Let's go."

"Go ahead I'm taking Jamilah back to camp." Dragonbrush insisted.

We're leaving too," Maria added.

"You are not going hunting either." Faheem queried.

"Next time," Lexus said dryly.

"Your loss," the small hairless said, dashing off into the woods with blinding speed.

"What are you guys going to do?" Dragonbrush asked the two that changed his life

"For now we're going to head back to the house where we've been staying and get our stuff then we need to talk to you about what to do after that."

"Then lets get out of here," Jamilah said getting on Dragonbrush's back, Before they could leave, Judas, the Saint Bernard and several of the Wolfen surrounded the three dogs and human.

"Your presence is required at the hunt," Judas pressed.

"We're not going" Dragonbrush answered.

"I wasn't asking," the Saint Bernard insisted.

"I don't care," Dragonbrush challenged feeling the hairs on his back lifting as he slipped from underneath Jamilah. After years of being bullied by Glock, Dragonbrush was not going to be bullied again.

"They have the right to choose to stay or go," Sandia's growled, interrupting the confrontation. "All they need to know is that they are welcomed whenever they choose to return. This is Anubis's will and I intend to enforce it" The Timber wolf challenged the Saint Bernard, openly.

"As you would like Sandia," Judas said falling back. "I will take my place in the hunt." He added, before scurrying into the forest. "Stay put." Sandia ordered the Wolfen.

. "Thanks a lot," Lexus said expressing the gratitude of all present.

"You know your pack don't trust Judas," Dragonbrush said, wanting Sandia to know the feeling of some of his supporters.

"Judas and I go back centuries. I should toss him aside because some questioned his commitment to the Union?" Sandia asked giving a response that none could answer, "As with all things we will wait and see."

Just don't wait too late, Jamilah thought.

Sandia turned to the Wolfen and ordered them to escort the leaving pack beyond the hunt so that they would have no more interruptions. Then he left the departing group, to also participate in the hunt.

25

11:05 p.m., Unknown, Yosemite Valley

The three canines escorted Dragonbrush and company for several miles then stopped in the thick patch of the woods. "This is as far as we go," the blue Doberman Pincher named Rabies spoke. "The hunt does not extend beyond this point. There are too many human ahead to risk attention to ourselves."

"Thanks for you help," Dragonbrush said.

"We did as we were ordered," Star, a black Doberman with a white star on his chest expressed. "To be honest, we have been told that you three are supposed to be superior to us, one day we would like the chance to see if that is indeed true."

Dragonbrush wanted to explain that he, Lexus and Maria had never said that, but knew it would be a waste of words, so he kept silent.

"The Wolfen has long been recognized as the most fearsome of the Union." Remus a red Doberman spoke, "So when we do meet, here's a demonstration of what we can do." Remus bit an enormous chunk out the side of a one hundred year old oak, sending the massive tree toppling over into their direction.

Before they could move, Star redirected the tree with the force of one mighty leap, sending the ancient tree crashing to the earth shaking the forest upon impact.

"Remember what you have seen here, when we face off." Rabies said before he ran headlong into the falling tree obliterating it upon impact. When the smoked and splintered filled air cleared, the Wolfen had gone and only the four remained in a state of awe.

"I wouldn't mind having a couple of those Wolfen's as guard dogs," Jamilah said in nervous jest.

26

11:15 p.m., Unknown, Yosemite Valley

Telma and Louisa quickly left the crashed vehicle escaping through the foggy night. They walked silently along the shore of the Merced River knowing that if they staid on the path despite the fog, it was just a matter of time before they came across a campground. When that happened, they would have food, and a vehicle. Whom ever they met unfortunately, would be the first in their planned killing spree. The two planned to die in a bloody gunfight, the kind that created headlines, movies and legends.

"Do you smell that?" Louisa whispered.

"Yeah, that's smoke," Telma acknowledged, "Smoke from a campfire." The two looked ahead and could see one large, lighted tent, inside was the silhouettes of two adults and three small children. In front of the tent a recently extinguished campfire. The two looked at each other and pulled out their guns and made their way toward the tent making as little noise as possible. They were several yards away from the tent when a Dachshund and a Chihuahua calmly walked between them and the tent and sat.

"I guess they have pets," Telma snickered to her partner. The two lifted their firearm toward the sitting dogs when their guns were removed from their hands before they could get off a round. They looked at each other stunned, noticing their trigger hands were aching and bleeding as something sharp had wrest the pistols from them. They then realized as if in a surreal nightmare, that they were surrounded in the fog by wolves, dogs and foxes. Their glowing eyes focused on them. The two females moved slowly backwards toward the Merced River, only to see even more wolves emerging from the river, wet and determined.

Louisa realized the only chance they had was for her to scream, alerting the tented campers of their plights. But, she was denied the opportunity as a red fox launched itself around her throat. Louisa's last images of Telma was her partner in crime being pulled to the ground by the back of the neck by a German Sheppard another fox attached itself to her throat before her world went black. The family of nearby campers would never know of the viscous attack that took place so close to their tent, or how the two killers were ripped asunder with pure savagery. The following morning they would question how two pistols were left lying around where someone could get hurt.

27

11:21 p.m., Unknown, Yosemite Valley

"You know what?" Coffy asked Shady and Slim Style as they wandered aimlessly through the woods. "If I get out of here, I'm giving up the life and going to church." He confessed to the others.

"Man, you always say that," Slim Style, answered with a smirk. "But, once we get out of the situation, then you ready to put the good Lord on hold."

Coffy, Slimstyle and Shady had split up in order to find Jamilah. When they began to hear the howling of wolves they found each other and began searching unsuccessfully for Glock. When the howling grew louder, the three gave up their search for Glock and with guns in hands headed back to the rendezvous point, hoping Glock would be there so they could get back to the business of finding their vehicle or a main road.

"You think Glock is alright?" Shady asked, as they made their way through the night, noticing that the fog was starting to break.

"Where-ever he is, we can't help him til we get ourselves straight," Slimstyle said leading the way.

"Hold up," Coffy whispered gesturing to the others to stop "Do you hear that?" The others complied, and they could hear the sound of growling and the rustling of bushes, becoming louder from every direction.

"Forget the dumb shit!" Slimstyle cried, "Back to back, just start firing til you hit something!" The three stood back to back firing aimlessly until the air was filled with fog, smoke, and the sound of automatic weapons.

" Think you hit anything yet?" Coffy asked Shady, who stood at his left.

He turned to his friend and to his shock, noticed that Shady's face had been ripped off. Coffy stood back in horror, "What happened?" He asked Slimstyle who held his hand over his mouth hoping it would prevent nausea, as Shady's bloodied body collapsed to the ground.

"How could this have happened?" Coffy cried, wondering how his friend could have been attacked inside the space of seconds. He turned his attention to Slimstyle, and screamed when his friend stood before him headless. His body continuing to move as if it had a life of its own before crumbling to ground where it continued to flay.

Coffy ran in a blind panic, screaming hysterically until the last thing he saw through his night visors was a Jackal lunging at him, its bloodied mouth opened and aiming at his face.

28

11:31 p.m., Unknown, Yosemite Valley

Dragonbrush picked up the sound of a car radio as the two made their way back to the camp. Following the sound until they came to the overturned Range Rover pinned between two trees.

"I wonder what happened," Jamilah asked, remembering the SUV from earlier "Oh man, clothes!" Jamilah said excitedly, able to clearly see through the side window of the truck with her sunglasses, longing to get out of her still damp garments.

"Are there anymore in there?" Dragonbrush asked, as Jamilah entered SUV aware that it belonged to Glock and company but also noticing that there was something else that smelled human in the vehicle.

"Yeah, why," Jamilah asked, sorting through the bags of dry cleaned clothes trying to figure out what she would wear.

"Because you don't' want to see me when I change back into human form" He replied.

"Uuugggh, you're naked, all of you were naked, gross!" Jamilah said with disgust after selecting what she would wear she placed the remaining garments on the ground before Dragonbrush "Now turn your back while I change clothes"

"I'll walk over there," he offered.

"You are not leaving me!" she ordered, tossing Dragonbrush more clothes. "Just turn around and get dressed. If you peek, I'll smack you on the nose with a newspaper or something."

"I wouldn't do that." Dragonbrush said complying with her request, transforming into his human self while Jamilah's back was turned.

"I know you wouldn't," Jamilah agreed, while pulling off her wet clothes.

"I was so afraid that I had lost you," Dragonbrush confessed, revealing his true feeling as he pulled the matching blue *Triple Five* hoody over his head and placing on oversized sweat pants

"I thought so, too," Jamilah agreed, acknowledging her own fears. "I kept hoping Omari would find me because he was the only person that I knew that would not rest until he did" she confessed. "I knew it would be just a matter of time before he found me." She said placing the blue down jacket over the white body contoured shirt that felt great and oversized jeans. "But when I heard your voice, I remembered that there was someone else who cared about me as much Omari." She said turning around to see that Dragonbrush's back was still to her "You can turn around now," When Dragonbrush turned he could see the tears in her eyes "Thank you" she whispered,' through choked tears. The radio broadcast then captured their attention.

"Right now, the Yosemite Mountains is the focus of FBI and every nearby law enforcement bureau as the area has become the host of multiple concerns for both Yosemite County and a little girl right here in Oakland. The bodies of city of Hayward officers, Ted Warner and Michael Yorkshire were found. The two officers were transporting Telma Harris and Louisa Alvarado, who were arrested for the murder of a Hayward businessman. We have learned that the two carjacked a courier that was delivering a liver for a local girl who is now awaiting a transplant. Fortunately the courier was spared, but we do not know if the escapees are aware of the liver they are carrying or if they even care. Hard Data Software is offering a reward of fifty thousand dollars for the safe return of the liver in the limited amount of time that the body part is still transplantable. But a word of caution, Telma and Louisa should be considered armed and dangerous, do not approach them instead, call your local authorities. To add to the FBI's troubles, two teenage campers have been reported lost in the woods, possibly even drowned as the two slipped into the Merced River and have yet to be found. Making matters even more difficult, the area has been hit with an intense fog rare for this time of year suspending any means of search. So right now it's a waiting game of praying that there are some happy endings. Again, if anyone has any information please contact their local authorities right away."

"That's what I smelled," Dragonbrush exclaimed, as he looked into the truck and saw a large metal case "This must be it!" he said excitedly.

"A cell phone!" Jamilah screamed, picking up the small phone that was wedged between two seats. She dialed 911 and after several transfers she was speaking with the proper authorities.

"We found the liver," Jamilah informed them

"Where are you?" The voice asked.

"In the middle of Yosemite park, duh!" Dragonbrush yelled.

"Are there any clearings where a helicopter can land?" the voice pressed.

"There's a place called Patterson's field you can land there," Dragonbrush added remembering it from when they passed through.

"We will be there in thirty minutes."

"Good, but we need you to do one thing first," Jamilah stated.

29

11:53 p.m., Unknown, Yosemite Valley

The fog had completely cleared up when Steven ran from his tent because of the unsettling dust that the helicopter generated.

"You have any word on the kids," he asked praying, the helicopter was not there to deliver bad news.

"Great news!" Ace yelled, over the sound of the propeller, "We found the teens, both are safe and they also found the missing liver."

"Thank you Jesus!" Steven said in a high-pitched voice, "Where are they now?"

"We are on our way to pick them up and rush them to the hospital but we were asked to pick up her brother Omari."

"Just a moment," Steven yelled as the propellers woke up everyone at the camp. Seconds later a confused Omari was running out with Steven with Tioni, Julie, Issues and Gustav close behind.

"Get in young man your sister needs you," the co-pilot said.

"I'm going, too," Tioni insisted getting in behind Omari.

"We don't have time for this" Ace argued.

"Then lets go," Tioni said, shaking her hand for the copter to fly.

"Anyone else?" the co-pilot offered after Steven entered.

"I'm not flying in that!" Julie responded "And if I'm not going," she said looking at her friends.

"We will make sure your things all make it home," Issues commented before watching the copter take off.

30

12:22 a.m., July 29 Patterson's Field Yosemite Valley

It took Dragonbrush ten minutes to transform into a Rottweiler, carry Jamilah to Patterson's field and transform back, there, they waited admiring the full moon.

"How did you get the lambs meat?" Dragonbrush asked.

The old guy Vaticinator gave it me, that and these glasses." She lifted the sunglasses from her face and handed them to Dragonbrush

"Really," Dragonbrush replied, looking through the glasses before handing them back, "all he gave me was a CD."

Jamilah noticed that her protector was becoming distant as they continued to watch the moon, "Hey, is everything okay?" she asked, concern showing in her voice.

"Kinda," he answered, "I'm just thinking about my sister Gwen."

"You have a sister?" Jamilah asked, immediately thinking what type of person she was.

"Had a sister," he answered. "She had Leukemia. She would draw pictures for me and take me places." Dragonbrush commented looking at the moon. "I think sometimes, I loved her more than my parents, but she died." He said fighting back the tears in his voice, "It was the worst thing that ever happened to me."

"Dragon, I'm so sorry," Jamilah said, placing her arm around him and pulling him close.

"I remember the doctors telling my parents on the night she died, that there was nothing else they could do for her, my parents just sat in the room with her, until she passed away".

Jamilah placed her arm around his neck and placed his head in her lap. "When I saw you fall into the river" he continued while wiping his eyes, "It was like I losing my sister all over again, and I couldn't let that happen again."

"I understand," Jamilah said stroking his hair as he sobbed.

"But you know what?" he said sitting up "This time I was able to do something and nothing stopped me from finding you, nothing and nobody. He said with pride as he closed his eyes and placed his head back in Jamilah's lap and began to relax.

"Thank you Dragonbrush," Jamilah whispered.

"You know when I first met you," he giggled "I thought I wanted you to be my woman."

"Me and you? Get out of here!" Jamilah laughed, "That's what you thought? But what you really wanted was another older sister, which is better anyway."

"It is? Why is that?" he asked

"Boyfriends come and go, but brothers are forever, I can always depend on Omari and I can always depend on you. I love Omari and I love you little brother."

"And I love you too big sister," he responded. The sky became loud again as they could hear the helicopters and could see the spot lights.

"Don't those bright lights get on your nerves?" Dragonbrush asked.

"No," Jamilah responded, taking off her glasses. "I think those spotlights are the coolest thing in the world, right up there with little brothers."

31

12:45 a.m., Rose Avenue Apartments,

Janet's mother Sylvia, her sister April and her boyfriend Leonard, all arrived to console Janet regarding the bad news she received about her daughters liver replacement. Janet appreciated their efforts to reassure her that things would work out for the best, but the evening's events had left her depressed, only wanting to go to bed and try to forget how cruel life could sometimes be. Janet did not remember hearing the telephone ring, only her mother shoving the phone in her face yelling, "It's the doctor, talk to him!" In her disoriented state she heard Doctor Collins saying excitedly, "We found it! We need you to get to the hospital as soon as possible!"

"Oh my God, thank you!" Janet shouted scooping her sleeping daughter in the bed with her, blanket and all. They all rushed to Children's hospital, Janet still in her nightgown.

32

1:52 a.m., rooftop, Children's Hospital

The helicopter carried the small crew directly to Children's Hospitals heliport, where waiting doctors received the organ; an attendant escorted them downstairs to a waiting area where reporters were waited with questions. Elder Charles Anderson was contacted by Tioni while still in the air and Sergeant, Norbert Bright, were on the scene. Once the reporters dispersed, the crew waited until they heard that the operation had gone well. While waiting, Jamilah and Tioni wandered the ground floor and parking lot just outside the emergency room.

"How come you're not taking any of the credit for finding the missing organ?" Tioni asked Jamilah, as they watched several ambulances arrive carrying small bodies on large gurneys into the ER.

"Because, Dragonbrush saved my life, and he was the one that found the SUV and the organ, and that's the truth. Of course I told him that I want five thousand dollars."

"Why if you had nothing to do with it," Tioni asked.

"Because had I not have slipped into the river for him to rescue me, we would have never even seen the SUV with the liver in it." Then she sighed "You know the worst part about getting the reward money?" Jamilah asked.

"What?" Tioni asked.

"Omari told me I have to give him half of my cut because of all of his clothes that I destroyed," She pouted, "Life is so unfair!"

Tioni wondered was the time she spent consoling Omari, Good for a couple of hundred? She would definitely ask.

The two purchased hot chocolates and were joined by Omari and Dragonbrush while they waited for Tioni's dad to finish his conversation with Bright and take them home when they heard. "Hey!" from across the street.

The group turned to see who was yelling, and it was Vaticinator, in the back of a yellow taxi cab that had stopped at a red light across from the parking lot where they were standing.

"Did the meat and the glasses help?" he shouted.

"Allot, thanks," Jamilah yelled back as the car drove off. Jamilah turned to the others and with concern in her voice said "I don't ever want to see him again."

"Nor do I," Omari echoed.

"You know that guy too? Dragonbrush asked, remembering Vaticinator from the BART station.

"Sure, we'll tell you all about it," Omari answered.

33

1:45 a.m., Madayag Residence, Fairmont Street

Joseph Sr. had dozed off in his chair in front of the television, ever since he and his wife received the news that their son was lost, the two had remained frozen in front of the television with the telephone within arms reach. Waiting and praying for good news, any news. An upset and exhausted Esmeralda had gone to bed an hour earlier and Joseph resolved to join her and to sleep light in case they received a phone call in the wee hours of the morning. He reached to push the off button on the television remote, when the reporter Lisa Chow interrupted, with a late breaking bulletin.

"This is Lisa Chow standing outside of Children's Hospital, where the liver transplant for little Lauren Azzaro has gone well, the doctors report that she is stable and recovering fine. As I reported earlier, the liver to be used for Lauren transplant was stolen but was recovered by a Joseph Madayag, Jr., a superhero in the form of a teenager."

"That's Dragonbrush," the teen said to the camera.

"You got lost in the woods, with another camper," the reporter continued.

"You mean my big sister" Jamilah, Dragonbrush corrected her again.

'Well apparently Mr. Madayag while lost stumbled upon the stolen vehicle that held the liver and immediately contacted the authorities. Do you have anything you would like to say to the world Joseph?"

"Yeah, I want to give some shout outs to all my dawgs, Omari, Mila, Yes, T, Jen, Aunt A, and uncle U, the Bright officer and I want to say to my Mom and my Dad, your son did good, this is Dragonbrush and I approved of this interview."

Madayag looked at the television with total astonishment, "Honey!" he called, running to the bedroom.

Part 10

Cleaning up after Dawgs

"there was about him a suggestion of lurking ferocity, as though the Wild still lingered in him and the wolf in him merely slept"

Jack London

1

July 29, 5:00 p.m., Yosemite Valley

"This is Lisa Chow reporting live from Yosemite National Park, where the remains of five victims of animal attacks were located. Their bodies reduced to nothing more than clothes and clean bones. Dental records identified the victims as the escaped murderers, Telma Richards and Louisa Mixon. The others belonged to Noris Dunn, Jamil McDonald, and Mac Brigham, whose street names were Slimstyle, Coffy and Shady. Although it is not known why they were in the woods, the three have had deep roots in the Cobalt gang and have lengthy rap sheets for mostly violent crimes. The only survivor is Henry Johnson, another Cobalt gang member whose street name is Glock, Johnson also has a history of violent crimes, to quote one officer, Johnson's rap sheet is as long as a *Harry Potter novel.* Johnson survived, but unfortunately, both of his hands, his nose and lips were completely removed, apparently by a wild animal. He was found in a state of shock, unable to talk. We will be reporting updates as they arrive, back to you Lorraine."

2

July 29, 7: 02 p.m. South Hill Court

"I'm glad you could make it," Ayanna greeted Esmeralda and Joseph Madayag. "Come on in" she smiled as she led the clearly pregnant woman of same height and her mid sized, gray haired husband in faded blue jeans and white shirt carrying a cake covered with aluminum foil into the living room

I baked a Makapuno pound cake," Joseph said in a soft tone.

"Joe is a baker for Safeway," Esmeralda said with pride. "But this is not sold at Safeway it is a family recipe."

"Thank you, we are honored," Uhuru responded. "We'll definitely have it for dessert."

"We can't stay long," Joseph expressed, "but we wanted to personally say thanks for taking care of our son and didn't want you to think that we don't care, because we do. I also plan to pay you for all your troubles when the reward money arrives."

"That is not the reason for inviting you over," Uhuru assured him. "We just thought it would be better, if we were not such strangers, Dragon loves you all very much, and we know you care for him. That is something for us to build on, would you agree?"

"Very much," Esmeralda answered, nodding her head in agreement. "Of my forty seven years on earth." she confessed slipping off her shoes allowing her swollen feet to breathe. "The last eight years have been the hardest, maybe Joseph Jr. told you but our only daughter Gwen, passed away from Leukemia, eight years ago. We spent most of our savings on second opinions and experimental procedures, I mean if it's your child what do you do?" She explained to the sympathetic couple. "That's when my Joe was laid off his job at the bakery and the medical insurance with it. Gwen died eight months later this was also the time Joseph Jr. started having problems in school and with the law. As much as we wanted to get a handle on out son we were so devastated by our lost, and so far behind on our own bills that we almost lost our home. My husband and I are both responsible for family members in the Philippines as well as a son in college which is why we allowed my nephew and his wife to move in, to help us pay the mortgage. Before going on maternity leave, I worked for Walgreen's and as a second job Joe is doing security." Esmeralda looked into her half filled glass, "But God is still blessing, we still have a roof over our head. When Joseph started associating with your son and daughter he stopped getting in as much trouble."

"Nephew and niece," Ayanna corrected her.

It was obvious to all that Joseph sr. was very uncomfortable with the open conversation Uhuru asked to him, "Do you watch boxing?"

"Yeah, I like boxing" he responded showing interest.

"I have an excellent copy of the *Pancho Villa, Jimmy Wilde* fight" Uhuru offered standing up. "Do you have time to watch it?"

"Really," he asked, "you know, he had over 100 fights before he was twenty-two." He responded, standing also.

"We can watch it in the family room," Uhuru said leading the way "you like imported beer?" Uhuru asked his interested guest.

"Not really," he answered.

"Will you drink it, if it's all we have?"

"Sure," Joe responded.

"Babe", Uhuru said to his wife "we're going to eat dinner in here, have the boys join us."

Esmeralda looked at Ayanna and smiled, "This is progress."

3

7: 48 p.m. South Hill Court

After a long conversation about the camping adventure, dinner and helping with the table and kitchen, Jamilah went to her room and immediately got on the phone. Omari had promised himself that he would make progress on *World of Warcraft* that night if killed him. Placing his headphones on Omari lost himself in the game.

Dragonbrush wanted to know what his parents were saying about him, lying on his futon bed and focusing, he could hear their every word. His father and Uhuru's conversation was restricted to boxing, with his father explaining to Uhuru how despite being just over five feet tall, and dying at only twenty four years of age, With one hundred and five fights, seventy seven of which he won, twenty two by knockouts, losing only five and either splitting or no decision on the rest Pancho Villa was the greatest Asian fighter in boxing history. The conversation between Ayanna and his mother was more informative.

4

8: 18 p.m. South Hill Court

"Do they talk?" Ayanna asked, about how Dragonbrush and his father communicated

Esmeralda smiled at the question as if she had an inside joke. "Joe's mother likes to say that when the good Lord realized that he didn't give Joe enough to say, that he made up for it by giving his son twice as much to talk about. Joe is a man of very few words, arguing is something that he doesn't do well; he says what's on his mind and is not always the most skillful at how he says it.

Joseph on the other hand is never at a lost for words and wants things explained to him and sometimes wants his father to express his feelings just to reassure him that his feeling's are correct. I have watched Joe try to express his feelings, but he holds everything in and is not sure how to release it, other than through anger. None of the others are like Joseph, who wants so much from his father but only seems to irritate him. But Joe is a very proud man that truly believes in providing for his family. When we lost our daughter, he could never talk about it, but the hurt has aged him and he speaks even less. He hates himself for the way his relationship with his son has soured." Esmeralda reached for the edge of her blouse to wipe her eyes but was handed a box of Kleenex by Ayanna "Even though he put his son out the house, he wouldn't sleep at night. He would just walk around the house with the photo albums looking at baby pictures of his son and daughter praying that he would be safe. Sorry for what he did and for not being smart enough to know how to be better." She sniffed and smiled again "But God answers prayers, because when you took him, and we knew he was doing well, it was the first time any of us were able to sleep, knowing he was somewhere safe. When we learned that Joseph was lost, Joe prayed that if God was fair by sparing our son he would be fair by taking him in and being a better father." Looking at the Ayanna with tears in her eyes" Esmeralda asked, "Does he sound like such a bad father?"

"No he doesn't," Ayanna answered wiping the tears down her eyes.

5

9: 16 p.m. South Hill Court

As the Madayag's were preparing to leave, Ayanna approached them with their son's sketchbook that she pulled without his permission from the boy's bedroom.

"Before you go," Ayanna spoke handing them his book "I have to ask, have you really looked at Dragon, I mean Joseph's artwork, he's really talented. You may want to consider sending him to art school."

Esmeralda and Joseph browsed through the book impressed by their son's talent, until they came to a page that got both of their attention. Esmeralda looked at the two drawings of a funny looking winged dragon holding a paintbrush and laughed,

"Remember this character?" she said pointing it out to Joe, handing the book to him." Then turned it toward Uhuru and Ayanna said, "Our daughter created this cartoon character and would draw it everywhere and on everything" She turned to her husband "Remember the time the nurses were upset because she drew it on the hospital sheets," turning back to Ayanna and Uhuru "She said that one day," choking on her own words, fighting back long biting emotion, "everyone in this city would know her character Dragonbrush," She looked at her son with searing red eyes, The revelation striking her and her husband simultaneously, "You were doing it for her, you didn't want the world to forget your sister." Dragonbrush looked at his father who held his hand over his brow and said, "I wish I had died instead of her," He looked at his son from the couch. "No, we need you too, he said with a crackling voice before burying his face into his hands. Dragonbrush looked at Uhuru through his own storm of emotion wanting to know what to do? Uhuru pointed to the space between his parent Dragonbrush sat between them, then placed his head on his mothers lap and continued to cry.

The rest also overwhelmed by the emotional scene walked out of the room to get more tissue, beer and juice.

"Will they be alright?" Jamilah asked, welling up at all the crying.

"This is a good start," Uhuru answered.

"Think he's going home with them?" Omari asked, handing his aunt the Madayag's serving tray as she had instructed.

"It will be good for him to be home with his parents to heal with them, we'll have to wait and see."

"You okay?" Omari asked Jamilah, her face covered with tears.

"Yeah, I'm happy for Dragonbrush, but why couldn't that be our parents together and us in there?" she asked before going upstairs to her room.

6

August 2, 10:05 a.m., Monday, Alameda County Courthouse, Juvenile Division

Dragonbrush hated standing before the judge, especially Judge John Yamiguchi. For one thing he used his real name, Joseph Madayag, rather than Dragonbrush. He knew that Yamiguchi hated Filipinos and no matter how well his behavior was; the judge was determined to make an example of him in front in his court. His bias was very obvious. Less than thirty minutes earlier Carlos Ramirez, the leader of the Crimsons gang stood in front of the judge. Carlos last public crime was throwing a man off a roof, in broad daylight, yet with no one willing to testify. The best the judge could do, was bring him in on a failure to appear. Yamiguchi told Carlos that he would not pursue charges if he would participate in group counseling otherwise his parole would be revoked and he would be sent back to the Youth Authorities the teen agreed. As Carlos walked out of the court the lean, dark, Latino with dark slick hair looked at Dragonbrush and said, "I'll see ya," exposing one of his fangs, though not as sharp, still noticeable, sending a quick chill up Dragons spine.

"Joseph Madayag vs. the County" The Bailiff called.

Dragonbrush felt his mothers' hand on his leg as he approached the bench and without turning around knew that Sergeant Bright had entered the court.

"Is Madayag's court representative here?" Yamiguchi asked looking out at the court.

"I'm here, your honor," a flushed overweight male that was as sloppy as he was disheveled, spoke as he walked toward the bench, accompanied by Dragonbrush. Yamiguchi was clearly annoyed.

"There is a new complaint against Mr. Madayag by BART officers Malcolm Walker and Edward Stansfield, The County Prosecutor, a professionally dressed blonde spoke handing the documents to the bailiff who presented it to the judge. "This report states that the two witnessed the tagging activities of the long haired boy in the Station. The prosecutor said, handing a copy to the Bailiff, for the judge and to the other attorney that was trying to find Dragonbrush's folder.

"Are either of the officers here?" The judge asked

"No they are not" the prosecutor replied

"This report fails to give time, or date of the alleged incident or any specific information that would suggest there are any photo's or a clean up cost, and if they witnessed him committing the crime, why wasn't he arrested at the time of the incident?"

Dragonbrush knew that the two officers that he had embarrassed in the BART station were seeking their revenge, and had picked the perfect judge, to use. He was going to Juvie.

"Can I speak to that your honor?" Dragonbrush's sloppy attorney spoke after finding the lost folder. We would like to recommend that Mr. Mayag," he said, quickly reading his name "be allowed to spend weekends at the Juvenile system to assure that he will not be a problem with his tagging addiction."

Dragonbrush and his parents looked at the attorney with rage and shock.

"Have you discussed this with your client?" Yamiguchi asked.

"No, but when I do, that will be my recommendation." He spoke holding files for the other eighteen cases he would poorly represent that day.

"You seem to forget that the person you are supposed to represent can choose to reject your offer if they don't feel it represents their best interest." The judge said to the attorney with little patience. "What do you think Joseph?" the judge asked Dragonbrush.

"I think you are going to do what you think is best, your honor," Dragonbrush spoke resolved that he was going to jail.

Yamiguchi smiled, "I read about you in the paper the other day, you found a missing organ that allowed a little girl the opportunity to live a fairly normal life. The word for people like you is hero. Now that word may not mean much to others, but it means something in this court. There will be no additional charges and your probation is being suspended. But, you will be back here to see me next month in chambers. So that I can know your progress" He looked out into the audience. But I think I will appoint Norbert Bright who seems to make a point of being at all your hearings to speak on your behalf. I tend to think that the County defendants can use one less case."

Dragonbrush looked at his parents as they walked out of the courtroom and said, "I can't believe he gave me a break."

7

4:32 p.m., House of Faith Church Child Care Center

Jennifer walked out of the childcare center with a pouting Soapy several steps behind her. Soapy was not ready to leave and resented her older sister forcing her.

"I'm in no mood for this dude," Jennifer barked, before picking up her sister. She stopped by the store to pick up dinner. When she arrived home, Jennifer could look forward to cooking dinner, cleaning up after and studying for her school entrance exam.

"You're never in the mood, dude!" Soapy barked back, showing the potential for causing future headaches. Jennifer was about to give the smallest of the Twan's a piece of her mind when she heard, "You want to trade?" She turned, and it was Omari, and in his hands were flowers, some fresh, some slightly wilted.

"Where did you get those?" She asked feeling slightly insulted by such an ugly assortment of flowers.

"When we went camping, I went out and looked for flowers for you. The plan was to pick flowers for you everyday that I was there and keep them on ice until I saw you. But you know what happened."

"So while everyone else was horseback riding, swimming, and taking pictures, you were out picking flowers for me?"

"Yeah," he nodded "I don't like having you mad at me."

Jennifer looked at the bouquet of flowers and blushed a beet red, they were the most beautiful floral arrangement she had ever seen. She handed him the heavy bag and took the flowers holding them close to her heart.

"I wanted to tell you that someone at the Nightcrawler was playing the same song as you," Jennifer commented.

"Oh that's cool." Omari replied unfettered.

"That doesn't' bother you?" Jennifer asked surprised that Omari wasn't upset.

"No, like me he probably downloaded it from the internet and was just sampling, beats from someone else's sounds. When a DJ spins they're just playing a beat, you know, in a different way. That new song is called a remix or given a new title by a different artist and then played by many different DJ's, even in the same city or area!"

"Oh," Jennifer responded, waiting for Soapy who was starting to lag.

"You don't like my music do you?" Omari asked.

"Omari, I like old school. Your stuff is too fast for me, but everyone else there loved it. In fact even some vampires that were sitting down got up to dance to your set."

"Vampires were dancing to my set?" Omari asked flattered.

"They were ready to kill for you," She grinned.

"Cool," he said with a smile. "Do you want to go to the Old Skool Café for a burger later?" He asked.

"I have to go home and cook," she said woefully.

"What if we order a pizza for them?" He asked.

"I want pizza" Soapy interjected, Jennifer agreed.

"So we get the pizza, drop off the bags, Ms. Sophia and get a couple of burgers." Omari agreed. They reached the corner and waited for the light, just before the light turned green, Jennifer snuck Omari a kiss on the cheek.

"Oooo! Jennifer has a boyfriend!" Soapy shouted.

Omari's phone rang "Let me take this call" he smiled, "and I will catch up with you" he said to Jennifer "hello."

"Thanks again for the flowers, you are so sweet" Makemba cooed on the phone. "You want to go tagging tonight?"

"No, not tonight," Omari said glancing at Jennifer who would turn around any second "Let me call you later" then ran up and caught up with Jennifer who automatically extended her hand out to her little sisters hand before crossing the street. Soapy responded mechanically, taking her older sister hand, watching her place her head on Omari's shoulder as they walked across the street together. Omari wondered *how hot was the fire he was playing with.*

8

9:48 p.m., Corner of 61st and International Blvd

Justin pulled over to the curb after he saw the flashing light behind him, then watched as two officers, a stocky Latino and an older, white male approach his vehicle.

"Is playing music loud against the law?" Justin yelled, turning *"Mama"* by Eminem down to a reasonable volume.

"Actually it is," the Latino cop answered. 'May I see your driver's license?"

"Sure, no problemo senor," Justin responded handing over his license.

"You mind if I check your vehicle?" the older of the two officers asked.

"Not at all," Justin answered looking at Edwin as he spoke. "You might find some empty beer cans, but that's only because I recycle. He continued as he popped the trunk. The gray haired sergeant looked in the trunk.

"There's nothing back there is there? Justin whispered to Edwin who whispered, "No" in return.

"Pedro could you come here," the older officer called seconds later the Latino officer walked to the drivers side of the car.

"Would you two mind stepping out of the car?"

"Why, what's up?" Justin asked with disbelief.

"Are theses yours?" Sergeant Bright asked showing him a crumpled brown bag filled with smaller Ziploc bags containing pills and vials.

"No!" Justin responded with astonishment, as he was face to face with the bag of drugs that had been confiscated from Omari "Those are not mine, I've been set up!"

"When we get to the station, we will run this bags and vials for fingerprints." Bright said "If your prints come up clean, then we will have to look into what you said, if not, you better have a lawyer."

Omari would be going down with him, Justin seethed, then he realized that Omari was wearing gloves that night, only his and Edwin's prints would appear, he was busted.

9

11:12 p.m. Jennifer' residence

After the second pebble hit her window, Jennifer opened her window and could see Dragonbrush standing in the driveway. After being greeted by the chilly night air she heard him whisper loudly "I'll meet you on the roof," and with a mighty leap, the teen landed upon the branch of one of the tall trees that lined her street and with another he was atop the roof of Jennifer's three story apartment complex.

Scanning her block to see if anyone was watching Jennifer glided up to the roof in her *Badtz Maru* pajamas where Dragonbrush waited knowing that when they last met it was confrontational. "What's up?" she asked affably.

"Jennifer," Dragonbrush confessed "I am so sorry for the other night I don't know what happened."

"I know!" Jennifer agreed, sharing the same feeling. "You're a werewolf now, and I guess werewolves and vampires are not supposed to get along."

"I'm a werewolf, until I can figure out how to get rid of it, he affirmed, "but if the Union and the Circle got funk, then it's their funk, not ours."

"That's what I'm saying," Jennifer agreed. "We have to stick together, we all we got."

"I'm not letting someone else's funk become mine," Dragonbrush acknowledged.

So I guess it's us against them."

"Oh well," Jennifer answered. The two could hear one of the other adults in Jennifer home walking and knew Jennifer had to go. "I'm glad you came by little Dragon," Jennifer embraced her Filipino friend.

"Me too," Dragonbrush returned, knowing that his friend, was still his friend.

10

8:49 a.m., Tuesday August 3rd, South Hill Court

While waiting for Tioni's mother to take them to the University of California, Berkeley, to register for the summer youth program, Omari, Jamilah and Jennifer finished their breakfast while Dragonbrush and Tioni sat on the porch.

"How does it feel to be a werewolf?" Tioni asked her gray eyes gleaming with the morning sun

"Strange," Dragonbrush answered knowing no other words to describe it.

"Okay, so are your folks going to pay off that graffiti bill that you owe?" Tioni changed the subject accepting the situation as it was.

"Naw, dad said that he and mom are going to continue the payment schedule. They have to put a lot of it in the bank for my college fund, like they teach tagging techniques in college." Dragonbrush replied with a smirk, "Jamilah gets five of it. And they want to go to the Philippines to see family."

"Are you going?" Tioni asked.

"Probably,"

"You're going to be gone a long time?"

"Dragonbrush leaned over and kissed her on the cheek.

"Don't be doing that," she said with a nervous giggle.

"I'm sorry," Dragonbrush said, "I'm also sorry for not calling you. Jamilah said I was spending so much time with her because I missed my big sister."

"I'm sorry, too," Tioni confessed. "I should have told you something, instead of getting upset; I just thought you didn't care about me anymore."

"Do you know how scared I was when I jumped into the blazing building?" he asked, "If I didn't care, would I have done that?"

Tioni sat quiet, then answered, "I still can't remember everything that happened that night."

"You don't want to," Dragonbrush commented, reflecting on the harrowing experience

Tioni leaned over and kissed Dragonbrush on the lips.

Then the sound of a blaring horned stunned her, the teens looked up and could see a stern faced Diana. "You young lady get your hot hips in this front seat now! And you, young man need another conversation with the pastor." The lecture would continue the remainder of the trip.

11

6:02 p.m., The Madayag residence, Fairmont Street

Joe Madayag was resting before he would have to get dressed and go to his second job when the telephone rang. "Hello" he said with sleep in his voice

Mr. Madayag, This is Harold Letterman from Rolling Hills Cemetery, and I regret to inform you that some hooligan attacked the tombstone of your departed daughter.

"What?" Joe said in outrage.

"We will do what we can to remove it." The comforting voice said, "Unfortunately attacks on tombstones are not uncommon, but your daughter's tombstone featured the strangest word"

"What does it say?" Madayag asked, suddenly getting a clear picture of what took place.

"The words: "Dragonbrush lives forever", was etched in the stone, how strange."

"I don't want it touched." Madayag said with a thoughtful tone in his voice, and a lump in his throat.

"Sir, you realize that it mars the name of your departed daughter?" The grounds attendant asked.

"No," he answered with a warm glow in his heart, "actually it beautifies it."

12

9:04 p.m., The Yamiguchi residence Layfeytte, CA

"How's the new guest?" Pastor Charles Anderson a solid, African American with chestnut tone skin, and short salt and pepper afro asked Flora, as he handed his wife Diana a glass of ginger ale. "Are you able to handle them okay?"

"For all of their powers and pain, Lexus and Maria are no better or worse than any other teen their age, just as lazy, mouthy, and attentive, and in need of structure. They are just kids and good kids at that," Flora answered, also accepting a cup.

"I'm jealous, while some of us have to hunt down our wards, Flora here leaves the door open and her's find their way to her." San Francisco, Chief of police Ron Kennedy spoke, a slender, bald, bespectacled, almond colored, African American whose penchant for black suits, white shirts, and black, neckties by American, designers, earned him the nickname, *"Salary Man."* "Maybe the doc here is not up to the heavy lifting which is why for her it was so easy." Kennedy smirked

"Or maybe so skilled, that I nake everything look easy unlike let's say, a police chief," Flora countered.

"It's agreed, everyone is good at what they do, we are just checking in to acknowledge that what was predicted is indeed happening," Diana added, diffusing the war of egos that began decades ago, when Flora, and Kennedy both attended UC Berkeley.

"How did Maria and Lexus find their way to you?" Captain Tony Hicks asked Flora. Captain Tony Hicks was an African American in his late fifties, with short, white hair, and a chestnut complexion. Hicks, was always well dressed and rarely seen without a Fedora on his head or a cigar stub somewhere on his person. Flora turned her attention to Sergeant Norbert Bright.

"Dragonbrush contacted me," the heavy, officer, whose French ancestry was evident by his dark hair that was now graying, answered. "When the girls refused to join the Union, they were no longer allowed at the resident they were living. I then contacted Flora, who took them in."

"It is becoming very clear" that the prediction is coming to pass" Flora confessed.

"Perhaps we are jumping to rash conclusions, brought on my cryptic, hallucinations maybe we should devote some time to logical explanations." Warden Douglas Adams the lean, dirty, blonde, and gray haired, Warden of Alameda County Juvenile Hall added, rolling up the left sleeve of his white button up shirt, before adjusting his round metal-rimmed bifocals.

"Did those metal doors that were ripped to shreds like paper at juvenile hall, a cryptic, hallucination?" Kennedy asked. "What's happening is real, stop fighting the inevitable and get with the program."

Looking for logical explanations is not fighting the inevitable, and nothing is above reproach when we are talking about saving the world," Douglas fired back.

"We must stay focused on the true objective, not our personal perspectives," Judge Mark Yamiguchi the slight, graying Japanese judge, appearing less authoritative in his navy blue, velour, Fila sweat suit than he did in his robe added. "We have Jennifer, Dragonbrush, Lexus and Maria, and there is no denying their abilities. Things are in motion, and so must we. What is the status of our other charges? The judge asked Pastor Anderson.

"I've met with Carlos Perez several times, and currently, he has no stomach for gang activity." Pastor Anderson responded, adjusting his glasses.

"That could be a problem," Tony Hicks noted.

"But he is also a natural leader. He'll come around" Anderson reassured the group.

Let's hope so;" Judge Mark Yamiguchi commented, "I've made enemies with the prosecutor's office for letting him back on the street."

"Speaking of wild cards," Flora interjected, flipping her hair over her shoulder. "Isn't it time you bring one of your charges out from the cold." She said speaking to Kennedy and Adams

"I don't think Young is ready yet," Kennedy countered, "he's extremely hardened for a youth."

"There are always the Stephen King's novels," Hicks ribbed Adams.

"Stephen King's novels?" the Warden asked, not getting the reference.

"You know, Carrie, and Fire Starter," the captain smirked.

"Don't call them that," Diana interjected, her gray eyes chastising the high ranking officer. "LaRhonda is grateful for the help, but where he is?" Diana asked, bringing the groups attention back to the pale warden.

"He's moved from LA, to New York, and currently headed toward New Orleans," Douglas answered, "and it appears his abilities are under control."

"Are his pursuers still on his trail?" Bright asked.

"They are but have had no success, it's like he's has a guardian angel" I can't figure it out," Douglas explained.

Bright looked at Kennedy and rolled his eyes, in unbelief.

"Of the three, I'd say that Young was the most essential to our immediate needs." Flora offered, to the agreement of the others.

"Fine, Young it is." Kennedy resigned, looking at Sergeant Bright he said, "I may need your help."

""Not a problem," Bright approved. "But I agree with Flora it is still important to remember that these are just kids"

"I second that," Yamiguchi added "but enough about saving the world," Yamiguchi cajoled. "Jan has prepared an excellent meal let us go to the dinning area eat, drink and be merry."

"For tomorrow we die," Tony Hicks added.

Epilogue

Mount Lyell, California

The lone human figure stood amidst a dozen canines atop Mount Lyell, Yosemite's highest point

"I don't know if you can be trusted EnOlive,` Judas spoke, the Saint Bernard's eyes critical of the tall, striking man with braided ponytail and braided beard.

"Why would that be?" EnOlive` questioned, the Saint Bernard.

"I just find it hard to believe that you would have the Unions best interest in mind" Judas snarled questioning if it was even safe for his small pack to be with the evil one.

"I have my own best interest in mind, make no mistake about it, EnOlive' spoke stroking his beard "but it's in our best interest to work together to eliminate the vampires."

"As long as Sandia is the leader of the Union there will be no opportunity for the Union to advance into the vampires territories." Judas growled with frustration.

"Then maybe the Union needs a new leadership" EnOlive` whispered slyly

"I like the way you talk," Judas said with a laughed that sounded similar to that of a hyena.

"Excellent," EnOlive smiled placing the tips of his fingers together. "I'm asking for patience not trust, it will all come together you'll see."

About the Author

A J Harper is the author of ***Night Biters,*** the first in the
Tales of Urban Horror series
Smoke & Demons the 3rd book in the series will be released in
2010
He lives in the Bay Area
You can contact him at urbanhorror@gmail.com
or visit his web urbanhorror.com.

"Night Biters is an action-packed horror novel"
Alternative Teen Services

Night Biters

A Tale of Urban Horror

Part 1

When 16-year-old Jamilah and her 14-year old brother Omari arrive in Oakland, CA A mysterious stranger gives Omari a magical compact disc and crucifix. Upon listening to the CD the siblings learn that the lyrics and the crucifix can aide them against the danger of vampires.

But danger has never been as attractive as the handsome and charismatic heartbreaker Tyrone, or as beautiful and deadly as the vengeful Jennifer.

Soon the siblings find themselves in twined with rival gangs, the Crimsons and the Cobalt's. Their leaders transformed into vampires whose hatred for another threatens to destroy the city.

Fasten your seat belts, you're going to a place bustling with taggers, skaters, gangs, girls that literally kick butt, hip hop and vampires.

Smoke & Demons

A Tale of Urban Horror

Part 3

By

A J Harper ©